CW00553698

BLOOD of the ROSE

BLOOD
of the
ROSE

Kevin Murray

urbanepublications.com

First published in Great Britain in 2014 by Urbane Publications Ltd
20 St Nicholas Gardens, Rochester
Kent ME2 3NT

Copyright © Kevin Murray, 2014

The moral right of Kevin Murray to be identified as the
author of this work has been asserted in accordance with
the Copyright, Designs and Patents Act of 1988.

All rights reserved. No part of this publication may be
reproduced, stored in a retrieval system, or transmitted
in any form or by any means, electronic, mechanical,
photocopying , recording or otherwise, without the prior
permission of both the copyright owner and the
above publisher of this book.

All characters in this book are fictitious, and any resemblance
to actual persons living or dead is purely coincidental.

A CIP catalogue record for this book
is available from the British Library.

ISBN 978-1-909273-12-2

Cover, text design & typeset by Julie Martin
Printed and bound by CPI Group (UK) Ltd, Croydon, CR0 4YY

urbanepublications.com

With grateful thanks to my wife – the most patient story listener and the greatest story of my life.

And to my children and grandchildren, who have kept the storyteller in me alive.

ACKNOWLEDGEMENTS

There are so many people who have helped me with this novel over the years, and I would like to thank you all for your support and encouragement. I would especially like to take this opportunity to thank you, the reader, for supporting me. I hope you enjoy the ride.

Finally, I would like to recognise the enthusiasm and energy of Matthew Smith at Urbane, with special thanks for his help in bringing this story to life.

PROLOGUE

HE SIGHED as he bent his face to the cold stock of the crossbow. Through the weapon's illuminated night sights he could make out every detail on the head of the Siamese cat twenty yards away. He drew another deep breath and took up the slack on the trigger. The animal watched him, the fur on its back slightly raised, whiskers trembling.

The man wondered whether it could see him clearly in the darkness. He was dressed head to toe in black. Only his eyes were visible, exposed to the cold night through the slit in his balaclava. He lay flat on his stomach, his left elbow on the grass to hold the crossbow motionless. He assumed the cat was a pet from one of the houses which surrounded the small square park in which he now lay.

He smiled, knowing his camouflage had to be good to fool a cat. He wondered which way it would leap. Left, he decided, towards the street. He let the sights drift slowly, marginally towards the hedge, keeping the crosshairs level with the animal's chest. He exhaled slowly, gently increasing pressure on the trigger. Still the cat watched him, absolutely motionless. The bowstring jerked free of its restraints. The recoil jolted him as the bolt surged from the crossbow, whirring in the air as it hurtled toward its target. The cat sensed the danger and scurried for the street, seeking refuge in the hedge.

It was too slow. The missile lanced into the centre of its chest, bursting through the other side to drive three inches into the tree behind it. The animal was stunned by the impact, impaled, hanging limp and breathless from the shaft of the bolt.

The man let the air explode from his lungs, keeping the weapon steady. He adjusted the sights on the crossbow, setting them for 30 yards. Then he put the crossbow down and crawled purposefully toward the tree. Still alive, the cat saw him coming and struggled to free itself. The movement wrenched flesh, lungs and bone, and the animal let out a dreadful screech. It sounded like the wail of a terrified child, filling the night air and rebounding around the square. The man leapt up and broke into a run, heaving a kick at the cat's head as he got within range. The crunch of bone against wood savagely ended the cat's eerie cry.

He put both hands on the shaft of the bolt and heaved it out of the tree with a grunt. The cat came with it, hanging in an inverted U from the quarrel. He put the point of the bolt against the ground and placed a booted foot on to the furred corpse, leaning his full weight on the limp body to slide it off the missile. Blood glistened wetly on his toecap, and he could see a pool of shining blackness gathering on the ground beneath the stricken cat.

He kicked the limp body of the animal towards the hedge, followed it, and bent over to gouge out a shallow grave in the flower bed. He dumped the cat in the hole and covered it with earth and dead leaves. He scooped up a handful of earth and crawled back to the tree, scattering the soil to disguise the sinister evidence of the blood.

He picked up the stained bolt and crept back to the fence, searching for his weapon. It was one of the world's most powerful crossbows – a Barnett CMX Commando. Equipped with a telescope, it was also one of the most accurate. The stock, telescope, limbs and bowstring were all matt black. The side plates and cocking slides were made of polished brass. He located the crossbow when he caught a glimpse of a reflected streetlamp off those slides.

Then he pressed against the fence which surrounded the

square and stretched for the top strand of wire. He hauled himself up, eyes peering over the top to sweep the street. The road was slick with recent rain and he had only the sounds of slumbering suburbia for company. A distant horn, the dull hiss of car tyres on a road nearby, scrapes and creaks and the whistle of wind through the branches. Somewhere, a television was still on. The late night movie.

Only then did his attention turn to the house directly across the road. It was one house in a terrace of many, yet he was in no doubt it was the one he wanted. He had been here often enough. He scanned the front of the building, a double storey Georgian-style house, set about 15 yards back from the pavement. The house was one of twenty four on the square, in the centre of which was a small park, in turn surrounded by the hedge which now served to hide him. In the middle of the park, two benches and a row of three children's swings stood eerily in the faint mist.

His eyes fixed on a first floor window of the house. The curtains were open, as usual. Inside the room he could see a middle-aged man and a young woman. They were arguing. It was a heated exchange. The girl stalked from the room in anger. In the darkness of his hiding place, and in spite of the tension, the man with the crossbow smiled.

He lifted his weapon and placed the stock on top of the fence, careful not to allow the crossbow to project into the street. He bent his head to the sights, once more adjusting the telescope. He bit his lip as the figure in the window seemed to dance in a heat haze. Another adjustment and the figure snapped into focus, quartered by the crosshairs of the sights.

The front door of the house slammed. He drew away from the crossbow in time to catch sight of the girl. She was dressed in a long coat, striding purposefully towards a car parked in the short driveway of the house. Plumes of vapour billowed from her mouth as she fumbled with a set of keys and cursed. The breeze carried the sound of her voice. Finally she opened the door of the car, got in, started the engine and reversed out of the drive in a squeal of tyres. On the street, she gunned the engine aggressively before racing away. The sound of her car's exhaust bounced off the buildings as she raced clockwise around the square towards the single exit, heading for Kensington Road.

His hands were sweating inside his gloves. He put down the crossbow to take them off, never taking his eyes from the man at the window. He wiped his palms on his trousers, stopped, then hissed. His quarry had moved out of sight. Anxious now, he felt for his gloves and drew them back on. His hands reached for the crossbow and took hold of the butt.

A scuffle from up the street turned him rigid. Footsteps, and drawing closer. He withdrew into the bushes, blood pounding in his ears. The footsteps drew level with his position and stopped. An animal was snorting and sniffing. A chain clinked.

"Chester? Come on boy. Chester!"

The voice boomed in the darkness.

"What's the matter boy? Find something?"

A head loomed over the top of the fence, peering into the hedge. He withdrew further into the bushes, gently rustling leaves and branches. The face at the fence froze. In the darkness, the crossbow was inches from the head of the intruder. The dog whined, and the face turned away.

"Come on boy, it's probably just a cat."

The chain rattled; the dog whimpered, then pedestrian and dog moved away, in the direction from which they had come. Thirty seconds passed before the man with the crossbow dared to exhale. He wiped his brow on his sleeve, then peered down the street in time to see the pedestrian and his dog turn a corner out of the square, and walk out of sight. Only then did his gaze return to the house across the road.

There, the target had returned to his desk, his back to the window. The crossbow was snapped open and the bowstring cocked in a fluid, practised movement. The Commando had a unique cocking system. It broke, like a shotgun, exposing two hooked levers which engaged the bowstring and drew it back into the trigger mechanism.

He looked down at the quiver strapped to his leg. His fingers ran over the feathered vanes on the backs of the bolts. He could tell the difference without looking, recognising each one by its weight and feel. His hand stopped on a plain-tipped 14-inch fibreglass quarrel. He ignored the ones he knew carried the more vicious three-bladed arrowheads, aptly named Razorbaks. The shaft of the missile whispered against the side of the quiver as he withdrew it. He dropped it into the crossbow's track, checked to see one of the vanes was in the groove, then slid the bolt back to touch the cocked bowstring. Then he removed the bolt, and slid it back into his quiver. He retrieved the bloodstained bolt he had dropped at his feet, and placed that, too, in the quiver. Once again he bent to the sights, taking quick, deep breaths. The crosshairs converged on the centre of the back of his quarry's head. He waited until his breathing had returned to normal. Then he took a deep breath, held it, exhaled again. He took a third deep breath, exhaled slowly, all the while gently squeezing the trigger.

This time the bowstring made an empty thwacking sound and the stock vibrated against his cheek. Around him, the night was undisturbed. He knew that firing the crossbow without a projectile in the groove could damage the bowstring. He didn't care.

He lifted the crossbow off the wall, glanced at his watch,

crouched down and crept back to the gate on the north side of the square. Once there, he slid the crossbow into a holdall he had left at one of the gateposts. He slipped off his balaclava and gloves and stuffed them into one of his trouser pockets. After a moment, he stepped on to the pavement, seemingly huddled against the cold rain, and walked to a car parked 50 yards away. He opened the boot and threw in the crossbow. He looked around before quickly unstrapping the quiver and flipping it in after the holdall. He closed the boot firmly. Another quick check and he moved briskly to the driver's door, all the time looking up and down the street. A light breeze flicked at his hair, and spittle on the beard at the corners of his mouth glistened in the light. He unlocked the door, opened it, and slid into the seat. Again, he checked his watch.

He started the engine, put the car into gear, and pulled away slowly. Once he had turned the corner into Kensington Road, heading towards Hyde Park Corner, he relaxed, stretched back in the seat and began whistling to himself.

Perfect. Just perfect. Tomorrow, he would be back...

ONE

JENNIFER CHAPMAN marched out of her father's study in a rage, crashing the door shut behind her. Hugh Chapman, editor of the London Evening Courier and one of the city's most influential men, sat helplessly as the walls of the house – and his world - shook.

"Damn him. Damn his stubborn, arrogant attitude," he heard her say.

For once he couldn't blot out the words. He knew she was on the point of storming out of the house. She would disappear for hours, perhaps days. He couldn't face that again tonight.

He stood up from his desk and walked to the door, opening it in time to hear Jennifer again.

"He says it's the work of a crank. He says he can't take it seriously. But I think he's scared. I think he's really scared. He just won't admit it."

He walked to the railing, looking down at his daughter and his wife as they stood at the bottom of the stairs. Close together like that they looked like twins. Except for the tell-tale lines around Sheila's eyes. Smile lines....but hard earned, thought Chapman.

Sheila had her back to the stairs, and her voice was muffled as she asked: "What did he say?"

"He says he can't count the number of threats he's received and insists these are nothing new," said Jennifer.

Chapman was always quick to describe his wife and daughter as beautiful women. Few disagreed with him. His wife was a short, petite brunette, always elegant, even while sleeping. She had a narrow face, high cheekbones, deep brown eyes, full, sensual lips and even, white teeth. He had witnessed her render men speechless when she smiled. Where Sheila wore her hair to her shoulders – thick and wavy and gleaming – Jennifer kept hers close-cropped, almost severe. But she had her mother's eyes, skin, lips and teeth. He had passed on only his stubbornness, his pride and his single-minded determination. Studying them from a distance, he was shocked to see how fear and the red eyes of sleeplessness had given them both a haggard, aged appearance.

"How can he ignore threats like these, and my feelings about them?" said Sheila, still unaware her husband was watching.

"I don't know, I've never really understood…" began Jennifer.

"I could understand him ignoring one letter," said Sheila, "But not three! Especially three like these."

She turned to peer at the hall table. "Where are they?" she asked. There was loathing in her voice.

"I don't know. They were there. He left them there before supper."

They both stared at the table, bare save the telephone.

"They're in my study," said Chapman. The two women started and turned to glare up at him. In spite of their concern for him he was still very much the target of their outrage. Jennifer's eyes were narrowed, her lips pursed. He noticed Sheila glance at her daughter. A fleeting smile. He knew why she was smiling. There was no doubt Jennifer was her father's daughter. They had fought often and violently over the years. Both were battering rams in their day-to-day lives, destined to clash time and again. Or, at least, whenever Chapman found the time to break away from the obsession he called his career. Sheila's years with her husband were the perfect preparation for a relationship with her adult daughter. She often said she had long ago learned to treat them both like cats. She never forced herself on them, but responded willingly when they wanted affection. She told friends she knew they would always come home but couldn't be tied there. He found the analogy fitting. That was the way to describe Jennifer now thought Chapman. Those eyes are fierce and mysterious, independent and distant. Just like those of a cat.

"What are you going to do about the letters?" demanded Jennifer. Insolence flashed in her eyes.

Chapman stifled an impulse to rebuff her. In spite of the fact she was 24, he still hated it when she challenged him so disrespectfully. The previous night, in his study, he had been unable to stop himself. He had lashed out at her in his rage until she finally fled his barrage to drive off in a gut-wrenching screech of rubber. He had not slept until she arrived home shortly before dawn. Last night their argument had been over his disinclination to do anything about two anonymous threatening letters delivered in the mail. But tonight a third letter had arrived, and even he felt shaken.

His first reaction had been to put on a show of bravado and not let Sheila see his concern, in case he intensified hers. His attitude had evolved into a stubborn refusal to admit to himself that he was wrong. When Jennifer had arrived home, he had become even more determined not to let them see that the letters had rattled him. He knew he was wrong. The three letters were too consistent to be the work of a one-off crank. While it was true he had often received death threats, he had never before received three in one week. And they appeared to be the work of the same person. He had to take some sort of action.

"What are you going to do about the letters, father?" Jennifer asked again, louder this time.

He shrugged. "What do you suggest?" he asked, conceding defeat.

"Call the police," said Jennifer.

"Why don't you call Jan?" asked Sheila.

He nodded before turning away and walking towards his study. Jennifer followed him up the steps. He waited for her at the door, staring past her at Sheila. "Will that make you happy?"

"No. But Jan is a policeman. He'll know what to do. I'll feel better knowing something was being done," said Sheila.

Jennifer stood at the door.

"I'll call Van Deventer, and see what he advises. You go and watch television. I'll tell you what he says."

Sheila nodded. She knew when to leave him alone. She would be waiting for him, he knew, anxious to hear what Van Deventer advised. But for the moment, she would leave his pride enough room to recover. He was grateful for her understanding. He walked into his study. Over the years it had become the curse of Sheila's life, almost like another woman. If he was upset, angry, or thoughtful, he would retire to his study. She had never dared go in when he went there angry, for fear of an explosive reaction from him.

Sheila stared after him as he disappeared from view. Her eyes flicked to Jennifer, still standing at the door. For a moment their eyes met, then Jennifer followed her father.

From his desk, Hugh Chapman studied his daughter. He was proud of her, almost as proud as he was of his newspaper. He was proud she was turning out to be a good journalist, proud of the glowing reports he received daily from his news editor. She had begged him to allow her to join The Courier, even though her appointment as a junior reporter in the newsroom smacked of nepotism. Yet she was showing them all the wisdom of his decision. Her persistence had brought her rewards in the guise of several solid investigative features that had broken new ground on drug abuse.

It was the same persistence she was showing now.

Chapman felt once again edges of his fear of the previous night, when he kept imagining she was dead or injured in a car crash. After she had left the house, Sheila said: "Is that the way you'd like your daughter to remember you?". The words had haunted him through the long hours of waiting for his daughter to return, and through most of the day. He had determined to tell Jennifer how much he loved her as soon as he got in from the office. But something in her posture strangled the words before he could utter them.

She seemed to recognise his difficulty. "I wouldn't do this if I didn't care,"

He nodded. "I know. I care too."

"Do you?" she said.

Silently, he mouthed: "Yes."

She came to stand in front of his desk. He ached to hold her. They stared at each other.

"I'll leave you to it, then," said Jennifer.

Again, he mouthed: "Yes."

She turned to the door.

"Jennifer," he said, so quietly she might have missed it had she not been straining for the word.

"I do love you. You are my only child. No matter how old you are, you will always be my child. You must understand that."

"I do. Sometimes, though, I want to be more than that. I want to be your friend. A support. I want to be able to help you. Can you understand?"

"Yes," he said. "And you can be my friend. Will be my friend. You can be whatever you want to be."

"Then give us more time for each other. That's all we've ever needed."

"I know. But right now I have to speak to Van Deventer alone. I hate to...I can't ask for help at the best of times."

"I know. We'll talk later?"

"Yes, all you want."

She smiled, her mother's smile. He was harried by the grin until he felt one come to his own lips. The radiance of her smile dispelled the signs of strain on her face, and she was as beautiful as he had ever seen her.

"I'm going out now. I'll be back at about 11. Can we talk then?"

"Where are you going?" he asked.

She smiled, indulgently. "To the cinema with Neville."

"Who is Neville?" he persisted, smiling in return.

"Just a friend, father. No-one you should worry about."

Chapman had heard about Neville from Sheila. He was one of the physical training instructors at his daughter's health club. He was young, fit and tanned and, according to Jennifer, "incapable of thinking about anything other than sex." This young man, thought Chapman, was EVERYTHING to worry about. But he decided to ignore this particular problem for the moment. Instead, he said: "Good. Then I'll wait up."

She smiled then left the study, closing the door gently. He heard the murmur of voices as she said goodbye to Sheila. The front door opened and closed. He listened as she started her car; listened as she drove away; listened long after the brassy exhaust of her Mini had faded to nothing.

"Sometimes, though, I want to be your friend," was what he heard. He was struck by an overwhelming sense of loss. All those years, he thought. Their daily routines were so different, in spite of the fact they worked on the same newspaper. He preferred to get to the office early, in time to organise his day before the madness began. Jennifer always slept until the last possible moment, showered on the run before dashing to catch a bus or tube. Occasionally she would wait for him after work in order to drive home with her father, but mostly she would leave well before he did. By the time he got home, she was usually at dance class, aerobics, or out visiting friends. Even at weekends, they found little time to be together. He usually worked, or was out at an official function. She would be partying, living life with her friends.

He wrestled his consciousness back to the present. The thought of the letters was enough to induce a wave of panic. All the letters had arrived by post. The first had been addressed to him by name, so Sheila had not opened it. When he got home from work that night he had gone through the mail, and found the letter. The paper was standard writing paper, available in dozens of stores. The message had been cut out from a newspaper or magazine, and pasted on to the page. It was made up of different sized headlines, and looked like one of those crude ransom notes Chapman had so frequently seen on television.

It said:

LAY OFF, OR WE'LL LAY YOU OFF. PERMANENTLY!

Sheila read over his shoulder. "Oh my God. Hugh, this is terrible. What's it all about? Who would do this? What must you lay off doing?"

Chapman shrugged impatiently, and walked into the sitting room. He hadn't wanted to talk about it, but Sheila insisted.

"What is it Hugh?"

"I don't know. It could be any one of a hundred stories. I have more than 100 journalists on my newspaper. Half of those are reporters. All of them are working on at least one story every day, and most of them deal with several different stories every day. How am I supposed to know what story that note is referring to?"

"Who says it is a story?"

Chapman sighed. "What else could it be?"

"Alright. If it is a story, then how about the most important one for the newspaper? The one you are helping with? Could that warrant a death threat?"

Chapman walked to the drinks cabinet, reached in for a bottle of Scotch, poured himself a stiff one, topped it with soda, added ice. He moved to the sofa, sat down, and looked at her. She stood at the doorway, hands on her hips, daring him to ignore her question.

"It really is not that big," he said. "A Tory MP is screwing his secretary and some jealous rivals are trying to make sure his affair receives maximum exposure."

He was uncomfortable talking about a current story with his wife. Usually, he avoided discussing these, telling her instead about personalities in the office.

Chapman forced himself to continue. "I suppose some crank connected to our love rat could have sent a letter like that. But then he'd have had to send it to every editor in town, because this is certainly not an exclusive story. And anyway, the note is not at all specific. Someone serious would tell me exactly what I should lay off. Believe me, it's just another nutcase, that's all." He had thrown the letter on to the floor, hoping Sheila would just throw it away.

A second anonymous letter arrived on the evening of the third day. This time, when Sheila recognised the type of envelope, she abandoned her respect for Hugh's privacy and opened the letter herself. It said:

WE WARNED YOU. WE WON'T WARN YOU AGAIN.
DOES YOUR LIFE MEAN SO LITTLE?

She had telephoned Chapman at his office. "There's another one. It's just come. It says they won't warn you again. They threaten your life. Hugh, don't keep things from me..."

"Honey, I give you my word. I know of nothing that could be causing someone to feel so threatened. Honestly, Sheila, I know what I'm talking about. The first time I got one of these letters, when I first took over as editor here, I nearly went out of my mind with worry. I called in the police, I looked over my shoulder for weeks. It was terrible. But I soon got over it, and the next one, and the next one. All of those were on stories that really were dealing with hot potatoes. Relax. This is nothing."

That night she had been quiet and withdrawn. The letter had shaken her. Hugh had looked at it when he got in, and casually tossed it onto the hall table next to the first one. Sheila had saved it. Conversation had been stilted during dinner, and when Jennifer arrived home from her evening dance class, she had looked from one to the other and said: "A little domestic bliss going on here? Something I should know about?"

"Your mother's worried because some crank has sent me two threatening letters."

Sheila looked at Jennifer and said, quietly: "You should have a look at them. They're evil. And very menacing."

Jennifer read the notes. Then she went to speak to her father. As soon as Jennifer entered Hugh's study she had exploded.

"Jesus Christ, father! These are not jokes."

There had been contempt in her voice. It had been enough to send him into a rage. Sitting at his study desk now, it was a rage he deeply regretted.

"Is that the way you want your daughter to remember you?"
His wife's face flickered in front of him, her eyes accusing.

"Sometimes, though, I want to be your friend."

Now his daughter's eyes rounded on him.

ENOUGH IS ENOUGH. NO MORE CHANCES. YOU WILL DIE.

The words of the latest letter. What the hell were they after? What did they want to achieve? Was there something he was doing that could be regarded as serious enough for death threats?

He held his face in his hands. He was exhausted. But he knew he wouldn't be sleeping tonight. Not with all this going on. He looked around his study. On his desk was a photograph of Sheila. He picked it up and gazed at her image. In 25 years of marriage, Sheila had never complained about his passion for newspaper work. She had never complained about the trips away, the calls late at night, the social functions, the working late, home entertaining, his neglect of her. He would always be grateful for that. She demanded nothing more than that he promise to be with her for life. For she knew one day his newspaper would turn its back on him, and she would be the one he turned to for solace.

Chapman thought of how Sheila had clung to him throughout the previous night. Never one to be brazen about her physical desires, she had astounded him on waking. Her appetite had presented an opportunity he had not been able to resist. As a consequence he had been 40 minutes late for work. Normally fanatical about being on time, Chapman had not been at all concerned today. His contentment, however, had not lasted. Sheila had called to tell him yet another letter had arrived. This time the words were even more sinister. She had been hysterical. He discussed the letters with his friend and colleague Bob Channing, who was also his deputy editor.

"Each of them threatens me. The final one indicates that I have run out of chances to stop whatever it is the person wanted me to stop. The hell of it is that I haven't the faintest idea what the letters could be talking about. I've thought about it, and I can't find anything that ties up."

"It wouldn't have anything to do with the Metcalf story, would it?" asked Channing. He was a small, rotund man who always looked cheerful, even in a fury.

Chapman paused before answering. "No, I don't think so. Brian Metcalf is small fry. His desire to expose Barry Jurgens as a runaway political Romeo is petty-minded. It won't hurt Jurgens, and Jurgens knows that. Nor will it hurt the Burroughs girl, his mistress...I can't remember her name –"

"Kristin," said Channing.

"Right, Kristin. She has nothing to lose from all this, and a great reputation to gain. The only one who might lose a little ground is Philip Whallen. As Jurgens' assistant he has been denying the relationship for months, so Whallen may get a little egg on his face. But that's it. Unless there's more to it than meets the eye...?"

"Okay, so on the face of it, you may be over-reacting," said Channing. "And you don't think there is any other current story that comes close to warranting this type of action?"

"No," said Chapman.

Channing knew he was dismissed, and Chapman saw him bristle. But as he left, he said: "If you want any more help, just shout."

Chapman didn't reply. His attention had wandered to the

galleys on his desk. That day's editorials awaited his undivided attention. By the time he got home, however, the letters had taken their toll on him. Even though he'd been focusing on problems at the office, they had been there all the time, bubbling away like an evil brew. It had taken an extreme effort of will to keep his temper in check through the cross-examining he had been subjected to by Sheila and Jennifer.

At first he had given Sheila a hug, always a slightly incongruous act for the two of them. Chapman stood 6'4" in his socks. Sheila just made five foot and two inches. But his brittle cheer had cracked under the barrage of questions, until he had stalked off to his study to be alone. Jennifer had pursued him, resulting in a row for the second night in succession. He was pleased they had managed to part tonight on friendly terms.

Looking now at the photograph of Sheila, Chapman felt a surge of concern. What if something happened to her while he was away? He had always been away on business when Sheila most needed him. When Jennifer was born, when her father had died, when their last house had caught fire and burned to the ground – he hadn't been there. What if he were out when this maniac came?

Chapman was an impressive man. His silences were more terrifying than other people's tirades. His dark hair, always worn short even though it was thinning, topped a deeply lined but forceful face. His dark eyebrows rode over brooding, piercing eyes. He had once been a county swimmer, and as a result had broad, powerful shoulders and the physique of an athlete in his prime. His burning dedication to his newspaper lent him the air of a man not to be trifled with.

Sheila had always given him his head, and as a result she was the only person with whom he had ever been able to share his fears. In spite of her own competence, she had drawn on his strength for her own existence. But he realised his one glaring weakness was his passion for The London Evening Courier. He knew it was his wife who was most vulnerable to this kind of lunatic.

Chapman stood up and walked to his wall safe, hidden behind a row of books on his floor-to-ceiling bookcase. He opened the safe and withdrew a pistol. It was a 9mm Luger, a relic his own father had brought back from the war. Over the years he had kept it in perfect working order, even though he knew it was illegal to own an unlicensed firearm. His father had given it to him when he became editor of The Courier and had received his first threatening letters and telephone calls. He walked to his study door and stood listening for Sheila.

The television was on, and he could picture her sitting there, staring blankly at the screen. She always did that when she was troubled. If you asked her what she had been watching she would not remember. He smiled, hefted the weight of the gun in his hand, and walked through to their bedroom. He knew Sheila was able to use the Luger. They had sometimes taken it with them on holidays in the country, and fired at tree stumps for the fun of it. She was almost as good a shot as he. There were still several bullets left for the weapon. His father had supplied him with 40 rounds when he had handed it over. Chapman had not asked how his father had got the bullets, nor whether they would still be live rounds after all the years in a cupboard. He knew his father wouldn't have taken any chances.

Chapman checked the magazine was firmly clipped into the butt of the pistol, then slipped it into Sheila's bedside table drawer. He would tell her about it later, after he had called Van Deventer.

He walked back to his study, shut the door, and sat down at his desk, studying the letters. Look at me, he thought. Terrified and resorting to a firearm because of three anonymous letters. This was ridiculous. Why let himself get worried? It was probably exactly what the author wanted. Perhaps he should not even bother with the letters?

He was struck by a vision of himself lying on a street pavement, mouth agape, surrounded by pairs of uniformed legs. How many times had his own newspaper carried photographs like that? Every time a European or South American leader was gunned down by the Red Brigade or some other terrorist organisation, the result was always the same. An undignified death syndicated all over the world, witnessed by millions of people. He could clearly see his own face in this imaginary photograph. The image sent his heart racing. Without thinking, he pulled the telephone closer and picked up the receiver. He wanted to get hold of Van Deventer as soon as he could.

Detective Chief Superintendent Jan Van Deventer was a man he could rely on. The policeman owed him, and would always owe him. How long was it now? Close on five years since the Campbell affair. Eighteen years since they had first met. He had been introduced to Van Deventer while acting as assistant to The Courier's crime reporter. In those days Van Deventer was still a rookie on Scotland Yard's fabled murder squad. Their relationship had been forged in the crucible of the gangland reign of the Kray twins. Van Deventer had been one of the detectives who helped put them in jail. From the first meeting the two men had struck up a bond of friendship that had lived on through their separate careers. Van Deventer had helped Chapman achieve many exclusive stories, trusting the journalist implicitly.

He shook his head as he dialled the policeman's number, hoping he would catch Van Deventer in. He knew the detective was now assigned to a desk job at New Scotland Yard, and that the Dutchman, as he was known, was no longer at the leading edge of police work in London. But if there was anyone he could talk to about this, it was Van Deventer. He would give it only ten rings, then try again he decided, employing a habit he had developed so many years ago.

He didn't have to wait his 10 rings.

TWO

CHIEF SUPERINTENDENT Jan Van Deventer, at 51 still a boy at heart, was watching his favourite television programme when the phone rang. It was a detective series which made a mockery of the police, but which he thoroughly enjoyed.

"Damn, who could that be?" he said, turning to his wife. "It's probably for you."

But Tessa, who shared his love of the programme, would not be drawn. Reluctantly, the policeman heaved himself out of his chair and padded down the hall to the telephone, muttering. He could hear Tessa chuckling.

He picked up the receiver, craning to peer into the sitting room so that he could keep an eye on the television. "Yes?"

"Jan? This is Hugh Chapman."

"Hello Hugh. You okay?"

"Yes. You?"

"Oh, I'm fine. In a great mood today. I broke ninety for the first time this afternoon."

"Say again?"

"I broke ninety. At golf. For the first time."

Chapman laughed. "I didn't know you played golf."

Van Deventer gave up trying to keep track of the programme and sat down at the telephone table, squeezing his bulk into the tiny seat. "Oh yes. I love it," he said. "I took it up when they transferred me to training. I lost interest in nursemaiding recruits and took up golf as an alternative passion. I play as often as I can get away from the training school."

"I'm sorry to hear that, Jan."

"Don't be. I'm happy. I've settled into an easier way of life. You should come and have a game with me. You'll find I hit the ball a million miles. Trouble is, I've not yet learned to master direction."

"A common problem, I hear," said Chapman.

"Yeah, but it costs me a fortune in golf balls," said Van Deventer, ruefully.

Chapman paused for a moment. "Jan, listen, I'm glad I caught you at home. I have a small problem. I was wondering whether you could lend a hand or steer me in the right direction?"

For the first time, Van Deventer noticed an edge to Chapman's voice. He raised his eyebrows, but still managed to chuckle. "It's been a while since I've heard those words. I must warn you, though, I know of very little on the go right now."

He heard Chapman laugh. A short bark. He knew the sound well. Chapman went on: "I'm not looking for information on a story. Actually I have a personal problem. Someone has been sending me threatening letters."

Van Deventer's attitude was abruptly hard. Professional. "What kind of threatening letters?"

"Jan, I really wouldn't have bothered you if I wasn't -"

"Never mind that, just tell me about these letters."

"Well, I've received three. Each one is on the same kind of paper. Each one has been made up using magazine cuttings.

And each one threatens my life."

Van Deventer reached for the notepad next to the telephone. He picked up a pencil and started to write. He asked: "Any idea who it could be?

"No."

Van Deventer sighed. "What kind of intervals between each letter?"

Chapman was silent for a moment. "About two or three days -"

Van Deventer heard a crash. It sounded as if Chapman had dropped the telephone. He waited.

"Hugh? You there?"

Nothing.

"Hello? HELLO!"

Still nothing, not even the sound of breathing, just a hissing on the wire.

Van Deventer cut the connection, and reached for his address book. Hastily he flicked through the pages. Years of police work had instilled in him an intuition he had come to value. A bell was jangling inside his head. Had he heard the sound of breaking glass?

Quickly, he dialled Chapman's number, punching the buttons with short, powerful fingers, and then waited impatiently.

Engaged. He tried again. Still engaged. Damn.

He stood up with surprising swiftness for such a big man, and shouted to his wife. "Tessa! I'm going out. Something's up at Hugh Chapman's place. I'm going over there."

She came to help him with his coat, handing him his car keys, concern on her face.

"Is it serious?"

"I don't know. He's had threatening letters. We were talking and our call was interrupted. I'm sure he'd prefer to talk this out face to face."

Tessa helped him do up his coat, clucking when she saw how much strain his belly placed on the buttons. "You're still fond of him, aren't you?"

"Yes."

"In spite of all that's happened?"

"Because of what's happened. Chapman kept everything to himself, in spite of coming under intense pressure to reveal what he knew. As far as I know, he's never opened his mouth. If I can do anything to help him, I will."

He opened the door, standing with an arm around Tessa. "I won't be too long. But don't wait up if I am."

He walked to his car, then waved to Tessa as he got in and started the engine. Breaking glass? He tried to recall the sound. He reversed out of the driveway too fast for Tessa's liking, ignoring her screech of protest, which reached him over the revs of the engine.

Steering the car into the street, his thoughts turned to Chapman again. Although the editor was only ten years younger than him, he had come to regard Chapman as something close to a surrogate son. He was one of the few men who had been able to get past the brusque, offhand manner of the policeman. They had forged a relationship in spite of different personal circumstances and the impacts of their chosen careers, making meetings far too infrequent. Later, after Campbell, the friendship had continued in the face of the obligations which arose from the affair. There was a strong bond of affection, and over the years an occasional lunch or drink together had been enough to sustain the relationship. Even so, thought Van Deventer guiltily, it was easier not to be reminded of the scandal. Which was why he seldom took the initiative to contact Chapman these days. He briefly wondered whether the editor still lived in South Kensington. If Chapman still had the same telephone number, he argued to himself, he must live in the same house. Chapman had been so proud when he announced he had bought a house there. Van Deventer had had drinks there several times, and regretted not getting to know the editor's family better. Sheila. And Jennifer was it? The daughter must be grown up now, he mused.

Van Deventer lived in Whitton, about 20 minutes away by car. He realised he was breaking the speed limit. Simply because of an interrupted telephone call? No. More. Something was wrong. He knew. On the way the thought struck him that maybe Chapman's number HAD changed, maybe he had tried to get through to an old number? Instinct told him otherwise. He accelerated.

Ten minutes later he pulled up outside Chapman's house and looked up at the building. Lights were burning upstairs and downstairs. Everything appeared normal. He sat in his car and laughed at himself. The years behind a desk must be getting to him, he thought.

Now that he was here, he may as well go up and say hello.

He got out of his car, locked the door, and stepped through the gate, walking up the path in his usual brisk manner. He rang the bell and waited. He could hear voices from a television or radio show, and rang again, the noise inside obscuring the ring of the bell. Sheila opened the door and a puzzled look came over her face as she recognised the policeman.

"Jan? Hello. What are you doing here?"

"Hello Sheila. I was talking to Hugh on the phone, and our call was interrupted. I tried to get through again, but the line was continually engaged, so I thought I'd come round to discuss things personally."

"That's funny," said Sheila. "Hugh said he was going to call you. But I've been watching TV and I haven't heard anything from upstairs for quite a while..." Her voice trailed off. Then she began again: "What do –"

Van Deventer shouldered his way past Sheila into the hall.

"Where is he?"

For an instant they stared at each other, then Sheila ran to the stairs and climbed them three at a time. Van Deventer was on her heels. She reached the top of the stairs, slowed to a walk, and halted in front of the study door. Her hand went to her mouth. She looked up at Van Deventer. He nodded at the door impatiently and she knocked. Nothing.

He reached for the handle, turned and pushed the door open. The sudden draft billowed the curtains and for a moment his attention was diverted to the window. The pane was shattered. A gasp from Sheila brought his gaze down to the desk.

"Oh my God. Oh dear God," whispered Sheila. She was immobile, her eyes wide with horror.

Hugh Chapman lay face down on his desk in a pool of blood. His face was tilted to one side and Van Deventer could see only his left eye. An arrow jutted from the back of Chapman's head. The feathered vanes of the shaft quivered in the breeze. Chapman's open eye was staring at three letters lying a few inches from his face. The telephone receiver was hanging over the edge of his desk.

Sheila started to groan. It started low and soft, increasing in pitch and volume into an unceasing scream so loud and so desperate it pierced Van Deventer's primeval soul. The policeman was stunned, his mind blank. On the ragged edges of his consciousness a prophecy took hold. He could see, with shattering clarity, that there would never again be a time in his life when he would not be able to hear Sheila's scream.

THREE

MARCH 28, 1986. *Keep thinking of the moment before pulling the trigger. In that instant, wielded the ultimate power. Power over life. Felt charged with menace, acutely aware of everything, especially my own fear. A lot can happen to a bolt fired from a crossbow over a distance of 30 yards. Wind can throw it off course – up, down or sideways. Gravity and friction play their parts too. Held my breath. Committed the trivial act of moving my finger. Pulled the trigger. Even as the missile flew towards its target the thought was in my head: what if it misses?*

No matter how much practice, no matter how expert, in the critical microseconds of flight always paralysed with doubt. The window behind Chapman shattered, and as glass rained down, saw the bolt strike home. It was over. After all the careful planning, all the anticipation, all the rehearsing, it was over.

Waited. Nothing. No screams, no sirens, no alarms.

Marvelled at how little seemed to have changed. Yet knew that nothing could ever be the same again. Dropped the rose, then walked away. A life was over. So far, no-one knew. Only me. Thought about it all. The more thought, the more conviction. Chapman was the right choice. His death would cause every editor in the country to be alarmed, fearful they might be next. As a consequence, they'd give the story front page treatment for days, if not weeks. The notes I'd sent him would be enough to confuse the police. Those notes were designed to make his death seem complicated. The police will never discover my true motive. There was something about Chapman I found abhorrent. That was enough. Hope the satisfaction of the killing will come later.

Mentally thanked Dan Stockton. That decrepit, smelly pig gave me the right weapon, and the right advice. Not that he'd had much choice. The Commando is rugged, easy to handle, powerful and accurate. Remembered his fearful face, his trembling words: "For rapid fire the crossbow has a unique cocking system that enables its user to fire, load and fire again very quickly."

He sounded like a salesman. In a way, he was. His trade is under-the-counter weapons. No questions asked. "These illuminated telescopic sights will make it perfect for night shooting," he'd said, handing it over.

He'd been perfectly right. Those sights had enabled me to watch Chapman closely, night after night, without him sensing me at all. Because of that, seeing him during the day always had a special significance. Once, without him being aware of me, I managed to get up really close. So close I could smell his after-shave. How animalistic that was. For a while, I actually had the scent of my quarry hot in my nostrils.

FOUR

"EVERYTHING INDICATES a professional hit," said Van Deventer. The two men with the Dutchman looked up. All three were standing in the hall of the Chapman house. Commander Philip Maxwell paused before speaking.

"An assassin?" he asked, not expecting a reply. "Yes, perhaps you're -"

"I'm sure of it," persisted Van Deventer.

Maxwell, head of the Serious Crimes Division of the Metropolitan Police Force, was a man used to authority and not used to being pushed. He especially did not enjoy being interrupted. Throughout the force, his colleagues widely regarded him as in line for the post of Commissioner.

Watching the two men was Chief Inspector Alan Winters, a detective directly under Maxwell's command. Knowing his superior, Winters expected it would not be long before Maxwell erupted. Van Deventer saw a hint of danger in Maxwell's eyes and fell silent. As the most senior officer on duty in the Serious Crimes Division office, Alan Winters had automatically assumed command of the murder investigation when Chapman's death was reported by the Dutchman. His was the name at the top of the list of three detectives posted for duty that night. Winters realised that the Dutchman was trying to convince Maxwell to let him assume command of the investigation. "The old bastard wants my job," he thought, indignantly.

For the past ten minutes he had been standing in the cold hall, surrounded by several police photographers, a scenes-of-crime officer and uniformed constables, listening to Van Deventer try to manipulate Maxwell. Around them, the scenes-of-crime officer was directing his colleagues in a comprehensive search for evidence, inside and outside the house, while a Home Office pathologist studied the body. Van Deventer was not able to stay quiet for long.

"An assassin. I'm certain of it. Chapman was taken out by a deliberate and cold-blooded killer," he said.

Winters was surprised when Maxwell merely nodded and said, quietly: "We'll see, Jan. We'll see."

Winters remained silent. He studied the Dutchman. Chief Superintendent Jan Van Deventer was a legend who had been put out to grass. After a long and distinguished career in the field, he had been piloting a desk for the past three years, assuming a backroom role at New Scotland Yard. Years ago he had commanded the Murder Squad. Among the famous cases he had been involved with was the Black Panther investigation. He was now in the training department, the only place his superiors had been able to assign him. They had taken him out of the criminal section, thought about detailing him to administrative work, then finally asked him to put his vast experience to good use by helping to establish training procedures for future detectives. Winters had heard many rumours, but no-one was sure why Van Deventer had not made it higher up the rung. Perhaps the sideways shunt had been a reaction to one clash too many with senior officers in the force?

Van Deventer had an imposing presence. He was a large man who had slowly allowed his age to get the better of his looks. He had a receding hairline, bags under his eyes, a double chin. A huge crooked nose was testimony to his willingness to engage in physical clashes. But the eyes were still young. They were always alert; a piercing blue. Those eyes were fixed on Maxwell now. The Commander, however, remained impervious.

"There is going to be an enormous outcry over this one," said Maxwell. "The death of an editor will attract a lot of heat. Do you feel up to handling that, Alan?"

"Of course, sir," said Winters. No more. He knew Maxwell well enough not to go on.

Winters was the youngest of the men, but not one to consider himself their inferior. He thought himself the luckiest of human beings – independently wealthy and pursuing his first love - police work - because that was what he wanted to do with his life. He recognised the opportunity solving this case represented. His tailored three-piece suit, combined with the dark blonde hair and lightly tanned complexion, marked him out as a man who looked after himself.

"I want it, Philip," said Van Deventer. "I know this family, I know Chapman's past, I know newspapermen and how he worked. Moreover, I OWE him."

Maxwell had obviously been asleep when the call came

through but he was awake now. He turned on Van Deventer, uncaring of the curious glances his raised voice attracted:

"Listen, Jan, you've had your years of doing this. There are enough men here now with the experience to handle the case. You may be the most senior officer here but you should know you have no jurisdiction. You did what you needed to do – now go home and let my men do their jobs."

Van Deventer would not relent. He shook his head. Winters watched as strands of silver hair, grown long to comb over the top of his bald patch, fell loose and hung over his ear. "No, Philip, you don't understand. I KNEW this man. He was talking with me on the telephone when the bastard shot him."

"All the more reason for you to stay off it. Your personal feelings might cloud your judgement," said Maxwell.

"Bullshit, and you know it."

Maxwell glared at Van Deventer. The Dutchman scowled back. Somehow, the faint Dutch accent still in Van Deventer's speech served only to accentuate his insolence. He had left Holland as a child, Winters knew, but still carried traces of the language of his youth.

Maxwell kept his temper in check, looking instead up to the first-floor landing. The paramedics clattered out of the study, manoeuvring a stretcher through the door. The body of Hugh Chapman lay shrouded beneath a white sheet. Winters knew the medics had to turn the body on its side, in order to prevent the bolt through Chapman's head from bending or breaking. A macabre discussion had followed as the men debated how best to lay the corpse on the stretcher.

The three officers watched in silence as the stretcher was carried down the stairs, through the hall and out to the ambulance. What an undignified way to leave your house for the last time, thought Winters. Who had kissed him goodbye the last time he had passed through this door? This time he would not return.

The three men continued to watch as the stretcher was loaded into the back of the ambulance. Several photographers were standing in the street. The arrival of the stretcher caused a barrage of camera flashes, which went on after the doors were slammed shut. The driver got into the vehicle and started the engine, pulling away slowly from the front of the house. There would be no lights, no siren. Chapman was beyond their skill.

Winters turned back to Van Deventer. Was that a film of tears in the Dutchman's eyes? Winters could see the distraction had served only to fuel Van Deventer's desire to command the hunt.

"You underestimate the impact of this case," said Van Deventer, addressing Maxwell, sniffing.

"How so?" asked Maxwell.

"The death of Chapman will be big news to other editors, especially when their lives now also may be at risk. I'm the only one who can cope with the attention this case will attract. It is going to be YOUR reputation on the line here, Philip, and you want to entrust it to relatively inexperienced people."

"I think you're out of line," said Maxwell. "They're not inexperienced. Winters here is a top rate man."

"You know what I mean. He's a good policeman. But he's not had this kind of experience, I bet."

The Dutchman spoke as if Winters was not present. The younger policeman, until now largely indifferent to the Dutchman, felt the first faint stirrings of hostility. Van Deventer turned to Winters and addressed him directly for the first time. "Well, have you?"

Winters was tall, with green eyes and a trim physique. In his suit he looked more like a successful businessman than a tough policeman. His appearance was deceptive in more ways than one. He looked gentle, considered. Yet he was superbly fit – a black belt in karate, a deadly pistol shot, and a first league squash player.

"No sir, I haven't. But this is a murder case, like any other, and I've dealt with many of those."

Van Deventer snorted in exasperation. "That's just my point. It isn't. I believe this will be unlike anything you've ever experienced before."

Winters stared into the Dutchman's eyes, pointedly refusing to be drawn. Van Deventer turned back to Maxwell. "I want this case Philip, for reasons I can't begin to explain. There are forces at work here only I will be able to deal with."

"What on earth are you talking about? What forces?" demanded Maxwell.

"I don't know. I can sense them. This is not going to be a straight up and down case."

Maxwell looked doubtful. In spite of his 53 years, he was still possessed of a youthful face, a good head of hair, and kept himself in trim. Many a colleague had learned the hard way that to underestimate this "boyish" policeman was to court disaster. Van Deventer seemed on the brink of doing so now.

Maxwell looked around the entrance hall of the Chapman home, watched as a police photographer's assistant came up the stairs from the garden, before squeezing between them and walking up the stairs. The man, wearing a white coat, wore his hair long. He could not have been much older than 19 or 20. Maxwell watched the youth until he reached the top of the stairs, sighed, hunched his shoulders and gazed down at his feet.

"All right. I tell you what. I was going to insist that you leave well alone. Instead I'm going to assign you a watching brief. I will approve your assignment to this investigation. However I must stress that you do not have any command authority over Winters and his men. Is that clear?"

Van Deventer hesitated a moment, then showed some sense. "Fine."

Maxwell turned to Winters. "What have you got so far?"

By the time Winters had arrived on the scene, Van Deventer had already begun supervising the activities. He had taken a back seat for a while, knowing Maxwell was on his way. He hadn't wanted to step on any toes. Besides, he knew Maxwell was a stickler for procedure, and he relied on that to wrest back control of the case. In the meantime, he had spoken to each of his team and quickly established background. He was glad of his foresight now.

"Not much," he said quickly. "Chapman received three anonymous letters in the post, at two-to-three day intervals. The author had cut out the words from a newspaper or magazine and pasted them on to ordinary letter paper. Each letter was vague but threatened Chapman's life unless he stopped what - "

"I was on the phone to Chapman," interrupted Van Deventer. "He called me to say he was worried about the letters. During the call, he was shot. I raced over here to find him dead at his desk. While waiting for the squad cars to arrive, I looked out of his study window, and figured the arrow-"

"It's called a bolt, or a quarrel," said Winters.

"- must have come from the road." Van Deventer went on. His attitude was still infuriatingly dismissive. "Perhaps a car stopped in the road and the driver or passenger seized his chance to shoot? Chapman's wife is heavily sedated. His daughter is out. We are trying to contact her now." Maxwell turned back to Winters, who was watching with a look of mild amusement. This was going to be a tough case, made even more difficult by Van Deventer's attitude, he thought.

"What else?" said Maxwell.

"I got the scenes-of-crime officer to take a look at the pavement and square across the road. He agreed with me that the bolt could only have come from the far side of the road, and there are officers looking there now."

"Who is the scenes-of-crime man in charge here?" asked Maxwell.

"Garner Patterson," said Winters.

"He's a good man," said Maxwell. "Give him his head, he'll produce the goods."

"Yes sir," said Winters. He waited to see if Van Deventer was going to butt in again, but the Dutchman was staring into the darkness.

Winters went on: "I've also got officers going over the letters, more men interviewing members of Chapman's staff, and all press calls are being diverted to Scotland Yard. Those press or media who have come here have been given very little." Winters was first and foremost a dedicated, ruthless and thorough policeman. His record was well known to Maxwell. "We are trying to establish exactly what the anonymous author could have been trying to dissuade Chapman from doing. We hear there was a story Chapman was currently working on."

Maxwell seemed pleased. "Good. Anything else? No? I'm going to go, then. If you need anything, call me. In the morning." He took one more look at the landing, turned on his heel and walked out of the house. He hunched his shoulders against the cold, hands deep in the pockets of his overcoat as he strode towards the gate. Halfway there, he stopped.

"Winters," he called.

"Excuse me," Winters said to Van Deventer, and walked to meet Maxwell.

When Winters had drawn close to him, the commander nodded towards Van Deventer. "He'll get on your nerves, he'll act as if he IS the boss. He'll be rude and abrasive. But listen to his every word. Consider his every suggestion. Then make your own decisions. If it gets too difficult for you, call me."

"If I need to, I will. But I don't think I'll need to, sir."

"Don't be so sure. He was a top man once. He knows his stuff. He's as coarse as sandpaper."

Before he could stop himself, Winters asked: "Why the fall from grace if he was such a top dog?"

Maxwell studied his junior officer. "You don't know?"

"No, I don't, sir."

"I guess you'll find out yourself anyway. I may as well tell you. Years ago there was a departmental investigation into the affairs of three members of the Drugs Squad, including an officer named Ivan Campbell. They were alleged to have been running an extensive drugs ring from behind the cloak of the law."

Maxwell turned back to look at Van Deventer, still standing in the hall, at the open door. "The investigation was kept secret and took months. Rumours became more and more persistent that they were going to be let off the hook because of a lack of evidence. Then someone leaked the story to the Press, and all hell broke loose. The headlines carried chapter and verse, naming each of the men involved."

After a pause, Winters asked: "What happened then?"

"Campbell committed suicide. He had a wife and three children. The remaining two officers went through hell. A witch hunt broke out for the source of the story, without success. Everyone had strong suspicions about who it was, but it could never be proved. A little later, an official inquiry cleared Campbell and his colleagues of any involvement with drugs. I'll never forget the look on Mary Campbell's face when the verdict was announced. It was indescribable. Hate. Relief. Pride. Vindication. Mourning. All in one look. She's married again now, but I hear she still wakes up calling for Ivan."

Maxwell's gaze returned to Van Deventer. This time his lips were curled in a sneer. "The author of the original newspaper story was Hugh Chapman. In the face of incredible pressure, Chapman managed to keep his source secret. But most people thought his source was Van Deventer. When asked, the Dutchman always denied it. Even so, his career took a nose dive. It says something for his character that he's managed to stay in the force despite the inordinate amount of hostility levelled at him."

Maxwell turned back to Winters. "I always have to remind myself that he was never proven guilty of ratting on his colleagues. I have to apply the principle to everyone. But, I find it hard to be civil to the man."

"I understand, sir," said Winters.

"No, I don't think you do. And don't let this affect your judgement, particularly when it comes to his advice. He WAS a brilliant policeman."

Winters nodded. As Maxwell walked away, Winters looked at the doorway, at Van Deventer, who was still staring into space. He wondered whether the Dutchman was going to be a help or a hindrance. He wondered whether the Dutchman was capable of helping anyone at all. For the moment he chose to sidestep a confrontation, and walked past Van Deventer up the stairs to Chapman's study. Fingerprint experts, photographers and detectives were working there. One of them was trying to deduce the trajectory of the missile that had ended Chapman's life. Watching the policemen searching for evidence, Winters gained some assurance from the steady competence with which they carried out their jobs. He felt sure he would crack the case, reasonably soon. After all, he thought, an editor was a very public man. There must be thousands of leads out there.

He was startled by Van Deventer's voice. He hadn't heard the Dutchman walk up behind him.

"Chapman once told me that he did not want a lingering death."

Winters nodded. He didn't know what to say. Instead, he asked: "Do you think the killer was the same one who sent the letters?"

Van Deventer shrugged. Winters went on: "Why were the letters sent? What did the senders - every letter spoke about 'we'- want Chapman to stop doing?"

"That's what we're going to find out," said Van Deventer.

In spite of himself, Winters felt drawn to the Dutchman. He seemed so solid. So dependable. Assured.

"What did you do after you discovered the...body?"

"I called Scotland Yard. Someone there must have passed the information on to you. Then I called a doctor, for Sheila, Chapman's wife. She is going to be devastated by his loss."

"Where is she now?"

"In her room. The family doctor is with her, along with her sister and brother-in-law."

Winters heard the sound of a car pulling up outside. "Excuse me," he said, and walked quickly out of the study and down the stairs. He strode out of the house in time to hear the engine of the car being turned off. It was parked in the short, sloping driveway of the Chapman house. The occupant, however, did not move. Winters caught sight of the whites of a pair of eyes in the darkness. They were large and staring. He walked down the stairs and ambled over to the car. Was this a reporter? he wondered. He reached the car and bent down to look in the window. Behind the wheel was a young woman who he found instantly electrifying. He had often imagined, in the moments just before sleep, what his perfect woman would look like. This stranger came close to being the physical embodiment of that dream. Seeing her now was almost a physical blow.

"Excuse me miss, could I..." he started, but realised the woman had not seen him approach. Her eyes were fixed on the front door of the house. He turned to see two uniformed policemen standing under the porch light. Oh shit, he thought. He felt chilled and unable to take the next step, which he knew he should make immediately. Still he remained rooted, staring at the woman, who was staring at the house.

Finally she turned to him. Her eyes were beginning to register fear. Her bottom lip trembled. She tried to speak, but her voice died in her throat. Winters wanted to take the girl in his arms, stroke her hair, hold her. Instead he coughed and opened her door.

"My name is Alan Winters. Do I take it you are Jennifer Chapman?" he asked, bending at the knees in order to look into the car. He knew he sounded horribly pompous, but he didn't know what else to say.

"Has something happened to my father?" she said, grabbing his coat lapel, pulling him off- balance. She was still seated in her car.

"Uh, I am afraid..." he began, but the girl pushed him aside, standing up and then setting off for the front door in one fluid, lithe movement that caught him unawares. One hand was still in his coat pocket, the other stretched for the handle of the car door, but Winters was unable to stop himself. He lost his balance and toppled gently into the flowerbed alongside the driveway. He struggled to free his trapped hand from his coat pocket, pushing himself off his side with his free hand. He felt so damned undignified. Thankfully nobody had seen him. The two officers at the door were equally taken with Jennifer Chapman, but just as afraid as he was to tell her the bad news. They pointed in the direction of the study, and Jennifer ran inside the house.

Winters finally managed to stand up, before the constables turned back to discover him brushing the earth off his coat and pants. He walked to the front door in time to see Van Deventer, his arm around the girl, leading her into the sitting room. The girl did not resist. Winters walked to the door and peered inside. Van Deventer was now kneeling in front of her, talking quietly. She was sitting on a couch, leaning forward, her arms clenched across her chest, rocking back and forth. Van Deventer looked up, saw Winters; shook his head. Out, he mouthed. Winters backed away, clenching his teeth.

For the second time that night he had to suppress a flash of jealousy and possessiveness. First the investigation, now the girl. Jennifer Chapman. Van Deventer was going to help to make this case more than a little challenging, he thought.

FIVE

WINTERS FOUND his attention wandering. His eyes felt gritty and sore. He felt dirty, shabby and hungry. His resentful gaze fell on Van Deventer, who had managed to get home for a wash and shave. Winters looked at his watch. It was 7am, more than 24 hours since he had last slept. He wondered whether he looked as awful as Garner Patterson. The scenes-of-crime officer had also been up all night. He and his men had scoured the square which was still closed off to the public. They were going back there later to see if daylight could help in their search. Winters was still wearing the same suit he had on when first alerted the previous night. By now it had lost its glamour, looking creased and disheveled. Patterson was wearing the same tweed sports coat, with a knitted tartan tie. Van Deventer was in a fresh suit, a simple grey off-the-rack item. His tie clashed horribly. Winters thought the Dutchman probably always dressed this way, with little regard for appearance. Clothes were clearly just functional items.

A wash and shave hadn't done much to change the surly look on Van Deventer's face, thought Winters, still smarting at the offhand manner in which the Dutchman had dismissed him a few hours ago. Van Deventer had summoned the doctor for Jennifer, seen her to her room, then spent time with Sheila Chapman. Later Winters had seen him leaving the house. He had stopped him, and asked him whether Mrs Chapman had been able to tell him anything.

"No. I'll tell you what she said in the morning. We'll speak to her again then, when she may make more sense. Don't disturb either of them until then."

He had left without saying goodbye. Irked by this, Winters had stewed while waiting for the scenes-of-crime officer to finish his work. He took a call from Maxwell, who ordered him to establish a command post at Scotland Yard the next morning. He had derived grim pleasure in calling Van Deventer at home. He was delighted to discover he'd woken the Dutchman.

Winters waited for Patterson to complete his search for clues, assisting where he could. His mind kept going over the moment he first saw Jennifer Chapman. He tried to brush thoughts of her aside, but failed miserably. He found himself hoping she would come out of her bedroom for something to drink, to allow him another look at her. Was she really as beautiful as his mind was reminding him?

Winters knew one of her aunts was staying the night with Jennifer and her mother. He was tempted to ask if he could do anything to help, but decided against it. There would be other, more appropriate opportunities.

By the time Patterson finished it almost had been time to meet Van Deventer at Scotland
Yard, so he offered to drive Patterson back. The scenes-of-crime officer had earlier loaned his car to one of his assistants, who was taking items of possible evidence to the Home Office laboratory for examination.

In the car Patterson had leaned back on the seat and groaned. "I envy you this machine, especially after a night like this," he said, looking around the interior of the BMW 535i. "Police work is a shitty life. On my salary I can only dream about something like this. Lucky bastard."

The car was the constant envy of his colleagues. "Being rich has its rewards," he said, turning the key. The engine burst into life, and Winters engaged first gear. He drove away slowly, restraining an urge to show off the power of the car. He had learned the hard way that accidents cost lives, and his driving was meticulous. His family had been decimated in a car accident. He did not need to explain to Patterson how he could afford a car like the BMW. And he was beyond apologising for his wealth.

Patterson was well aware of the detective's background. Winters inherited a fortune when his parents had died. Like many others, Patterson had begun by underestimating Winters.

But his rise through the ranks had not been meteoric because of his money or position. Winters was known as a fiercely determined policeman who if necessary would work inhuman hours to solve a case.

Patterson had worked with Winters on several cases. He had a healthy respect for the detective. He sighed again. "I was dragged away from a warm bed and a hot lady to come to this," he said.

Winters smiled. Traffic was beginning to build up, but he was still able to drive in a relaxed manner. The sun was coming up as they entered the roundabout at Hyde Park corner, Winters slipping his car into the traffic with ease. He reflected that Patterson's complaint was a common one. It was also one of the reasons he had remained unmarried for so long.

"I know what you mean," said Winters. "This life requires a dedication to the exclusion of family life and private interests. Hard."

"Oh God! You sound like you're quoting from a training manual."

"I am. I have a good memory."

"Hmmm. Were you alone last night? I suspect you must have been, or you'd be complaining as much as I am."

Winters laughed. "None of your business."

"Whatever happened to your air hostess friend? It looked like you two were getting things together."

"I didn't know you'd met her."

Patterson smiled. "I didn't. But you told me before you went on leave you were going to Spain for a week. With an air hostess. I think you said you'd met her during your hunt for the Glove rapist?"

"That's right. She was one of his near-victims."

"Well?"

"Well what?"

"What happened to the air hostess?"

Now Winters smiled. "The first three days were great. Then she started getting a little serious. The last three days were hell. The last time I saw her was when we said goodbye at the airport."

"You make it sound as if it took place months ago. You only got back from leave last week," said Patterson, lighting up a cigarette and looking for the ashtray.

Winters pointed at it, at the same time pressing the button which opened his electric window. He hated cigarette smoke. Opening the window allowed in the noise of the traffic and forced him to raise his voice slightly.

"After a night like tonight, it feels as if it WAS years ago."

They slipped into a companionable silence. Patterson gazed out the window, watching the passing shops and buildings. Winters concentrated on the road. He loved driving in London at this hour. Before very long it would be bedlam.

The two men knew they would soon be back in the thick of this case. They wanted a brief chance to relax, so the topic of the killing was avoided for a while. After all, they had spent most of the night examining the scene and speculating about the case.

Patterson took occasional drags at his cigarette, leaning forward to tap it in the ashtray.

Looking at the burning tip, he said: "You did well on that investigation. The Glove was a pretty difficult bastard to track down. I hear you received a commendation?"

"Yes. For what it was worth." Patterson opened his own window and flicked his cigarette out. Winters scowled his disapproval. They were nearing Scotland Yard.

Patterson continued: "That hunt took you three months.

How many victims did the guy rape? Seven? You don't have to play down your effort. It was a job well done."

"Thanks," said Winters. "I really was lucky. The guy virtually gave himself up."

When they reached Maxwell's floor at Scotland Yard, two of Patterson's assistants were already waiting. Winters went straight to his desk, and looked at the morning papers, folded neatly on his blotter. Chapman's murder occupied the front page of most of the papers. Those that did not carry a report were obviously printed too early to have caught it. He read the reports of Chapman's death while Patterson discussed the case with his assistants. Winters decided to wait for the Dutchman before reviewing the evidence. Van Deventer had not rewarded his politeness. He burst in through the squad room door - "What have you got?"

Winters had to suppress yet another flash of irritation. He was about to tell Van Deventer to wait for him to ask the questions, when he realised the Dutchman was renowned for his lack of subtlety. Now was not the time to take issue.

Winters was the first to speak. "We have a lot, we have nothing."

"What do mean? Don't be cryptic."

Patterson butted in: "What he means, Superintendent, is that we have made progress, but we have no clues that provide us with red hot leads."

"Well, what HAVE we got?"

Winters and Patterson started talking at the same time. Both stopped, looked at the other, and waited.

Van Deventer's irritation was acute. "Come on, damn it. Winters!"

Winters looked up at the Dutchman. He knew the shadow of his heavy beard made him look gaunt and drawn. Girlfriends had told him he always looked particularly fierce early in the morning. He stroked his bristles as he tried to contain his mounting rage. His eyes pricked and for a moment he feared tears of anger would humiliate him.

Once again, Patterson butted in. "As you know, Superintendent, physical evidence can be a critical cog in the solution of crimes."

Van Deventer grunted his acknowledgement. He was still staring at Winters.

Winters had heard Patterson delivering lectures throughout London, to anyone who would listen, about the importance of science in crime detection. He always made the point that too many investigators were clumsy in their attitude to evidence, and through their ignorance let criminals get away and crimes go unsolved. Patterson said even the tiniest piece of evidence could be a great help in providing critical clues in tracking down criminals.

It sounded as if Patterson was going to launch into another of his lectures.

The scenes-of-crime officer went on: "Wherever a criminal steps, whatever they touch, whatever they leave behind, even without knowing they are leaving it behind, will give us clues - silent testimony against a perpetrator."

"Yes, yes, I know and understand all that. Get to the point," said Van Deventer.

Winters could see Patterson was more than taken aback by Van Deventer's abrasiveness. The tall, balding officer blinked his surprise.

Winters stood up, his chair rasping on the floor. "Garner," he said, looking at Van Deventer, "forgive the Superintendent. Chapman was a personal friend."

Van Deventer looked from one to the other. "Go on," he said.

"All right, I get the message," said Patterson. "Look, briefly, what we have is this: The killer was a man, of average height, about 73kg in weight. He used a high-powered crossbow to fire a bolt with a three-bladed, barbed head. It is not legal in the U.K. even though it was manufactured by a company called Barnett International, based in Wolverhampton. Assuming the man also used one of their crossbows, it might be a good place to start looking. The killer fired the bolt from behind the fence of the square opposite Chapman's house, and used the top of the fence as a rest for the stock of his weapon."

Winters nodded. He was taking in everything, trying to picture the scene. Van Deventer said: "If the man was in the square opposite, and not the street as I first surmised, then standing at Chapman's open window as I did meant the killer could have had me in his sights as well?"

Winters grunted. The sound expressed the thought that it was a great pity the killer hadn't made use of the opportunity.

Patterson went on, seemingly unaware of the tension between the two officers. "Further, it is obvious the killer spent several nights before the murder at the scene from where the bolt was fired. "

"Anything else?" asked Winters.

"No, not at the moment. But we will have more by tonight when the forensic laboratory has completed tests on everything we found. We are going back to look again in daylight."

"The letters?" asked Van Deventer.

"We're still considering those. At the moment all we can say is that they were made from magazine cuttings, and the paper and envelopes were standard items available in many supermarkets or shops. We hope to be able to tell you which magazines the cuttings came from, what fingerprints are on the letters - though we think these will be from members of the

Chapman family only - and perhaps more after a microscopic examination."

"Such as what?" asked Van Deventer, impatiently.

"I don't know. More. Sir." Patterson spoke softly, but Van Deventer was clearly upsetting him.

Once again, Winters stepped into the breach. This was getting to be tiresome. "The newspapers have had a field day. But nothing in any of the reports helps."

He noticed both of Patterson's assistants, neither of whom he had met before today, were edging their way out of the circle. Van Deventer had successfully intimidated them. Still Van Deventer ignored him, and finally Winters exploded.

"Shit! Are you always this difficult?"

Van Deventer looked at him, surprise on his face. "Who's being difficult?" he said.

"You could at least listen to what we have to say."

Van Deventer, who until now had been standing with his hands in his pockets, jabbed a finger at Winters. "Chapman was a friend of mine. Now he's dead, and I'm determined to find out who killed him and why. That's my only interest. Forgive me if I lack social niceties at the moment. I find the situation difficult enough without having also to deal with a rich boy who wants to be a policeman and a scenes-of-crime officer who wants to be a prima donna."

Winters and Patterson gaped at the Dutchman. Winters leaned back on one of the squad room desks. One of Patterson's assistants broke into an uncontrolled coughing fit, distracting Van Deventer. Winters regretted his outburst. He was usually able to contain his temper. Now he felt undignified, as if the Dutchman had won a victory by riling him. He wondered how best to back away from this situation with some dignity.

Then he thought: To hell with it! "I'd like to make a point

here Superintendent. I wish I didn't have to." His voice was calm, almost a whisper, each word precise and clipped. "Let me remind you I am in charge of the investigation. From now on please remember that. And remember also that I have enough to worry about without having also to tiptoe softly around you, simply because the victim was a friend of yours. If you find that too difficult to cope with, please don't let me prevent you from leaving."

To his surprise, Van Deventer smiled. "Fine," he said.

Winters waited for more, hoping someone would break the growing silence.

Van Deventer spoke, still smiling. "Okay. We have letters. We know someone tried to warn Chapman about the danger before he was killed. We know someone had been watching Chapman, even while the letters were in the post. So someone was preparing for the kill even while there was a chance Chapman would stop whatever he was doing. Why? Was he watching for some other reason? Was the killer the one who sent the letters? Or was he hired by others? What was Chapman doing that warranted his death?"

Van Deventer had been thinking aloud. But the others nodded. They were wondering the same thing.

"All right Winters. We found out last night Chapman was working on a story about an affair among politicians. Have you got any more?"

Winters wanted to bellow at the Dutchman. Van Deventer persisted in leading the meeting.

Winters managed to reply, civilly. "No sir, not yet. As you know, Mrs Chapman couldn't tell us much last night. Neither could the daughter, Jennifer. We couldn't get hold of any of the journalists Chapman was working with. I'm going to see his deputy, a man called Channing. Other detectives are talking to friends, neighbours, and colleagues right now. By this afternoon we should have much more."

"What about the newspapers. You were saying they didn't have much?"

"That's right," said Winters. "They didn't even mention the threatening letters. Most speculate he was shot from a car in the street, others say it was someone in Chapman's garden. But every paper has this as their front page lead. A crossbow is a spectacular weapon, as far as they are concerned. Judging by the initial response, you were right. There's going to be a lot of flak."

"Has anyone spoken to the owners of neighbouring houses?"

"Yes. Nothing untoward to report. Yet."

Van Deventer swung to Patterson. "Okay. Garner, you say we should have more from the lab by this afternoon?"

"Yes, by about three."

"Winters, when you go to see Channing, you should take three or four men with you and let them talk to people in the newsroom. See if any of them have noticed anything lately."

"Right." Winters clenched his teeth. He was going to do it anyway, but the fact the Dutchman suggested it now as if it was his idea compounded his irritation. Winters cut across Van Deventer and addressed Patterson. "I have to brief the detectives assigned to this case before I go to see Channing. Maxwell has called a press conference for four pm. I think we should all meet back here at three sharp. Bring whatever you can give me. Everything will help. Is there anything else you need from our side?"

"Yes," said Patterson."I need you to tell your men to be more careful if they are the first to investigate the scene of a crime like this. Luckily I got some good casts of the killer's footprints. The different depths of the several tracks in the area showed us the prints were made at different times, some during or immediately after rain. But even those tracks, and God knows what other evidence, would have been destroyed by ignorant behaviour from your detectives had I not been there to stop them."

"Okay, I understand. See you at three."

Van Deventer turned to Winters again. "You would do well to send other men to talk to every informer we have. Find out if anyone knows what's going on, or has heard anything. Find out where the crossbow came from. Go to every arms dealer and sports shop in London. Once you've spoken to Channing - is it Channing? – get more men. Follow up everything he says. Send someone to talk to everyone who lives in the square, or regularly visits the square."

"I've already arranged all that," said Winters.

He stood up from the desk and walked to the squad room door. Before leaving he turned back to Van Deventer, unable to bite his tongue. "What are you going to be doing for the next seven hours, Superintendent? Anything useful?"

Van Deventer smiled, sweetly. "Yes. I'm going to see Maxwell. You're going to need some extra manpower on this one. I'm going to see if I can talk him into arranging us access to the regional crime squads."

As Winters left the office he saw the Dutchman was smiling again. Bastard, he thought.

SIX

THIS TIME, Van Deventer was the one waiting impatiently in the squad room. He was sitting at an empty desk, watching the other policemen in the room. His eyes kept roaming to the clock on the wall, then back to two detectives who had been standing at a filing cabinet, talking, for the past fifteen minutes. Every time he watched them, a disapproving look came over his face.

Winters tramped in, talking to two detectives who had been assigned to his command for this case. He had shaved, showered and changed since last in the room, and his step had a renewed spring. He was dead on time.

"Let's wait for Patterson, then we can go into the conference room," he said. He deliberately did not greet Van Deventer. The Dutchman did not seem to notice the slight. He ignored the two detectives and spoke directly to Winters. "Maxwell has promised you anything - anything at all. You have only to ask."

Before Winters could answer, Patterson walked into the room, looking around deliberately as he headed toward the group. He seemed to be taking in his surroundings as if he were studying the scene of a crime, looking distastefully at the desks, the typewriters, the notice boards, the coffee machine. He too had changed. Winters noted a trend towards tartan ties.

"Afternoon," Patterson said. Winters felt a rush of affection for Patterson. He was so damn ... cool. He should have been an artist. In a way, Winters supposed, he was.

Winters ushered them in to the meeting room. "This will be our operational headquarters for this case. Let's hope we won't be here for long. Superintendent Van Deventer, this is Detective Sergeant Ian Hawkins, and Detective Inspector Matthew Boyer," said Winters. "You all know Garner Patterson."

Van Deventer nodded briefly in acknowledgement. The two detectives, primed by Winters on their way over to the Yard, knew they could expect a difficult character. They said, in unison: "Good afternoon, sir."

Boyer was a small, rotund character who always played Father Christmas at the annual children's Christmas party. He exuded good cheer. He wore his dark hair close-cropped, and hid behind a thick pair of spectacles. Hawkins was of medium height, average except for his pipe, which he always carried. He had an ageless appearance and was one of the squad's stars when it came to tailing people. He was the kind of man you could easily miss seeing, even if he was the only other person in the room. Everything about him was nondescript, including his brown hair, his average build and his plain, dark suit.

Both the detectives had surprised Winters by knowing all there was to know about the scandal which haunted Van Deventer. While Winters had been aware of the affair, he had never paid much attention to the story. At the time he had been too busy trying to make a name for himself.

"He wasn't always a sourpuss, know what I mean?" said Hawkins. "But since Campbell, he's never been the same. Used to be a cheerful fella. Bitterness got to him, if you ask me. I worked with him once. Bloody good copper in them days. Bloody good."

Winters couldn't care less about Van Deventer's bitterness. He felt largely indifferent to the story of the scandal. It didn't seem right to rat on another policeman, but then again, he didn't know all the details, so he couldn't judge the Dutchman. All he was concerned about now was that the Dutchman was an aggravation he had to cope with while trying to solve a murder.

Consequently, he quickly assumed command: "I interviewed Bob Channing this morning. He told me Chapman had spoken to him about the letters for the first time yesterday morning."

He could see Van Deventer looking at his fresh suit, obviously impressed. He suppressed a smile. So Van Deventer judged a book by its cover, eh?

He went on: "Channing felt Chapman was genuinely puzzled. That he had no idea who could be sending the notes. They both wondered whether it had anything to do with the story Chapman was working on together with the newspaper's political writer, a journalist by the name of William Bennett."

Winters looked up to see Van Deventer was staring at Hawkins. He stopped talking. Van Deventer did not appear to notice. Still staring at Hawkins, the Dutchman asked: "Do I know you?"

Obviously embarrassed, Hawkins muttered: "Uh, yes sir. We worked together a good few years ago."

Winters waited, irritation welling up. Hawkins coughed, looking from under his brows at Winters. Van Deventer turned back, a puzzled look on his face.

"Sorry," he said, distractedly.

Winters continued, but now his voice was icy, his speech slow and deliberate. "Apparently Tory MP Barry Jurgens is having an affair with a girl called Kristin Burroughs, his secretary. A Labour backbencher called Brian Metcalf leaked this news to the newspapers in the hope the exposure would hurt Jurgens."

Hawkins, Boyer and Patterson listened attentively. Winters had learned the hard way to command respect through his years in the force. When he had first joined, colleagues often called him (to his face) an arrogant little rich boy. They had been especially tough on him. But he had been top student at the police training school at Hendon, and from then on had built a solid career in the force. These days people seldom remarked on his penchant for flashy cars and clothes – and reputation with women. They knew he had the money and the confidence. More importantly, they knew he was good at his job.

"The only one who was worried about the affair was Jurgens's assistant, someone called Philip Wallace. He is a bit puritan, and was worried the affair would lead to a Party scandal." Winters paused, looking out the window. It was a bright and cloudless day, he noticed, for the first time.

"Go on," urged Van Deventer. It was the first indication that the Dutchman was listening.

Winters waited a while longer, deliberately. He looked at Boyer, then Hawkins, then Patterson. They were all leaning toward him, anxious to hear more.

"Channing said Chapman was convinced none of these people could be behind the letters. The story simply wasn't big enough. We spoke to all of the people today, except for Wallace. I don't think there was anything they were worried about from Jurgens's side, and Metcalf was merely disappointed his exposé would now take a back seat to the murder. Bad timing, he said. According to Metcalf himself, the most that could have happened to Jurgens was a slapped wrist, as the Burroughs girl did not present any kind of political threat. But anything that could have dented Jurgens's image was good enough for Metcalf."

"Anything else?" asked Van Deventer.

"The bad news," continued Winters, "is that not one of the neighbours can remember anything odd. I'm afraid that, on face value anyway, we have nothing to go on."

Winters turned to Boyer.

"What about the men on the street? Have their contacts turned up anything ?"

"No, not yet. Those we got hold of say there hasn't been a breath about this. We haven't contacted many of the known arms shops and sports shops yet, let alone any of the illegal ones."

"Okay, keep on it will you? Stay for the press conference, then put a watch on the Chapman home for the next few days, in case the killer returns. By the way, are we sure the notes were meant for Chapman? As I recall, they were pretty vague, and could have applied to anyone in the family."

"Yes," answered Patterson. "The envelopes were addressed to Hugh Chapman."

"Well, perhaps he WAS working on something else. Did any of the other members of his staff have anything?"

"Not a thing," said Boyer. "They all said Chapman was a little aloof. That he mixed with one or two senior members of staff, but otherwise ruled at arm's length, leaving day-to-day decisions to his departmental heads."

"What about this political journalist? Betten?" asked Van Deventer.

Boyer looked at Van Deventer, but turned back to address Winters. "It's Bennett sir. But no, he couldn't add anything, and echoed the feeling that the Jurgens case didn't warrant a reaction like this. He felt Chapman may have been working on something secretly. Apparently that's not uncommon among journalists."

"Oh hell!" exploded Van Deventer. "There must be something we can go on?"

Winters saw that Hawkins and Boyer looked chastened. "If it was a professional hit, an imported hitman, we may have some way of checking with the airlines?" suggested Boyer in desperation. Van Deventer gave him a withering look. They all knew this was an impossible task with so little to go on.

"The streets must know something. They always do. Boyer, I want it found," said Winters.

"Garner, what can you tell us?"

Patterson, too, had smartened himself up. Even though his eyes were still red and puffy behind his circular horn rimmed spectacles, he looked fresh and alert. He sat upright in his chair.

"We've turned up a couple of oddities, one of which is pretty gruesome," he said. "In the

daylight we found a partially buried cat. It had been skewered, probably by a crossbow bolt. It appears our man used it for target practice some time before shooting Chapman. The body of the cat had begun to decompose. We found a hole in a tree near the cat, where again the killer may have been practising. But as we found some blood near the base it is more likely the bolt that killed the cat is the same one that made the hole in the tree."

"Jesus," said Hawkins. He sucked on his pipe, and the gurgling sound distracted all the men for a moment.

"We also found a single rose near the entrance to the square."

"Why should a rose interest us?" asked Boyer.

"Because it didn't come from the square. It may be it has nothing to do with the killer, but we keep anything that doesn't fit," explained Patterson.

"What sort of damage did the bolt do to the cat?" asked Winters. Van Deventer leaned back in his chair and folded his arms. He was listening to every word now.

"That's the strange thing," said Patterson. "Not much. The bolt the killer used on the cat must have had a plain tip, looking something like a sharpened pencil. It went straight through the cat. But the poor thing's skull had been crushed."

"Cruel bugger," said Hawkins.

"Yes, yes, but what does all this mean?" asked Van Deventer.

Winters stood up and walked to the window, staring down at The Embankment. He clenched his teeth, trying to suppress an urge to tell Van Deventer to shut up. He watched Patterson's reflection in the glass.

"Well, it confirms my suspicion that the man rehearsed the murder," said Patterson.

"We don't know he rehearsed it for sure. I thought you knew only that he had been there on different nights, or at different times," said Van Deventer.

"Correct. But fibres we found on some of the branches of the hedge indicate he was wearing different clothes on the different occasions. Those same different fibres are on the fence, in various positions near the spot from where he must have fired the crossbow at Chapman. Fibres are really very useful. They transfer easily from one cloth to another, or to a non-cloth surface."

"And from that you surmise he rehearsed the murder?" asked Van Deventer. He was leaning back in his chair again, an arm hooked over the top of the back of the chair. Winters turned back to the table, and leaned against the window sill. He had to suppress irritation each time Van Deventer asked a question.

Patterson glanced across at Winters, but continued talking. "Yes. It would seem to indicate he had the crossbow with him on the other nights as well, and aimed at Chapman."

"Perhaps he was merely waiting for the right opportunity, and had to come back several nights to get it?" suggested the Dutchman.

"Possible," said Patterson. "But I doubt he would have killed a cat in that case. We also know from the fibres that he was wearing, at different times, a dark brown woollen jersey, and a dark blue jersey, also woollen."

Winters imagined a dark figure creeping into the garden, taking up his station, aiming at Chapman across the road. He shuddered, then walked back to his chair. Both Hawkins and Boyer looked relieved to see him back. They had found it uncomfortable craning to see him.

Van Deventer tried to continue probing Patterson, but Winters butted in. "He must have
had telescopic sights," he said.

"Why do you say that sir?" asked Hawkins, immediately more interested in this new thought.

"Because it is a distance of about 30 to 40 yards across the road to Chapman's study. In the dark, it would be too risky a shot to take with an illuminated front sight only. He would have to be very sure of his shot, knowing he would probably only get one opportunity."

"I'd buy that," said Patterson. "The bolt took Chapman at the top of his neck, travelled upwards through his brain and exited just above the right eye. It was a good shot, from that distance."

Van Deventer glared at Patterson, horrified. This time Winters sympathized with him. Sometimes Patterson's clinical attitude to murder took his breath away.

Van Deventer spoke, and now his voice was frosty. "Mr Winters, I suggest all this information is circulated. Also, get our men to go to every known illegal arms dealer. The crossbow must have come from somewhere, and probably locally."

Patterson said: "I've got more."

Winters turned back to the scenes-of-crime officer, a slow, calculated gesture of insult to the Dutchman.

Patterson went on. "The letters were posted at different post boxes. The envelopes and paper were common types as you know. What might be of help, though, is that the sender used cuttings from International Finance Week magazine. It is published in the United States and distributed here on a limited circulation every week. Within a day or so I'll be able to tell you which issues of the magazine."

Hawkins snorted, a queer sound what with his lips still wrapped tightly around the stem of his pipe. "How'd you find out that?" he asked.

Patterson nodded. He enjoyed being tested. "The type and character of paper are almost infinitely variable, the result of which is a tremendous number of distinguishable papers. We knew that the particular type on which the headlines were printed is used mostly in the United States. We also know it is used in magazines. Narrowing it down to a weekly finance journal circulated here was the easy part."

"You could try getting their mailing list in the UK, specifically London. That may give you some names," said Van Deventer, looking at Winters.

"Any fingerprints?" asked Winters. He took pleasure in a faint redness which began to suffuse Van Deventer's face. The Dutchman was feeling the effects of the silent war they were waging.

Patterson shook his head before answering. "Only those of the Chapmans, and Mr Van Deventer. We did take some dust samples from the letters though, which we are subjecting to microscopic examination. We may have more by tomorrow morning. The laboratories are working on it full time."

"What will the dust tell us?" persisted Hawkins.

Patterson smiled, patiently. "I don't know, yet. It might have something in it that will help us. Pollen maybe, or traces of some substance that can provide us with clues."

Hawkins was not satisfied, sucking fiercely on his pipe, but he decided to drop this line of questioning for the moment.

"Anything else, anybody?" asked Winters.

Except for Van Deventer, they all shook their heads.

"Okay, let's go see the chaps from public relations. They're going to have to work out what we should say to the Press."

"One moment, Mr Winters," said Van Deventer. "I'd like to talk to you when these gentlemen have left the room." It was not a request.

Winters indicated to Boyer and Hawkins to wait outside. They stood up, joined by Patterson, and left the room.

The Dutchman waited until the door was closed, then softly said: "You have been rude and insolent throughout this meeting Winters. Do you always behave this way?"

Winters gaped. "That's rich, coming from you - "

"You may be in command of this investigation Winters, but I would caution you against ignoring the opinions of officers senior to you in rank and experience. The way you cut across a line of thought I was exploring there was offensive in the extreme. It was also immature and short-sighted."

"I have not ignored you at all. I merely find it - "

"What? A nuisance having to tolerate me? I have a funny feeling that with your intense self-centredness you won't last very long on this case Winters. And if you carry on this way, I assure you I will do everything in my power to have you removed from the case. Don't underestimate me."

Winters stared back for a moment. "Is that all?" he asked.

"For the time being."

"Good. Now, if you have no objections, I'd like to talk with Commander Maxwell. Feel free to join me, if you wish."

The two men rose together. Winters, nearest the door, opened it and walked out of the room without waiting for Van Deventer. He was seething, and he did not want the Dutchman to see it. He set off for Maxwell's office without looking at the three men who stood waiting for him.

Boyer, Hawkins and Patterson followed in his wake, Boyer looking back over his shoulder to see if Van Deventer was joining them. When he looked directly into the Dutchman's eyes, he felt obliged to wait.

Winters intended telling Maxwell he doubted whether he was going to be able to work with Van Deventer, but rapidly changed his mind when he opened the door to the Commander's office.

Maxwell had with him three Metropolitan divisional CID chiefs, as well as the Chief Public Relations officer. Maxwell summoned all five newcomers into his office, quickly introducing everyone.

After a short briefing, the press officer advised Maxwell that the investigating team should not release any details about the clothes worn by the killer, the slaying of the cat, nor the letters, and to stress the police were following up leads. Obviously, they should say they hoped for an early arrest.

The group moved through to the special press office in Scotland Yard. Nothing could have prepared Winters adequately for the conference. He had never seen so many press men in one room. He was introduced as the investigating officer. After he had made a brief statement, the first thing the press men asked concerned the letters. That day's London News had printed the full story about the threats to Chapman, and, after some hasty on-the-spot advice from the press officer, he told them about the three letters, and what the letters had said. He refused to comment on speculation that the killing was the work of a professional assassin.

During the conference, Van Deventer was asked what his involvement was. He explained he was on the telephone at the moment Chapman was killed.

Where Winters had been deliberately restrained, Van Deventer embellished. When Winters had made his statement, few of the journalists had bothered to write anything down. But, as Van Deventer spoke, most of them were bent to their notebooks.

"It was carried out as precisely and as clinically as a surgeon would conduct an operation," he said. "This is as cold a killer as I have ever seen."

After the conference, Maxwell congratulated Van Deventer on the way he had diverted the journalists with colourful quotes.

"It could have got tricky there," said Maxwell. "But they seemed very happy with your quotes."

On his way home that night, listening to his car radio, Winters heard the first news reports of the conference. The radio reporter focused on Van Deventer's quote. Then he went a stage further. He said already detectives assigned to the case has started referring to the man they were hunting as "The Chiller Killer."

It was news to Winters. He had not yet heard any of his men use that phrase. But he felt sure of one thing: he soon would. Incessantly.

SEVEN

APRIL 16, 1986. *The dream. It has haunted me since childhood. Always the same. Always a storm.*

There is no real beginning, no definite end. Standing in a street of my childhood. Brighton.
It is a steep street. Slopes downhill towards the sea, about two miles from where I stand.
Around me, like canyon walls, are terraced houses typical of Brighton, all with their peculiar bay windows, bright and multi-coloured. All the houses feel empty. Windows are bereft of curtains.

Watch the storm clouds gathering. No-one else around. The street is empty of cars, of people, of all signs of life.

Stand there in the middle of the road. Can smell the rain coming. Wind licks at my hair. Moisture is in the air, against my cheeks, on my ears. The sun sinks into the sea and the last rays of the day light up the clouds with a brilliant purple light.

The clouds are on the distant horizon, moving in from left and right to a central point. There they meet, collide, swirl, form up and begin marching toward me, like columns of soldiers.

I stand, leaning into the wind, challenging the might of the storm. The clouds march on, growing in size and menace. The wind slaps at my clothes.

Before the first clouds reach me, I see still more racing in from both sides to that meeting point on the horizon. They swirl in a demented, frenzied way, then charge off in pursuit of the leading clouds.

Now the wind lashes at the trees along the road, and it is like an evil portent. I stay. I recognise my personal Armageddon. Prepared to take on the storm, standing fast as it rages all around me, prepared to endure the full might of the elements.

In all this fury, there is no sound.

Just an eerie silence as the wind whips at the trees, as the lightning bursts from the clouds as my clothes flap and lash at my skin.

Then the rain comes. First one drop, one giant drop, followed by more, then the clouds open up and unleash their pent-up rage. The drops crash down, flattening everything.

My perspective changes. The clouds are moving, I can see that. But they don't get any closer. It is as if I am being whisked away from them as fast as they travel toward me. But still I lean into the wind, motionless. The clouds aren't getting any closer, and still more clouds are racing in, joining forces with those already at the mustering point, more and more setting off towards me.

I am not afraid. I am fascinated. As I watch, the raindrops change colour. Gradually they darken, become black, then scarlet, then blue, then green, then yellow, forming rivers of coloured water, covering everything.

Then, the first sound. A man hissing. I look around. See a figure in a doorway several houses away. He is in the shadows.

He makes sure I can see him. Steps out of the shadows and walks towards me. I peer at him, trying to see who he is. Even though he stands clear of the doorway he still looks shadowy and mysterious. Medium height. Medium build. He gets no closer. He spots a chair standing in another doorway. He walks to the chair, turns it to face the storm, sits down. The chair has a high back. I can no longer see him.

But I can HEAR him.

He tells me things. His words have no shape. Like words whispered in another room. Just the rise and fall of a human voice, the sound familiar, but the words indistinct. I strain to determine the sense, but the words fall bafflingly short of meaning.

I call out that I cannot hear. He starts to shout, but as he does the wind starts howling. Like one piece of an orchestra leading off, followed by another. Then the thunder starts, and I can hear the lightning crackling in the air and the thunder rolls and rolls, even as the man speaks.

Don't know who he is or what he wants but he is talking to me, telling me things. I cry with the frustration of not being able to understand him. Try to get closer but even as I walk I stand still and around me the wind gusts and the rain falls and the thunder claps and the lightning flashes and the clouds race and race and the man talks and the drops turn black and run in rivers and the man screams, a long wail that rises over the sound of the wind and thunder, rising and rising until finally it drowns out all sound and then there is nothing, no clouds, no storm, no man, no houses, just whiteness, blinding whiteness and the sound of the scream, on and on and on.

I grasp for the light, awake, terrified, the scream still ringing in my ears.

I have looked up several books on dreams.

Most say a dream about rain is an omen of difficult times. If the downpour is heavy, then the difficulties will be serious. The books say different colours of rain have different meanings.

Black rain is sinister.

Sometimes the dream leaves me alone for several days. Then it comes two nights in succession, then stays away for several more nights.

After killing Chapman, it left me alone for ten consecutive nights.

But during this past week, I have experienced the dream every night. Last night, I woke up seven times, always at the same point in the dream.

This buildup of dreams is almost like my own personal storm gathering. First one cloud, then another, then several more, and more, and more.

Legions gathering for the tempest.

EIGHT

ALAN WINTERS abandoned his restraint. He had to see her again. After all, he had a reason.

He wanted to find out more about Chapman. He wanted answers to questions his detectives had not yet asked. Questions such as: who WAS Hugh Chapman? What were his interests? What did he do with his spare time? Who did he mix with?

Every little bit helped in an investigation like this.

The past four days had been a whirl of inquiries and interviews, official memos and newspaper reporters. Detectives were pursuing every possible angle, attempting to find out who or what was behind the murder. Terrorist organisations were top of the list of suspects. The theory was that Chapman was a victim of a radical group. Winters found himself agreeing with Van Deventer's skepticism about this. If it was terrorism, someone would have claimed his scalp. There had been no such claims, but every angle had to be followed up, even if it meant having to deal with police forces all over the United Kingdom and Europe, along with all the irritations this brought.

In all, it had been a frustrating few days, and the tension between himself and the Dutchman had not helped. It seemed to ferment at a subliminal level, colouring his attitude to the case. Thank God for Patterson and Boyer. The two of them had managed to keep Winters from boiling over into a rage that threatened physical violence. He knew he was going to have to watch his every step with Van Deventer around. There had been no further angry exchanges since the meeting prior to the press conference, but the Dutchman's threat to have him removed from the case still worried Winters. He knew Van Deventer wanted the case for himself, and was waiting for Winters to slip.

This was why he was away from Scotland Yard now, driving to interview Jennifer Chapman. Any break from the disappointments of a frustrating investigation was surely a good break. There was always the chance she might be able to tell him something that could help the case.

Or so he told himself.

He told Boyer he would be at the Chapman house and, without informing Van Deventer, drove there in his BMW. It was the middle of the fifth morning after Chapman's death.

He knew Jennifer had taken a week's leave. He also knew there had been a church service for Chapman the day before – despite not being able to bury the body while it was part of an ongoing investigation, the family had wanted to recognise the loss of a beloved husband and father. He did not know what to expect. When he pulled up outside the house he turned the engine off and sat in his car for 10 minutes, watching her front door and rehearsing his opening lines.

Before he got out of the car, Jennifer appeared at the front door and Winters forgot every rehearsed word. She was as striking as he remembered.

As he watched he realized she had opened the door to let some visitors leave. A young man and two young women. The man was tanned and lean, dark-haired and good-looking. He bent toward Jennifer and put a hand on her arm as they talked. After a brief exchange, he kissed her on the mouth. Winters felt instantly depressed.

The three waved goodbye and walked to a small sports car parked at the bottom of the Chapman driveway. They got in, one of the girls having to contort her legs to fit in the back seat. They did not notice Winters in the car parked opposite. Close-up, Winters could see the young man was extraordinarily handsome. He found himself hoping this man was a family relative.

The front door had shut by the time his attention returned to Jennifer. Winters got out of his car and paused on the pavement. He turned to look at the square, realising he was more or less in line with the spot from where the bolt was fired at Chapman. In the bright sunlight of a cloudless day, it was difficult to conjure up the menace of the thought.

Shrugging his shoulders, he hitched at his tie. As usual, he was impeccably dressed, in grey flannel trousers and a navy blazer.

Winters walked up to the front door and rapped on one of the glass panes. After a few seconds, he could see the blurred outline of someone moving in the hall. It was Jennifer.

She opened the door to the limit of the chain which restrained it. As she peered out at him, he noticed she was tired and drawn. There was no sign of recognition in her eyes.

"Ms Chapman?"

"Yes."

"My name is Detective Chief Inspector Alan Winters. I'm in charge of the investigation into your father's murder. May I come in, please?"

She stared at him, and he felt as if she was staring through him.

"Um, do you have any...I mean, shouldn't you show me -"

"Identification," he finished for her. "Yes, you're right. Here you are." He flashed his Metropolitan Police card.

Still Jennifer did not move.

"Please?" he repeated.

"Sorry. Yes. Yes, come in."

She closed the door again and Winters heard the chain

sliding in its bracket. The door opened wide and Jennifer stood aside, waving vaguely at the sitting room.

He walked into the room and looked around. Cards of condolence and flowers were everywhere. But the house was cold and still.

She motioned to him to sit, and he chose a single chair nearest the door. She sat down on a two-seater couch directly opposite him, crossed her legs underneath herself and leaned her elbows on her knees. Still she said nothing.

"I wondered whether I could ask you a few more questions? I know this must be trying, but we need your help." He placed his hands on the arms of the chair, aware that his palms were moist. He was amused to find he was a little nervous.

She studied him intently, ignoring his question. "Have we met?" she asked, eventually.

"Yes, briefly. On the night your father ..."

"Oh. I'm sorry, I don't usually forget a face."

Good start, he thought. "Not to worry. Are you all right? Is there anything we can do to help?"

"Find him," she said, and he was shaken by the ferocity in her voice. She spoke through clenched teeth, looking down at her hands, twisting and untwisting on her lap. "Find him soon."

He tried lamely to respond. "We'll do everything in our power to -"

She continued to gaze at her hands. "That's not good enough, Mr Winters. Whoever did this to my father has got to pay. You don't seem to be getting very far."

"That's not true. We have made a lot of progress -"

"Then why haven't you made an arrest?"

"These things sometimes take a little -"

Her hands froze. But still she spoke into her chest, with a

voice tired and old. "Can't you hear yourself? You're spouting clichés. You've got no further than you were on the night he was killed."

If there was one thing Winters hated, it was being interrupted. Even so, he found himself talking gently. "If you let me finish you might find out what we HAVE got."

She looked up at him, mildly surprised at the rebuke, and he felt she was seeing him for the first time. He watched as her eyes travelled over him slowly, soaking in detail. He was relieved he had taken care dressing that morning, while planning this interview.

"What do you know? Where are you looking? Every time I speak to Van Deventer he fobs me off with the same answers." He was surprised to hear she had spoken to Van Deventer. The Dutchman had said nothing.

"Then give me a moment without interruption and I'll tell you everything we know." He challenged her with a direct gaze, watching as she straightened up, staring back. She squared her shoulders.

"Well?"

He started with the plaster casts of the footprints, describing the assailant, his clothes, the type of weapon used. He told her about the cat the killer used for target practice, and about the rose. He told her about the results of the forensic reports on the letters, and the avenues the police were exploring. He moved on to the story her father had been working on, the questioning of all his contacts. He concluded with the so far fruitless search of sports and arms shops.

As he was speaking, he was scrutinising Jennifer. She looked lean and fit, supple and strong. She was small, but projected the presence of someone larger. She had long legs for her size, a flat belly, small, high breasts, a Mediterranean complexion. Her few movements were lithe and graceful, almost measured. She moved with feline grace, he thought.

He talked without stopping to think. But he spoke without emotion, reciting the facts as he would while giving evidence in court.

Her eyes never left his. They were the most striking thing about her; pale green, almost yellow in certain light. Riveted as she was, they were also hard, unyielding. Also like a cat, he thought, when its eyes are focused on prey.

He finished by saying the police were doing everything they could, that every available man was on the case, tracking down leads.

"Five days have passed. What you've got doesn't sound like very much." She was almost contemptuous.

"You must realise, Ms Chapman, this seems to be the work of a professional killer. It could take us months to get to the bottom of all this. So far we have only scratched the surface."

For the first time, he began to have his doubts about Ms Chapman. She was beginning to irritate him.

She sat very still. With her legs crossed underneath her, she was in an attitude of meditation. He began to toy with the idea of leaving, feeling disillusioned.

She snapped her fingers suddenly and pointed at him. "I remember you. You're the one who fell into the flower bed."

So, she HAD seen, after all.

She laughed then, and it transformed her face. In an instant the drawn, pinched look was gone, and her laughter rang out, filling the room. In spite of his renewed sense of indignation, Winters laughed, resonating her merriment. He was ashamed yet relieved, delighted at the contact they were making, blushing at his humiliation.

"You should have seen your face as you fell," she spluttered.

"You have the same look on it now."

Her words renewed the laughter. He sensed the brittle nature of her jollity, and tried his best to sustain the moment.

"I felt pretty foolish. It wasn't the sort of moment for high comedy," he said.

She stopped laughing, almost choking. A veil dropped over her eyes. They were cat's eyes again. He cursed. What was wrong with what he'd said? Then he saw she was looking beyond him at the door.

He turned and immediately started. Standing at the door was a wizened image of Jennifer, years of suffering and pain heaped on her, an awful image of sorrow.

Sheila Chapman wavered at the door, clutching the frame. She was dressed in a nightgown. Winters had seen photographs of her, pictures Chapman had kept in his study. The woman he saw now was barely recognisable as the same person.

Jennifer stood up and walked to the woman, taking her arm. "Mother, this is Detective Alan Winters. He's the one trying to find out who killed father."

Sheila stood, blankly looking at Winters. Her head was nodding, and shaking. After a moment there was a glimmer of comprehension in her eyes. She pulled her arm free and turned to walk back to the stairs. Jennifer remained at the door. Winters could hear Sheila dragging herself up the stairs, one at a time.

When he turned back to Jennifer he caught her staring after her mother, unguarded. He looked into eyes that suffered every step. He felt as if he was intruding on an intensely private moment and stood up to leave.

"Don't go," Jennifer said. Softly. Without looking at him.

He didn't need any more. He sat down as quickly as he could without appearing to be anxious.

"She worries me. I don't think she will be the same ever again. She didn't just live for him, she lived because of him."

He didn't try to answer. He could understand her concern. He wanted to share some of the load. But then he thought: What am I doing? This isn't the time or place for an involvement. But still he watched her, intrigued, fascinated by her every movement.

She caught him watching. A smile flickered for a moment. She looked down at her hands. Then she sat down again, assuming the same cross-legged position, her hands on her lap. After a moment, she looked up at him again, her eyes bottomless. Behind them was a dam of words, he realised. Come on! Let go, he willed.

"I ... it's been, well...I'm not used to - "

He smiled. He wanted to take her in his arms. She looked frail, and frightened, and confused.

Then it came. She started falteringly. As she spoke she looked at him frequently, to gauge his response.

"I, WE, have both been, well, in a state of emotional suspended animation. I'm not used to it. The feeling came over me when I arrived home that night and discovered the police cars." She held the index finger of her left hand, rubbing, stroking. He watched her hands, entranced by the long fingers. There was a sense of suppleness even there.

"I knew he had been killed. The letters. By the time I got to the top of the stairs I was numb. Van Deventer stopped me, took me downstairs again.

He muttered, acknowledging but not interrupting her flow.

"Van Deventer asked me a lot of questions I don't remember. Our family doctor gave me a sedative and my aunt escorted me to bed. The pill was powerful, and knocked me out. I woke up halfway through the next morning."

Winters leaned back in his chair. Her voice was soft, nearly without accent. It was also deep and throaty.

"I went through to my mother's room, and she was still heavily sedated. My aunt was at her bedside, and asked me how I was doing. I asked her what was to happen next and she said your detectives wanted to speak to me again, and would be back at lunch."

For the first time, she stopped. Winters urged her on with a nod and smile.

She smiled back, wistfully. He sensed she was still scared, perhaps terrified, but not willing to admit it, even to herself. "The next few days were a blur of people and voices and places. The worst moment was at the service for my father. It was yesterday, four days after the murder, and still the pain had not come. Everything seemed to be taking place on the other side of a glass tube. Even voices were that degree removed."

She pursed her lips, shook her head. She was no longer seeing him. "The weather was kind, a few wispy clouds, a bright sky. But it was cold, inside and out."

She stopped, lost in the memory. Winters did not want the moment to break. He said: "I know the feeling. My own parents were killed in a car smash. At their funeral I couldn't cry. I wanted to. I never did. It took years to warm up again."

"I'm sorry," she said. She started to ask him a question, but he went on quickly, not wanting her to stop.

"Were there a lot of people at your father's service?" He wanted to hear her speak, even if it was about such a painful subject. Usually when he was with a woman, he steered away from difficult subjects, preferring to keep the topics light and suggestive. But this was different. Why? He couldn't understand his motives.

"There were more people than I expected. Faces from the

office, relatives, family friends. Every time one of them spoke to me I could only nod. I couldn't meet their eyes – those intense stares. I didn't want them to see what little emotion I was feeling. It seemed so wrong."

"It takes a while. Sometimes a day or three, sometimes years," he said. But he didn't think she'd heard him. No matter.

"During the sermon my mother sobbed so loudly the priest had to stop and wait for her to calm down." She paused. "Finally it was all over, we were back in the house, and I said goodbye to the last guest. Mother was alone in bed upstairs, having cried herself to sleep again. It's strange. In spite of the fact I feel so much pain for her, for some reason there is a kind of distance between us. I can't describe it."

Her hand fluttered a dismissal. She wasn't going to try to analyse it now, either.

"Last night I sat down on my father's favourite chair – the one you're sitting on now – with a glass of his Scotch."

Winters felt invasive. He wanted to move to a different chair, but there had been no resentment or malice in her remark.

"I thought of the day he had taken me to the station, when I caught the train to go off to university for the first time. I was doing a degree aimed at getting me into journalism. He said he was glad I was doing it. He said we would be able to talk about so much more together." She looked at Winters, raised her eyebrows. "I'm still waiting. Only now I'll never stop waiting. My life will always be acted out with a question mark, an expectation that can never be fulfilled."

For the first time, Jennifer's eyes sparkled with a hint of moisture. She struggled to contain the tears.

Winters spoke, if only to give her room to compose herself. "I remember the agony of realizing I would never see my parents again. For me it was made worse by the fact we had barely been speaking at the time of their accident."

"Why not?" she said, dabbing at her eyes with a tissue she pulled from her sleeve. When she had finished she slipped it underneath her thigh.

"They were applying pressure on me to get involved in the world of publishing, so I could be groomed to one day take over my father's empire. I'd been insisting on a career with the police. The worst part was knowing I'd never be able to tell them I was sorry I'd hurt them, and that I loved them. I know I'll always miss them."

For a moment he was lost in his own memories. He realized Jennifer was watching him.

"Thinking about your parents?" she asked. She seemed concerned.

"Yes," he said. "I don't think a day goes by when something doesn't remind me of them. I was lucky. I had a very warm childhood. But, as I said, at the time they died we weren't speaking. I never got over the guilt of that."

Jennifer snuggled more comfortably into her seat. She was responding warmly to him, almost excited at being able to express her pain to someone who understood. "I feel the same way. I had a terrible row with my father the night before he was killed. Then again an hour or two before he died. We finished by saying we would talk. He said he would wait up for me. I came home looking forward to some time with him -" She broke off, sniffing, looking around for her tissue. He offered her the clean handkerchief he always carried in his top pocket. She took it from him and smiled her thanks.

"In the darkness of the sitting room, with just the smell of his whisky, I felt the first grief. A powerful sense of loss. I cried then, until this morning. I sort of slept and woke, cried and slept. I feel drained now. I must look awful."

"You look ... just fine." He had been about to say beautiful, then thought better of it. But he knew she knew what he meant. She smiled. He felt he could watch that smile forever.

"Most of all I feel bleak. I resent the time he spent on the newspaper. We worked in the same place, but never saw each other. He was always too busy, working long hours at the office, rushing home to change and go out to this function, or that dinner, or this meeting, and there were precious few weekends we could call shared. I grew up longing to spend more time with him, to learn what made him so dynamic, to learn why other people respected him so much. I wanted to have a part of him no-one else could reach. But he had no time for anything but his newspaper. There were no interests or hobbies I could share with him. We developed our separate lifestyles."

Winters saw his opening and took it. "What do you do with your spare time?"

"Oh, I –" she started. She shook her head. "Not a lot, really. I took up modern dance. I go to the gym often. My friends are all dancers and physical fitness fanatics."

"As I arrived, I saw some people leaving. Were they your dance friends?" He tried to sound merely curious.

"The two girls were. The fellow was my boyfriend. He's an instructor at my gym."

"I see," said Winters, striving to keep the disappointment out of his voice. He performed a mental shrug. What the hell.

As if to answer his thoughts, she said: "Perhaps boyfriend is too strong a word. We've just started going out. His name is Neville. My girlfriends would gladly park their slippers under his bed, but he's a bit shallow for me to take too seriously. Vain too."

"Seemed he had ample reason. Good looking young man."

"He likes to party, and go to all the 'in' places. He's fun, if you like that sort of fun on a non-stop basis."

Winters smiled, shrugging his shoulders.

She went on: "He's also a bit of a coward. Afraid of the dark."

"We all have our weaknesses," he said, trying to be gallant.

"Oh really? What's yours?"

"Heights," he said, without hesitation. "Ever since I can remember, I've had a dread of heights."

"Heights. Heights? How did we get on to this subject?" she asked. She seemed amused.

Before he could reply, Winters heard his stomach grumbling. He cringed in embarrassment. He had forgotten the time.

Jennifer smiled. "May I make you something to eat?"

"No. Thank you. I didn't realise how late it was. I have an appointment at Scotland Yard. But first finish what you were saying about your attempts to get close to your father."

She looked blankly at him for a moment. "Am I a suspect?" she asked suddenly.

"No. Although, theoretically, I should say everyone is until we can definitely count them out."

"Oh. Yes. Well, I was saying that my becoming a journalist and working on my father's paper was an attempt to share in his future by making myself a part of his dreams It all seems so pointless now."

"Will you go on working on the paper?"

"Yes. What else is there? I go back to work tomorrow."

Winters stood up. Reluctantly. Where had all the time gone?

"Uh, I was going to ask you a few questions, but we didn't get a chance to fit them in - "

"My fault, I shouldn't have gone off like that."

"No, I'm glad you did. I wish I had more time now. Perhaps I could come back tomorrow evening and we could talk some more?"

"That would be fine."

Winters walked to the front door. He bowed his head then left. He didn't want to say goodbye.

When he opened the door of his car he looked back at the house. She was still watching him.

He was careful not to bump his head on the door frame as he got in the car. She'd think him a right idiot then.

As he drove away she was still watching. She waved a farewell.

Winters knew he had one great failing in life. Women. He found them too attractive, too intriguing. He fell in and out of love several times a day. His father used to call him "rubberneck". He had never been able to resist looking at a pretty girl, even from a speeding car. Jennifer was undeniably pretty. She was a forceful character, sporting a complex facade against the world. Usually exactly the kind of woman he shied away from, believing them to be too much trouble. But something about her held his attention. She WAS like a cat. Independent. Capable of gentle affection yet deadly rage.

He realised he felt rewarded, even though he had not learned much that could help him with his investigation. He was going to have to come back, after all.

As he drove back to the Yard, slowed by the thick lunch-hour traffic, he smiled. What had she said? "That would be just fine."

NINE

APRIL 17, 1986. *Dreams have always been a part of my life. A dark and terrible part. At least, ever since my mother died.*

Don't remember her well. Bits and pieces. Remember her smell, her love of flowers, particularly roses. She used to say my father had courted her with roses. A ceremony with them. Every time he visited, he brought a rose. Consequently, she used to have roses everywhere. She continued to keep them around the house after they were married. I remember they used to last for such a long time, and she gave each one a name. She never ran out of names.

My father called her The Rose. Used to get home from work and ask me: "Where's The Rose."

Mother enjoyed the name, I could tell.

She enjoyed me too. She enjoyed most things. Our walks. Our long talks. My father. Even when he began to change.

He started work in a lawyer's office and after that I hardly ever saw him, not even at weekends. He would come home late at night, tired, and I would hear him walking around downstairs, pacing for hours, back and forth across the living room. He seldom came up to say goodnight, and when he did, I always pretended to be asleep. At weekends he was at his office. My mother used to say he was very busy. It was why we could live in a nice house. Some kind of clerk, he was. They never explained it to me. He helped to investigate. Did the legwork for his employers. So they said.

They never explained why my father hated lawyers. He frequently made comments about them. Said they had locked him in with them forever. Said they had suckered him.

Mother tried to help. She used to say he was always tired because he worked so hard. She used to say the bruises on her face didn't hurt. She used to say the bottles were because he didn't enjoy his work.

She loved him, and me.

My dreams started when her bruises began to occur regularly. The dreams were merely minor disturbances during the long nights when I would hear another bottle crash against the floor boards. When I could hear the sound of flesh bruising flesh.

Still, she worshipped the roses. She told me each one had meaning. She told me to remember her for the roses. She told me always to remember the roses, and that I was blood of The Rose.

I don't remember a lot else about her. I have tried, but I don't believe there is much else I have stored away about her.

I remember better my sense of bemusement when she stopped putting up roses. She would sit in a chair next to the fire and I remember how white her skin seemed, how the flames seemed to reflect on her cheeks. She became very thin. I asked why she didn't put up flowers any more. She smiled, but never answered my question. That scared me more than anything.

My father, for a while, stopped with the bottle and the bruises.

He would come home at night and they would send me to my bedroom, and I would listen to them whispering in the sitting room, straining to hear what they were saying. It was maddening, not being able to hear them clearly. Sometimes, though, I could hear something I didn't want to hear. The sound of my father crying.

Then they told me my mother was going to visit a special place, where she would be able to put on some weight and be happy again. She asked me if I would be a good boy, whether I could cope with coming home to an empty house for a while. I said that would be fine. I remember how sad and old she looked, how she held her head up especially high, how she trembled a smile for me at the door. I remember my sense of loss when she was gone.

And then, the dreams.

I would wake to find my sleep had been replete with violence and death. Horror and panic. Running away. Losing things. People disappearing. People dying.

On waking, would be left with a sense of dread, of having got into terrible trouble, of being on trial.

One day I came home from school and found our neighbours in the house. They were very quiet and kept asking me if I wanted something to eat. I didn't know them very well. Finally my father came home. He said goodbye to the neighbours and sat me down on a chair. He said my mother would not be coming back. We would have to cope without her.

For a while he tried to see to my needs. I was about eight, maybe nine. I don't remember. But then he gave up, started with the bottles again and stopped going to work.

It was strange having him home. Sometimes I would come home from school and find him still dressed in his pyjamas, unshaven, unwashed. He would be looking at a photograph of my mother. In this photograph she was holding a single rose. She looked so beautiful. Whenever I got a chance, I would sneak down and stare at the picture myself. It was the one thing my father and I shared.

One day, while staring at her image, his chest started to heave. His hands trembled and tears filled his eyes and then he threw the picture against a wall. The glass inside the frame shattered and the photograph fell on the floor.

I picked it up and he flew into a rage, hitting and kicking me. I ran away from him, dropping the print.

He was shrieking horribly, sobbing, almost hoarse.

But he wasn't shouting at me.

He was screaming for my mother.

TEN

"**HIS CHOICE** of weapon intrigues me," said Van Deventer.

"Indeed," said Winters, coldly.

He marvelled at the Dutchman. Minutes ago they had been bellowing at each other; now Van Deventer expected to carry out a normal conversation as if nothing had happened.

They were sitting at opposite ends of the table in the meeting room at the Yard. Winters reflected that they had now had several ... exchanges ... in this room. Probably, they would have many more. Working together with the Dutchman was proving to be one of the more unpleasant tasks of his career.

When Van Deventer discovered he had visited Jennifer Chapman without telling him, he had flown into a fury, then had sulked for two days, refusing to speak to Winters at all. Winters had enjoyed those two days, taking malicious pleasure from the Dutchman's silence.

But Van Deventer had soon started interfering again, and it was this interference which had sparked yet another confrontation this afternoon. The Dutchman had once more sarcastically been questioning the ability of Winters to supervise the case. Many of his remarks were made when other people were in the room. Winters suspected it was all part of a campaign designed to erode his position and allow Van Deventer the chance to assume control.

After yet another cutting remark, Winters had not been able to help himself. "If you didn't have such a murky past you'd probably be commanding this yourself. Sir."

Van Deventer had been momentarily stunned, a hurt expression on his face. The remark had silenced him for a while. He had closed off and become guarded again. Enjoying the silence, savouring his brief triumph, Winters read through the reports which were flooding in from his detectives. He and Van Deventer had annexed the meeting room as their headquarters for the investigation. The filing cabinets in each corner of the room were filling up rapidly.

Van Deventer tried again. "I said, his choice of weapon -"

"I know what you said. I was merely reflecting on it. If you're asking me, I think he used a crossbow because it was quiet. Gave him time to get away," said Winters. He found it difficult keeping his voice neutral. The words of their row were still swirling around in his head. After every exchange, Winters found himself thinking about what he SHOULD have said to the Dutchman, if only he were more quick-witted. He realised the tension between them was diverting his concentration from the case at times, and he begrudged it intensely, further fuelling his dislike of Van Deventer.

The Dutchman grunted. "Could be. But I think there may be another reason."

"What, for example?" asked Winters, reluctantly putting down the file he was reading.

"I don't know. He took a big chance firing from that distance. A crossbow is more risky than a rifle. It might not have killed his victim. Why was he prepared to take that chance?"

Winters dug among the files in front of him, finding what he wanted and then waving it at Van Deventer. "If you'd only read all these reports, you'd know Boyer has established that crossbows these days are deadly accurate. Crossbow shooting is a fast developing sport in the UK and in competitions high scores are common over distances of up to 80 yards. Perhaps there wasn't that much chance involved?"

Van Deventer shook his head. He took his feet off the table, his heel dragging the cord of the telephone and dislodging the receiver. He replaced it, then sat erect. He had been staring out the window. Now he looked at Winters.

"Has Boyer been digging up information on crossbows?"

"Yes. It's all here, in this file." Winters knew he sounded petulant, and his resentment grew.

"I asked him to do some research on them. The biggest problem we face is that they are freely available to anyone who cares to buy one. No licensing, no paperwork. There is a group, called the Crossbow Archer Development Association, which works on a national basis, but it concentrates on field target shooting. Officials of the Association may be able to tell us something useful."

Van Deventer was impressed. Grudgingly, he said: "That was good thinking. I'd like to talk to Boyer when he has a moment."

"Be my guest," said Winters, returning to his file. "He's also looking up the history of the crossbow, to see if there may be some significance in the choice of murder weapon."

"What has he found out?"

Winters sighed, dropping the file again. "Oh, not much. From what I could gather, crossbows have been around since the 6th century BC. They were first used in China, then gradually knowledge of the weapon spread to Europe. They were used by the Romans. Boyer notes one of the Popes in the 12th century issued an anathema against crossbows, describing it as 'a deadly art, hated by God'. They died off in popularity, but there has been a resurgence in interest in recent years."

"Yes, yes. I know the crossbow was used in the Crusades. Richard the Lion-heart was apparently a fine shot with one."

Winters was surprised. Occasionally Van Deventer plucked information from a personal store of general knowledge that seemed very wide-ranging.

"Boyer says he can find nothing that might point at it being used for a particular reason. I had hoped it might be a sign, rather like knee-capping or stilettos are a sign of the IRA or the Mafia."

Van Deventer leaned back on the chair, lifting one foot on to the table again, crossing the other at the ankle. It was a mannerism Winters had grown used to over the 10 days they had worked together. He was also used to Van Deventer staring out the window at passers-by in the street below. The Dutchman spent hours at the window. The view from the 20-storey New Scotland Yard building encompassed a large portion of Victoria Street. While staring at the traffic, Van Deventer churned thoughts over and over, jotting down suggestions for Winters on a pad he kept handy all the time.

The only reason Winters had not yet gone to beg Maxwell to remove Van Deventer was because of this flow of notes. The suggestions contained in them were often inspired thoughts, and Winters was forced to admit the Dutchman's experience was often helpful. He knew what he was doing - the Dutchman had been involved in many legendary Murder Squad cases.

Van Deventer seldom spoke of his experiences. However, these were proving to be invaluable now. The endless supply of suggestions was born of ideas from these cases. In a way, Winters was grateful, in spite of the fact he had a backlog of suggestions to deal with.

Van Deventer wore a pair of silver-framed spectacles, and had a habit of pushing them up the bridge of his nose frequently. He had little dress sense, which Winters had noticed from the first day, but now it began to irritate him. Van Deventer mixed ties and shirts and suits with abandon. In moments of anger, when his face suffused with blood, the overall effect could be stunning.

Winters knew that Van Deventer had taken up golf with a passion. He wondered what he looked like on a golf course, given the loud nature of some golf clothes and the Dutchman's lack of taste. Winters caught Van Deventer reading all the golf reports in the newspaper, muttering to himself about professional players in awed tones. From what Winters could gather, the Dutchman played and practiced as often as he could, without managing to master his spectacularly erratic play.

Winters preferred squash, regarding golf as "an old man's game." He didn't enjoy squash, but he played it as fiercely and as often as he could, as a means of staying extremely fit.

"Have you asked Interpol about any known assassins who've used crossbows in the past?" asked Van Deventer.

"Yes, days ago. They still haven't come back to us."

"They sometimes need to be chased."

The two men fell quiet. Winters returned to his file, but couldn't concentrate. His mind was on Jennifer. He found his thoughts returning to her again and again. He had not yet been able to go back and see her, although he had twice spoken to her on the telephone. By the end of the second conversation, she was teasing him coyly. She had pressed him for information about the investigation, but he had been mindful of the order issued by Maxwell not to make any more comments to the Press. He wasn't sure how far he could trust Jennifer. Even so, he ached to see her again. If he could just find the time.

Van Deventer broke into his daydream. "What do you make of the forensic reports?"

"Which ones?"

"The ones which say the letters were composed in a room full of flowers. Roses, to be precise."

"Yes, very strange that, considering we found a rose at the

square. No-one knows what to make of that at this stage. Do you?"

Van Deventer shook his head.

Winters continued. "In the meantime, we've already sent men to interview as many florists in London as we can find, trying to discover if there is anyone who spends money regularly on roses."

"How do they trace pollen on paper, or in envelopes?" asked Van Deventer. "I mean, can they be sure it is pollen and, if so, can they also be sure of the flower from which it comes?"

Once again, Winters rummaged pointedly among the files spread out in front of him. "Here it is," he said, flicking one open. "According to Garner Patterson, pollen grains are so tiny they adhere to almost anything, and will invariably be found on clothing, in sweepings or even in ear wax. He says that because their presence is never suspected by the person carrying them, no special effort is ever made to eliminate them. Even if someone tried, they'd probably be unsuccessful. All this makes pollen significant evidence."

Van Deventer tapped his fingers on the table, which was clear in front of him except for his note book. He scribbled on the paper. "They found pollen in the envelopes? And in the glue on the threatening notes?"

"That's right," said Winters, quoting directly from Patterson's report. "Pollens, like other plant structures, are highly individual to each species. Garner has seen the evidence of pollen prove a suspect was at a place he claimed he had never visited."

"Yes, yes," said Van Deventer. "So this means that a pollen is significant in that it can prove a person has been at a particular locale."

"I suppose so," said Winters, closing the file and wondering what the Dutchman was getting at.

"Then, if there is a significant amount of rose pollen, our man could be a gardener? Possibly a rose gardener?"

Winters cursed. Why hadn't he thought of that? "Yes," he said curtly, dreading the inevitable suggestion that was bound to follow.

"Yes, yes, then I suggest you have someone explore the possibility. Rose gardens, nurseries and so on." Van Deventer scribbled in his note book again.

Winters felt sure the Dutchman was keeping a record of his every idea to use it in evidence against him later. Either as proof of how many ideas he contributed, or that Winters had been neglectful about following them up. "I'll get Hawkins on to that first thing tomorrow morning," he said.

Both men were feeling the pressure. They knew this case could take thousands of hours to get anywhere. Past experience showed that if a crime was not solved in the first 48 hours, it was a safe bet it might never be solved. One of the harsh realities of life on the force. Yet there was mounting pressure from above to make a breakthrough, any kind of breakthrough.

Van Deventer looked at his watch, and yawned. "Well, if there's nothing more to do today,
I'm going home," he said.

"Sure. I'll see you tomorrow," said Winters. The Dutchman took his coat off the back of the door. They exchanged nods and Van Deventer closed the door behind him.

Usually he could expect to hear Van Deventer booming a farewell to whoever was still in the murder room, but tonight Van Deventer was strangely quiet. After a moment, Winters thought he could hear Jennifer Chapman's voice. What was she doing here? He walked to the door, opened it slightly, and peered out into the squad room. He saw Jennifer kissing Van Deventer on the cheek. The Dutchman pointed towards the meeting room, and she thanked him before saying goodbye.

Winters opened the door, unable to contain a broad smile. He was puzzled, but hugely pleased.

She was dressed in a full skirted dress, in white and pale grey. Winters thought she looked beautiful. He noticed that every eye in the room was on her. Quickly, he ushered her into the meeting room, shutting the door behind him.

His hand went to his tie, which was hanging loose from his unbuttoned collar. His sleeves were rolled halfway up his forearms, and he knew his shirt was crumpled from a hard day's wear. He wished he'd had a moment to compose himself before she arrived.

"You look nice," she said, as if reading his mind.

"Not as good as you look," he said, admiringly.

"Forgive me, I met your Detective Boyer downstairs, and he escorted me up here. I hope you don't mind." She looked at a seat, and Winters quickly took the hint. He pulled the chair out for her and waited for her to sit.

"Not at all. I'm glad to see you. Why did you come?" He went to his own chair, sitting heavily.

"I was hoping you wouldn't ask that."

"Why?"

"Are all police officers so insensitive?"

"No. Just me." He was still smiling, even though he was unsure of her true motives. Was she flirting with him? In their telephone conversations, he had detected a softening in her attitude towards him. But he also detected a growing determination to have a hand in finding her father's killer.

Several times, Jennifer had said there was nothing she wanted more than to see the man who had killed her father. He had asked her why and she had said it would mean he was in custody. But he suspected she was entertaining thoughts of taking the law into her own hands, as ridiculous as that may sound. Even as she spoke with him now, she was flicking her gaze at the files on the table.

"I came partly to find out if you had any more information, and partly because I wanted to see you again." She cocked her head as she spoke. It was coy, and challenging. Unlike the Jennifer he thought he knew. His suspicions were instantly alerted. Would someone with the obvious class of a woman like Jennifer be so flirtatious so soon after her father's death? Or did she have a deeper, revenge-inspired motive? He could think of little to say. "Oh," he ventured.

"Oh? Oh? Is that all you can say? I come miles out of my way and all you can say is oh?"

He smiled, leaning back in the chair, putting his hands behind his head. With horror, he realised he was exposing patches of sweat under his arms, and hastily dropped his hands to his lap. He recovered as quickly as he could. "No, I could also say: May I buy you a drink, or even better, some supper?"

"Yes, you may." And in case there was any doubt. "I'm ravishing."

That you are, thought Winters. He smiled. "Do you by any chance mean 'famished'?"

"What did I say?"

"Ravishing."

She smiled. No embarrassment. "That too."

Winters hurriedly escorted her from the building, ignoring the stares of his detectives as he left the squad room. Jennifer was suitably impressed with his car, commenting that white was her favourite colour in cars. He did not think it wise to ask why she drove a black Mini. He resisted the urge to show off the BMW on the way to the restaurant he suggested. It was a small

Italian in South Kensington, near his apartment. He said it was a good idea because he would be able to park his car at his apartment and they could walk from there to the restaurant, which in any case was en-route to her house.

He parked his car in the courtyard and they walked from there to the restaurant. On the way, dodging traffic at the interchange at the South Kensington tube station, he took her arm. The instant he touched her, she seemed to lean towards him. Her bicep was firm and hinted at strength.

She smiled secretly all the way to the restaurant.

After being seated by the owner, who greeted Winters warmly, they chose a bottle of wine and their food. The mood was warm, and Winters found it difficult to relate what was happening to the night ten days ago when he had first laid eyes on Jennifer. For a brief moment, he wondered again whether Jennifer was using him.

She spotted his scowl. "Something wrong?"

"No, not at all. I eat here several times a week, and I was wondering whether I had settled my account." It was all he could think of to say. The truth was, he settled up after every meal.

His attention drifted back to the thought that he was being used. It was quite possible. Probable, in fact. But he couldn't resist.

The more they spoke, the more he felt his attention being engaged. He asked her to tell him more about herself. At first she was reluctant, claiming there wasn't much to tell.

"That can't be true," he urged.

"Well, I have a great love of things historical. Old buildings, antiquity, historical novels English history. I love any play or film that has a sense of history about it. One of my favourite films was 'A Man For All Seasons', about Sir Thomas More."

"I know it well. Paul Scofield starred in the title role. He was marvellous. From a play by Robert Bolt, directed by Fred Zinnemann."

Jennifer giggled. "My! How do you know so much about that film."

He shrugged. "It was nothing."

"No, really, is it a favourite of yours?"

"Promise you won't laugh?"

"You're about to tell me some deep secret?"

"Yes."

She leaned forward, putting down her wine glass. "I'm all ears."

"You won't believe this, but I have a rather unusual hobby."

"I'm listening." She was smiling in anticipation, and Winters was pleased he could take her mind off harsh realities for a while.

"I collect movies."

"You mean you see as many as you can see? That's not so unusual. I love films as well."

"No, I mean I collect movies. I have a room at home full of old films. Wall to wall, ceiling to floor. Ones I have seen and loved and been able to source. In the room, I have a projector and screen, as well as two extremely comfortable armchairs. My viewing room. "

She giggled. "You're kidding?"

"No, I'm serious. Films are my passion. I see as many as I can. I have books on films stars, guides to movies, guides to Hollywood, guides to the guides, even. Ever since I was a child, I've loved cinema."

"You're right. That IS the last thing I would suspect you of being. A cinephile."

"Oh yes," he laughed. "And proud of it."

She sipped at her wine, obviously intrigued. "Do you specialise in any particular genre?"

"Uh, this is the part I hate. I always feel so childish."

"Why? Why should you feel childish at all? I think it's marvellous. There can't be many people I know who have whole film libraries of their own, I can tell you."

He smiled, looking boyish. He ran a hand through his hair. It fell back into the style he always preferred - specially cut for him by his stylist - a casual windswept look that somehow seemed tidy and presentable at all times.

"Uhm, well, I seem to have collected a rather large number of westerns. Somehow."

Jennifer laughed, delighted. "I'd love to see your collection some time. Have you films other than westerns?"

"Oh yes, hundreds. If I see a film I enjoy, I make sure I track down a copy. I may never watch it again, but I like keeping it in case I have the urge to watch. I have a very good memory. I can remember nearly everything about films I see, so I seldom have to watch a second time. If I view a film more than once, it is because I really love it and I'll watch it countless times."

"Do you have a favourite?"

"Many, depending on my mood."

"Who starred with Scofield?" she shot at him.

"Robert Shaw, Susannah York, uh, John Hurt -"

"Okay, okay, I believe you. Do you have any films that might interest me?"

"Plenty."

She nodded, breaking off to receive her meal from a waiter. She had chosen lasagne. He had joined her. He used the break in conversation to remove his jacket, wishing he'd had time to change into something less formal.

"This is terrific," she said. "I'm dining out with an acrophobic detective who is a film fanatic."

"I'm surprised you know that word. It's not commonly used these days."

"I'm a wordsmith. It is my business to know words."

"I'm impressed."

"Then I must admit I looked it up, the other day, after you told me you were scared of heights." She jabbed her fork at him. "Were you joking?"

"Unfortunately not. I'm literally terrified of heights. I become dizzy and ill and sometimes I have an almost over-powering compulsion to jump. I'm not sure which of those scares me most. Being dizzy and falling by mistake, being ill and embarrassing myself, or giving in to the compulsion to jump and then wanting to change my mind halfway down."

Jennifer laughed, almost gagging on her food. "Don't," she said, "you'll make me choke."

He waited for her to regain her composure. She dabbed at her mouth with her napkin. "Ever traced the source of your fear?"

"No, and I have no intention of doing so either. I can live with it, as long as I don't expose myself to situations which involve heights."

"What about flying?"

"I look at the floor, not out the window. In any case, that's different. I'm afraid of heights where I feel exposed, that's all. No big deal."

"You'll have to confront that one day, you know."

"I'll cross that bridge when I come to it – no pun intended," he said, a little impatiently. "But enough about me, tell me more about you. About your work."

"There's not a lot to tell," she said, between mouthfuls. "I find my work interesting, but depressing. I'm unlike my father ... was." She hesitated, but decided to press on. "I have no compulsion to find out, to dig out news. I enjoy people and I enjoy writing stories and, happily, the two go well together. If I write something, I prefer to explore solutions to problems, rather than simply attack. I only took up journalism to prove to my father I could do it. I never had any great drive to start with, but it does tend to grow on you."

Winters used the opportunity to catch up with the meal, nodding his encouragement to her to proceed.

"I don't like the environment, nor the pressure of deadlines several times a day, but I can live with them."

Winters asked: "What do you do for fun?"

"I ... love trying new things. I have a great sense of adventure. I'm game to try anything at least once. That's got me into trouble sometimes, but not much. I love sport, climbing, hiking, outdoors. That sort of thing."

Winters finished his meal and pushed his plate aside, reaching for his wine. "What do you plan to do with the rest of your life? Any goals or dreams?"

Her eyes dimmed. She looked down at her plate, dropping her fork. "I can't finish this," she said. "Do you mind?"

Winters waved a hand in dismissal. "Your goals?" he prompted, realising too late his insensitivity.

"I don't really have any now. None that I can think about at the moment. I haven't sorted myself out yet. Things are still too fresh, too painful. My mother needs a lot of attention. Perhaps I should convince her to move away from our memories? I just don't know right now."

He realised he had inadvertently changed the tone of the evening, wondering whether he could recapture the warmth and closeness that had been developing. She seemed cold and distant.

"Tell me," she said, sipping at her wine, clutching the glass to her mouth with both hands, "do you remember any films in which a crossbow was used?" There was bitterness in her voice.

"Yes," he said, flatly, trying to end this line of talk.

"For instance?"

"Several. One you may have seen was the James Bond film, 'For Your Eyes Only'?"

"Yes, I saw that," she said. Her voice was now even more bitter. "I remember enjoying that, at the time."

"Why do you ask?"

She ignored his question. "How far have you got with your investigation?" There was a coldness in her eyes again. It was as if she was talking to a stranger.

Winters gave up. The moment was lost. He signalled for two coffees before answering. He leaned back in his chair, noting that Jennifer was now sitting with both arms tightly folded across her chest. "I'm afraid not far enough to please you. But we are making progress. There is a lot we know about our man. We still can't put our finger on a motive. A lot of theories, but no hard evidence."

"Will he get away with it?"

"Not if I can help it. But I have to say it is possible."

"Shit! I can't believe it. How can there be no clues when a prominent newspaper editor is murdered?"

Winters could see the flame of the candle on their table reflected in her eyes. "I've told you already. This man was very, very careful. He made few mistakes that we can find. We are tracking him down the slow way, through hours and hours of plodding investigation. Something will come up."

Tears welled in her eyes. They were tears of anger and

frustration. "It all seems so unreal. I still can't accept what has happened. I find it so hard to accept someone can cold-bloodedly kill another human being and walk away from it so easily."

Winters watched, sipping the last of his wine. Enough, he reminded himself. He still had to drive Jennifer home.

She dropped her hands to the table, drumming her fingers in and agitated fashion. She stopped, and took the tablecloth in her hands. She clenched her fists, crumpling the material. He reached out, took one of her hands. She started to resist, but he held tight. Her hand went limp, then responded to his grip.

Still, he sat quietly. He was trying to judge whether he could take her in his arms. He wanted to comfort her, carry some of her pain. She recognised his intent, and she choked back a sob. More tears. He covered her hand with his free hand, gently stroking her skin. It was soft and silken.

Without warning she jerked free her hands and thrust the table away from her. She stood up and walked off to the ladies room.

The restaurant owner saw her pass. He shot an angry look at Winters and stalked over to the table. "May I get you something else?" he asked, coldly.

"Just the bill, thank you."

Winters had paid by the time Jennifer emerged. She had recovered. She kept her distance as they walked back to his flat. When they reached his car, he opened her door, stood back and offered his hand to assist her. She took it, but remained standing where she was.

For a moment they looked at each other. He stepped towards her and she moved into his arms He could feel her strong back beneath his hands. He was intensely aware of her breasts against his chest. She snuggled into his shoulder and rested her forehead there. They stood that way for several minutes, in silence.

Then she shivered, and he stepped away, ushering her into the car.

On the way to her house they drove in silence. She stared out the window at the night people still in the streets. When they finally reached her house, he turned the engine off and sat.

"Thank you," she said.

He knew she meant thank you for being understanding. "My pleasure. May I see you again?"

"Yes, I'd like that," she said, opening her door.

"When?"

"Whenever you like."

"Tomorrow night?"

She thought for a moment. "I'd enjoy that."

He got out the car and walked round to help her out. As he walked her to the front door of the house, Winters noticed that she smiled as she passed the spot where she had pushed him to the ground. When they reached the door she was composed again.

When the door closed behind her, he walked slowly back to his car, thinking of Van Deventer, annoyed that the Dutchman had thrust his way into his thoughts. He decided, at all costs, to keep from Van Deventer the news of his developing relationship with Jennifer.

He was convinced the Dutchman would not approve.

And that would only make things even more difficult.

ELEVEN

SHEILA CHAPMAN was waiting up for Jennifer, and called out from the sitting room. Jennifer joined her mother, who had been watching television, knitting.

Once again, Jennifer was surprised at how rapidly her mother seemed to be recovering.

Sheila had made an effort to dress well, had put on make-up, and although still looking drawn, was more like her old self.

"Some coffee?" asked Sheila.

"Please."

"Go and sit down. You look tired. I'll bring it through."

Jennifer sat down in her father's chair. Her mother had started a fire. The room was warm again, for the first time since...that night.

When Sheila came through with a tray, Jennifer was staring at the flames.

"Who was that man?"

"Detective Chief Inspector Alan Winters. One of the youngest chief inspectors on the force, and probably one of the most attractive policemen - real or fictional - I have ever seen. I had supper with him."

Sheila chuckled quietly, but ended by chewing her bottom lip as she poured the coffee and handed Jennifer her cup.

For a while they sat in companionable silence, sipping at their coffee and watching the flames together. Jennifer was the first to speak. "I feel so guilty. I mean, I enjoy his company. I LIKE him, I'm attracted to him. But it seems so wrong. How could I feel this way? I mean, it is only ten days since ... since ..." She paused, catching her breath. "I can't let go and be myself with him. Because of what happened to father. Because he's the man trying to find out who killed father. There is no escape from that terrible truth. It hangs over me now like a pall."

"How does he feel about you?"

Jennifer recalled the evening, felt again his fingers on hers, his arms around her. She had drawn such strength from him. Being in his embrace had been easy and natural. "I think he is interested. Not just because of his job."

"I see." Silence. Then: "I can see no harm in it. You are a human being, in need of comfort and attention. Some may criticise, but you have no need to feel guilty."

Jennifer looked at her mother. Where was she getting this strength? She seemed to have shaken herself free of her debilitating grief. There was still an ancient mourning in her eyes. But also resolve.

For the first time, Jennifer felt confident enough to ask: "How are you feeling now, mother?"

Sheila sighed before answering. As she spoke, she continued to stare into the flames. "Empty. But life will go on. It always does. I'll find something to keep me going. Perhaps I'll go back to teaching. It's been a long time, but I'll need something."

They fell into easy discussion, and slowly Jennifer drew her mother out, encouraging her to talk. Sheila spoke of her childhood, recalling her own parents. She said, sadly, they had been happiest in retirement together. She had been holding that as her goal in life with Hugh. She had known she would never be able to share completely with him until then. He had been her life.

Jennifer did not feel resentment or jealousy. She understood. In her own heart, she knew she too had been focused on her father. A part of her had always mourned not having her father around, and as a consequence her relationship with her mother had never quite been complete.

They spoke sitting together in the darkness until the fire burned down to a dull glow. Then they went up to bed. After changing Jennifer went through to her mother's room. Sheila was lying in her huge king-size bed, looking so alone Jennifer was again pushed to the edge of tears. She walked to the bed and leaned over to kiss Sheila goodnight. Straightening up she glanced into the open bedside table drawer. In the drawer was a pistol she recognised as being her father's.

"Where did you get that?" she asked, concerned.

"Don't worry. Your father must have put it there just before he was killed. I think he knew something terrible was going to happen. I'm keeping it there, just in case."

Just in case what? Wondered Jennifer. She was fearful her mother would use it to end her own life. What then? She resolved to remove it later, when she got a chance to do so unobserved.

In her own bed she reflected on the events of the past ten days. She felt helpless. She was a passenger and she hated the image. How could someone do this and get away with it so easily? What could SHE do about it? Sub-consciously she had already started on a course of action by getting close to Winters. He might well be useful. How? She wasn't sure. What about her feelings for him, indecent as they seemed? No answer to that, she decided. She would have to live with her emotions, as confused as they might be. She tossed in her bed for more than an hour, unable to sleep. As she finally drifted towards sleep the answer hit her with startling clarity. She would do what her father would have done, she would find out for herself what was going on. By doing what she did best. Being a journalist.

TWELVE

APRIL 18, 1986. *Kept trying to find out from my father what happened to mother. Often the question made him furious. Mostly he would look at me, vacantly, and wouldn't answer. He was changing, worsening by the day, and I began to sense a menace growing in him that frightened me and spurred on my nightmares.*

For a while I lived with dread and mystery. What had happened to my mother? What was happening to my father? What would happen to me?

Once, I even went to our elderly neighbours. They looked concerned, but said it was none of their business. I kept thinking there was some kind of conspiracy. Finally one of my teachers asked me to stay after school. He said he would have to talk to my father about my homework, and find out why I was never up to date. He gave me a note.

When my father read it, he surprised me. Instead of the violent outburst I anticipated, he finally tried to explain why mother had died.

He said her blood had turned to water.

Water?

Something in her blood, he said, planted there by HER mother, had killed her. Tears were in his bloodshot eyes, rolling down his unshaven cheeks. He talked about disease, and cancer, but none of it made sense.

My inability to understand eventually drove him into a rage and he punched me. I fell in front of him and he kicked me in the ribs, muttering again and again that I was a "useless bastard."

It was the first of many beatings. Soon they became something I had to face every day. He would find any reason, then he would pull me over his knee and beat me with his bare hand. He would be crying all the time. He would be sobbing my mother's name.

Over the following months I learned to hate him. He mutated. He became flabby and derelict. He was always half shaven, his eyes red. His hair turned white. He carried about with him a pall of gloom. He looked defeated. And he was nearly always drunk.

When he drank, his beatings were less painful. He seemed to lack the co-ordination to really hammer me. I was relieved when I saw him drunk.

Then he stopped me going to school. He made me take a note to my teacher. The teacher seemed surprised when he read it. He asked me where we were going. I said I didn't know.

We didn't go anywhere. Instead, my father would sometimes beat me several times a day. I would hide in my room, eating whenever he had drunk himself into a stupor, too scared to go out for any reason. Kept hoping someone would come to take me away from him. I was too terrified to try running away. He would kill me when he caught me. So I stayed, preferring the lesser, ritual beatings. He would go out, locking me in my room, to buy his drink and a little food every week, while I would sit in my bedroom, looking at my few toys, trying to remember what life had been like when my mother had been alive.

I remembered the roses. Her roses. And I wished she was back.

Then father started what he called his night games.

After dark he would turn off the power and there would be nothing but darkness, blacker than anything. For a while, I'd see a torch's light flickering on the walls around the house. The light would draw closer to my door and he would come into my room.

He would shine the torch under his chin to make terrifying faces. I always knew it was him.

It was his face. But something about it would make me scream, and then he would come closer and hit me with a wooden spoon. I never knew where the blow would come from and all the time his unshaven, blurred face would leer at me and he would tell me it was my fault my mother died and he'd hit and hit and sometimes I would faint from the pain and the terror.

I always knew it was my father, and not a ghost, but somehow that made it worse. There was never any escape. I just didn't know how to get away.

On some nights he would get his hands around my throat and I'd lose my breath and he'd go quiet and put a pillow over my head and I always felt I was going to die.

I tried to will myself to disappear. If I could do that, or if I could will myself to die, then everything would be okay. Whenever the lights went out, I'd try to die. But it never happened.

After he left me, having shambled off to his own room, I would lie awake and try to fight off sleep. For sleep held even more terrors in store. My dreams, fed and nurtured by my father, would be rampant.

Those night games seemed to go on for years. But it was only months.

One night he got very drunk. I could hear him lurching about the house downstairs. He seemed worse than ever, which scared me, and I took the key to my room and locked the door from the inside.

The lights went out and I could hear him stumbling up the stairs. He tried the door, and as he did I could see the torchlight through the keyhole. He stood outside my door and screamed at me until I was compelled to open it.

He was in a dreadful rage. The faces and the wooden spoon went on forever. I begged him to stop. He dribbled on me as he made his faces, and I wept in terror. When he put the pillow over my face, I passed out.

Daylight greeted me when I regained consciousness. My waking expectation had been that I would still be looking at his leering face. I woke up whimpering.

I waited for hours before leaving my room. The house was silent. Had he gone out?

Finally, I crept downstairs to see if I could get some food. I found him in his favourite chair in the sitting room.

Three bottles lay next to his chair. All empty. Permeating the room was a stench of vomit even more powerful than the smell of stale sweat and brandy. The vomit was all over his face and vest. I looked at him and knew the night games were over.

But that the dreams had truly just begun.

THIRTEEN

"HOW DO I know you're a policeman?" asked the woman, peering suspiciously at them.

Winters knew the door would remain firmly chained until he proved his identity.

"Hang on a minute," he said, reaching into his jacket pocket for his police card. As he did so he glanced at Hawkins, standing at the door with him, out of sight of the woman. Hawkins raised his eyebrows in exasperation.

Winters found his card, which he kept in a small leather folder, and flipped it open to show the woman. She peered at the card from beneath her hair rollers.

"Okay," she said, shutting the door. The chain rattled and the door was opened wide for the them to enter. Winters walked in ahead of Hawkins. He was irritable and tired. Normally he wouldn't get involved in legwork, but he had left the office to get away from Van Deventer, and now he was beginning to regret it. His feet were killing him from pounding the pavements for the last six hours.

Together he and Hawkins had interviewed twenty-three residents of Kensington already. After failing to uncover anything among the immediate neighbours of the Chapman household, he had decided to spread the net to all residents within a mile radius of the editor's house. So far it had proved to be a fruitless exercise. A telephone call to the squad room had proved that the same was true of the other thirty uniformed policemen and plainclothes detectives currently out on the street. Van Deventer was quick to point out they had all been wasting their time. This interview promised to be equally disappointing, thought Winters, as he introduced himself and Hawkins to the woman. She told him her name was Myra Kendall, mother of three boys and long-suffering wife of a busy banker. They were entertaining clients that night, thus her hair in rollers now. She didn't have much time.

"We're investigating the murder of Hugh Chapman, who lived in the square up the road, and we wonder if you can help us?" started Winters.

"I know nothing about it, except what I read in the papers and saw on television," said the woman.

Winters smiled, trying to be charming. The woman scowled. He said: "I'm sure you think you're right, Mrs Kendall, but often people may have seen something odd that they don't realise is significant, and even the smallest detail can help us."

"No, I'm positive I haven't seen or heard anything," said Mrs Kendall. She did not invite them further than the hall, and Winters felt hunted by its heavy wallpaper. Claustrophobic. He smiled at the thought of developing another phobia, to complement his fear of heights, and wondered what Jennifer would make of it.

"Perhaps a man in the neighbourhood who hasn't been here before, Ma'am?" suggested Hawkins. Mrs Kendall looked at him, as if surprised. Hawkins had stood to one side in the hall, and it appeared Mrs Kendall had forgotten he was there.

"No. I'm quite sure. We've seen nothing. The only one around here with anything to say about the murder is old Mr Goodman, who lives on the corner there." Mrs Kendall pointed out the door. "He's always telling us stories we can never believe, and now he's telling us he thinks he bumped into the killer the night before the murder. But he's such a liar - you should HEAR some of his war stories. We all laughed at what he said, and none of us have thought about it since."

"Where did you say Mr Goodman lived, Ma'am?" asked Hawkins, scribbling on his note pad.

Winters leaned against the wall, trying to take some of the weight off his feet. He felt depressed. Another nutter was all they needed. The squad had been flooded with calls from people confessing to the crime, others who thought they had invaluable information, still more wanting to tell the police their theory about the murder. Each call wasted valuable manpower. Yet nothing could be left unchecked.

Mrs Kendall walked to the open door and pointed across the road, toward the house on the corner. "He's retired, a grandfather, living with his son in that house. He should be there now, if you want to talk to him."

"Thank you Mrs Kendall, we will. Sorry to have wasted your time. If you should happen to think of something, or if you hear about any unusual incidents, please -"

"I know, I'll call. But I assure you there is nothing we can tell you. Now if you'll excuse me, I still have to get dressed AND finish cooking, and it's nearly five o'clock already..."

She ushered them from the house. Winters stepped out into the pale sunlight, looking up at the dreary sky. He sighed.

"I should be back in the squad room. This is pointless," he said.

"Van Deventer still making your life 'ell, sir?" asked Hawkins.

Winters shrugged. The tension between the Dutchman and Winters was no secret. Still, he would not be drawn. He did not think it wise to talk about the disharmony to his officers, although he knew the squad was seething with gossip. Several shouting matches from behind the closed doors of their joint office did nothing to boost morale, and Winters thought it better not to fuel talk by commenting on the dissention.

Instead, he clapped his hands together and said: "Come on. Let's go talk to our war hero friend. You can come back and speak to the people in these other houses tomorrow."

As the two detectives stepped into the street and crossed to the opposite pavement, Winters thought about Van Deventer, suppressing a surge of resentment. He hated being beaten at anything in life. He was intensely competitive. The ongoing rivalry with Van Deventer, though, was something he would gladly forego given the choice. As each day slipped by, the Dutchman became more and more pointed about the failure to turn up any clues. It was why he was out on the street now. Anything to escape Van Deventer, and to feel more involved in the case. If he could just dig up something to keep the investigation moving along, he would be happy. He would also get the Dutchman off his back, at least for a while.

The two detectives stopped outside the Goodman residence, and Winters was happy to stand and wait for Hawkins to fill and light his pipe. He was grateful for the chance to do a little more brooding about Van Deventer.

The Dutchman had been more tetchy than usual this morning. Winters wondered whether he had found out about his evenings with Jennifer. It would answer some questions, like why he was picking on everything with even more intensity than normal. Yet no mention had been made of Jennifer. His negative observations about the case were damaging, especially as what he said was true. The investigation was choking on paper, most of it containing useless information, and being goaded by Van Deventer wasn't helping.

In two weeks he had been unable to uncover much more on the Chapman case. Maxwell, contrary to his word, was beginning to lose faith. The Murder Squad Commander was spending more time checking their every move. Mind you, Winters admitted, he couldn't blame him. There had to be something, somewhere, he had overlooked.

Even the Dutchman was clutching at straws. This morning Winters had heard Van Deventer on the telephone to Patterson. He had hoped there might be something new from the forensic laboratories, some tiny piece of evidence to give them a break.

The conversation had been barren. Winters had heard the Dutchman talking about some of the interviews he had conducted, and had been annoyed to hear him telling Patterson they weren't doing very well.

Van Deventer had said, talking to Patterson: "We're doing pretty badly as well. We've had no luck tracking the crossbow through any local legitimate arms dealers or sports shops. It could have come through customs, which is unlikely, or been bought from an illegal dealer, or brought here from another city by some contact of the hitman. We just don't know anything. The investigation is beginning to lose direction."

Van Deventer had said this while looking directly at Winters. He had continued, talking softly, so that Winters had to strain to hear, even though they were separated only by the table between them. "Well, we're working on finding as many of the known illegal arms dealers as we can. First we have to find them. Then we have to try and convince them they should admit they've committed a crime by selling a weapon to a professional killer. It will not be easy."

Winters could hear the sound of Patterson's voice on the phone, indistinctly.

Van Deventer said: "I saw one chap this morning, a fellow called Stockton. He was a shifty bloke. He definitely had something to hide. But then, they all do. I'd love to have been able to torture a few scraps of information out of him. I left him my card, suggesting he should call me if he learned anything."

Finally Van Deventer replaced the receiver, his ear glowing red. "Got nothing better to do than listen in on my calls?"

Winters had not bothered to reply. He had picked up his coat and walked out of the room. In the squad room he had called Boyer and Hawkins and told them of his plan to widen the net around the Chapman house. He had assembled the other detectives and, taking a grim delight at leaving Van Deventer out of the planning, arranged for the house-to-house inquiries to be extended. Then, somewhat impulsively, he had assigned himself to assist Hawkins on his beat. He was cursing that impulsiveness now.

Hawkins finally got his pipe drawing well and, from behind a plume of smoke, reminded Winters of the unsuspecting Mr Goodman.

At the door, Winters banged lustily on the glass panes. Waiting for the door to be answered, he thought of Jennifer. After the second evening he had spent with her, he had to admit to being confused. They had returned to the restaurant near his flat, and spent the evening talking about their respective childhoods. Everything about Jennifer fascinated him. He had to keep stifling impulses to touch her. At times he ACHED to hold her. She was sensual and intelligent. He felt she would never bore him. She was just too unpredictable. All the rules he had learned while courting other women had to be thrown out the window. Jennifer saw through his every move, and forced him to relax, to be himself. At one point she said: "You don't have to pretend to be so cavalier about life. It doesn't become you." This had taken him by surprise, and they had drawn closer over the rest of the evening.

But still there was something keeping them apart - some kind of invisible barrier. He could not crystalise his thoughts. Perhaps if he gave it time? He mused about what would happen when they broke through the ice. His thoughts turned to imagining her in his bed. Before he could get too far, Goodman's front door was opened.

Goodman was a tall man, wide and grand, like a stately home. He had a bush of vividly white hair and pale blue eyes under equally white and bushy brows. His face was heavily lined, but a dense spray of lines around his eyes gave the impression he was amused. He wore a crimson cravat under an old cardigan. On his feet were mismatched, fluffy slippers.

The man caught Winters staring at his slippers and looked down at his feet, wiggling his toes. "Slippers are important. Dog got hold of one pair, chewed the right slipper to bits. Grandson got hold of another pair, sunk the left one carrying one of his toy tanks in the fishpond. Never was the same. This pair does fine. Couldn't see the point in buying more. May I help you?"

Winters and Hawkins smiled at each other. Winters warmed to the man immediately.

"Sir, my name is Detective Chief Inspector Alan Winters. I'm investigating a homicide which -"

"My name is Ira Goodman. I thought you'd finally get here. Come in." He stood aside and extravagantly waved his arm towards the door at the end of the hall. "Let's sit in the kitchen. Warmer there. Make us some tea."

Hawkins led the way through to the kitchen, a bright and large room, an oak table and four chairs at its centre. "Sit," ordered Goodman.

He switched on the kettle and began assembling the tea service.

"I know why you're here. You want to know what I know about the killing of Chapman," he said.

"Yes," said Winters, simply. He was relishing the chance to rest his feet. He sat on one of the chairs, Hawkins opposite him, watching Goodman. Hawkins had his notebook open on the table.

"First, you must understand that I've been away. Got back yesterday after a three-week stay with my daughter in Birmingham. I'm living here with my son these days. I like to get away every now and then and give him room to breathe. He lost his wife two years ago. Lost mine fifteen years back. We all miss them. Now I look after his two children. Love the job, but my son needs to find himself a woman. Won't do it with me here all the time."

The kettle boiled and he broke off to tend to the tea. His movements were quick and economical. Mr Goodman was not the fool Mrs Kendall thought him. He brought the tea to the table, and sat down between the policemen. As he poured the tea, Winters studied the man.

He was well dressed, and in good shape, probably in his mid- sixties. His face was full, his skin almost translucent. His eyes had seen many things, good and bad.

"Go on," said Winters.

As he spoke, Goodman offered them milk and sugar, preferring his own black. "Reading the paper last night I saw something that jogged my memory about the Chapman murder. I heard about the killing while I was away. Never realized it took place in my neighbourhood until yesterday."

That explained why we haven't heard from him, thought Winters, mentally crossing off one of his questions. Sipping the tea, he replaced the question with a mental note to compliment Goodman on his cuppa.

Goodman continued: "The Courier last night published a sketch of the murder scene. Showed where the killer stood when he fired the arrow. In the square opposite Chapman's house, right?"

"Yes," said Winters.

"Well, a few nights before Chapman was shot, in fact, the night before I left, I was walking my dog down that same street."

Winters was sipping his tea, enjoying every mouthful. Goodman had paused for dramatic effect. Hawkins had his pen poised, his pipe in his free hand. Finally, Winters said: "So?"

Goodman looked pleased, shaking his head like a large shaggy dog as he launched into his explanation. "So, I think I disturbed the killer."

The man wanted an appreciative audience. He sat forward on his chair. Hawkins spoiled the moment.

"What's your point, Mr Goodman?" he asked.

"That IS the point. I passed by the spot where the killer sat. When I passed it, I heard noises from the bush. My dog turned around at the noise as well. I thought it was just a dog or a cat in the garden. Ignored it. Carried on walking. Never paid it another thought, until last night."

"Did you see the man?" asked Hawkins.

Goodman slapped his cup down in its saucer. "No, I told you. I thought it was an animal. I didn't see anything."

Hawkins persisted. "Well, what time was this?"

Goodman brushed his hair from his brow. Then he emphatically tapped the table with his index finger, rattling all the cups in their saucers. "Must have been quite late. About 10:30. I usually walk Chester just before retiring myself. Doing battle with fresh air helps me sleep better."

Winters was enjoying the man's theatrics. Hawkins was drawing on his pipe. It had gone out, to his added annoyance. It was obvious he thought this all unnecessary. "What kind of noises did you hear?"

Goodman turned to Winters, smiling secretively. "Just rustling in the bushes. I felt Chester straining on the lead, so I was looking at him, not at the bushes. Chester was nervous. He always is. Nervous that is. Don't know why I got him. Anyway, I was trying to calm him. Didn't want him barking and setting off all the dogs in the neighbourhood."

"What night was this?" asked Hawkins, still taking down Goodman's every word.

"It was a Tuesday. Or it could have been Wednesday. I'd have to check my diary. I keep a note of what I do in my diary. It was the night before I left, so I'll be able to tell you by looking in my diary. Tomorrow."

Winters smiled. "Why tomorrow, Mr Goodman?"

"Because my son needed some telephone numbers in my diary. Took it to work with him today. Don't suppose you want to wait till he gets back, probably about seven or eight."

"I'll send one of my men around tomorrow, if you don't mind?"

"Not at all. It will make me a bit of a celebrity. I was getting round to calling you tonight, when my diary came back, just in case it could help you in some way."

Hawkins put away his pen and flipped closed his notebook. But Winters was not ready. He felt sure there was more. "Mr Goodman, thank you for your assistance. We've been up and down that street and no-one could tell us a thing. I'm not sure what you've told us can help, but I'd like you to think about it. You might recall something else you can tell my officer tomorrow?"

Goodman was silent, his large hands clasped behind his head. He was rocking back on the chair. He was staring out the window.

"Mr Goodman?" said Winters.

"Yes? I'm here. I was just thinking."

"What?" said Hawkins.

"Well, there was one other thing. I remember it struck me as a little strange, otherwise I wouldn't have noticed it."

"What?" repeated Hawkins, his voice rising.

"Walking this area as often as I do, you get to be able to feel the pulse of the neighbourhood. You know what belongs, what doesn't. Know who's got a new car, who's banged an old one."

Hawkins and Winters were both leaning forward again, listening attentively.

"On this night, there was a car there I didn't recognise. Bright red Golf. Looked out of place, if you know what I mean?"

Winters waved a hand. "Yes, exactly. What can you remember about the car? Anything. Anything at all."

"It was a red Golf, that I know. Not much else. It was dark. The car was between pools of light cast by streetlamps. But I do vaguely remember the letters on the number plate."

Winters felt a surge of excitement. "Yes, yes?"

"I think it was something like KLJ, or KLK. And a C registration, new this year. I don't remember the numbers."

"Anything else? Anything at all?" said Winters. Hawkins had caught up with his note-taking.

"No. That's really it."

Winters sighed. "Mr Goodman, you've been a great help. One thing. As you know, this is a very serious case. Please don't breathe a word about this to the Press. We need to work as quietly as possible on this one. A leak could jeopardise the whole investigation."

"All right. I'll keep my mouth shut. But I've already told my son. And Mrs Kendall up the street. My son is so busy he didn't hear me. Won't remember a word I said. Mrs Kendall didn't believe me."

Winters smiled, understandingly. "That's fine, Mr Goodman. Keep it to them, will you?"

"Only about the noise. I didn't remember the car until now."

"That's fine, sir. Even better. If you think of anything else, call me at Scotland Yard any time. One of my officers will take a statement from you in the morning. Thank you for your help. I wish there were more people like you."

They got up to leave, and Goodman fell silent as they walked to the front door. Hawkins stepped out and walked to the pavement. Winters hung back. He was looking at a faded photograph hanging next to the front door, above the telephone. It was of a group of men dressed in dark clothes. They all carried rifles. At the bottom of the picture hung a medal.

Inscribed on it were the words: "For Valour".

Winters turned to Goodman and asked, quietly: "What did you do in the war, Mr Goodman?"

The old man looked surprised. "Mostly, I fought with the French Resistance. Earlier on, I was a foot soldier. Got caught but managed to escape. Wound up with a band of resistance fighters and saw out the war with them. That's a group of them there," he said, nodding at the photograph.

"Saw some action then?"

"Yes, quite a bit. Why do you ask?"

Winters smiled. "I have a hunch that you could tell some interesting stories, sir, nothing more."

He left Goodman holding open the front door, a puzzled look on his face. As he joined Hawkins he jammed his right fist into the palm of his left hand. "Come on. Let's get back. Quickly."

It took them fifteen minutes to reach the car, walking at a brisk pace in breathless silence.

As he unlocked the door, Winters crashed his fist on the roof the car. "At last," he said.

"What?" asked Hawkins.

"This time, Hawkins, we've got something. At long last we've really got something. And I can't wait to see that old bastard's face."

FOURTEEN

WINTERS HAD to move heaven and earth, and several senior officials at the DVLA in Swansea, to get the information he needed.

As soon as he and Hawkins got back to the Yard, he sent officers to the Police National Computer at Hendon, and then contacted the police liaison officer. He asked him to get a listing of all red VW Golfs registered with the letters KLJ or KLK. The police computer was unable to help. They had no cars with that registration which were listed as stolen. The liaison officer said Swansea would not be able to help until late the next day. Winters used some high-ranking names and extracted a promise direct from the centre that he'd get the information first thing the next morning.

"I just hope that they weren't false plates. It's a slim chance, but perhaps this is his first mistake?" he whispered to Hawkins.

The next morning Van Deventer greeted Winters curtly, before isolating himself by reading through the previous day's reports from the squad room. Hawkins and Winters whispered excitedly to each other outside the meeting room, enjoying their conspiracy. They waited with a mounting sense of impatience, and telephoned Hendon and the liaison officer several times to try and speed them along.

"This sort of thing normally takes days to find out," said the liaison officer, "and you want it in hours. I'm doing the best I can."

Just after lunch – which Winters and Hawkins ate beside the telephone - the liaison officer called back.

"You'll have a printout of all the cars you asked about tomorrow morning."

"That's not good enough," said Winters.

"Slow down, I do have one thing you can check out first. There are apparently more than 75 red Golfs with that registration on their computer. Of those, 15 are registered to a car hire company in London."

"Really? That's interesting. I'll get on to that immediately. Which one?"

"A fairly small operation called Chartercar."

After informing Maxwell of the breakthrough, Winters went to tell Van Deventer what he had.

The Dutchman was watching him over the top of his spectacles. He kept his face impassive as Winters explained his decision to widen the net around Chapman's house. Winters gave vent to his pleasure when he described how it had been successful.

"You look pleased with yourself," said Van Deventer, when Winters was finished gloating.

"I am."

"Good work. I have to hand it to you. That was well done. I'll tell Maxwell immediately."

"No sir, don't bother. I already have."

Van Deventer was annoyed. He recovered quickly. "Right, let's go see them now. It's a long shot, but it's worth doing while we're waiting for the printout."

Winters called Chartercar, and arranged to see the hire company's public relations officer, Ian Gilmore.

The trip across London to the Chartercar head office was conducted in frigid silence, with Van Deventer choosing to stare morosely out of the window. But, by the time they had parked and found the office, the Dutchman was beginning to thaw.

"Please God, let this be something," he said.

Winters knew that, in spite of their animosity, they both badly wanted to solve this case. Van Deventer had been driving himself over the past two weeks. He marvelled at the older man's stamina. Van Deventer was usually in the office before him, nearly always the last to leave. He would spend long hours going through reports from the various detectives assisting on the case, often conducting many interviews himself. He was supposed to have been there as a "guiding hand", but had thrown himself into the field wherever and whenever he could.

Van Deventer stepped aside at the entrance to let Winters lead the way.

They were shown to Gilmore's office, to be greeted by a short, plump, balding man who wore the thickest pair of spectacles Winters had ever seen. His eyes appeared grossly distorted, and Winters found it easier to stare at Gilmore's nose.

"I have everything waiting here, gentlemen," he said. He had a deep and resonant voice.

Gilmore pushed over some computer print-outs. Van Deventer looked at Winters, who was quick to take the hint. He reached over and took up the sheets himself. He had seen Van Deventer struggling with these sheets before. Usually they wound up in an untidy bundle on the floor.

After a minute, Winters said: "I'm afraid I can't make any sense of these records. Would you mind explaining them to us?"

"Not at all. Ummm, let's see, thank you. Okay." He peered at the list, making notes in the margin in pencil.

"What this means, is that of the 15 cars registered to us on this sequence, 10 are in other parts of the country, one has been written off in a crash, and only four are still in London."

"Anything else?" asked Van Deventer.

"Not on this sheet, but if you wait a minute, I'll look up the records on those four cars."

"Thank you," said Van Deventer. Winters studied the office while Gilmore was out. It was small, and contained only a desk, two small bookcases, a filing cabinet, two guest chairs and a coffee table. Nearly every flat surface was piled with magazines, newspapers, posters and books. Several used plastic coffee cups adorned the desk.

Not a tidy man, thought Winters. How the hell would he be able to find the necessary records? He was being uncharitable. Gilmore was back within five minutes.

"I think I've got all you want," he said, clearing space on his desk for three large files he brought in with him.

"These are the records of those cars for the past three months. We can tell when they were hired out, to whom they were hired, which of our staff did the paperwork, which branch saw the car out, and so on. What do you want to know?"

"We want to know about any movements of those cars between, say, March 21 to the first week of April. Particularly on March 28," replied Winters.

"Anything in particular we are looking for about those dates? Any long journeys? The state of the car when it was returned to us?"

"Everything," said Van Deventer brusquely, avoiding the trap of telling Gilmore what this was all about.

"Okay, let's see," said Gilmore, as he paged through the first file.

"Here we are," he said, putting a finger on one page while he moved on through the file.

Presently he flipped back to the page he had marked.

"Two of those cars were not out on March 28. One was being serviced, the other was on our floor. The third one was out on the night of March 28, and brought back the next day. But then, so was the fourth one, brought back the next day, I mean. That one was hired out on March 23."

"That's the one," said Winters, standing up. "Let me see that file, please."

"Certainly," said Gilmore, "although it won't show you much more than what I've told you, except which branch it was hired from and the name of the employee who conducted the transaction."

"I thought you said those files would have all the information we required?" said Van Deventer.

"Uh, well, I'm sorry if I misled you. These files here won't.

The individual branch files will. But you'll have to go to that branch yourselves."

"Which branch?" said Winters. "Who hired out the car?"

Gilmore looked at the file again. "Anne Chartham. At our Chancery Lane office. Would you like me to tell her you're coming?"

"No, don't worry," said Winters. "Waiting for us might make her nervous, which tends to inhibit a person's memory. We'll go there now ourselves."

The two policemen stood up, towering over Gilmore, whose paunch had popped one of the buttons on his shirt. Winters could see what Gilmore lacked on his head, he more than made up for on his body. It was like a jungle in there.

"Thank you for your time, Mr Gilmore. We're sure to be back at some stage, and we'd appreciate your assistance then as well."

"Anytime," said Gilmore, glancing down at the file still open in his hand. "By the way, the name of the person who hired that particular car was a Mr Harold Hastings."

"What?" asked Van Deventer.

Winters, who had already started for the door, stopped. There was something in the way Van Deventer reacted...

"I said the name of the man who hired that car was Mr Hastings. Harold Hastings. Do you know him?"

"No," said Van Deventer. "No, I can't say I do."

"Oh, It sounded like you knew him."

"No. Thanks for your help."

Gilmore showed the policemen out of his office. They walked in silence to the car.

When they had got in, and Winters had already pulled out into the traffic, Van Deventer said: "Do you know where the Chancery Lane office is?"

"Uhh, no. And I forgot to ask which end of the Street."

Van Deventer chuckled. "Fine detectives we are. Just when we stumble onto something big, we stuff it by forgetting to ask the obvious."

Winters was relieved. He had expected another verbal pasting from the Dutchman. It was the first time Van Deventer had smiled in days. Winters was shocked to find he was actually beginning to be a touch scared of the Dutchman. He had been worn down by a steadfast process of attrition.

For no apparent reason, Van Deventer turned to Winters and asked: "Tell me, did you do history at school?"

"Yes. Why do you ask?"

"Perhaps nothing. We'll see. But I wager our Mr Hastings didn't produce any ID when he took the car." Winters looked across at Van Deventer. The Dutchman was smiling mysteriously.

By the time they had driven along Chancery Lane twice in search of the Chartercar office, Van Deventer's good mood had vanished. He managed to spot it on the third pass, and was steaming by the time they found a parking spot several minutes' walk away.

When the two men strode into the office, an attractive woman in her late twenties stood up from her desk behind the counter and walked briskly towards them.

"Good morning, gentlemen. May I help you?" she asked, smiling generously.

Winters stopped dead in his tracks. It was a dazzling smile.

"Sorry to bother you, but we're looking for Anne Chartham," said Van Deventer, as he shouldered his way past the immobile Winters.

"That's me," she said, still smiling, less certainly now.

"We're police officers, investigating an incident that took

place in March. We are particularly interested in a red VW Golf hired out on the day of March 23. I believe you would have the information?"

The smile died slowly during the speech, to be replaced by a frown. Anne Chartham looked very worried, and acutely vulnerable.

"Yes. Am I supposed to ask for your identification? I mean, neither of you looks like a policeman."

"Yes, you're right. Let me show you my ..." started Van Deventer, but Winters was already holding his ID under her nose. She was forced to lean back to bring the card into the correct focus.

"Thank you," she muttered. "What exactly did you want to know?"

"As I said, a red VW Golf, was hired out from this office on March 23, to a Mr Harold Hastings. We'd like to know more about this transaction."

"Would you mind waiting here for a moment? I'll go through the records..."

It took just a few minutes to find the correct file. "Oh. Oh yes," she said. "I remember now."

"What do you remember?" asked Winters.

"This car. The man. These records are like staring at photographs in an album. Some bring back memories, some don't. This one does."

"What do you remember?" repeated Van Deventer.

"Not a great deal. Just that the man had to hire the car because his had been stolen that morning."

"What did he look like?" asked Van Deventer.

"Nothing very unusual. A beard, spectacles, medium height. He walked with a limp, that I remember clearly."

"Right. Anything else?"

"Well, he came in about mid-morning, and asked if we had

anything he could drive away in. I told him all we had was one of our Golfs. He seemed disappointed when I told him it was red. I asked him if it worried him and he said it was a little too obtrusive for him, but it would do."

"Those were his exact words?" asked Winters.

"No, not exactly, but more or less."

"Go on," urged Van Deventer.

Anne Chartham glanced at Winters, and hesitated for a moment. She seemed to lose concentration, patting her hair. "He said his car had been stolen the previous night. He was in need of transport until he could buy himself another car."

She looked at Winters again. He took his hand off the counter, shot a glance at Van Deventer, and nodded at her to proceed. He hoped Van Deventer wouldn't notice it was the intensity of his gaze that was distracting her.

With a trace of irritation, Van Deventer said: "I'm listening."

Winters looked away, pretending interest in the file on the counter.

"I remember him telling me he wasn't sure how long it would take to get his insurance company to pay for the car. He said his licence and ID had been in the car when it was stolen. That was going to create enormous problems for him in terms of getting all the necessary paperwork done."

Van Deventer nodded, sharply. He had been expecting that. How? wondered Winters.

"I told him we needed to see a credit card or some form of ID before he could take our car. He said he knew, but what could he do? He would pay in cash. Did I want to check with the police? I said no. After all, he looked respectable. I told him that would be in order."

She looked at Van Deventer. "I know that's not normal company policy, but he seemed okay. And he DID bring the car back, on the 29th. Did I do wrong?"

"No, in fact, right now, you're being a great help. I'd like to impose on you to see if you can be even more of a help. I'd like you to describe this man again, to one of our photofit specialists. I'm sure you'll be amazed at what our men can do."

"Yes. Certainly."

"I'll send a car round here immediately, if I may?"

"No. I'm here until five, then someone else takes over until eight. Will five o'clock do?"

Winters coughed. "Uh, Ms Chartham? Is that particular car still here?"

"Yes. But it has been out several times since then. And if you're hoping to find something in it or on it, I'm afraid it has been cleaned several times as well."

"I thought as much. Still, we'd like to have a look at it, if that's at all possible?"

"Yes. I'll just clear it with head office. Will you want to take it away?"

"I'll get back to you on that, before you leave. But until then, will you make sure the car stays where it is?" Winters smiled, and was rewarded with a tentative, quick smile in return. It was good enough for him.

Van Deventer had been staring out of the office window during this exchange. He now glanced at Winters. "Finished?"

"Yes. I think that's all."

Van Deventer turning to Anne Chartham again, "Do you have the papers this man signed? We'd like to have a copy of his handwriting."

Winters cursed himself. Immediately Van Deventer spoke he realised he had missed it. He clenched his fists, digging his fingernails painfully into the palms of his hands. His mood was soured.

"Yes, but that could take me a while to dig up. Is it all right if I give the papers to your driver when he comes?"

"Thank you for your help. I'll see you when you meet our photofit man. His name is Andrew MacNeil, and he's very good at his job. He'll draw up this man you saw, and I'll watch his every move. You see, I'm very anxious to see this Mr Hastings."

She smiled.

The two men left the office and walked back to their car. Winters, even though he was taller than Van Deventer, had to quicken his pace to keep up.

As they walked, Van Deventer said: "I can smell him now. We're on his trail. And once we have that photofit we'll have something solid to go on. I just don't want this to leak to the Press yet. I want time to circulate the face to all stations. I want time to study the face of our man. It's him, I just know it."

"How can you be so sure? And how did you know there would be no ID?"

Still striding out, Van Deventer turned to look at Winters again. His irritating smile was back.

"Because of the name, Harold Hastings."

"Well, who IS he then?"

"It's not so much the name as what it signifies."

Winters was beginning to feel sorely irritated. His lips pursed, and he scowled at the pavement. After a few more brisk paces he stopped. A pedestrian collided into his back, dropping several files he had been carrying. Winters stared absently at the man as he stooped to pick up his scattered documents, all the while casting hatred-filled glances at the policeman.

Shit! thought Winters. Of course. He should have seen it sooner. Hastings. The Battle of Hastings. Harold. King Harold. King Harold was killed at the Battle of Hastings.

By an arrow through the eye.

FIFTEEN

"HELLO, JENNIFER? Good news. We've finally made a breakthrough." Winters was relieved that Jennifer was still at her office.

"What sort of breakthrough?" she asked.

"Oh no. Not on the phone. Let me take you for dinner. I'll tell you then."

"You don't have to make up excuses to see me."

"Same place?" he asked.

"That's fine. When?"

"At six. We can have a long drink and a leisurely meal."

"Alan, that's only an hour away. I want to go home and take a bath and get myself ready."

"Forget it. You don't need any time to improve yourself. I'll take you as you are."

He had wanted that to sound light and breezy. It sounded sincere. There was silence on the line. In the background he could hear telephones, typewriters, a burst of laughter.

"I have a meeting at five thirty. It will take an hour. I can be at South Kensington at seven. Is that okay?"

"Of course. What meeting?"

"Oh, just some colleagues. We get together now and then to discuss stories."

"What sort of stories?"

"Not on the phone. I'll tell you later. Let me take you for dinner. Tomorrow night. I'll tell you then."

He laughed. "Great, see you at seven. Tonight AND tomorrow night."

She laughed and put down the receiver. No goodbye. Damn, but he liked her style. The way she dressed; the way she talked;

the way she moved. Was that a song? He couldn't think. Well, there should be one if there wasn't already.

Winters fell into fantasy. He could see himself on holiday with Jennifer, walking arm in arm along a deserted stretch of beach. Dressed in white. Wasn't that the way the films always portrayed it? Oh well, he shrugged. He had some leave due. As soon as this case was over. Perhaps Jennifer ...?

He felt a strange tension. Something about Jennifer still worried him. It was her reserve. He couldn't explain it. She was so natural, so open, and yet he felt there was something deeper she was keeping hidden. A part of her was aloof from what was happening. He couldn't shake the feeling she was using him. Perhaps she felt inhibited by the speed at which their relationship was developing, so soon after her father's death. She had said nothing direct about it, but often alluded to the subject. She confessed to still crying at night over Chapman's death.

Yet Winters sensed she responded to him. Perhaps in a way she responded to few other people. He did not think she was vastly experienced with men. But she was self-possessed, calm and serene around them. Tantalisingly so. Again he found himself fantasising about her in bed.

Winters often felt a woman would one day be his downfall. Where strong men had failed to bring him down, an attractive woman had an inside track and a running start. He simply could not resist. Trouble was, those relationships were fast and furious, but seldom lasting. That was the way he liked it. At the age of 35, he had lost count of the number of girlfriends he had waved goodbye. He knew he often appeared shallow and a lothario, but he liked the chase.

Now the shoe appeared to be on the other foot. He had always been the stronger one in relationships, the one who was able to take it or leave it. That was an enviable position of strength and normally he wouldn't have it any other way. Now, it was he who might be vulnerable with Jennifer. He was power-less to resist.

He worried about his developing feelings for her through the final briefing, through his meeting with Van Deventer - now a daily ritual - and all the way home. In the shower he looked at his reflection in the full length mirror on the wall opposite the cubicle. He critically appraised his lean body and wondered whether he was putting on weight. During the Chapman case he had not had much time to exercise. He had not played squash in two weeks. Normally he played four times a week. Although he had never focused on weights he had well-defined muscles, broad shoulders and a flat, hard belly. His karate training had been enough to hone him physically. He felt another twinge of conscience. No practise for close to a month now. He HAD to watch it. This was the way you slipped into a lazy and unhealthy lifestyle. He towelled himself dry, then dressed. He left a few minutes before seven.

Jennifer was late. He went to their usual table and summoned a waiter. He ordered wine. Again, the same wine they had sipped the two previous meals they had shared. He knew this, too, was unusual. His normal style was to wine and dine a woman at different places, to dazzle her with a variety of good food, drink and entertainment. With Jennifer he had elected to visit the same restaurant, sit at the same table and drink the same wine three times in a row.

Finally, Jennifer arrived, out of breath. "I've been running. I caught a bus and forgot which stop I needed. I wound up on the far side of the Natural History Museum. Sorry."

Perspiration glowed on her forehead and along her hairline. He found himself excited by her flushed appearance.

They ordered their food. The waiter treated them like old

friends. While Winters poured their wine Jennifer flicked at her hair, and re-arranged her blouse.

"Well?" she asked.

While waiting for their food, sipping at the wine, he told her about the interview with Goodman, the car, the licence plate, and the visit to the hire car firm. He did not tell her about the attractive Ms Chartham, nor the possibility of a photofit of the killer.

"What are you going to do now?" she asked.

"Share a meal with you."

"You know what I mean." For a moment Winters saw something new in her eyes. It was a hint of ruthlessness. In that instant he decided not to reveal anything else. After all, he hardly knew this girl. He decided to trust his instincts, and tried to banter away the question.

"Take you home with me?" he laughed.

She failed to disguise a flash of anger. Then she smiled. It transformed her face.

There was an uncomfortable moment before she broke the silence. "When did you decide you wanted to join the police? You somehow just don't seem the type."

He smiled. This was better. "I had a very warm childhood. I wanted for nothing. My father was keen for me to take over his business, so he'd arrange for me to work in his office during my school holidays. His publishing business was in Oxford, and we had a house in Witney."

Jennifer looked bemused. "What's all this to do with police work?"

"You show little patience you know. I'm getting there." It was said with a grin, but the grin hid his irritation. Winters felt the evening was going to be a tough one. "During one of the spells at my father's office, there was a burglary. I was interviewed by the investigating detectives, and I'll never forget how impressed I was with their self-confidence and presence. They were completely assured and conveyed a strong sense of purpose. From then on I devoured everything I could on police work, and I became very well known at the local police station. For the right reasons!"

Their food arrived, and Jennifer tucked in with enthusiasm. He continued speaking between mouthfuls.

"At first my parents indulged me, then my father slowly realized I was intent on becoming a police officer. He suffered in silence until I got to the training college. We had a terrible row and he refused to speak to me for weeks. They were killed before I made up."

"What did you do then?"

"Well, I inherited a fortune. I sold his business and invested the money. I have enough to do precisely what I want. I bought myself my flat, a car, clothes, furnished my home, indulged in exotic holidays and generally I live exactly the life I choose. I have more money than I need. But it can't buy the one thing I truly want – the knowledge that my father forgave me, and that he still loved and respected me when he died. Dying the way they did, without us speaking, took away a large part of me I have never been able to recover. As a result I've always been afraid to get too close to anyone. Too scared of suffering another loss like that one."

"Oh," said Jennifer. She looked disappointed.

"The truth is," he hurried on, "it is also likely I just haven't been involved with the right person, until now."

She looked up at him. After a moment, she nodded. He sipped at his wine, staggered at what he'd said. It embarrassed him.

"You're blushing," she said. "Don't feel foolish. I know

what you mean. I feel the same way. Somehow, being with you has taken some of the edge off losing my own father. I mean that."

She reached across the table and took his hand from his wine glass, turning it over to look at his palm. Her finger traced the lines on his hand, touching softly, whispering across his skin.

They stayed that way for several minutes, not eating, just watching each other, until the waiter came to top up their wine glasses. After he had left, Jennifer continued. "I always tried so hard to win his affections and his attention. I always tried the very best at everything I did. Not for me, for him. Consequently, I never had time for other relationships."

Winters squeezed her hand. He was feeling acutely uncomfortable. This was too intense for him to feel sure of himself. Unchartered waters. He coughed. It gave him an excuse to remove his hand and break the searing contact. He picked up his fork and picked at his food. It was cold and unappetising now. He pushed his plate away.

"Something has puzzled me for a while," he said.

She cocked her head. Her hand was still in place, awaiting the return of his.

"How is Van Deventer involved with your family? I work with him every day, and it seems as if he was very close to your father. Very protective of him - and you, for that matter. I just can't understand it. He wants to handle this case so badly that he has taken ME on as his enemy. He wants to have me removed so that he can do it all his way. The rivalry is highly disturbing. It could get in the way of our investigation if I don't watch out."

Jennifer picked up her glass. "Can I trust you?" she asked.

"Yes," he said, without hesitation. "Implicitly."

"Swear your secrecy."

"I swear."

She paused, looking at him intently. "Some years ago, my father published a story about an investigation involving some drug squad officers."

"I've heard about it."

"What you may not know is that Van Deventer was his source. My father refused to divulge this to anyone. He has a...HAD...a safe in his study. One day, when I was still at university, he went out with my mother, having forgotten to lock his safe. I was curious and I looked in it. I found a notebook. It contained all the information my father had gathered about the case. When he came home and discovered that I had been in his safe, he took the notebook and burned it immediately. He never discussed the incident with me, but there is no doubt about it, Van Deventer was his source. I think the Dutchman has felt obligated to my father all these years."

Winters sipped the last of his wine. "That sort of information could finish him off forever. There were a lot of hard feelings about that case, especially after an inquiry cleared the officers of any guilt. Those feelings still exist today. I've encountered them myself."

"What I've just told you is in confidence. You can't use it in any way. Promise me you won't."

"Okay," he said.

"Okay what?"

"Okay, I promise. I won't use it in any way."

"Nor tell him you know."

"That too."

Jennifer sat back, relieved.

"You look beautiful," said Winters. He blushed, amazed at himself yet again. He had never felt this way. Normally those words glided off his tongue so easily. Tonight he felt like a boy again.

"Thank you," said Jennifer. Then: "Have you thought about the fact you are a lot older than me?"

"Only 12 years."

"That's a lot."

"All the more to show you," he said.

She chuckled. "Why don't you show me some of the shops around here? There might be something I can come back and buy."

After settling the bill, they left the restaurant and walked arm in arm looking in shop windows. They were going nowhere in particular.

"It's starting to rain." Winters held out a hand, watching as drops splashed on his palm. "Come on, let's make a dash for my flat. It's only a couple of minutes away."

They ran, she half a pace behind him, keeping up with him effortlessly. In spite of the rain-slicked pavements, she ran with an easy, sure-footed grace. He grabbed her hand. The rain - heavier now - was like ice on his face. By the time they reached the entrance to his block they were both drenched. They stood in the foyer, dripping and shivering.

"Come on, my place is warm. I left the central heating on. You can have a hot shower while I change and make us a drink."

They went up to his flat, on the top floor of a four-storey building. When he opened the door she looked inside and whistled.

"Very nice. Did you do the decorating yourself?"

"No. I hired someone. I'm usually too busy with work to spend a lot of time doing this sort of thing, as much as I enjoy it."

"It's beautiful. Very masculine. Is that a real fire?"

"No, it's gas. Move inside, I'm freezing."

They stepped inside and he took her bag and coat. Her blouse was wet and clingy. His throat went dry. She was studying the flat. Her eyes swept over the hall and sitting room.

Winters had chosen a high tech style for his home, a look described by his decorator as "hard edge." It smacked of a tough, no-nonsense approach, with all angles sharp rather than curved. The hall, sitting room and dining room were separate segments of one large, open-plan area, resembling a converted warehouse loft. Furniture was mostly in metal, glass and rubber, with little wood.

"Organised," said Jennifer. "Everything has its place. But very elegant."

"What does your room look like?" asked Winters.

"Quite the opposite. I enjoy the cottage feel. A kind of organised clutter. Things left lying around. But I like this. Very much."

"I'm glad. For your information, the bedroom is through there. The shower is en suite. Help yourself."

"Thank you, I will," she said.

She suppressed an involuntary shiver, and Winters chided her. "You should have got straight into a warm bath. There's plenty of time to see the other rooms later."

"You're right," she said. She went into the bathroom, while he went to open a bottle of wine. He changed his mind and put the kettle on for coffee. After a few minutes he heard the shower running. He ventured into his bedroom, saw the bathroom door was closed, and went to a cupboard to get fresh clothes. He quickly put on a tracksuit, then went out into the sitting room and took out a bottle of wine for after the coffee.

He decided to put on a record. Great Romantic Movie

Themes. For orchestra. That would do nicely, he thought. He put it on, turned up the volume.

He heard her calling.

He went through to his bedroom, then knocked on the door.

"What is it? I'm listening."

"There are no towels in here." Her voice was muffled by the shower, still blasting away.

"Hang on, I'll throw one in."

He found two towels in his airing cupboard, two huge, woolly brown towels still warm from the heat of the boiler.

At the door he paused a moment, opened it a crack, then thought: What the hell!

He stepped into the bathroom into a cloud of steam. He could barely make out her outline in the shower and he wondered if she had heard him enter. The outline was enough to push him another step forward.

"Need any help?"

"Oh! You gave me a fright. Where are you?" He could dimly see her back was toward the door.

"I'm on the other side of the glass. You're still safe."

"Am I? What a pity."

"Your towel awaits you." His heart was racing. She had not objected. Yet she had not accepted the bait.

He decided to give it a minute. Then he would leave. This would be an ideal moment for her to respond to his initiative, if she was of a mind. He waited while she continued showering. The steam swirled and eddied around him, flowing and dancing a giddying but formless pattern. Winters glanced at the mirror. It was covered in steam, and all he could make out was the vague image of a human form. He coughed.

"You still here?" She called out.

"I'm just leaving," he said, quickly. He felt the crush of disappointment, and left the bathroom.

By the time he was in the sitting room again he had cooled off. He had been pushing his luck, he reasoned. It was much too early in the relationship, and too soon after the killing, for that kind of thing. No harm in trying, though, he smiled to himself.

He turned the music down, and busied himself opening the wine and pouring two glasses. He took them to the fire and stood in front of it, leaning against the mantlepiece. Winters heard the shower being turned off.

He was staring into the fire when she walked into the lounge, wrapped in the towel. He resisted looking at her.

"Messy young man, aren't you?" She said.

"What do you mean?"

"You've left your wet clothes all over your bedroom floor. They were soaking the carpet, so I put them in the wash basket."

Winters smiled. "You shouldn't have bothered. But thanks. Here's some wine. Come and warm yourself next to the fire. I've also got some coffee coming."

Jennifer took the glass from him, but as he moved to walk past her to the kitchen she placed a hand gently on his chest to stop him.

She placed the glass on the mantelpiece. Facing the fire, her back to Winters, Jennifer let the towel drop slowly to the floor. Her reward was a sharp intake of breath.

Jennifer turned to watch him. His eyes met hers, then he could no longer resist the urge to look, to devour her with his gaze. She stood proud under his awed bold scrutiny – there was no shyness there. Only anticipation.

Running one finger gently along his cheek and jaw she brought his rapt attention back to her eyes. "Kiss me," she said. And he did.

SIXTEEN

THE RADIO alarm came on – a Beatles song: Yesterday. It was still dark.

He yawned, then turned on the bedside lamp.

Jennifer muttered, snuggling closer to him.

He smiled. He could feel the silken skin of her buttocks against his hips. He pushed against her.

She groaned, stretched, opening her eyes slowly.

"Morning," she said.

"Breakfast?" he asked.

"Yuk. Coffee."

He laughed. "Coming up."

He went through to the kitchen, still naked, thankful he had left the heating on. Quickly he made two cups of coffee, using instant granules. He placed the cups on a tray. Milk? Sugar? He didn't even know if she took milk or sugar. Then he remembered the restaurant. She took it black.

He padded into the bedroom again, carrying the tray. The cups were steaming. He looked around the room. Clothes and towels still lay scattered around. The bed was a mess, most of the blankets on the floor. It had been a long night. Only a sheet covered her, and even then, only parts of her. The best parts, he thought.

He made her sit up and stretch for the cup, and the sheet fell away. He sat down on the edge of the bed, sipping at his coffee, watching her frankly.

"You like?" she asked.

"Very much."

She smiled. She was still tousled with sleep. Now he knew. It was wonderful to wake up with her beside him.

"I'd better get going," she said. "I have to get home and change in time to get back to the office."

"Got much on today?"

"Nothing, at the moment."

"So I see. That's not what I meant."

"I know what you meant."

She held the mug with both hands, her knees drawn up to her chin. The sheet lay at her hips.

"There's something I want to tell you," she said.

"What's that?"

"I want to get it out into the open now."

"Well?" He was still smiling. He felt nothing could shake this mood.

"I can't sit by and wait any longer for you to find my father's killer."

His mood was broken. "What's that supposed to mean?"

"Please don't look like that. I just mean I can't wait for the police."

"I am the police."

"I know, but you are just one man. You are bound by rules. Perhaps I can do better."

"How can you do better? You're just one person."

"I know. But I've managed to talk several of the reporters at The Courier into helping me with an investigation of my own."

"You must be mad. This isn't amateur hour. We're dealing with a ruthless assassin." He stood up and paced around the room. Suddenly he felt the need to cover up. He searched for, and then put on his gown.

"You're angry," she said.

"No. Yes. You don't need to get involved."

"Why? Because I'm a woman? Well bollocks to that. I'm involved already. He was my father."

"I know. But you don't know what you're doing." He hastily added: "In this field."

"What makes you so sure? Journalists are trained to dig up information. And we have done so time and time again, sometimes when even the police have failed."

"I don't want you endangering yourself. Or endangering the investigation."

"Because it would offend your male ego if I did uncover something?"

"No, dammit. Think. This is not some small-time murder. Or hadn't you noticed?"

She threw off the sheet, jumped out of bed. "Who do you think you're talking to? I'm not some floozy you can order around as you please."

She stalked to the bathroom, found her clothes, dragged them into the bedroom. "Oh shit," she said. "They're still wet."

"You can take one of my shirts and a jersey if you like."

"Where are they?"

"The shirts are in that drawer, the jerseys on a shelf in that cupboard."

He watched as she walked to the cupboard, opening drawers to find a folded shirt, then haul out a chunky aran sweater. She dressed angrily, not bothering to check her appearance in any mirror.

"Jennifer, I'm sorry. Please try to understand."

"No. You understand. You do what you have to do. I'll do what I have to do. It's as simple as that."

She grabbed up her bag, and he followed her to the door.

He was staring at his jersey, which looked better on her than it did on him, even if it was a little too big for her.

"Don't worry. You'll get it back."

"That's not what I'm worried about."

"Well, don't worry about anything else either. I'm a big girl and I can look after myself."

"I want to look after you."

She stopped and turned to look at him. He felt his flush reappearing. She smiled, in spite of her anger. "I know. But not now. I have to go."

"You owe me a dinner."

"I know. Tonight. I'll call you."

She shut the door behind her, leaving him standing in the hall with his coffee.

He looked around.

She was right. It was masculine. Too masculine? He had bought this flat soon after his parents had died. Then he had contracted a designer to decorate it. The designer had asked him how he wanted it done. "I'm a bachelor. I want to keep it that way," Winters had said. Well, now he wasn't so sure. That worried him, but not as much as the news Jennifer had broken. Sure, every newspaper would have a team of journalists working on this story. He could hardly prevent that. Yet he still wasn't sure if Jennifer was using him, in spite of the feelings she professed. If she was, that would make her one of the most calculating people he had ever met. He shook his head. He felt sure her attraction was genuine. But was she motivated by a more powerful force as well? Revenge? Would he be crushed by that force?

He didn't want to find out.

Besides, this complicated things somewhat. How could he develop a relationship with her when he had to watch his every word? What would Van Deventer say? If only he could shake a sense of foreboding. This was getting far too complicated. Too many hands were on the oar. Maxwell. Van Deventer.

The so-called Chiller Killer. Jennifer. Himself. What next? he thought.

Or, to be more precise, who next?

SEVENTEEN

HIS CHEST. It was the tension. It always brought on the heart-burn. He braked his new Ford Granada, looking for the street which would take him to the local shopping centre.

What the hell was going on? he wondered. The man had said so many strange things. Vital information? Police? Car parks in the middle of the night?

Where WAS the bloody street?

Ballantine and his family had recently moved to Farnborough. As he spent most of his time in London, he still wasn't sure of his way around. His wife was the expert, but the man had said come alone. He had taken hasty directions from her. According to those directions, the car park had to be around here somewhere.

He drove on, careful not to rev the engine too hard. He believed that being gentle with a car helped it to last longer. He was proud of his car. Like most other things in his life, he had researched it carefully before making a decision. He had researched where to locate his offices, where to live, his business partner, the sort of legal practice to start. He had never been disappointed as a result.

He seldom used the car, preferring to catch a train into London every day. This hour on either side of his working day gave him time to catch up on his paperwork. He enjoyed his paperwork. Just as he also enjoyed his car, revelling in the luxury every time he got into it. He took maximum pleasure from the ten minute drive to and from the station every day.

He recognised the road to the shopping centre and slowed to a crawl. Did he really want to do this? It all sounded so crazy. The man had given him no time to think about it. Now he felt harried and desperately uncertain of himself. What had the man said? That he had vital information that could turn the case around? Something like that. What could he have meant? Well, really, what was a man supposed to do when he was disturbed so late at night? He had been in the bath when his wife had knocked on the door. There's someone on the phone, she'd said. Tell them to phone back, he replied. He can't, he's in a phone box. Ballantine had wrapped a towel around himself and trudged, dripping, to the main bedroom.

"Hello?"

"Mr Ballantine?"

"Yes, speaking."

"I have some information that will interest you. It might possibly turn the case upside down."

"What case?" Ballantine had asked.

"Don't be ridiculous. Nick Graham. I have information that might be worth something to you." The voice had been low, husky. Someone was trying on an American accent.

"What sort of information?"

"The type that could see Graham wind up in jail for life if you don't know about it."

Ballantine had drawn a breath. Damn. Just as he had been thinking all was well. He was defending a notorious gangster named Nicholas Graham, reported to be one of the richest underworld drug dealers in Britain. Graham was prepared to pay handsomely for Ballantine's efforts. It had helped that the evidence against Graham was mostly circumstantial. The police seemed desperate to hang anything on Graham, to make some sort of bust. Ballantine judged that if he had the jury on his side he could win this one easily.

But this man had said he had information which could put Graham away for life! Ballantine had tried to find out more, but the man had cut short the conversation.

"Look, I'm not going to talk about this on the phone. I'm running out of time. Let's meet, tonight, before it's too late."

"But where? How? When? I mean, where are you?"

The voice had muttered inaudibly. The lawyer thought he heard the word "Farnborough".

"What about my place, tonight?" asked Ballantine.

"No, that's too unsafe. I can't risk it. I tell you what. There's a shopping centre near your house. I'll meet you in the middle of the car park."

"Which centre? Which car park?"

The man gave him directions.

"When?" asked Ballantine.

"In ten minutes. Come alone. Park your car in the middle of the lot and then get out and open all the doors. I want to make sure your car is empty before I make contact. I can't risk police involvement. If you are not alone I won't show."

"And then?"

"Be there in ten minutes."

Click.

All far too mysterious for Ballantine's liking. So what the hell could it be? He made a note to add a hefty amount to Graham's charges for this one. He hadn't become successful by being shy with his fees. He steered into the car park and drove around the perimeter, checking to see if anyone was around. He tried to pierce the gloom. Too many shadows.

He stopped in the middle of the car park, facing the shops. He turned off his engine. His parking lights were still on. He could see no-one. The centre and the lot were deserted. He had expected to find another car, even though the man had said he would not appear until Ballantine proved he was alone.

What sort of information could he possibly have? Ballantine wondered whether he had got in way over his head when he decided to represent Graham. He had seen the case, and a notorious client, as a watershed in his career. If he could successfully defend Graham he could start a new way of life.

What had the man said? Open all the doors. Or else he wouldn't show.

Ballantine sighed, then opened his door. He hitched his coat firmly across his neck, hugging it with one hand to make sure it didn't flap open. He had dressed quickly, pulling on a polo-neck jersey and some jeans, and grabbed the first coat he had seen. It had turned out to be one of his light summer coats.

He took one more look around. Still no-one. Well, it seemed safe enough. The closest building was about 40 or 50 yards away. Anyone who wanted to get up close would have to move like lightning to prevent him jumping back into his car. If the character looked dangerous or threatening, well, screw Graham, he would just take off.

Ballantine heaved himself out of the car, once again regretting his bulk. It seemed he had always been bulky. He had to squeeze himself past the steering wheel. He walked to the back door, pulled it open, thankful for the central locking. He walked to the far side of the car, beginning to shiver in the cold, opened the two doors, then walked back to the driver's door.

He was struck by how similar this was to a scene from a recent television show he had watched. He remembered the man waiting at his car had turned on his headlights and then gone to stand in front of the bonnet, so that the lights shone in the eyes of the person approaching. Seemed like a good idea, he thought. He reached in the car and turned the key. The headlights blazed into the darkness, two distinct beams which fused somewhere ahead of him, shining towards the buildings of the shopping centre. He walked to the bonnet and stood between the headlights, glad of the light they cast on the scene. Still, the man hadn't shown himself. Where was he? Watching right this moment? He was going to be relieved when this melodrama was over.

Ballantine was about to lean back and sit on the bonnet when he thought his rear pocket button might scratch the paintwork. He twisted to his left to undo the button.

Something whirred past him in the night. It clattered on the ground behind his car, scraping and hissing along the tarmac. What was that? he wondered, alarmed, his eyes scanning the darkness. Was someone throwing something at him? It must have come from beyond the range of the car lights, in front of his car. He turned back towards the shops, hoping his headlights would pick up something. Silence.

He was struck a stunning blow on his left shoulder.

The force spun him around to face his car. He lurched on to the bonnet, sprawling face down for a moment, feeling the warm metal of the car against his face. He slid to the ground.

His arm was numb. He was shocked senseless.

He turned and stared out between the headlamps.

Pain coursed through him, emanating from his arm and sweeping over his body in wave after wave of an agony he had never known. He stared blankly at his shoulder.

What was that?

It looked like the back end of a dart.

But it was too big for a dart.

What then?

An arrow? No. It was a bolt. Someone had shot him with a crossbow bolt.

He stared at it with horror, his mind numbed by the pain, until he was shocked rigid by a terrifying realisation.

Jesus Christ. The papers were full of it. That newspaper editor had been killed by a bolt.

Through the head. Now me. But why me? he wondered, still dazed and confused.

Ballantine tried to stand up, but the pain made him dizzy. He started to retch, but nothing came. He pushed himself onto his knees, his back to the shops, leaning against the bumper. Into the car. Get home. Quickly. He would think about what to do then.

The bolt had penetrated deep into his shoulder. It felt as if the tip was threatening to burst out of the skin on the back of his arm. Only the last six inches protruded from his coat. Blood had seeped through the material. Shit. It would get all over the seats.

Ballantine forced himself away from the Granada, wavering. His power seemed to be seeping out of the hole the bolt had made in his arm. Thank God I turned, he thought. Otherwise it would have hit me in the chest! He took a step towards the driver's door; another.

Behind him he could hear shoes crunching on the loose stones on the tarmac surface of the car park.

Ballantine had forgotten that the man was still around. Jesus. COME ON. Into the car.

He tottered forward. The car was spinning, his vision telescoping backwards and forwards. He took another step. Behind him, the footsteps were getting closer. Unhurried.

But closer. Or maybe it just seemed like everything was taking so long? Ballantine had read how time seemed to warp out of perspective in moments of extreme danger.

For pete's sake. THIS was a moment of extreme danger. Stop messing around. Get in the car.

He took another step, and another. The momentum carried him to the car door and he put his good hand out to steady himself. The door closed and he fell, tearing his trousers at the knee. He felt the sharp lance of pain as shards of gravel dug into his kneecap. Ballantine tried to haul himself up again. He pulled open the door. He could see the keys now, hanging from the ignition. All he had to do was pull himself into the car, shut his door, turn on the engine and get away.

The footsteps were closer. The man was somewhere off to the right of the headlights.

He was clutching his left arm to his chest. He leaned forward on his right hand. He tried to push with his legs, but he could feel his hand slipping on the gravel. It shot out from underneath him and he banged his chin on the door sill. This time he didn't feel the pain.

He heard a sharp slap and then that odd whirring sound again. An instant later a dull thud. He looked up, dazedly. Another bolt was embedded in his car, inches above and to the left of his head.

JESUS. It went straight into the metal of a car door!

Terror gave him renewed strength. Ballantine hauled himself up, grabbing at the steering wheel. He pulled himself erect, still clutching at the wheel. He tried to lift a foot into the car. His leg stayed rooted to the spot. He turned back to see if the man was any closer.

What he saw filled him with dread.

His attacker stood no more than 30 yards away. He was dressed in black. He was smiling. And inserting another bolt into his crossbow. Brass plates on the weapon were shining. The rest of it was black. On top was a scope. But it was the bolt that filled Ballantine with horror. It looked like the leading edge of a rocket, with three sharp vanes trailing back from the point. It, too, was brass. He could see that each vane had jagged teeth.

Ballantine tried again to lift his leg into the car. This time, he succeeded. He sat down, with a jolt. He looked again at his pursuer.

The man had taken up an odd stance.

His feet and legs were pointing towards the headlight beam, while his upper body was twisted from the hips towards Ballantine. The man's pelvis was pushed slightly forward. It seemed as if his whole upper body had been allowed to sag onto his hips, angled backwards, counter-acting the weight of the crossbow in his hands. The archer rested his left elbow on his left hip, seemingly transferring the weight of the weapon to the ground via his bone structure.

The man's trigger finger, wrist and arm formed one straight line.

Pointing at Ballantine!

The lawyer was galvanized into action again. He hauled his right leg into the car, then leaned forward to wrench at the car keys. His voice was rasping in his throat. He was wheezing and whimpering, his breath as ragged as the teeth on the vanes of the bolt.

His fingers closed on the keys, slid away, and he fell back in the seat. The man was closer now. Ballantine could see his eyes. They gleamed. The man was still smiling. He took a crab-like step forwards, his stare never leaving Ballantine's face.

The lawyer leaned forward again, reaching under the steering wheel for the keys. "Please, oh please, oh please," he blubbered. "Just start!"

His fingers closed on the keys, fumbled, gripped tightly. He turned the key.

The engine burst into life!

He fumbled for the automatic shift, but the pain in his shoulder prevented him from reaching the lever. He tried to reach the gearshift with his right hand, but his stomach butted up against the steering wheel. He was sobbing, tears blinding him, spittle foaming on his lips.

The man was closer now. Twenty yards.

Summoning all his willpower, Ballantine reached out with his left hand, leaning forward and to his left to increase his stretch. The pain shot through his body. He could feel the head of the bolt was deep in his shoulder, somewhere under his collar bone. He glanced over his good shoulder. His attacker was adjusting the scope on the crossbow.

Drive, his mind screeched. Just get moving. He revved the engine. The car strained against its brakes, the engine screaming. Oh God. The handbrake. It was still on. In its lowest gear the car would not be able to fight free of the brake. In panic, he looked at his pursuer. His right hand was crushing the steering wheel. The engine screamed in his ears.

This time he didn't hear the missile.

It smashed into his upper chest at an angle, just below the armpit, tearing open his ribs, driving through his right lung, ripping through flesh and bone.

Ballantine arched his back, frozen in an instant of mind-searing agony. Then blood gushed from his mouth on to his chest, rushed over his stomach and pooled on the seat between his legs. His eyes were wide, his hand still locked on the steering wheel. His was head shaking and trembling, as if on a spring. Ballantine looked down at the blood on his clothes, and on his car seat. His eyes became saddened. He sensed, rather than felt, the car stall. Then he looked back at his attacker. The man had inserted yet another bolt in the hideous weapon he was using. He had stopped walking. The smile was gone. He took careful aim, gently squeezing the trigger. The string was unleashed and the bolt flashed from the bow, ripping across the divide to spear into Ballantine's neck. The force jolted Ballantine backwards, but he was locked against the steering wheel, his hand now frozen in place. He rocked in the seat, a dreadful grating groan escaping from his mouth. Even more blood was running down his neck. He sat frozen for another second, then he fell forward, his head crashing against the steering wheel.

He didn't hear the sound of the horn blaring out in the night.

EIGHTEEN

APRIL 19, 1986. *We had no relatives. No-one else wanted me. I was taken to an orphanage. I have only indistinct memories of my first years there. Nothing is clear. Remember, vaguely, fighting with other children. They tried to tease me. I was always bigger than the others. Soon, the teasing stopped. During that time it seems I had no mind nor will. They said I was trying to escape my past, coping the only way I knew how.*

I remember, years later, one of the doctors at the orphanage talking to me. He wore a white coat, and we sat in a small, stark room and talked. He spent days trying to find out how I felt about my parents. I told him I didn't feel anything. It was true. He asked me if I remembered what my father used to do to me. I said I didn't know what he was talking about. Also true. He spoke of a report about my condition when I was admitted to the orphanage. Social workers had said I was badly bruised, had written in their reports that I cried a lot, that I kept everyone awake at night, that I refused to speak to anyone. I couldn't help him. Nor could I help any of the other doctors who tried to speak to me.

Not then, anyway. Parts of my past came back to me slowly, swimming up from the deep during sleep, revealing themselves in the endless nightmares that have been a constant feature of my life.

Learned in the orphanage to keep to myself. Other children came and went. Used to stand at the office and watch them with their new parents. They would leave, and I would go back to my bed, and sit there for hours, hearing the sounds of the other children playing – after a while, I wouldn't even hear that. I would sit and stare and see nothing, think nothing. Nobody could touch me in that state.

I went to school. I got good marks, without much effort. I did enough to get by, and that was okay, because people left me alone. I used to sit in the homework room at the orphanage and pretend I was studying. I was really in my empty state. The other children left me alone. They called me a bookworm. I heard some of them calling me strange. It didn't bother me.

Finally the time came for me to leave the home. I overheard one of the social workers talking about me. She said she was going to be relieved to have me out of the place. It seems I used to depress everyone who came into contact with me. I learned then that was a mistake. So I developed a mask that helped me in my 'relationships' with people. I could never be totally isolated, and that the only way to get by would be to pretend I enjoyed their company. I learned to handle longer and longer periods with other people.

That served me well when I started to work. Eventually I was offered a job in London. I had heard big cities were lonely places, so I accepted. Over the years I gradually improved my standard of living, moving from place to place until I finally arrived at this small, two-roomed apartment in Chelsea.

It does its job. I do not have a lot of pictures and paintings up. Never found any that I liked. I've never let myself grow attached to anything. Even when I moved so often, to wind up here, I never missed any of the places I left. Nor any of my neighbours, whom I spent most of my time trying to avoid. Even my current neighbours have now finally got the message. I don't want a relationship. I want to be left alone.

My only companions are the flowers.

I keep a lot of them in the flat.

Roses.

They remind me of my mother. Even though I do not remember her well, these flowers somehow make me feel...well...better. On the bad nights, when the storm dream wakes me and the scream goes on and on and I feel lonely and scared of I don't know what, I come to look at the flowers.

If I knew where my mother was buried, I would make sure she always had a rose on her grave.

I know that would please her.

NINETEEN

"CHRIST, HE'S been used a pin cushion," said Winters, his face pale.

"Too right," said Patterson. His teeth were clenched and a knot on his jaw jumped and twitched with a life of its own.

Police cars were everywhere. Their lights flashed grim and eerie shadows on the scene. The lights of the ambulance were also flashing, but out of synchrony, adding to the discord of the scene. Occasional camera flashes seemed to hollow out the cheeks of the people looking down at the body, creating a disquieting impression of skulls.

Garner Patterson tapped on the rim of his spectacles and looked around. He was crouching next to the Granada, peering at the body. A press photographer's camera flash blinded him. Winters saw Patterson resist the temptation to hurl abuse.

"Idiot!" he whispered, between gritted teeth.

Winters smiled in sympathy. Patterson shrugged. "I must ask that bastard which newspaper he represents. I'll send my wife out to buy a copy in the morning."

Patterson had only just arrived. When the call had come through from the Murder Room at Scotland Yard, Winters had insisted on Patterson being brought to the scene. It wasn't that he didn't trust other officers to collect evidence, it was just that he had faith in Patterson.

The detective who called Winters had been apologetic. It had been obvious that he had caught Winters at an inopportune moment. If only he knew what he interrupted, thought Winters, wryly. He told Jennifer he had been called out on an emergency, but refused to give any details. He said simply that he didn't know any. She elected to dress with him, and go home. He told her he would call her the next day. Jennifer would never have forgiven him if she knew he deliberately withheld details of what appeared to be another victim of the Chiller Killer.

It had taken him 40 minutes to get to the scene. He still felt charged with the exhilaration of blasting his BMW along the M3 motorway at more than 100 mph. Van Deventer was still on his way, as was Philip Maxwell.

"What's his name?" asked Patterson.

"The policemen first on the scene established it as John Ballantine. A solicitor. When he saw the man bristling with arrows, he called his local station and they called Scotland Yard and the murder squad."

Patterson grunted, still peering at the body.

"The body was discovered by a young college student and his girlfriend, out for the night in his father's car. They were on their way to the car park to find a quiet corner to ... 'talk'.
The couple heard the horn, saw the car with all its doors wide open, and drove closer to inspect it. It was only when they got out of their own car that the girl saw the body."

Winters stopped to look around. The car park seemed to be crawling with people. Police, paramedics, scenes-of-crimes officers, the Home Office pathologist and his staff, newspaper photographers and reporters, and local residents who had been attracted by the noise.
He shook his head.

"According to the student, they both immediately went back to their own car. They were afraid they had walked in to 'the middle of something.' They drove to a nearby telephone box and called the local police. The officers who responded to the call met the young couple at the telephone, and then drove together to the car park. By then a few local residents had arrived to see what the noise was all about."

"Where are they now?" asked Patterson.

"They've long since been escorted home. We can get back to them tomorrow. Nothing either of them said throws any light on the situation."

For the first time, Patterson said what was on both of their minds. "The Chiller Killer again. Almost certainly. If you think the shit had already hit the fan, think again."

"Yeah. I know. I know."

Patterson stood up and pointed at one of the detectives. "You there! Please put out that cigarette and don't allow anyone to smoke around here for a while. Keep your stub in your pocket. We'll be looking for exactly that sort of thing in a minute. I don't want to have to investigate any extraneous crap."

Already, police had cordoned off the car park. The scene was enough to sicken even the most hardened policeman. Ballantine had bled profusely, from the mouth, chest, neck and shoulder. The first policeman on the scene had turned off the car's ignition, silencing the horn. Ballantine still lay forward against the wheel.

Winters knew this was one car that would be difficult to sell again. The smell of blood – THIS much blood - was difficult to extract. It would live with the car forever.

Patterson broke his train of thought: "I wonder what happened here? Why are all the car doors open? Did Ballantine bring passengers? Did one of them kill him?"

The two men turned to watch a police car as it pulled into the car park and came to a halt at one of the police barriers. Winters was expecting Van Deventer and Maxwell. He watched as a uniformed constable got out. He approached one of the local CID officers. Winters saw the men turn to look at him. The constable walked towards him and Winters stood up to receive the man.

"Inspector Winters?"

"Yes?"

"Sir, I've just come back from the victim's home. His wife is in a terrible state. She was on her way out here with us, but collapsed. A doctor is with her. She said Ballantine was summoned to this car park by a mystery caller earlier this evening. Ballantine received a telephone call at about eight.

Apparently the caller said he had information vital to the case Ballantine is...was...working on, involving Nick Graham."

"Yes, I read about the case, this evening, in fact. What else did the caller say?"

The officer's eyes kept drifting back to the body. Under the glare of spotlights the corpse seemed to have shrunk, startlingly alone in the middle of the crowd.

"The wife was hysterical. I could only establish the man insisted her husband come alone. Ballantine had to prove he was alone by opening all his doors. The caller said he would be watching. If Ballantine wasn't alone, he would leave. Mrs Ballantine had suggested she go with her husband, but he had refused, and explained why."

"Right. Anything else?"

"No sir, that was all I could get from her. The family doctor is with her now. I doubt anyone could talk to her before tomorrow."

"Thank you. You've shed a lot of light on things here officer. Well done."

The constable smiled proudly. Winters saw his gaze switch to the body, and the smile dropped off his lips. He understood. To smile now was to flaunt life in death's face.

Patterson called him to the front of the car, pointing at the ground. Winters walked to him, hands buried in his pockets. He felt chilled to the bone, even though the weather was fair.

"Blood on the bonnet, more on the ground here, leading to the door. Ballantine was hit first while standing here. If he had been standing between the headlights, it is unlikely he would have allowed anyone armed with a crossbow to approach him. That bolt must have been fired from some distance away, possibly the line of shops. Another bolt was found about 200 yards away, behind the car. One that missed."

Patterson scanned the buildings, his gaze stopping at several alley-ways. He glanced at Winters, who nodded.

The pressmen had by now gathered in a huddle near the barriers. Police would not yet allow them into the restricted area. A television crew was setting up lights and Winters could see the TV reporter doing practice takes.

A sense of dread hit Winters.

"Another public figure murdered. In what seems like a carefully planned hit by a professional killer. Who uses a high-powered crossbow," he said, quietly.

"Uh huh," said Patterson.

Winters sighed. He looked pointedly at the television crews. "Jesus," he said. "What are those reporters going to say now?"

"God knows," said Patterson.

They stood together, peering into the darkness of the alley-ways between the shops. After a minute, Patterson said: "Well, let's go see what's in there."

"First let's get some torches," suggested Winters.

"I've got them in my murder bag."

The murder bag was standard equipment for scenes-of-crime officers. The bags contained all the equipment they were likely to need to search for and collect evidence. "I've got tweezers, bottles, tape measures, magnifying glasses, tape recorders, dusting powder...why shouldn't I also have torches?"

Patterson handed one to Winters. "We'll do a quick scan first. Don't touch anything. You take the alleys on the left there. I'll take these."

As Winters began his search he found himself having to overcome a strange reluctance to enter the first alley. What would he find? Did he want to find it?

As he stepped into the lane he heard Patterson calling

him. Now what? He took another look into the darkness of the alley, shrugged, then turned and went in search of Patterson.

He found him in the first entrance. The scenes-of-crime officer was kneeling behind a pile of empty cardboard cartons, his torch pointed at something on the ground. At first Winters could not distinguish what it was that Patterson had discovered. As he knelt to take a closer look he froze. "What on earth...?" he began.

Then he turned to his colleague, his brow furrowed. Patterson was shaking his head.

In the glare of the torch beam, the object fluttered. A slight breeze had caught one of its petals.

"A flower," said Winters, bemused.

"Yes," said Patterson. "And if I'm not mistaken, it's a rose."

"Oh Christ," said Winters.

TWENTY

ANOTHER SLEEPLESS night. Tension showed on all their faces. Maxwell wanted results. So did the commissioner.

"Take every available man. As many as you need. But for God's sake come up with something," Maxwell said.

It was always the same. In spite of the fact some murder cases took months to solve, and literally hundreds of thousands of interviews, they always wanted instant results. When Maxwell suggested a new special squad to handle the case, Van Deventer surprised Winters and stood firm.

"You have your best men on the case. I am with them every step of the way."

Winters wondered whether this was simply to make sure he wasn't taken one further remove from the case. It was unlikely Van Deventer would support him for any other reason. Only eighteen hours after the discovery of Ballantine's body, Winters felt as if a lifetime had passed. Winters, Patterson, Van Deventer and Maxwell were sitting in the Murder room at Scotland Yard, each glumly staring at the photofit picture of "Mr Hastings." When the men had first seen it, they had been thrilled. Anne Chartham declared it a "near perfect" version of the man she knew as Harold Hastings. The face was plump and bearded. A long, straight fringe drew attention to a pair of silver-rimmed spectacles. The eyes were set wide apart, and the brows were dark and heavy. The beard was full, perhaps shaggy.

"Even though this has been posted at all stations, even circulated around the country, we've heard nothing?" Maxwell asked.

"Not a whisper. If we give it to the press, we wouldn't be able to move for leads," replied Patterson.

"No. Not now," said Maxwell, firmly. "The press is guaranteed to use it at the moment, but with all this fuss we are likely to be led up so many blind alleys we'd wind up in chaos."

As Winters had predicted, the press had gone crazy. Newspapers, television and radio were in a frenzy. Headlines screamed: "Chapman, Ballantine killed by terrorists?", "Paid assassin behind killings of editor and lawyer?", and "The killer who leaves a rose."

Already many of the newspapers had changed the now accepted name of The Chiller Killer to "The Rose."

One of the popular dailies - Winters couldn't remember which - had used most of its front page to print a photograph of Ballantine's body slumped over his steering wheel. The headline had said: "Blood of 'The Rose'."

Maxwell saw one positive element in the killing. "At least our man is still around."

It was, Winters thought, bitter consolation.

"But just what the hell is going on? What connections are there between Ballantine and Chapman?" persisted Maxwell.

Van Deventer stood up, running his hands through his hair. "Already a special task force of more than 100 detectives drawn from divisions throughout London has started looking for links. They discovered Chapman and Ballantine apparently met at one or two official legal functions in the past two years. But that's it."

Winters was struck by a sudden fear. Unless they found out what was happening pretty quickly, they may find another body. Then what? He knew well the pattern of many investigations. A slow, inexorable gathering of information, then one clue, and another, and suddenly you were home and dry. But sometimes cases went unsolved. Would this be one of the latter? So far, luck had been running against them.

Van Deventer went on: "Around the country we have been checking florists, sports shops and arms dealers. Neighbours of both Chapman and Ballantine, as well as residents in surrounding streets, have been interviewed. Known criminals all over the country are being hauled in and leaned on for information. Every informant has been tapped, and the records of known assassins have been scoured. Forensic scientists have tried in vain to piece together enough leads from the clothing fibres found at the Chapman murder to provide clues our detectives can follow up. Officers have been trying to trace the sales of the notepaper on which the anonymous notes were written and we have spoken to every British recipient of the business magazine. Hundreds of crossbow enthusiasts around the country are being interviewed. The records of the crossbow manufacturer have been followed up and a hunt is on for every Razorbak bolt ever made. Detectives have interviewed members of Chapman's staff, and are now interviewing Nicholas Graham and many of his known associates."

Winters coughed. Maxwell turned his attention to the younger officer. Winters took up the story, ignoring a glare from Van Deventer. "Interpol has been asked to make inquiries about arms dealers. The process of eliminating the terrorist organisations has begun. Could it be IRA, or PLO, or some other terrorist organisation? We don't know, but most of us feel this is the work of an individual, or a small group. But not terrorists."

Van Deventer took his place at the table. He said: "Local detectives are interviewing every illegal arms dealer we can trace."

"The truth is," said Winters, "the list of leads is endless. The list of genuine clues is pitiful."

"It's funny how this investigation has been going," said Patterson. The others looked at him, blankly.

He continued: "The security guard on duty at the centre had gone off to another location nearby. Apparently the night watch there had feared trouble, and called his colleague for support. The Rose has luck on his side."

Winters saw Van Deventer frown. He objected to the killer's nickname. He felt it glamourised the murders. He did not approve of any police officer using the term.

"Either that, or this is one of the most thorough killers we've ever come up against," said Maxwell.

Van Deventer moaned. He looked at Winters. "We've gone through Chapman's life as thoroughly as we could," he said.

"Nothing, nothing, nothing. We're going to have to go through this Ballantine chap's life as thoroughly. Somehow I get the feeling we'll come up with exactly the same thing. Nothing. I don't know what's going on here, and it frightens me. I've never come across anything quite as barren of clues as this case. Never."

"I thought the fact Ballantine was defending that under-world chap, Graham, would open up a lot of avenues?" said Patterson.

"Yes, yes, yes, there's plenty for us to follow up," said Van Deventer. "Make no mistake. But I've a feeling this is not as obvious as it might seem. I feel neither Chapman nor Ballantine really knew they were in danger, in spite of the warning letters to Chapman. It all has a strange pattern."

"What do you mean?" asked Maxwell. "This is the second time you've mentioned this 'strangeness'. What are you on about?"

Van Deventer smiled, grimly. At last he had Maxwell's undivided attention. "Well, there are inconsistencies everywhere. Everywhere. Why send warning letters to a man without being specific about the warnings? Then, why kill him before he has had a chance to react to them? Why watch him for nights before killing him? Why a lawyer and an editor? Why not kill the lawyer at his home? I could go on. And on and on."

"Well, I can't," said Maxwell. "I need some sleep. So do you chaps. I suggest we go home for a few hours. Meet up again tomorrow morning. We're no good to anyone in this state."

"What are you suggesting?" asked Winters, irritated. He was staring intently at the Dutchman. He felt Van Deventer was merely trying to undermine his position in front of Maxwell.

Van Deventer said nothing for a moment, steepling his fingers in front of him. "Perhaps we should change the way we have been thinking. Perhaps."

"How? By thinking what instead?" persisted Winters.

"A psychopath, perhaps? A mindless, random killer?"

"No, definitely not," said Winters, his voice rising. "These men were carefully singled out as targets. There is a distinct pattern. What we have to do is find the motive."

"What if there was no motive?"

"I would reject that line of reasoning out of hand," said Winters.

Van Deventer smiled. Inwardly, Winters groaned. Shit. Couldn't he keep his temper around this old bastard? The Dutchman said: "It is a foolish man who closes his mind to possibilities. It is an even more foolish detective who does that."

"He's right," said Maxwell. "Keep it in mind as a possibility. But for the moment I have to agree with you Alan. I think there IS something carefully planned and co-ordinated about this. When, and if, we exhaust this line, we'll try yours Jan."

Maxwell stood up to leave. Patterson dragged himself to his feet, following Maxwell's lead.

"And now I'm going to go home," said Maxwell. He looked at Van Deventer. "Coming?" he asked.

"In a minute," said Van Deventer. "I need to clear up one or two things before I go."

Without saying goodbye, Maxwell and Patterson left. As he walked out the door Patterson tossed a salute at Winters, and a discreet thumbs up signal.

Van Deventer turned to stare out the window.

Winters felt morose. He momentarily thought of secretly revealing the truth about Van Deventer to Maxwell, then dismissed the idea as a cheap shot. Besides, he reasoned, if the truth came out now, Jennifer was bound to deduce its source. No. He was stuck with that secret.

Van Deventer was picking at the paintwork flaking on

the window sill. Winters thought that if he picked at the sill much longer, the bloody building would fall about their ears. There had been persistent rumours that the multi-million pound Yard building was shaky. Made more so by the thousands of tons worth of equipment packed into its walls. A morbid joke among staff at the Yard was of its imminent collapse. Perhaps it was more than a joke, thought Winters. The way their luck was running at the moment, he wouldn't be surprised.

The telephone rang. Both men were startled.

Van Deventer got to it first. He answered gruffly, then, without a word, handed the telephone to Winters. He went back to the window. It was Jennifer.

"Alan? I hope I'm not disturbing you. I called you at home last night until late. It was only this morning I found out why you were out so long."

Winters sensed Van Deventer straining to listen in on his conversation. He turned away from the Dutchman.

"Yes, it's been ragged here. How are you?"

"I feel terrible."

"Why's that?"

"Hard to explain. I feel betrayed."

Winters sighed. He hoped she wasn't going to resort to emotional blackmail. After all, SHE was the one who had said they should each do their own thing. He was about to remind her when she spoke again.

"Until now I believed there was a direct relationship between the killer and my father. I feel ridiculous. But it seems like the killer has been unfaithful. Or my father has been deceitful. He never mentioned Ballantine to us. Do you know what I mean?"

Winters was still mindful that Van Deventer was listening to every word. "Jennifer, that isn't an unusual reaction. I've heard other people in your situation saying the same thing. But listen, I can't talk now. Later."

"When?"

"You know," he said, trying not to give anything away to Van Deventer.

She insisted: "When? And where?"

He remained silent.

She took the hint. "Your place?"

"Hmm."

"At about eight?"

"That's fine," he said.

He replaced the receiver.

Van Deventer was still staring out the window, at the darkness and the lights. Without turning around, he said: "She's a beautiful young lady."

"She is," said Winters.

"I knew her when she was just a baby."

"I know."

Van Deventer turned around, looked at Winters, sighed, then walked to the door. He looked as if he was about to say something, then shrugged. He took his coat off the hangar on the back of the door. Slinging the coat over his arm, he muttered "G'night" and stalked out the office.

Winters exhaled slowly. The bastard knew. He had probably known all along.

He dismissed his concern about Van Deventer. Winters finally addressed a worry that had been building in him since hearing of Ballantine's death. It was now clear this was bigger than they had ever imagined. Jennifer and her team were prying into a viper's nest. Just what the hell was he going to do about THAT?

TWENTY-ONE

BAKER SIGHED. "It's a great story, Jennifer."

"I know," she replied. "But if we use my source's information now, he'll clam up. I think we should hold it."

Jennifer looked up to find the others watching her. They could sense a good story. She could see in their eyes a cunning patience. She felt irritated and pressured.

"Perhaps there's a way of making it seem as if it came from someone else?" Her own reluctance puzzled her. Was she trying to protect Winters as a news source, or protect and safeguard her relationship with him?

Jennifer, Frank Davis, Colin Baker, Morris Paynter, Trevor Bergman and Stuart Gibson were at Food for Health, one of the most popular restaurants in the Blackfriars area. It was ten minutes away on foot from The Courier's offices. As it was usually full, the reporters had arrived early.

Davis said: "We could ask Stuart to make contact with one of his police friends working on the case. Say he heard a rumour. We could source the story that way, under Stuart's byline, to shield you."

Jennifer seized on the idea. "What will we say? There are some things Winters would know could only came from me."

"Such as?" asked Paynter. Jennifer looked at the slight reporter. She wondered if he ate well. He was always so anaemic-looking. He seemed to wither under her direct gaze, and appeared even more agitated than normal.

"Well ... " she began. She paused. "Let's review what we CAN say," she said, instead.

"Come on Jen," said Gibson. He was clearly irritated. Jennifer noticed his eyes still seemed to be laughing in that infuriating way he had, as if he was enjoying a private joke at the expense of the person he was looking at. He had a face of prominent features – a distracting cleft on his chin, a large nose, a wide mouth, and badly stained teeth from a 40-a-day habit.

"Okay, okay," said Jennifer, quickly, glancing at her watch. They would have to be back in the office soon. The time had flown by, and her recap of the news Alan had given her the night before had taken up most of the time they had available. During the lunch she had lapsed into long silences as she tried to defend herself to Winters mentally. It was HER father. She wasn't using him, she DID feel deeply for him. But something was driving her. Alan would understand. He was so gentle and perceptive. He would understand, wouldn't he?

She wasn't so sure. She sensed in Winters a ruthless edge. She suspected there was a part of him that was violent and savage. Jennifer gritted her teeth. "We know the following. The police are desperate. They know the man rehearsed the murder of my father by killing a cat. That's news. It seems he rehearsed the Ballantine murder as well. That's also news. We have a vague description of him. That's news. He leaves a rose – but everyone has used that angle. The killer is cold-blooded and utterly ruthless -"

As she spoke, Jennifer looked at each of her colleagues in turn. Frank Davis was sitting back with his arms folded. As usual he looked relaxed and self-assured. He was a handsome man, clean-shaven. His shirt was open and Jennifer could see a dark mat of hair on his chest. Although he said he never did any form of exercise, Jennifer believed he was a powerful man, sexy in an oddly primal way. She knew he was a quiet journalist, only occasionally seen in the favourite pub of Courier employees. He was a prolific writer, and had been on the Courier for as long as Jennifer could remember.

Baker was her favourite. He was always such a good-humoured man. A world-weary attitude of cynicism belied his intelligence. He rarely smiled. It was unfortunate, for he just missed being a good-looking man. His full beard served only to accentuate how small a mouth he possessed. His nose had been broken somewhere, somehow. When Jennifer had asked, he dismissed the question with a curt explanation: it had happened so long ago he had forgotten. He also had a small scar on his left cheek, which wound into his thick beard, choking to a halt on the fringe of the hair. This, he said, he had obtained in a car smash when he first started working on newspapers.

Baker returned her direct gaze, a smile touching the corners of his mouth. Jennifer wondered about Baker. She didn't think he was gay, but there was something almost asexual about him. He seemed not to be interested in women. "Forget the review, Jennifer," he said. "We all remember the facts. I think the best angle for a story is the rough description of The Rose. It's great colour."

"Sure," said Gibson. "Until now he has been only a name. But with his height, his dark clothes, his weight, he takes on a shape, a form. His practice shot at the cat in the garden is spooky."

"What's so spooky about it?" asked Paynter.

"Christ, Morris, do you have no feelings? The man kills a cat as a try out, just before shooting his victim. Now that's professionalism, if you ask me. It shows just how ruthless and committed this man is," said Gibson.

Jennifer interrupted. "The police don't know it was just before he shot my father. It may have been on one of the previous nights."

"So?" said Davis. "He still practised. It shows him to be thorough, if nothing else."

"Drink up folks, we'd better get back," said Bergman.

The reporters finished their coffee and stood up from the table, scraping chairs on the wooden floor.

"Who's going to pay?" asked Baker.

"I thought we were going Dutch?" said Paynter. Jennifer smiled, looking away to hide her mirth. She knew he would be hurt if he saw her smile. He was such a complex soul. He hated confined spaces, was always ill-at-ease, tapped his fingers in a perpetual expression of nervousness; and blushed easily and often.

"What I mean is who's going to take the slip and hand over the cash?" said Baker, irritated. Baker found it difficult to hide his contempt for some of Paynter's characteristics. Most of all he hated Paynter's tight-fisted approach to their meetings. Paynter had yet to pay for a round of drinks. Jennifer often found herself stifling an urge to mother Paynter. His shock of blond hair above large ears, red lips, pale eyebrows and large eyes gave him an air of boyishness. People were often amazed when he revealed he was already 31. Jennifer knew several of the younger female reporters in the newsroom lusted after him. She wondered why. She preferred her men to be well co-ordinated. Paynter seemed to move around in bursts of energy, after which he would lapse into an intense and brooding silence. Smiles would fleet across his face, seldom reaching his eyes. At times he seemed almost vague, half-witted. She knew this masked an incisive mind.

"I'll go and pay," said Gibson, stepping into the breach. He gathered the money and joined the queue at the till. "You start out, I'll catch up."

Jennifer put on her coat, watching Bergman as he struggled with his. Bergman WAS a clumsy man, she reflected. He caught her looking, and smiled. She warmed to Bergman. He was the joker, always game for a wisecrack, sometimes at the most indelicate moments.

They trooped out into the street, gathering together against the cold wind. The sky was grey and overcast. They huddled down and began walking back towards New Bridge Street and Ludgate Circus. The icy wind attacked them. Heavy traffic prevented them from crossing the street, and Gibson soon caught up. Waiting for the lights to change at the zebra crossing, Jennifer and Davis were standing at the edge of the pavement, with the others behind.

They spotted a gap and crossed at a run. The others were held up and she stood with Davis, waiting for the pedestrian lights to change. Jennifer noticed that Davis seemed to have had a sleepless night. His eyes were red and looked sore. Slightly out of breath, she asked: "Something wrong with your eyes?"

Surprised, Davis shook his head. "Nothing. Why?"

"They look sore. I wondered if you needed drops, or whether you used contact lenses?"

"No. No contact lenses. Must be the wind," he said, dismissing her comments.

She shrugged and turned back to the others, in time to watch them stepping on to the pavement near her.

"So what are we going to do?" she asked Gibson.

"I'm going to call up some of my former contacts, tell them I've heard whispers, and ask them to confirm them," he said. "Then we'll write the story about The Rose and we'll hand it over to Rodgers. It's a good story and he won't be able to refuse it. We can say I came across it by chance. Or we can hint we're looking at this ourselves. Rodgers doesn't much care for our new editor. He might even encourage us."

The five men were trying to stay close to Jennifer, shouldering their way past the pedestrians rushing back to their jobs. Jennifer saw Davis collide with a large, elderly man. He turned to stare after the pedestrian and when he turned back, his eyes were filled with anger. A temper barely kept in check, she thought.

They turned into Fleet Street and headed towards their own office. Jennifer looked up at the stone edifice of the Reuters Building, opposite the Daily Express. She thought about the thousands and thousands of words pouring out of the building, to newspapers in Johannesburg, Sydney, Mexico City, New York. She wondered how many times her father was mentioned in those stories. The thought sent a chill through her, one much colder than the freezing wind. She had managed to build a shield around the hurt, but every now and then something sneaked through and an emptiness and sense of despair welled up inside. It was disconcerting, and she stopped suddenly, the men bumping into her and each other.

"What's the matter?" asked Davis, standing at her left elbow.

"Nothing. I had a thought, that's all."

"Well, hurry up. We haven't all day," said Paynter.

They swept into The Courier building moments later, took the lift to the fourth floor newsroom and entered en masse. They glanced furtively towards the news editor's desk, to see if he had noticed their late arrival.

"Okay, I'll get to it and draft a story. I'll show you all before I put it in the newsdesk In-tray," said Gibson.

Jennifer ignored them and walked to her desk, slinging her coat over the back of her chair.

She sat down, staring at her typewriter. She felt ill at ease. Her father haunted her. She was worried about betraying Alan's trust. She wondered why she was falling for the policeman – there was no denying she was - so soon after her father's death. She even felt guilty about THAT. How could she? She didn't know. It seemed almost indecent, but she couldn't help herself. Most of all, she found it so confusing that he could attract her so overwhelmingly. She had dated many men since leaving school. She had slept with three, not including Winters. At no stage had she ever felt out of control. It was almost as if there was a part of her doomed to stay aloof, watching from a distance, commenting cynically on her every move. She was always so cool and calculating with other men. They never measured up to her father – her constant yardstick. He had influenced every stage of her life, mostly through his absence. But now she found herself responding to Winters spontaneously, without thinking of consequences. Why did she feel so damned guilty? Jennifer hugged herself. Unless she found the killer, she would never be free of the chains her father had wound around her.

TWENTY-TWO

"AT FIRST Rodgers wanted to hand the story to William Bennett, for incorporation into a story he was writing," said Gibson. "But I stood my ground. I argued it was MY story. I didn't want it getting lost under Bennett's byline."

Gibson paused. drawing out the tension.

"He's bought it," he said, finally. "And moreover, he wants us to keep digging – unofficially.

He's putting the story through with the recommendation we use it as our front page lead tomorrow."

"Did you give anything away about my involvement?" asked Jennifer.

"Not a thing. I said I'd heard whispers and dragged the facts from a reluctant informant."

"Who?" she insisted.

Gibson folded his arms, adopting a defiant stance. Clearly, he did not enjoy being questioned by Jennifer. "A detective named Boyer. He owed me one."

Insensitive to the exchange, Bergman broke in. "Great," he said. "The first of many."

"Yes," said Gibson. "I should say we are on our way." He winked at Baker.

Jennifer turned away from the group and walked back to her desk. If the story did appear as the front page lead the next day, they would certainly be on their way. As she sat down at her desk, looking up at the clock, she shook her head. "But to where?" she muttered.

TWENTY-THREE

APRIL 20, 1986. *When the time came to leave the orphanage and find a job, no-one knew what to do with me. I couldn't help. One of the secretaries said her fiancé worked on the Evening Argus, a provincial paper in Brighton. She said she knew they were looking for two office juniors. A few days later I reported for duty. From the first day I found the job was just a job, something that provided me with enough money to be independent. That was the best part. When I turned 18, that independence enabled me to leave the orphanage to find a home of my own. They were relieved to see the back of*

me, and my dreams. By then, the storm dream was a part of me, documented in the doctors' notebooks, something I had to live with, but something they wanted no part of anymore.

During my first year of work I was used in the newsroom, doing chores, fetching and carrying, finding books at the library, running copy to the newsdesk, going with photographers on shoots, carrying their equipment. It seemed like an endless round of making tea, filing, pouring out pots of glue for the sub-editors to paste up their articles, and running messages. I didn't have a boss. Everyone in the newsroom was my boss. If there was something to be done they'd ask one of the secretary/typists or me. As the typists were usually too busy I wound up doing all the jobs no-one else wanted to do. Because they all looked down on me no-one bothered to try and find out who I was. No-one engaged me in conversation, and if they did, I discouraged it. I did everything I was told to do. I found that no-one seemed to notice me until there was something unpleasant to be done, which suited me in a way. When I moved into my own flat, I was very nearly entirely self-sufficient.

I used to enjoy that time of the day when the subs had finished doing the late Final edition, when I would file away any of the copy that hadn't been used. I used to wander around the near-deserted newsroom, roaming between canyons of paper and typewriters and telephones. Most of the journalists would be at the local watering hole. It was when the newsroom was at its quietest. One evening I was the only one in the newsroom, except for the night news editor. The two late duty reporters, who had just come on shift, were both out. They had come in to the office, been given assignments, and had left immediately. The day shift reporters had waited for a while, then one by one drifted away. The telephone rang and the news editor picked it up, spoke for a while, then called me over. He said there had been an accident on the main road to London, on the outskirts of Brighton. He wanted me to go and see if I could find out what had happened. I suppose he wasn't too worried about my failing on the job. If I botched it, someone else could have done it all the next morning, when a check would get the latest news anyway. A photographer came with me.

When we arrived on the scene, the police, ambulances and several people had already gathered. A car had strayed over the middle line to collide head-on with a van. Both had been travelling at well over the speed limit, it seemed, for there was precious little left of either. I walked over to the one vehicle and looked in the driver's window. There wasn't much left of him. Firemen were trying to cut open the door on the passenger side. Apparently that man was still alive. I reached inside and felt inside the driver's jacket pocket, found his wallet and looked at his calling cards. I wrote his name down. Nobody tried to stop me. I did the same with two other bodies on the scene. There were five. Not including the passenger, who was finally cut out of the cabin of the first car. He lived for another four hours.

I somehow managed to get blood on my hand. It soaked into the pages of my notebook. The photographer took a shot of the scene while I was in the foreground, looking down at my hand. I had a slight smile on my face. The hand was the one covered in blood. They chose that one for the next day's paper. Later, I went back to the office and wrote my first report. It was terribly simple. I just wrote down what I'd seen. I hadn't had to speak to anyone at the site of the crash. Later I'd telephoned the hospital, to find out the passenger had died. I thought it was a pretty simple way of making a living. The news editor thought I had promise. The next day he recommended to the editor that I be made a trainee reporter.

An accident got me into journalism. I've been with newspapers ever since. After the Evening Argus, I moved to Oxford for a while. From there I came to Fleet Street and The Courier. I'm glad I work on an evening paper. I far prefer the hours and deadlines. I hate night work. Mostly, I try to do stories that involve minimal contact with other people. That's easier than one might think. Speaking to people on the telephone is easy. No contact, no faces, no eyes, no emotions. For a while, when I got on to *The Courier*, I did court reporting, and then crime reporting. Hugh Chapman said I showed a lot of promise. I thought he was crazy, but I took his money, and made a life for myself. I was happiest when I had my weekends alone, and I was able to indulge myself in an orgy of books and films, television shows and videos, magazines and newspapers. There was a kind of predictable harmony and balance in that lifestyle.

It was a kind of balance that had managed to subdue the dreams. The storm and the man in the chair and the coloured rain were still a part of my life, but not so overwhelming a part. I thought I was on top of it all.

But now that balance is upset. With each passing day a sense of fear is growing in me. I can't put it down to anything in particular. A vague disquiet began when Chapman first started trying to take me under his wing. He wrote me a note of congratulations on a feature I had researched. He would go out of his way to encourage me. He used to walk through the newsroom, stopping to talk to various reporters, and he would always stop to have a word with me. He disturbed me. I couldn't tell why. Whenever he walked away I would feel relieved, without knowing what had upset me. He seemed to be trying to father me.

I will never forget the shock of realizing what it was that unnerved me so. One day Chapman stopped to talk and he waited a moment before speaking. The look in his eyes was the same look of appraisal and summing up my father used to give me. In making that connection, I was able to see other similarities between them. They were both tall. Both distinguished looking. Both had deep lines on their faces. Both carried the gleam of introspection in their eyes.

As Chapman turned to leave my desk, I was caught staring at him by the reporter who sat opposite me. The look of shock on the man's face was enough to warn me never to allow my hatred for Chapman to show again. I masked my feelings for years after that day.

But the dreams were back. And the balance was gone.

TWENTY-FOUR

JENNIFER STARED across the desk at Bergman, barely able to disguise her contempt. She decided he was a coward. Bergman blanched, but renewed his efforts to explain himself to the others.

They were all sitting in the newsroom, around the desks of Bergman and Jennifer. Baker, Davis and Paynter had drawn up chairs. They watched Bergman intently. Gibson watched from his desk across the aisle. It was the silly time in the newsroom after the final deadline of the day but before it was time to go home.

Bergman said: "The case is too big for us. Our continued prying into the murders could be fatal. We might suffer reprisals from people who might be linked to the killings, people we don't know we should fear."

Jennifer shifted in her chair and Bergman shot a glance at her, expecting her to comment. She remained silent.

Paynter snorted. "They'd have to kill every police officer, every crime reporter and every editor in the city," he said. "We're not the only ones investigating this thing. And so far, we've got nothing. We're not a threat to anyone."

"That's not true," said Bergman. "We shot into the

limelight with Jennifer's story two days ago. Jennifer is the daughter of one of the victims. Haven't you noticed how Rodgers is funneling all The Rose calls to us?"

Like most newspapers, The Courier received more than its fair share of "crank" calls. These normally followed major stories. The difficulty was sorting the loonies from those who had a real story to tell.

Bergman fidgeted, looking down at his desk. He stood up, in what seemed to Jennifer like an effort to gain advantage through height. It didn't work. She thought he still looked miserable and puny.

He went on: "What if we have brushed close to someone involved in this thing? Someone who would rather have us out of the way than risk us turning up something? I don't want to go on taking that kind of chance, and I'm not under any obligation to do so either."

"You're right," said Jennifer. "You don't have to stay. You can run away if you like. I'm not stopping you, and you certainly don't have to justify yourself to us."

"We understand," said Baker. His voice was soft. It held none of the menace of Jennifer's voice. "And Jennifer is right, you don't have to justify yourself."

Jennifer urged herself to give him the space to leave with dignity. She started to speak, but the words choked her and she fell back into silence. She thought for a moment about telling them of her nightmares, of the dark archer who pursued her in her sleep, but she rejected the idea. If she let the others think she was weak, her team might fold up on her and she would be forced into passively waiting for something to happen.

The thought of how that kind of inactivity frightened her. No. She had to keep them together. Make it hard for others to back out. Let them see how Bergman suffered. She sneered.

Bergman saw it, and paled. For a moment Jennifer thought he was going to recant. Instead, he said, lamely: "I'm sorry. But count me out."

Jennifer turned to stare at Paynter, and said: "How about you? Do you want to chuck it in?"

He sat upright under her glare, and Jennifer saw him look at the others, one by one. "Well, I've been frustrated at the lack of progress we've been making, but I'm still in," he said, finally.

She turned her attention to Baker. He shook his head. She looked at Davis. He smiled, saying: "I'm more interested than ever." Gibson, face grim, nodded. Jennifer went back to Baker. "Did that mean you were in or out?" she asked.

"I'm in. Oh, I'm in all right," he said.

Jennifer relaxed, feeling her shoulders slump. There was an ache along her neck; knotted muscles protesting. She looked at Bergman and was touched by the pathetic look on his face. "Well, thanks for your help so far Trevor," she said. In spite of herself she was unable to keep a note of condescension out of her voice.

Bergman took the offering gratefully. "Pleasure. If I do hear anything of interest, I'll be sure to tell you."

He sat at his desk while the others replaced their chairs. Without speaking they moved to gather around Baker's desk, further away from the news editor and about 30 feet from Bergman's desk. Jennifer watched Bergman from afar. He looked uncomfortable. He was sweating. He looked as though he were going to weep. He picked up a pen, threw it down, shuffled some papers on his desk, then got up to go and talk to one of the court reporters who had just arrived in the newsroom.

"I hope he doesn't make it difficult for us," said Jennifer.

"By doing what?" asked Davis.

"I don't know."

"Forget that for the moment. What are we going to do for a follow up to our story about The Rose?" asked Gibson. "Let's get something going."

"He's right," said Davis. "Stories should stir things up a bit. Especially stories with an unusual angle. Good stories may lead to more people calling us, even if they do so anonymously."

Jennifer listened quietly, enjoying Davis's deep, rumbling voice. He had a very deliberate delivery, she thought. She watched his hands playing with newspaper clippings on Baker's desk. His hands were strong and the fingers were chunky. Not like Paynter's hands, she thought. Paynter had the hands and fingers of a pianist.

Jennifer interrupted. "What if the killer –"

"What?" urged Paynter.

"Well, perhaps we've all been looking down the wrong track. Gibson has been asking Interpol about a hitman, we've been scouring the newspaper files for a known terrorist who might have used a crossbow, you and Colin have been looking at all sorts of angles involving my father and his contacts, as well as Ballantine and his contacts, and especially Nick Graham's mob, but ..."

"What, for goodness sake?" said Baker.

"Well, this may sound preposterous, but what if our man isn't a man? What if he's a woman? Why are we assuming it's a man?"

They lapsed into silence.

Jennifer toyed with the idea. It was a long shot. But she had never heard Alan mention it. What if she was right? It could open up a whole new field of investigation. Perhaps there was a jealous woman involved somewhere? No political motives. No power mongering. Just a woman scorned. Jennifer tried to think of her father being unfaithful to her mother. Surprisingly, the thought did not offend her.

"The biggest problem with this case is the inability of the police to discover the motive," said Gibson. "A motive always points the finger at possible suspects."

"That's right," said Jennifer. "The police have no motive. They think the anonymous letters must contain clues to the motive, but so far no-one has found one."

Another silence. Jennifer could see them keeping an eye on the clock.

Gibson rejected the idea. "No. This does not seem like a woman's work. It is not feminine in style."

"You're such an expert on women?" said Jennifer, her sneer back. She checked it, hating herself when she was like this.

"Well, I reckon it's time to buzz off," said Gibson, clearly irritated by Jennifer. "Let's finish this at Duff's Place." He was deliberately ignoring Jennifer's remark.

"Good idea," said Baker. "You coming Morris?"

"No, not tonight," said Paynter. "I have to finish a feature for an early page tomorrow. I'll catch up tomorrow morning."

Baker looked at Davis, who smiled and said: "Sure. Listen, Jennifer may have something there. A woman archer is an interesting thought. The one thing these file clippings show is that there are a lot of female crossbow archers."

Jennifer smiled gratefully at Davis. Already he had his coat on and, with Gibson and Baker, was waiting to walk with her to the door. "You're right," he said. "We must keep things on the boil. Let's do a speculative piece about a woman killer. Not now. Now I feel like some coffee. Coming?"

"I'll be with you in a minute," said Jennifer. "You go on ahead. Order me a coffee, please."

The three men waved cheerily and left the newsroom

together. Paynter walked back to his desk. Jennifer sat down at her desk, opposite Bergman. She could not bring herself to talk to him. She thought of Alan. She would tell him about her idea that evening. She found herself looking forward to their evenings together. As usual, he would be late. He was always late these days. He had given her a key to his flat, so that she could wait for him there. It was the police work, he said. No set hours, but usually long ones.

She smiled. And then frowned. She looked around the newsroom. Her father still walked this floor. His name was everywhere. She couldn't get away from him, didn't want to get away from him. Then another thought struck her. If she became even more involved with Alan, would she always feel scared, frustrated, pinned down, by having to wait for him? God forbid, she thought. Maybe it was best she keep her distance. Keep a part of her to herself.

"The part that belongs to Daddy." The words sprang to her mind and she smiled, wryly. She shrugged, then gathered her coat and shoulder bag. She did not see Bergman watching her every step as she walked out of the newsroom.

TWENTY-FIVE

VAN DEVENTER replaced the telephone receiver, looking thoughtful. The call had come as both he and Winters were preparing to go home.

"That was Trevor Bergman, a reporter from the London Evening News," said Van Deventer.

"What did he want?" asked Winters. He didn't like the

way the Dutchman was looking at him. Their open hostility had quietened to a dull dislike lately, but Winters felt it coiled and ready to spring to life at the slightest provocation. He wondered whether something would trigger it now.

"He said he was an ex-member of Jennifer's team. He thought we should know about it, for their sake," said Van Deventer.

Winters shrugged. "I know about it."

Van Deventer remained silent. But his pale blue eyes fixed on Winters, relentlessly.

"Jennifer told me about it herself," Winters said.

"Yes, yes. But what did YOU say to her?"

Winters stood up. He wanted to leave early for once, without a conscience. This could take a while. "I was hoping to get away on time tonight," he said. "You know where to reach me?"

"First tell me: What did you say to Jennifer about this team of hers?"

"I said what she was doing was dangerous. That she should leave it to us. She told me where to get off." Winters tried to sound as if it was an impersonal exchange. That it was none of his affair.

"No, no, no," said Van Deventer. "Answer my question properly."

"What does properly mean?"

"It means telling me whether you think you have any influence with her. This is dangerous. Very dangerous. She must stay out of it."

Winters sat down in his chair again, folding his coat in his lap. He tried again to evade the question. "Why did Bergman call?" he asked.

"Because he chickened out of their investigation. It appears Jennifer tore strips off him in front of the others. He claims to be acting in their interests, but I think he wants to sabotage their efforts," said Van Deventer.

Winters surrendered. He knew the Dutchman would not give up easily. "I have no influence in that regard," said Winters. "Jennifer will do her own sweet thing."

Van Deventer chuckled, without genuine mirth. "She's always been like that," he said. "Always. Chapman used to encourage it. He was proud of that streak in her."

Winters said nothing. He wasn't sure he liked the direction this conversation was taking. "I really must go," he said, standing up again.

"Alan. Wait. Just one more thing."

Winters sat down again, heavily, hoping this would deter the Dutchman.

"In many ways I feel obligated to Chapman. He was a friend for many years. Many years. I want things worked out as best they can, under the circumstances. I worry for her."

Winters stared at Van Deventer.

"When are you seeing her again?" asked the Dutchman.

"Tonight. Now."

"Then you must go. But do me one favour."

"What's that?"

"Do what you can to dissuade her from pursuing this thing. Convince her she must drop it. Tell her I said she is being foolish. Very foolish. Blame me, do whatever you have to. But stop her."

"I'll try," said Winters, rising from his chair. For once he found himself agreeing with the Dutchman. But as he walked out the door he was shaking his head. He knew Jennifer would explode if he tried to manipulate her. Tonight he wanted things to be peaceful and gentle, with good music and good wine, just the two of them.

TWENTY-SIX

"YOU HAVE a WHAT?!?" bellowed Jennifer.

"A photofit. It's a –" started Winters.

"I know what it is. Why haven't you told me about it before?" There was cold fury in her voice. Winters felt unnerved. So much for a quiet night, he thought. Until now the evening had been going just the way he planned. He wished he had waited until later to bring up the subject of Jennifer's team.

Jennifer had been waiting for him when he arrived home. Somehow that had seemed so right. She had greeted him with a kiss, wordlessly. Then she had led him to his kitchen, and he had been surprised to see the table laid for two. Whatever she was cooking smelled terrific.

"It's loaded with garlic," she said, reading his mind.

Jennifer had bought a bottle of wine, and they chatted easily and freely over their meal, the lights dimmed, only a candle burning on the table. After the meal they stacked the dishwasher and sat on the floor in front of his fireplace, backs against the couch. She had refused his invitation to watch a movie of her choice in his cinema room. She said they had watched too many lately, which was true. Together, they had viewed several of his favourites, including some westerns.

"Let's sit quietly together and talk for a bit tonight," she insisted. They turned off all the lights, and sat arm in arm in front of the fire, watching the flickering of the flames. Winters found himself relaxed and strangely at peace with Jennifer at his side. "I love being with you," he said, impulsively.

"Mmmm," she muttered, snuggling close to him.

"At moments like this, I feel as if I want to protect you and look after you and ... I suppose I'm being silly, really," he said.

"Not at all. I like to hear it. It makes me feel safe."

"I know what you mean. You make me feel safe as well. I think I could even forget my fear of heights with you at my side."

Jennifer laughed. "I'm pleased, though at times I think it is you who needs protection. From me," she said.

"That's not the way Van Deventer would see it," said Winters.

"What's he got to do with this?"

"Well, he feels very protective towards you," he said.

"I can't begin to explain why."

"Just before I left the Yard tonight he was asking me to try and dissuade you from continuing your investigation."

Jennifer sat upright, disentangling herself from Winters. She moved away from him and turned to face him directly, crossing her legs on the carpet. "How did he know about it?"

"Someone called Bergman told him."

Jennifer looked shocked. "When?"

"This afternoon. Late."

"Why, that little – "

Winters laughed. "You're not going to use unladylike language, are you?"

She shook her head. But he could see she was seething. She folded her arms tightly across her chest. It was a warning sign he had come to recognise with her. It signalled danger. Nevertheless, he continued.

"Perhaps Van Deventer has a point," he said.

She leaned back from him, and picked up her wine glass. For a few seconds she remained silent, looking into her wine. The flames lit up her hair, the side of her cheek. He couldn't see her eyes.

"What might his point be?" she asked, finally.

Winters sat upright, mirroring her, crossing his legs. He plunged in: "That you shouldn't go sticking your head into affairs about which you know nothing. He says what you're doing is dangerous and stupid."

Without looking up from her glass, Jennifer asked: "What do YOU think?"

"I happen to agree." Jennifer met his gaze. Winters couldn't be sure, but it seemed there was more than the reflection of the fire in her eyes. "Do you now?" she said quietly.

"Yes, and I want you to stop. I worry about you."

"On what grounds?"

"On the grounds that it's dangerous. On the grounds that you don't know what you're doing, or who you're dealing with."

"Who am I dealing with?"

Winters sighed, then sipped his wine. "I don't know. But whoever it is, is potentially lethal. Stop while you're ahead."

A defiant look took shape on her face. It was one he didn't like. Somehow, it was also arrogant and contemptuous.

"That brings me to a point of my own, Inspector. The fact that you don't know who killed my father. Perhaps if you spent less time worrying about what I'm doing and more time on the case you'd have more to tell me. I mean, what DO you know about the murderer? Next to nothing, I suspect."

Winters bit his lip. Mentally, he counted to ten. When he spoke, his voice was a whisper. "We know more than you Jennifer. We know this man is cold-blooded, thorough and that he has ..."

"Has what?" she said. She was taunting him. She was still sitting cross-legged in front of Winters, but she was leaning forward, jutting her chin at him.

"Nothing. Forget I said anything. Forget your investigation.

Let us do our work. You might already be in way over your head."

Another moment of silence. Both paused to gain their breath. The intensity of the exchange and abrupt change of mood left them reeling. Jennifer was the first to recover.

"The reason I started my own inquiry was because I lost faith in the police, Alan. In spite of my relationship with you I have seen no reason to reassess my feelings. So far you have nothing. I may be able to find out something."

It was his turn to be contemptuous. "What makes you think you can find out more than we can? I have at my disposal the power and influence of an entire police force. What have you got?"

When she replied, her voice dropped a tone. The scorn was gone. She was earnest. "The fact that he was my father. The fact that I can never rest, can never start a new life, until his killer is found. Until I can truly bury my father, and be free of this...this ghost."

"I don't understand why you're so stubborn about this. What is it going to prove?"

"I'm not trying to prove anything. It is important to me, and no-one else. What does this really matter to you? It's your job. No. I'm not trying to prove anything," she said.

"Yes you ARE. You most certainly are."

Jennifer put down her glass, not looking at Winters as she spoke. "You seem to be able to read my mind, when I can't. What IS my point then?"

Another silence.

He reached for her hand. At first she did not respond. Gradually she warmed to the pressure of his fingers, and he felt her hand squeezing back. After a few minutes, she said: "I've been thinking."

"Mmmmm."

"No, seriously. I have an idea."

"Well, what is it then?"

"What if the killer was a woman?"

Winters burst into laughter, but then choked on his mirth when he saw her face. Instead, he said: "It would have been a good theory, but I'm afraid it can't possibly have been a woman."

"Why not? What do you know?"

"Am I telling you this as a journalist or as a lover and confidant?"

"You're telling this to your lover, who happens to be a journalist."

"Then I have nothing to tell you."

"And if I promise not to write anything about what you tell me?"

"Or to tell anyone who WILL write about it?"

Jennifer gave him a strange look. Then: "Yes. All right. I promise."

"Well, we've actually found out quite a bit about this man. In fact, we even have a photofit of him."

"WHAT?!!?" she had shouted.

Looking back, Winters saw there was no way he could have steered the discussion any other way. Jennifer had been too single-minded. He should never have raised the subject. Now her nostrils were flared, her lips pursed. She looked beautiful. He was definitely in trouble. She sat staring at him for a while. He tried to return her gaze. After a minute he broke the deadlock, looked down at his glass then finished his wine.

"More?" he asked.

She handed him her glass. He walked to the kitchen and poured more wine, grateful for the respite. When he returned to the fire, she took her glass without thanking him. He was about to excuse himself and go off to the toilet when she spoke. "And you haven't bothered to show it to me? What kind of a policeman are you? Have you even shown it to my mother?"

"No. Not yet."

"Why haven't you shown me? I might know the man. I can't believe you ..."

"Don't you ever calm down? I didn't show you because I don't think you'll be able to help us. I don't think you WILL know the man. And in any case, he is obviously disguised."

"Not only should you show that photofit to me, but you should let the newspapers have it. I don't believe you're doing this," she shouted.

"Oh great. That would treble the number of crazies we've got calling us at the moment. Every one of those loonies has to be investigated. Do you know..."

"Are you going to give it to the press?" she asked, between gritted teeth.

Winters could stand no more. "Who do you think you're talking to young lady?"

"I'm not your young lady," she shouted.

"I wonder whether I shouldn't perhaps be grateful for that?" Immediately he said it, Winters wished he hadn't. He tried to placate her.

"Just calm down. Relax. This is getting us nowhere."

"You're right," she said coldly. "And unless you release that photofit to the press you won't be getting any further with me either."

"Jennifer, I shouldn't have to explain myself to you, but seeing as you're so hardnosed, give me one uninterrupted moment to say something, all right?"

"I'm waiting."

"That photofit is of a man in disguise. If I release it now it will just cloud the investigation. We'll get hundreds of crank calls, diverting our attention from finding the killer, finding the man who may kill again. We can't afford to waste that sort of time."

"That's all the more reason to have that picture published. You might also get one vital call that leads you to the killer's door."

"That's unlikely."

"Is that your final word?"

"No, we haven't finished talking about you and your investigation yet."

"Oh yes we have, Inspector." She stood up.

"Where are you going?"

"Home."

"Oh for pity's sake. Don't be so childish."

She walked out of the sitting room, into his bedroom. He heard his bathroom door slam shut.

He cursed. He had already discussed the issue of publishing the photofit with Maxwell. They were in agreement. It had to stay confidential until they had more. Until there was a more accurate depiction of the man. But Jennifer had a point about showing her and her mother the picture. What if there was even a remote chance they had seen the man? He still had to show them. Just in case.

He walked through to his bedroom.

"Jennifer?" Nothing. He stood at the door, his forehead against the frame. "Jennifer? Are you there?"

"Yes."

He raised his voice. "I don't agree about releasing it to the press. And you have no choice about that. But I think you're right about seeing it yourself."

Silence.

"Well?"

"Well what?"

"Would you like to see it?"

Jennifer paused, then said: "Yes. When?"

"Tomorrow evening?"

"No. Now."

Winters smiled to himself. "It's late. The photofit is at Scotland Yard."

"Are we going to go to Scotland Yard?"

"Yes, okay. But just get a move on, will you?"

"I'm on my way," she said.

TWENTY-SEVEN

HE PARKED his car in the garage, amongst the Flying Squad vehicles. The garage was easily accessible from The Embankment. He didn't need to show his badge. A uniformed policeman had waved him in, recognizing Winters's distinctive BMW. On the drive from South Kensington, Winters had tried to explain to Jennifer why a photofit was not always successful. He was at pains to say that a photofit of a man in disguise would be next to hopeless.

"The one thing we know about our man is that he was very deliberate. He would never make a mistake such as being caught without a disguise. In any case, the face was mostly hair," he said.

He told her all the details about their discovery of a car parked near her father's house a few nights before his death, and how they tracked it to the car hire firm. He told her of the killer's macabre sense of humour in using the name Harold Hastings. She said little, staring out of the window at shop windows.

As they drew up to Scotland Yard, she broke her silence. "I've always wondered; why is it called Scotland Yard?"

"Well, apparently the old Yard building was once the site of a palace. Kings and Queens from Scotland were received there when they visited the English Court."

She muttered, but would not be drawn further.

They stepped into the empty murder squad room, then walked through the squad room to the meeting room where Winters and Van Deventer had their office. When they got to the room, Winters told Jennifer to sit down. He was surprised when she did so without argument.

"First, I'm going to tell you in more detail about photofit. Then I'll show you what we have."

"I'm, waiting."

Winters sighed. For a brief moment he could see himself putting her across his knee. He relished the image for a while. Then he dismissed it, ashamed he could even think it. Still, she was being so petulant. He stood in front of her, theatrically. His voice became official and impersonal. "We have photofit kits for full frontal faces and profiles only. Each kit is made up of hundreds of different photographs of the five basic components of the face - the hair, eyes, nose, mouth and chin. There are also add-ons like glasses, beards, moustaches and hats."

Jennifer nodded. She was becoming more attentive again.

"The cards can be arranged to create a vast range of faces. In the kit for white European males, there are more than 1,000 pieces, and more than five billion possibilities."

"How do you start making one up?"

Winters nodded. "The officer doing the photofit asks about the strongest features. A catalogue of those features is shown, depicting variations. Building up a face is a gradual process. We don't put ideas into our witnesses' heads. We don't ask if the person had a moustache for example – this may sow doubt. We let them build it up."

"What's all this leading to?"

Winters raised a hand. Be patient, he signalled. "We rely on our witness. Everything depends on how clearly they remember the person. Unless they are extremely good, ten people will give ten different descriptions of the same man."

"So?"

"When someone clever disguises himself, he does so in a way that blurs recollection. He 'fuzzes' the lines. And he emphasises certain points to distract memories."

"Yes?"

"Well, we feel The Rose has done just that. I'll show you what I mean."

Winters went to his filing cabinet. Most of the information related to the police investigation was contained on thousands of cross-indexed cards in the murder room, but he kept a few personal notes in this filing cabinet. A copy of the photofit was one of the items.

He walked to Jennifer and told her to sit still. "First impressions count for a lot," he said. He unfolded the sheet on which the photofit had been printed, watching her face as he did so. She frowned, staring hard at the face. She shook her head. Nothing. Then she took the sheet off him, bending to examine it closely.

Finally, she shook her head and handed the photofit back to him. "You were right," she said.

"I thought ..." His voice trailed off. Instead, he said: "I'm sorry."

She was still shaking her head, still frowning. She took the sheet from him again. "No, I've never seen this man. But without his beard and glasses, and moustache, and long hair, there might be something."

"It was impossible to draw up a jawline. Notice how he chose thick, black-rimmed spectacles."

Winters was staring intently at Jennifer. He kept hoping. But still she shook her head.

"Are you sure?" he asked.

"Yes," she said, handing back the photofit. "I'm positive."

Reluctantly, he took the sheet from her, folding it slowly. He was puzzled. He had noticed something he suspected even Jennifer had missed.

For the briefest of moments, when she first looked at the picture, her eyes had narrowed, and she had cocked her head. It was only after a few seconds that she had shaken her head. Something about that picture had pricked her subliminally, he was certain. The question was, what?

TWENTY-EIGHT

APRIL 23, 1986 *The first day I met Ballantine he was in court defending a case. The sound of his low-pitched voice instantly jangled my nerves. Disliked him from the first encounter. Avoided him if I could. Dismissed it as one of those things. Until I understood why I found him so repulsive. It was for the same reason I hated Chapman. The editor reminded me of my father. And so did*

Ballantine. Each of them brought back my past, in different ways. When I heard Ballantine talking, it was as if my dream was manifesting itself in real life. His voice was the same as that of the man in my dream. The same as that of my father. Or, rather, close enough to remind me of him. And of those days when I would sit and listen to my parents talking, unable to make out what they were saying, straining to make sense of their words.

I came off court reporting, saw little of Ballantine, forgot about him. I even managed to live with my dislike of Chapman, though I saw him nearly every day. They never knew they were so closely connected. One and the same trigger for my dreams. The police are frantic for a link. They will never know. How could they?

After Chapman, when the dreams were back, when the storm was gathering again, I saw a photograph of Ballantine in the newspaper. He was about to start defending a criminal celebrity. It was enough. Ballantine was a lawyer. My father worked for lawyers. They made him what he became. It seemed fitting. The rest was easy. Except for one thing. For a while, I was afraid Ballantine would not die. I thought I would have to batter him with a club to finish him off. Never again.

I went back to Stockton, disguised again, for a revolver. Something powerful, I said. Something sure. For the dreams.

I wonder what they would say if they knew that it was really Dr. Mason who killed them? If not for him, both Chapman and Ballantine might still be alive. The first time I visited Dr. Mason he remarked that I was unusually healthy. I seldom made use of his services. He asked me what my trouble was, and I told him about the headaches, the blurred vision. After he examined me, concentrating on the sinuses above my eyes, he made several notes on my card.

Dr. Derek Mason, I gathered, was not given to words. We stared at each other. After a while he asked me whether there were any other complaints. I said now that he came to mention it, there were, and I told him about the sore throat and my coughing. I said the headache had been with me for weeks, in a mild way, but I decided to ignore it. When it became unbearable, I came to him. I asked him what he thought the trouble was. He muttered it was probably nothing, but it could be a growth in one of the sinuses causing a blockage. He arranged to send me for head x-rays. He suggested I come back in a few days. He would have an answer for me then.

I put the visit out of my mind. After all, it was routine, wasn't it? I went for the x-rays, irritated by the inconvenience. In any case, I was feeling better already. When I went back to him, his first words were: "I'm happy to tell you that there is no growth. You have a sinus infection and the mucous membranes are inflamed, causing the blockage. No worry about a tumour at all."

Tumour?

I was shocked. Dr. Mason had contemplated the possibility that I had a cancerous tumour in my head, and I didn't even know. A ringing started in my ears. The ringing prevented me from hearing what he had to say after that. I watched him, and all I could see was his mouth moving. There were no sounds. Over his shoulder, through his office window, I could see the branches of trees waving in the wind. Big oak trees.

I faced the thought of my own death for the first time in my life. The emptiness of my existence. The grave nobody would visit. The funeral only I would attend.

"So," he said, loudly. "If you take these antibiotics and inhale steam from a bowl of boiling water every night, you'll probably be clear of the infection within a week."

I left his office and walked for hours, my mind empty. Every time I started to think about my own death, the ringing started again and I had to block out my thoughts, attempt the empty state I used to achieve at will in the orphanage. I got home and I sat in my *favourite chair until it was time to go to bed. I was not thinking at all. Just empty.*

The dream was back that night. As usual, during the dream, during the terrible storms, the mystery man in the chair spoke. This time, I could hear him:

"Don't be afraid."

"But my life is such a waste. Few will know I'm gone, and when I do, after a while, even they'll forget."

"It doesn't have to be that way."

"What can I do?"

"There is much you can do. Think."

"No. I have nothing. All that I have left to do is what I've always done. Kill time."

"Not quite. What you have left is killing time."

I understood then." Why not? What have I to fear?"

"Precisely," he answered.

TWENTY-NINE

"**MUST YOU** check everything I do as if I was an irresponsible child?" Winters said, in exasperation.

"You know why I'm doing this. Not to get at you. Not at all. I just think we are all capable of missing something simple. None of us is perfect. None of us," said Van Deventer.

Winters glowered at him. The Dutchman was beginning to play at his games again, trying to undermine Winters as often as he could. After the burst of activity following the discovery of the rented car, the investigation had ground down to interminable rounds of routine foot-slogging again. Winters found his time comprised of daily conferences with Maxwell and other officers, constantly reviewing every scrap of information. Already three of the filing cabinets in their office were filled, and thousands more pieces of information had been stored in the murder room. Detectives were scouring the information every day. Was there something in there they could go on? Something they had overlooked? It was, he admitted, distinctly possible that he had overlooked something. Had it been anyone else who decided to check his every move, he would have been in wholehearted agreement. Seeing as it was Van Deventer, he knew what the Dutchman's true motivation was likely to be. The thought galled him.

Winters lifted his feet off his desk, dropping them heavily on the floor. He stood up and walked to the filing cabinets, putting both hands on the nearest. He tried to make his mind a blank sheet, tried to soak the information in the cabinet up into his soul. Let there be magic, he thought. But the cabinet remained cool, hard and inanimate.

What was in there he could try? What remote clue lay in those papers? He knew crimes were often solved as a result of following up the most innocuous of clues. Van Deventer himself had told him of a case he had cracked due to seemingly impossible coincidence. Winters knew the story was true. It was all part of the legend of Van Deventer. As The Dutchman told him, it had started on a stormy night. He and his partner had decided to park their patrol car near a major intersection and wait for the rain to subside. The crackle of their radio signalled a message from their controller, who dispatched them to a nearby block of flats.

"The scene that greeted us haunted me for years. Years," said Van Deventer. "It appeared to be a burglary that had gone horribly wrong. The flat was owned by an 85-year-old pensioner who must have walked in on the burglars. For some reason they stabbed her, several times, and then bound and gagged her. An 85-year-old woman."

Even as he repeated the story, Van Deventer could not hide the traces of horror he felt at the memory. "I searched her flat and found a small wall mirror had been broken. The sheets had been pulled off the woman's bed, and used to bind her, even as she lay dying. Apart from these disorders, magnified by the tiny dimensions of the apartment, everything else was neat. So neat and tidy. She was a tidy old lady. I was intrigued by the broken mirror, which had obviously been mounted by four brackets on a wall near the bed at about head height. It had been unscrewed from the wall, and then smashed on the ground. Why? I knelt down to look at the broken glass, seeing myself reflected a thousand times. A million times. I also noticed a small, triangular piece of metal, about the size of the nail on a man's little finger. Tiny. Careful not to touch anything, I tried to work out what it was. There was something maddening, tantalising about the piece of metal, but I couldn't identify it. I didn't have a clue."

When detectives arrived to take over the investigation, they complimented Van Deventer on the way he had conducted his search, but were able to add little by way of explanation. Apparently, nothing appeared to have been taken from the flat. It seemed as if some other motive was behind the killing, that this was not a routine case of an interrupted breaking and entering.

"The police could find little more to help them in their investigations, and after three months, the docket was finally laid to rest with others in the open file: unsolved. The woman had no living relatives. Nobody to care about solving the mystery. Nobody. Except me. I remembered her. Another six months passed. One evening, walking the streets of my division while off duty, I chanced upon a pickpocket in action. I had only to take two steps and declare the man under arrest. The thief surrendered without a struggle. Not a whimper. He looked down at the ground, his shoulders sagging, and followed me meekly to the station."

At the station Van Deventer had emptied the man's pockets, to find two stolen wallets, a pocket knife, a piece of frayed string, cigarettes and a lighter. It was the pocket knife that captured the Dutchman's attention. The main blade was missing its tip. As soon as Van Deventer looked at the blade he felt uneasy. While this was just another booking, a petty thief apprehended for a petty crime, there was something in the utter resignation of the criminal, something about the blade, something in the air.

"I questioned my captive for more than an hour, feeling I was on the edge of something. I didn't understand it, but I was sure one word, one gesture would solve my puzzle. I stared at the knife during the interrogation, not seeing it." Van Deventer's eyes glittered behind his spectacles as he went on. "Then the tiny piece of metal in the flat that night came to mind. Detectives had been puzzled by the metal. They had not known what it was, but had kept it anyway, along with other evidence collected in the flat. Nearly nine months later, I realized where the metal had come from. This knife. But how? And why?"

The Dutchman took the knife to the detective who had been in charge of the investigation. Together they found the evidence from that night. Like a piece in a jigsaw puzzle, the piece of metal seemed to fit perfectly to the knife's blade. They rushed to the Home Office forensic laboratory, and waited impatiently while one of the police scientists worked to confirm their suspicions. A perfect match.

Only then did Van Deventer return to question his prisoner.

Confronted with the missing portion of the blade, the man had begun to weep. He confessed to murdering the old lady in the flat.

"He and a partner HAD been interrupted during a burglary. The old woman had threatened to scream for help, and he had stabbed her. Fifteen times. Then he wiped clean the blade. Problem was, he believed in the supernatural. He feared the mirror on the wall had recorded their crime, and would reveal it somehow. Can you imagine? So he unscrewed the mirror, breaking off the tip of the blade in his frantic efforts, and smashed the mirror on the floor. He said he had been expecting a knock on his door every night since the killing. He was glad it was over."

Although Van Deventer had received a commendation for his detective work, he was the first to admit luck had played an overwhelming role in his discovery. Yes, he had been diligent when looking for evidence at the scene of the crime. And yes, he had done well to piece the two very different crimes together under what were entirely different circumstances. But above all else, fate had been the main player on that stage.

Staring now at the filing cabinets in front of him, Winters felt certain he was going to need just as much luck to solve The Rose murders. Somewhere in these files were the clues. Somehow, he had to find them, piece them together. Perhaps all the parts were not yet available. Perhaps they were, only no-one had seen them in the correct context yet. He tried to concentrate. Was there anything, anything at all he had not yet followed up? If there was, Van Deventer would be sure to turn it up, and make political capital out of it.

Winters turned to look at Van Deventer, who was steadily, meticulously, checking through Winters's files. The younger policeman felt tension flood through his muscles. The old bastard! Before he could stop himself, he said: "Who is checking your files, Superintendent?"

Van Deventer looked up, surprised. "Talking to me?"

Winters gritted his teeth. "Yes. You're checking my work. The thought occurs to me no-one is checking yours. After all, nobody is perfect."

Van Deventer looked squarely at Winters for a moment, his irritation only thinly disguised. He forced himself to be gracious. "You're right," he said. "Perhaps you would care to go through my notes yourself?"

"Damn right I would," said Winters, ashamed of himself for the warm glow that derived from his minor victory.

Van Deventer went to his filing cabinet and removed several fat files. "This one contains notes from the interviews I carried out myself. These contain my notes from our various meetings." He placed the files in front of Winters, who had moved back to his seat.

Winters said nothing. He was sure the notes would contain information the Dutchman had been storing up to use in evidence against him. He suspected the notes of their meetings would be revealing. He itched to read them. Instead, he reached for the file containing Van Deventer's interview notes.

"Let's see if there's anything in here," he said, and began reading.

The two men read without saying a word, with only the sound of pages flicking over to break the silence.

After an hour, Winters looked up at Van Deventer, held up a spiral back notebook, and said: "Did you follow up that Stockton person?"

Van Deventer looked at him, impatience showing in his frown. "Who was Stockton?"

"An illegal arms dealer. You noted here that you thought he

was hiding something. You wrote here that you should go back to him. Any reason you haven't?"

"No time. Simple as that," replied the Dutchman.

Winters was anxious to rub it in. "Well, don't you think we ought to try him again?"

"Why?"

"You've often said a policeman's nose is his best ally. And yet, you ignore your own. You clearly suspected something here."

Van Deventer scowled. "Get to the point."

"I want to see this man again. Now," said Winters, maliciously.

Van Deventer paused. "Very well. Let's go see him then. He lives in Earls Court."

They did not need to discuss what they had to do next. Together they walked down to the Yard garage, collected the car, and set out for Stockton's house. On the way to Earls Court Van Deventer described how he had already spoken to Stockton once since Chapman's death. At the time he had felt Stockton was fearful and hiding something, but he put it down to a natural fear of police, acquired over years of operating on the other side of the legal divide.

When they got to Stockton's house Winters double parked his car and watched the front door. It was early evening, and several neighbouring houses already had their lights on. In Stockton's house, all the lights were out. The policemen stepped out of the car, looking up and down the street. Nothing suspicious. They walked to the front door, knocked, waited and then knocked again. No reply. They looked at each other. The door opened suddenly, startling both of them. Neither had heard the sound of someone approaching. Stockton must have been standing at the door before they arrived. He kept the door chain on. Only his eyes showed through the crack in the door. They were wide and frightened. "Superintendent Van Deventer?"

Van Deventer nodded, looking pleased that Stockton remembered him. "Yes, and this is Detective Chief Inspector Winters."

"Oh Jesus. Go away. Please go away," said Stockton.

"We'd like to ask you a few more questions. Open the door," ordered Van Deventer.

"Please. You don't understand. If anyone sees you here, I'm dead. Go away. Please, just go away."

Winters raised his voice menacingly. "If you don't open the door right now I'm going to kick it open. Now do it."

Stockton hesitated. Then he said: "Step over here, towards the light. Let me see you."

The two policemen obliged, trying to peer into the house. They could not pierce the gloom behind Stockton. He shut the door, rattled the chain, then held the door open for the two men to enter. They walked in, peering around, talking in whispers, expecting something to leap at them from the shadows. Stockton was clearly a man in dread. His fear was infectious.

"What is it Stockton? What are you so scared about?" asked Van Deventer.

For a moment, Stockton seemed to cringe. He rubbed his hands together, hunching his shoulders, nervously looking at the open front door. Then he blurted: "I want some bloody police protection. This is out of my league. That man is the most terrifying person I've met. He doesn't try. He doesn't have to. He just looks at you, and you get scared shitless."

"What man?" asked Winters.

"The man who took my weapons. The one they're calling The Rose."

The two policemen looked at each other, incredulously. "He was here?" asked Van Deventer.

"Yes. Twice."

"Why?" asked Van Deventer, frowning at Winters to keep quiet.

"For a crossbow and a gun. And ammunition."

Before Van Deventer could react, Winters cut in. "Can we sit down? My feet are killing me," he said. He jerked his chin to indicate to Van Deventer they should get away from the door.

Stockton peered at Winters, as if seeing him for the first time. Cigarette ash clung to the front of his shirt, and a lifeless cigarette hung from his lips. Stockton's hair was awry, and Winters soon understood how it got that way. The arms dealer had a nervous habit of running his hand through his hair. His state of near-panic resulted in him doing it two or three times a minute. After a moment he shuffled out of the hallway to his sitting room. Van Deventer hastily closed the front door before following. Stockton walked in the darkness to the far side of the room and turned on a small lamp.

"This man can shoot. Keep out of sight of those crappy windows," said Stockton. Winters went over to the window to peer out between the edge of a frayed curtain and the wall. He could see up and down the street, as Stockton's house was close to the pavement. Nothing. He shook his head at Van Deventer and noted how the older policeman visibly relaxed. The Dutchman went to one of the most comfortable chairs in the room, turned it away from its position directly in front of a television set, and sat down.

Stockton sat down on the arm of a settee. Winters remained at the window.

"You said he came here for guns and ammunition? When was this?" asked Van Deventer. The Dutchman seemed irritated. Winters was elated. Clearly, they were on the verge of another breakthrough. As a bonus, it was one that Van Deventer had missed.

"Yes," replied Stockton, distractedly. "The first time he came, he didn't seem to know much about what he wanted. But he asked for a crossbow. A crossbow. Said he wanted to shoot the thing at night. I got him one. A beautiful Barnett Commando, with telescopic sights."

Stockton paused for breath, patted his pockets, found a lighter. He leaned forward over its flame. As he did so Winters saw the man's hands were shaking. As much as he despised this little thug, Winters knew both he and Van Deventer would have to be gentle with him. If they wanted all the information Stockton had to offer, they were probably going to have to strike a deal.

"Let's start at the beginning, shall we?" suggested Van Deventer.

"Yes, all right. But I'm not sure where that is. This man, The Rose, he ..."

"Why are you so sure he's The Rose ?"interrupted Winters. Van Deventer glowered at him. He wanted to conduct this interview.

Stockton said: "It's him. I just know it. I can sense it. I knew the moment I read about that editor. What was his name? Chapman."

Then why didn't you tell us straight away, you stupid little shit, thought Winters. He contained his temper.

"Start again," said Van Deventer, warning off Winters with a stern glance.

"Well, he just turned up at my door one day. Must be about a month ago now. I could see he was wearing a frigging disguise. He didn't explain how he had got on to me, and I can tell you,

I didn't ask. He said he needed a crossbow, for night hunting. He said it had to be capable of accuracy across some 100 metres."

While he was talking, Stockton dragged on his cigarette, looking at the window, at Van Deventer, his cigarette, back to the window.

"I got him a night sight and a crossbow. And 20 bolts of different shapes and sizes. He particularly wanted something with a large head, several blades – evil looking little bastard. He came back and collected it all a few days later."

Stockton looked up at Van Deventer. He did not make excuses for what he'd done. They all knew the man would have got a crossbow somewhere else anyway.

"I thought he must have had some heavy connections. How else would he have bloody-well got on to me? He said he had read about me, that he remembered me. But I'd have remembered if I'd ever seen HIM before."

Van Deventer nodded. He urged Stockton to continue. "I came to see you after Chapman's death. You must have known it was him by then. I can see why you didn't tell me about all this. What I don't understand is why you're telling me now."

Stockton shook his head. "Like I said. That bastard is evil. He smells of death. He came back, wanting a handgun. At first I pretended I couldn't get him one. He was wearing a different disguise, but I knew it was him, even though we didn't refer to the sodding crossbow."

He took another drag on his cigarette, now burned down to the stub. He squashed it out in an ashtray, took out a pack, shook free another cigarette, lit it. "He didn't say anything. He just looked at me. He said he wanted a Magnum. He said he wanted it immediately. I was about to say I didn't have any guns in the house, but I looked at him. He was looking at me, and

I saw something in his eyes. Me. Dead. I was so frightened I pissed in my trousers."

Van Deventer remained silent. Winters found a seat.

"I know you think I'm making a big thing out of all this. But I swear I'm not. This man carries death around with him. He wears it like a cloak. It's why he exists. He's a killer, a ruthless killer."

"What happened next?" asked Van Deventer.

"I went and got him guns, what do you think I did? A Walther P-38 automatic pistol, and a Magnum 357 revolver. He was very specific. He wanted the revolver. He asked for a silencer. I didn't dare tell him you couldn't silence a Magnum. But I said I didn't have a bloody silencer. He knew I wasn't lying. I was too shit-scared to lie." Stockton stood up, began pacing. "I'm telling you, he's lethal. And I think the bastard's going to come back for me. He was here last night, and I crap myself every time someone walks passed my front door now. He's going to come back."

"Why?" said Winters.

"I don't know. The way he looked at me. Like he was thinking I knew too much."

"When did he leave? Did you see what he was driving?" asked Van Deventer.

"No. He walked up the road. Towards the tube station. He knew I wouldn't follow him, that I was stiff with fear."

"When was this?"

"At about six. He just appeared at my door again."

Winters stood up. Stockton looked at him, alarm on his face. "Where are you going? What are you going to do?"

"What can we do?" asked Van Deventer. He had seen the sign Winters had passed. Make him sweat.

"Then take me with you. Lock me up. I've committed a

crime. You could throw away the key this time. Just get me out of this place. Anything is better than waiting here." Stockton's face was a pitiful mixture of terror and hope.

"All right," said Van Deventer, finally. "Come with us. You can help us draw up some photofits. Then we'll find you somewhere safe. And keep you there."

THIRTY

VAN DEVENTER shuddered. He hunched forward and rocked his shoulders, grimacing when he saw Winters watching him. They were back in their office in Scotland Yard. It was five hours after they had pulled up outside Stockton's house. "There is something frightening about all this. Very frightening. I can't put my finger on it. Stockton has imparted some of his fear to me, I suppose."

Winters was gazing at the original and new photofits. The three lay side by side on Van Deventer's desk, with only two bearing any resemblance - the two so recently described to the police by Stockton. Underneath the three photofits was a sheet of paper. This one bore a police artist's impressions of what the person UNDER the disguise looked like. With spectacles, without. With moustache, without. With plenty of hair, without. But somehow, Winters knew it wouldn't be close. Anne Chartham swore the version delivered by her was a perfect resemblance. Stockton was convinced both his versions were as near as it was possible to get to being photographs of the killer. The only thing the three drawings had in common was an intensity around the man's eyes. Almost as if he were in need of spectacles and was squinting to draw things into focus. There was something menacing about this characteristic.

Winters drew himself erect, folded his arms across his chest. "What are we going to do now, Inspector?" He had been talking to himself.

He looked at Van Deventer, saw the red-rimmed eyes, the result of an intensive interrogation of Stockton at the Yard. The tiredness on Van Deventer's face was underlined by failure. They had managed to glean very little of any further use from Stockton. When Van Deventer spoke, it was in a tired, soft voice. "Keep on trying to find him. Persist. Circulate the photofits. Spread the net further. And further. God knows what else, Winters," he said. "I certainly don't."

Winters thought about the look on Jennifer's face the night she saw the first photofit. He still hadn't got that out of his mind. Could she have seen the killer? Did she know him? Someone from her father's past? Someone Hugh Chapman knew?

He was about to confide his fears to Van Deventer, when he saw the Dutchman was about to leave. Under his arm he had several files. Van Deventer saw Winters looking at the files. "They're yours," he said. "I'm going to read them tonight. I might be able to find something else we've missed." The Dutchman waved a hand in farewell and left Winters in the office. Fuming. All thoughts of the photofit and Jennifer's reaction were forgotten as Winters glared at the Dutchman's retreating back.

THIRTY-ONE

APRIL 25, 1986 *The clouds gather. They race towards me. The coloured rain falls. The man appears in the doorway, takes the chair, starts his evil whispering. The wind whips my body. His terrible scream shatters my sleep and I know he has come back for me. I lie quivering, fitfully dozing, and then the dream starts all over again, a part of me trying to escape and wake up, but another part watching intently, in case the figure reveals himself.*

All the time I'm terrified. I feel as if the man knows all of my sins. His whispering is a recital of my darkest secrets. I try to hide from the storm and from him but I cannot move, for even as I walk I stay in the same place. Even as the storm clouds descend on me, they get no nearer. Even as he talks, I cannot hear his words. But I know he is waiting for me.

The worst part is I cannot see him. He sits in the chair and I feel...as if I KNOW him. I catch glimpses of his face, but it is like looking through frosted glass. His outline is blurred and vague. As if he is wearing a stocking, the way bank robbers do. Somehow, the outline is familiar.

Who is he? What does he want? Why does he torture me this way?

His visits are building up again. Last night, at least twelve times. Double the number of the previous night. Tonight, who knows?

He has brought with him something new. Thorns. And roses. As the storm flails at us, I see a rose is in his hand. As I watch, I see one of the thorns on the stem begin to grow. It snakes out toward me, sprouting more thorns, each in turn growing and sprouting thorns themselves. They writhe and grow and snake around each other, growing and growing until they envelope the man. They do not harm me, but it is not long before the man screams, and this time his scream is one of agony.

I wake frightened it is The Rose I'm dreaming about. My mother. Has she returned to wreak vengeance on my father? Is he the man in the chair? Is my subconscious trying to tell me something? I used to wonder whether my father had killed The Rose. Part of me still wonders. She took a lot of beatings from him. Like I did. Perhaps the beatings killed her? But no, says logic. She died as a result of a natural illness.

I still mourn her, even now. I think she is in search of a kind of vengeance. That is why she was with me the night I killed Chapman. I left her sign at the scene. She was with me when I went for Ballantine. Again, I left her sign.

Soon, the dreams will reach an intolerable crescendo and I will have to go out again. When I do, I will leave her sign anew.

In preparation, I've been watching a certain man for days. I chose him carefully. Since then I have been doing a great deal of reading about him. He is the chief executive of a rather large industrial company. Rich as Croesus. For some reason, his staff worship him. Which is saying something, because his company employs more than 20,000 people all over the United Kingdom. A newspaper report said he was regarded as a "father" by most of them. All that power and wealth and influence! It isn't right, for one man to be a father to and have so much of an influence over so many people. One newspaper feature said he liked to walk his dogs along the river in Richmond, in his local park. The report said he walked in that park every night, regular as clockwork. He explained it was a way of winding down from the stresses and strains of corporate life. He said his walks along the river were designed to get him away from people. I thought that rather a stupid thing for him to make public. You never know who's reading the papers. It could have been terrorists or kidnappers.

Unluckily for him, it was me.

THIRTY-TWO

STUART WHITFIELD was approaching the age when most men welcomed retirement. He would be fifty-nine on his next birthday, just four months away. Yet he had never been more active. Far from thinking about retirement, he was thinking about his next goal in life. Politics. That was where the real power lay, he decided. His life had been dedicated to the pursuit of power. As chief executive of Whitfield Industries, he was no stranger to being in a position of influence. His business empire had tentacles that spread throughout the western world.

Somehow, though, it had all begun to pall. More and more these days he was thinking about a successor. Someone who could take over the reins to free him to go after something more substantial. He smiled as he thought about his prospects. He had made many friends (and enemies) in his years in business. Many of those friends owed him favours. It was time to start calling in a few debts. He would use their influence to manoeuvre himself into position.

His dogs tugged at their leads and he called them to heel, aware suddenly that it was growing dark quickly. He had been walking for twenty minutes already, and his wife would soon start to worry. She fussed over him as much now as she had when they first married, more than forty years ago. She did not approve of his daily walk in the park. Especially as he insisted on always taking it alone with his two Golden Labradors. It was a time he treasured; a time when he could get away from people and do his thinking. He took a walk in this park every night he was in London. He religiously walked in Crane Park every evening. Alone. When he arrived home from the office, he sometimes did not even greet his wife before going straight out again. He would walk down to the River Crane with the dogs, immersed in thought. Some of his best ideas had been born during these walks.

He enjoyed the park, and the people in it. He had made casual friends with many of the regulars who walked the river, exalting in the uncomplicated warmth of their greetings. They did not know him for a wealthy man, and this pleased him. Here he was anonymous.

Whitfield was drawing close to the tower, built close to the water's edge. It was called The Shot Tower, so named because bullets were long ago manufactured in the building. Drops of molten lead were allowed to fall from the top of the tower into a water barrel on the ground, freezing immediately into the tear shape required. It was an old and ugly building, and few people bothered anymore to read the plaque mounted above the locked door, which carried an explanation of the building's origins.

The park ran along one side of the river. It was a public park bordered on the other side by residential properties. One of the entrances to the park was near the tower, and Whitfield contemplated taking a short cut to his car through this exit. Even after forty years, and even though he now influenced the lives of many tens of thousands of people with his decisions, he still feared his wife's wrath. The path branched after the tower. Normally he would have continued his walk, but he decided he would take the route that led him out of the park in order to get home quickly. He had arrived back from the office later than normal this afternoon, and his food would be now be waiting for him.

Movement from the side of the tower startled him. A man was sitting in the gloom, on the grass bank next to the path. He had thrown a pebble into the water of the river, on Whitfield's left. The businessman stopped for a moment. His dogs were straining at their leashes, anxious to investigate. Both Whit-field's pets were wagging their tails, anticipating someone new on whom they could bestow their affections. Whitfield watched the man stand up, looking worriedly at the dogs - he was scared of the animals. The man stepped backwards.

Whitfield could see he walked with a heavy limp. He was younger than Whitfield, wearing dark clothes, black gloves and a large, floppy hat which covered his eyes. He had a long, straggly beard, and his eyes kept flicking between Whitfield and the dogs. The man had been smoking a cigarette, which he dropped to the ground and trampled with his foot, still keeping his eyes on the dogs. Whitfield had seen no other people in the park this evening, and wondered why this man had been sitting alone in the dark. Had he been smoking something illegal?

The dogs were panting at their chains, putting up a tireless struggle to get away from Whitfield. The businessman was a big man, paunchy from too many executive lunches and too little exercise, and his breathing was laboured from the exertion of holding the labradors in check. Sensitive to the man's anxiety, Whitfield said: "Evening. Never mind the dogs, they won't hurt you. The most they'll do is kill you with an overdose of affection."

The man stayed in the shadows of The Shot Tower, his hands hanging loosely at his sides. His left arm seemed to be unnaturally stiff, and he held it slightly apart from his body, unbending. He eyed the dogs dubiously. After a brief glance to confirm the animals were not ferocious, the man looked back at Whitfield, unsmilingly.

"Mr Whitfield?" he asked.

A puzzled look come into the businessman's eyes.

"Yes," he said, squinting to examine the stranger. "Do I know you?"

The man shook his head. "No, but I've been waiting for you."

"Why?" said Whitfield, as he tried to pull the dogs to heel. The animals were intent on hauling in different directions. Whitfield staggered as one of the dogs suddenly stopped pulling on the chain, unbalancing him.

The man remained silent, staring at Whitfield, looking into the businessman's eyes.

Still Whitfield could not recognise the man. He could not return the stare because of the shadow cast by the brim of the man's hat. Whitfield frowned. His irritation turned his cheeks crimson. He resented this intrusion, which undoubtedly would turn into a delay he could ill afford if he wanted to keep his wife happy.

"Look," he began, "I don't want to be rude, but I ..."

Whitfield's voice trailed off as the man reached with his right hand into his shirt. His left arm stayed at the same odd angle to his body. Whitfield's eyes grew wide as he realized what the man was withdrawing from beneath his dark jumper. It was a revolver, one of the biggest Whitfield had ever seen. The man pointed the weapon at Whitfield's belly.

Puzzlement changed to fear in the older man's eyes. "Who are you? What do you want?" he demanded, bluster in his voice. "I have a wallet in my pocket. You're welcome to it if that's what-"

"I want you dead," the man said, and the flat statement of intent filled Whitfield with dread.

"What? Why? Who ARE you?" he whispered hoarsely.

The man looked around, the gun never wavering from Whitfield's belly. The two men were separated by a few yards, and Whitfield followed the man's gaze. Not a soul in sight.

The man smiled, and Whitfield stared into a bottomless pit

which opened darkly, pitch black against the descending gloom. The man lifted his chin, and Whitfield glimpsed the whites of his eyes for the first time, flickering dully, not a trace of the grin above his cheeks.

"I'm the man they call The Rose," he replied, and still his voice was flat, and chilling. The smile left his lips. Whitfield's eyes widened even further, reflecting shock. He knew the name. He had read about the editor, and that lawyer, Ballantine. But hadn't they died at the hands of someone who used a crossbow?

Hope stirred within him. Perhaps this man was using the name of The Rose to frighten him into obedience? "I thought you used a–" he started, but broke off as he realized this might provoke the man.

"A crossbow," the man said, his voice blank. He spoke slowly, deliberately. "It doesn't matter. Whatever is at hand."

As if to illustrate his point, the man cocked his left wrist, and bent his elbow. He held his hand up to the branches above him, and Whitfield could see the polished brass vanes of a lethal arrowhead jutting from the sleeve of the man's jumper. It was an intensely frightening missile.

"I don't understand. Why me? What have I done? Why do you want me dead?" Mindlessly, almost by reflex, Whitfield was clinging to the dogs, still resisting their efforts to scamper free. All the time the revolver was pointing at Whitfield's middle.

"You wouldn't understand," said the stranger. He held the missile at the feathered end, using it to punctuate his words, flicking the shiny tip at the businessman. "And it would take too long to explain."

But Whitfield did understand. Without being able to explain why, he knew suddenly that the police were wrong. There was no connection between the Chapman and Ballantine murders. The man who stood before him WAS The Rose. But he wasn't a skilled assassin. He was a deranged killer. There would be no reasoning with this maniac. He had to try and distract him somehow, so that he could make a break for the safety of the street. It seemed hopeless.

Whitfield was facing the river. The man with the gun was standing with his back to the water, and he kept looking around to see if he could see anyone. It was too late to hope for a passerby, and Whitfield knew it. The businessman was almost mesmerised by the weapons in front of him, his eyes darting between the arrowhead and the barrel of the revolver. He knew a bullet would blast out of the barrel, a bullet designed with one purpose, to destroy him. He wanted to try and fend it off.

"You won't know what hit you," the man told him, and Whitfield felt the dreadful words like a physical blow. He started to plead then. Fear distorted his face and there was no more power there, no more strength. He begged for his life.

"Please," he said. "I'll give you anything you want. Anything at all. Please don't do this. You can take anything. Anything at all."

His dogs were barking. The fear in his voice transmitted itself to them. They were jumping against the restraining chains. An idea pierced the panic blanketing his mind, and Whitfield choked off his pleas. He let go the chains, and the dogs pelted away as he started to lumber for the shadows of the trees near The Shot Tower.

The man had anticipated his move, and pulled the trigger.

The sound of the shot was shattering, but Whitfield did not hear it. The bullet hit him high in the chest, flinging him, spinning crazily, on to the slope which faced the river. The grass was covered in leaves, and as he rolled back down the slope, he gathered them on his cream-coloured jersey. It was a slow-motion roll, and the man with the revolver watched expressionless as first Whitfield's chest showed, with its brilliant flash of blood red; then his back, covered in leaves; then his chest, leaves glued to his clothes by the blood; then his back, with a new and different set of leaves showing.

Whitfield stopped rolling as the slope evened out, and the man stepped towards him, watching carefully. Whitfield didn't move. He lay with one arm under his body, his face against the grass, the other arm pointing up the slope. The man bent over the businessman and pressed the barrel to the back of Whitfield's head. He turned his face away, hesitating for a moment, flinching in anticipation of the gun blast. He did not pull the trigger. Instead he looked at the crossbow bolt in his hand, then back to Whitfield.

He smiled.

Using his foot to turn Whitfield on to his back, the man put the revolver in his trouser pocket and transferred the bolt to his right hand. He clutched the missile tightly, the feathers touching the thumb of his glove. He knelt beside the businessman. Whitfield's eyelids fluttered open. The man recoiled in horror. Whitfield tried to speak, but his lips quivered in silence. His eyes were filled with pain and terror. He tried to move – only his hand flapped feebly on the grass. The man leaned over Whitfield again, his right hand held high above his head, the arrowhead glistening.

Whitfield managed to lift his hand, and grabbed at the man's dark jersey. He tried weakly to push him away. The man smiled. Once again his eyes were flat and lifeless. Then he brought his hand blurring down in a sweeping arc, grunting with the effort. The arrowhead rammed into Whitfield's exposed throat. Viciously, the man jerked the shaft from side to side, tearing open a gaping hole in Whitfield's neck. Blood burst up in a fine spray, and began pumping from the wound in powerful spurts. Whitfield's eyes widened for an instant, then glazed over.

The man stood back, leaving the bolt in Whitfield's throat. He watched for a moment, aware of the horrible silence surrounding the scene. Whitfield's dogs had vanished. Quickly, the killer grabbed one of the businessman's heels and dragged the body to the edge of the river and rolled it into the water. The river was only a foot deep at the edge and Whitfield landed face down in the water. His weight pushed him to the river bed, forcing the arrowhead to burst through the back of his neck. As the body bobbed on the surface of the water, the man looked down from the bank. He could see the blades of the arrowhead glistening wetly above Whitfield's collar. A dark cloud spread around the body in the water.

He watched impassively for a minute. Then he reached under his jersey for his shirt pocket.

He took out an envelope and tore open the flap. He emptied the contents on to the path. The man turned away from the river. He began limping towards the exit. As he walked, he pulled the brim of the hat lower over his eyes. At the exit from the park he stopped for a moment, searched the grounds once more, nodding to himself, then turned and walked slowly towards the street. As he left the park, he was whistling. Softly.

THIRTY-THREE

PATTERSON WAS worried. He spoke quietly. He could not look into Winters' eyes. They were filled with horror.

"Whitfield was killed by our man. We're certain," said the scenes-of-crime officer.

"Oh Christ. Oh Jesus Christ," said Winters. He reached into his pocket for an antacid tablet, using his other hand to rub his chest. "This bastard seems to be escalating his agenda and his levels of violence. And I don't feel I'm any closer to him now than I was when I started."

He felt another rush of acid bile in his throat, and grimaced in distaste. Either he had an ulcer or he was going to have to stop drinking so much coffee he thought. He was feeling miserable, and irritable. He'd had to send out for the antacid tablets early this morning after getting back to the office from Crane Park.

"How can you be certain?" he asked, turning back to Patterson.

Both men looked exhausted and were still wearing the same clothes they had on yesterday.

Patterson reached inside his jacket and withdrew a manila envelope. He tore it open and unfolded an official report form. Winters was almost at a loss. What could possibly be going on now? What was this killer doing? Why? All prominent men. All killed by a man who used crossbow bolts to finish them off. All killed at night. And in each case a red rose had been left at the scene. He shook his head. His mind was whirling. He looked up to see Patterson watching him closely.

"Well?" he urged.

"Are you all right?" asked Patterson.

"Fine. Why?"

"For a moment there, you looked as if you were going to faint."

"No, I'm perfectly all right. Just very tired."

As he spoke, Winters smiled ruefully. If only Patterson knew exactly how tired. He and Jennifer had been up until the early hours of the previous morning. They seemed not to be able to stop talking when they got together, and that was BEFORE they got to bed. He had had just five hours sleep in the past forty-eight hours. He leaned back in his chair, and looked out the window. He was assuming Van Deventer's habit. The Dutchman was with Maxwell, discussing resource requirements, having suggested putting a watch on both the Ballantine and Chapman homes. He was now trying to get authorisation to detail several officers for the duty. Winters had supported the idea. It would provide protection for Jennifer, which consoled him. He longed to be with her again.

"Alan?" asked Patterson, leaning forward across the meeting room table. "You sure you're okay?"

"Yes. Sorry. Go on."

Patterson looked doubtful. Winters waved his hand, urging the policeman to continue. Patterson nodded.

"I'm first going to explain a few things. It will help you to know what we've done, and how we did it."

Winters ran a hand through his hair. "I'm listening."

"You'll remember I told you we found woollen fibres at the scene of Chapman's murder. They were on twigs and brushes in the area where the killer waited. The same fibres were on the fence around the square, which led me to believe he had rehearsed the murder. We couldn't find anything like that at Ballantine's shooting, but we were able to link the two by virtue of the crossbow, and the rose." Patterson paused for a moment, checking to see if Winters was still with him. "The scene of Whitfield's death was a quiet park. Whitfield's wife called the police out to search for him. It was an officer who found the body, so the scene of the murder was kept free of extraneous matter that might confuse the evidence."

Patterson put the report on Winters' desk. He ran his finger down the text. "We worked out that Whitfield was shot while facing the river, virtually at point blank range. Blood patterns on the ground show he was then stabbed in the neck with the bolt. The killer was vicious, and strong. Then Whitfield was dragged to the water's edge and rolled into the river." He paused for a moment, reading from the report. "The killer was also standing while the shot was fired. We were able to determine this from the path of the bullet, and the powder patterns on Whitfield's clothes."

Without knocking, Van Deventer swept into the office. He was humming to himself. "Oh, sorry, I didn't know..." he began.

"Never mind. You'd better hear what's going on here," said Winters. "Grab a chair."

"Should I recap?" asked Patterson.

"No, go on. I'll fill the Superintendent in later," replied Winters.

"We next looked under the nails of the victim and made an interesting discovery. Somehow Whitfield must have grabbed at the killer's clothes, because he had woollen fibres under his fingernails. Those fibres were subjected to a microscopic examination. At the same time the bullet which passed through the body was sent for forensic examination."

Patterson waited for a reaction. Winters said nothing. Van Deventer was still playing catch up. "When I heard about the fibres I called for the samples found at Chapman's place. We subjected those to the microscope as well, and as far as we can tell, they match. We have every reason to believe the dark blue jersey is definitely a link. We also know The
Rose took a Magnum off Stockton. The bullet fired at Whitfield was from a 357 Magnum," added Patterson.

"But why did he kill Whitfield?" asked Winters. His face was strained. "Why?"

"Oh shit!" said Van Deventer, suddenly comprehending. "So it's true. Definitely true. The Rose again."

Van Deventer's face was bleak. He looked at the two men in front of him. "We've just been talking about it. A minute ago. Maxwell was saying that if the evidence proved it was The Rose, he would begin to see things my way."

"Which is?" asked Winters, aggressively.

"Since you told me about Whitfield, I've been wondering again whether we're on the right track? Really wondering. Maybe we're not dealing with a hired killer? Maybe there is no reason for the killings? Maybe we're looking a madman in the face? A vicious random killer?"

"No," said Winters, fiercely. "I've got a pretty good feel for this man. A random killer doesn't spend time previewing his victim. He doesn't give him warnings. He doesn't study his victims the way this man so obviously has. There is - there HAS to be – some kind of deeper motive here. It's far more complex than random murders."

"Whatever the theory, we need to agree on one thing," said Van Deventer. "Unless we want to create an unprecedented panic, we are going to have to keep the connection with this one out of the press for a while. Out. Let them speculate, but no confirmation. Imagine if all the bigwigs in London were led to believe The Rose was after one of them? Imagine."

Patterson raised his eyebrows. Winters looked desperate. He had a glimmer of what would happen. The Dutchman put it into words.

"Pandemonium," he said. "Utter pandemonium."

THIRTY-FOUR

WINTERS CLOSED one eye. Well, he only needed one (at this range) to study Jennifer's breast.

She giggled. "What on earth are you doing?"

"It's not what I'm doing you should worry about. It's what I'm thinking."

"Don't you ever get tired?"

He opened his eyes wide. "Me? Tired out?"

Jennifer smiled and pulled the sheet around herself protectively. "Oh no you don't. Not until I've finished my wine."

Winters rested on an elbow. For the moment he preferred to imagine the shape he knew so well, tracing the outline of her under the crisp linen. As she leaned over to take her glass from the bedside table he caught a glimpse of a breast, and an eyeful of the alarm clock.

Jennifer turned back in time to see him shaking his head. "What is it?" she asked.

Winters rubbed his eyes. "Come to think of it, I AM tired. Especially after seeing the time. I don't know how I've made it this far without sleep. I grabbed a nap before you arrived, but that was an hour at the most."

"And now it's past eleven already," said Jennifer, sympathetically.

She reached for him and her fingertip traced lines on his shoulder.

"You should have let me make the supper," she said.

"It was my pleasure. I enjoyed it."

She remained silent for a while. "You're very domesticated, aren't you?"

"I don't know. I like everything tidy. And since my mother

was never around to tidy for me, I had to learn to do most things myself. I can even sew and knit, would you believe?"

"So you keep telling me. You can do everything." She said in a sing-song voice, mocking him gently.

He laughed. "'Cept climb a tree. 'Cos I get vertigo," he said, in a small boy voice.

"A man unto yourself," said Jennifer, thoughtfully.

He fell quiet. He thought about it. A desire to have and hold Jennifer forever struck him, dousing him in warmth and longing.

"What's the matter? Why've you got that look in your eyes?" she asked.

"Sometimes I look at you, and I don't ever want you to leave. I want to wake up with you every morning, not just some days."

"Watch out. Wishes have a way of coming true."

"Not true. Or I would have solved The Rose case long ago."

Jennifer sipped at her wine. She looked around his room. It was funny how she seemed to belong, thought Winters. "Do you think we'll ever solve it?"

He could not answer positively, as much as he wanted to. "Yes. I think we will. Eventually. But I don't know when. Your guess is as good as mine."

"I thought it wasn't. Or so you've told me."

"I wasn't referring to your ability to guess, nor your intelligence, nor to your determination. I was talking about your resources. You don't have my resources."

"What good have those resources done you so far?"

"Now, now, let's not fight. At least not until after we've done something about this." He lifted the sheet and peered down at himself.

Jennifer giggled. "So. That's all you want from me. Well, you're going to have to answer some questions first."

"Oh no you don't. That's blackmail."

"My prerogative."

"I'll remember that next time you start ripping MY clothes off."

"Fat chance."

Winters smiled. And slipped a hand under her thigh, squeezing gently.

She ignored him. She was studying her wine, a sour look on her face.

"What's the matter?" he asked.

"I was wondering what was going to happen. Whether you have something new. More photofits? Whether there was any progress at all. Any developments?"'

"Yes. There are. And we have some more photofits I'd like you to look at. Things keep moving, but sometimes I feel a chill wind around my ankles on this one. It could be my downfall. I can see it coming. Most detectives are beaten by at least one case in their careers. If I handle everything impeccably I might come through it with my record unblemished. The problem is I'm not sure I've covered my back. I still don't trust Van Deventer. Although he's been helpful, I still feel the Superintendent would love to be running the case himself. I just wonder if he'd have done it differently."

Winters was mindful there was so much Jennifer didn't know now. He was keeping it all from her, and he felt guilty about the secret between them. He knew she had been bursting to ask him about the connection with Whitfield this evening, whether the newspaper speculation was true. He preferred not to remember the scenes in his office that afternoon. After a heated meeting with Maxwell, they had decided to withhold confirmation of the connection for as long as possible. Television, radio and newspaper reporters were consequently divided over whether it was a copycat killing or another victim of The Rose. They played heavily on the fact police had adopted an official silence. Winters had fought hard for the silence, even though Van Deventer's theory of a random killer was beginning to gain support. Winters could feel his grip on the investigation slowly slipping away.

Somehow, Jennifer had managed tonight to avoid asking difficult questions, sensing his fragile frame of mind, and he admired her restraint. He lay back on the pillow, staring up at his ceiling. He sighed, and Jennifer began massaging his shoulders, her breasts swaying deliciously in front of him. "We're following every lead we can think of," he said, quietly.

"Every aspect of the case. For example, we're still working on those anonymous notes sent to your father."

Jennifer continued massaging his shoulders, working steadily as she listened.

"Van Deventer has gone to the London offices of Finance Week magazine, to learn there are 65,000 subscribers in the UK, and weekly sales in retail outlets of a further 40,000," continued Winters. "The damn magazines are everywhere. Patterson's men have been able to pinpoint specific issues of the magazine from which the cuttings were taken. Something to do with paper batches being different, and being able to match up the cuttings in the letters with headlines in five different issues of the magazine. These issues were spread out over a period of six weeks, from mid-December to the end of January."

"What does that tell you?" asked Jennifer.

"Ow, that's sore," said Winters. Jennifer had discovered a knot of tension in his neck. He rolled on to his stomach so that she could get at the knot more easily. "It tells us...I don't know. That the man had been planning the murder for a long time? I just can't say for sure. There are so many things about the case that puzzle me. As much as we do, we seem to only find a very few pieces of the jigsaw, let alone enough to start piecing a picture together."

Winters paused for a moment, reflecting on the aspects that puzzled him most. He thought of the look on Jennifer's face when she studied the photofit. Why hadn't he made an effort to try and show her the latest photofits? Because he still didn't trust her fully? No, he trusted her. But he didn't trust her emotions. He felt vaguely uneasy, in a way he couldn't explain. Would she abuse his trust? He mentally cursed himself. He shouldn't let that get in the way. He should show her the photofits. The look on her face that night was still vivid in his memory. It still worried him, but didn't make any sense. So much made little sense.

Jennifer stopped massaging and lay down on the bed beside him. Winters put an arm over her, pulling her close to him.

She nuzzled him gently. "Sometimes I feel a part of me is dying slowly."

Winters turned to face her.

"Oh, don't look at me like that," she said. "You ARE special to me. You're what's keeping me alive. But HE was my father. I can't let go. I've tried, but I can't. Information about this killer is the energy I need to sustain my whole being until he is caught. When it goes this long without hearing anything I begin to feel hollow and desperate. I can't describe the feeling. It scares me."

Winters watched her, keeping his distance. Even though all the lights were turned out, and the only illumination came from the sitting room lamps, he could see her face clearly. Tears had welled in her eyes as she spoke. The Jennifer who loved him, he adored. He would kill for her. But there was another Jennifer, a Jennifer growing stronger by the day, threatening to take over the more gentle of the two. He was scared of this Jennifer. It was the girl who wanted to avenge her father that frightened him. He felt sure she would be utterly ruthless.

Yet Winters felt the guilt rage through him. He felt he was holding out on her. He looked away from Jennifer, unable to watch the tears. He felt like a bitter old cynic, but he wasn't sure the tears were for real. Could he trust her? He looked back at her. She had picked up her glass and was staring into her wine. He felt a rush of anger. Why, when he had finally found someone he could care about, did there have to be so many complications?

He had been finding the case a drain in every way. He wanted to solve it as a matter of personal pride. He was supposed to be a good policeman. It would do wonders for his career. But also because... he didn't like anyone getting the better of him. He couldn't allow that. But every day he found something else in the way. Something was growing in him now and this might be a further hindrance. Finding The Rose was no longer a question of doing his duty. It had become much, much more. The woman he was growing to love was being kept from him, made ultimately untouchable, by her grim desire to see her father's death avenged. He knew that this force driving her might soon become too powerful for their fragile relationship. It might destroy them both before they had a chance to begin.

The Rose was beginning to make a mockery of the police, his killings brutal and swift and almost contemptuous. He was taunting the police with his roses, and Winters ground his teeth as he fought back the animosity. The case had become so much more than his duty. It was something personal now. Between him and The Rose. The prizes were Jennifer and his career. As he looked at Jennifer's face, he could see the pain there was genuine. How could he refuse to answer that?

"Jennifer," he said, softly. "What I'm going to tell you is confidential. I don't really have to caution you, but a lot of this is still classified, so to speak. The truth is, we HAVE been making progress. We found the man who gave the killer his weapons. And we have two more photofits." He saw the look on her face and he hurried on. "But, like the last one you saw, they are obvious disguises and these two look nothing like the original."

"You must let the newspapers have them," she said, quietly.

"No. Not yet," he answered, surprised at her mild response.

"When?"

"When I'm ready."

"When will that be?"

"Soon. Sooner than you think."

"When? A week? A month?"

"I don't know. The time must be right, and only I am the judge of that. But wait, don't interrupt. There's more." Winters sat up, crossing his legs, arranging the sheet around himself. He felt the need for some formality, and talking to Jennifer naked unsettled him.

"Jen, you may be angry with me for not saying anything, especially in view of ..."

"Of what?" she prompted.

"Well, of our relationship. But the point is, we have established beyond doubt that The Rose has killed again."

"Whitfield?"

"Yes."

Jennifer said nothing.

"This man is clever. Ruthless. Every killing has been carefully planned and executed. He has researched each of his victims, singling each one out carefully. Van Deventer is leading a movement to treat the bastard like we would a random killer.

But I'm convinced there's a reason for the killings. Something links the victims, I've just got to find out what that link is."

Jennifer put down her glass. Still, she was subdued. "Do you know anything else about him?"

"Not much. We found smoked cigarettes at the scene of Whitfield's killing. But the killer was wearing gloves. No finger-prints. And another rose."

"Does that have any significance?"

Winters hesitated. He wondered whether Jennifer was going to cry again. She seemed barely able to control herself.

"Uh, one of the lads at the Yard says there is a language of flowers. Roses have different meanings. A Yellow Rose means infidelity. The China Rose means grace or beauty. A red rose sometimes means pleasure mixed with pain. It doesn't tell us much."

Something in Jennifer burst, and he saw her wine glass start to shake, and she started to sob, slopping wine onto the sheet, onto one of her breasts. The liquid soaked into the sheet, which clung to her breast, taking the shape of her nipple. Winters was at once alarmed, yet transfixed.

He reached for her, expecting her, as usual, to pull away angrily. She always kept herself to herself when she felt vulner-able. Instead, she came into his arms He rocked her gently as she wept, the sobs racking her, and he wondered if this might be the end of it, or at least the beginning of the end, and he lay down, pulling her down with him, kissing her neck, her cheeks, tasting the salt of her tears.

After a while she stopped sobbing, and he could feel her breath against his shoulder. In all her years with her father, she had not been allowed to be vulnerable, he thought. It would take her a long time to find that out. It would take her even longer if she carried on working in the cynical world of journalists. Resentment towards Hugh Chapman smouldered in him. Did that bastard know what he was doing to his daughter? Had he known the pain he was inflicting on her? Did he ever suspect the legacy of unfulfilled dreams he would leave? And why turn your own daughter into a hard-bitten clone? Winters wondered what attracted her to newspapers. Somehow, he could not see her world, could not imagine what sort of environment she worked in. For some reason, it seemed suddenly important. An impulse struck him. He would like to see inside a newspaper office. Where she worked. Jennifer could take him.

He leaned back to see if she was sleeping. Her eyes were on his. "I want you to take me to your office. I want you to show me what it's like."

"When?"

"Now. I took you to Scotland Yard late. Now it's your turn."

She paused, looking at him quizzically. "You're really serious, aren't you?"

"I am."

"But you're tired. You need sleep."

"Come on Jen. I want to see where you work. Not next week. Not tomorrow. Now."

"I'd like that," she said, smiling. "I really would. All right. Let's go. Right now." The transformation was astonishing. She was all at once keen and gleeful.

The excitement in her grew as they went to his car and drove to Fleet Street. On the way, she started telling him about stories she had covered. She boasted of her series on drug dealers, the series of which her father had been so proud. They found a parking spot down a side street. Winters was amazed. Parking had not been easy to find, and there were many more people about than he had expected. It was near midnight. "Is it always this crowded so late?" he asked.

She didn't answer. Instead she led him into The Courier building. He could see she was pleased with his interest, and anxious to please. She started to do the grand tour, but stopped. She explained most departments would be shut at this time. "I'll show you the editorial department," she said.

"Which floor?" he asked, nervously.

"The fourth. Why?"

"I'd be happier if we took the lift, not the stairs."

Jennifer laughed, teasing him. "How can you stand being tall? It must keep you in a constant state of terror."

"Don't joke," he said. "You should see what I'm like on a double-decker bus. Terrified. And stairwells slay me. The lift, please."

After calling the lift and riding it to the fourth floor, Jennifer proudly showed him the newsroom, explaining how the journalists worked against deadlines every day of their lives, how they never knew what they were going to do one day from the next, how they soaked up long hours and junk food and stress and insults and very little praise, always searching out the story, pressing for the big break.

Winters listened, enrapt, catching a glimpse of another world, one he felt he could never understand. A reporter's life appeared so vicarious to him. They seemed to live on other people's disasters and successes.

However, Jennifer's enthusiasm was infectious, and he happily let her steer him around. Walking to the editor's offices, they passed racks of corridor. He asked what they were for.

"Oh, for record. We keep all the national newspapers on file, so that we can always go and read up a story should we be called in to handle something we know nothing about. It is part of our job to read every newspaper from cover to cover. But these are here because we can't be expected to remember everything.

You should see the library. We keep even more magazines and newspapers in there, and this is only a fraction of the information stored away there."

Jennifer steered him into the editor's wing. But she didn't stay for long. He felt her father's ghost stirring. On the way back to the lifts, she pointed out the library. "Come and see what I mean," she said.

Winters was acutely aware that few people were about. They had passed one reporter in the newsroom. Jennifer had explained he was on night duty, and would be going off soon. He knocked off at two o'clock, and would be most anxious to leave. The night shift was the least favourite duty of afternoon newspaper reporters. "Did you ever see so much paper in your life? We keep most magazines, over there, on that rack, most national newspapers, many English-language foreign magazines, over there ... Alan?"

"Yes?"

"Are you listening?"

"Yes. You said you kept most foreign magazines over there." He looked at the rack. Copies of the major international news and business magazines were stacked on the rack, including copies of Time, Newsweek, Fortune, Business, Punch and Finance Week. It made for a colourful array of covers. But his mind was no longer on periodicals, looking at Jennifer now, so vibrant and alive in this environment. He pulled her toward him, bending his head to kiss her. She received his kiss timidly, reservedly, but responded slowly as he pressed himself to her. He could feel her breath growing ragged. He backed her up to the rack of magazines, his hand sliding underneath the waistline of her sweater.

The sound of the lift door opening down the corridor

startled both of them. He sheepishly whipped his hand out from under her top. She tried to smooth her clothes.

"Come on," she said, taking his hand. "It's time I got you home, I can see."

"I'd be grateful," he smiled, looking down at himself.

They walked out of the library and stepped into the lift. As the doors shut behind them, Winters punched the ground floor button. He shook his head. "There's something that puzzles me," he said. "I can't picture the Jennifer I know in this environment. What attracts you about it?"

"Lots of things. Notwithstanding the fact my father was an editor, the job does have enormous stimulation. Everything else seems so humdrum after newspaper work."

"Everything? There must be other exciting jobs?"

"Yes, but none like this. I often feel I should leave newspapers, because of the cynicism. But I would always miss the people."

"I didn't realize other journalists were as interesting as you."

"I mean the people you get to meet as a journalist. You get to know all sorts in this business. Either through my father, or my own stories, I've met film stars, millionaires, businessmen, drug addicts, pushers, robbers, police -" she broke off to smile at him - "whores, sportsmen. I could go on. The truth is, I've met all kinds."

"Including me."

"Including you."

She kissed him then, in a way that made Winters believe it was going to be a long and uncomfortable drive home.

THIRTY-FIVE

DAVIS KICKED out at the pigeons around his feet in a flash of irritation. Three birds fluttered disinterestedly out of range. Nearby a tourist ran through the birds, most of which refused to take flight. Trafalgar Square was theirs too, they seemed to say. Davis stood with his four companions near one of the lions guarding Nelson's Column, watching the tourists and the heavy traffic.

"You call us all the way down here just to tell us about a story we can't use. What a bloody waste," said Gibson, his brow creased in a heavy scowl.

Baker took up the argument. "This time we have a fantastic story, Jennifer. Police confirm that The Rose slaughtered Whitfield. They withhold photofits. How can you suggest we sit on it?"

Paynter and Davis said nothing, but they were nodding in agreement.

"Yes, but what happens to our source?" said Jennifer.

"We have to weigh up whether this is a big enough story to run by ourselves, and do without him," said Gibson.

Jennifer shook her head vehemently. "Can't we do this the way we did the last story? By pretending one of you wrote it?"

Paynter snorted. "Come on Jennifer. He'd see through that straight away."

Jennifer dug her hands deeper into her coat. All five were huddled against a chilling wind.

This wasn't going the way she anticipated. She had broken the news to the journalists on the walk to the square in the hope it would keep them satisfied for a while, and keep them interested. She hadn't counted on them insisting on publication. She told them about the forensic links with The Rose, as well as the new photofits and the refusal of Winters to release them.

"He thinks they will be misleading. I haven't seen them yet, but I have seen the first one they got," she explained.

"Would you be able to get one of our artists to draw it up?" asked Davis.

"Perhaps. I don't know."

Baker looked at his watch. "We can still get this story into today's editions if we hurry."

"No, wait," said Jennifer. She was still undecided. Would Alan understand? Perhaps he would forgive her? But what if he didn't? Could she face that? She turned away from her colleagues and stared at the cars circling the square. The traffic seemed mainly composed of black taxis, she noted.

"What are you waiting for Jennifer?" asked Gibson. His voice was hard, each word clipped short. "Isn't this what it's all about? You're meant to be a professional, yet you're sitting on a front page lead."

"Only because I think we should wait for something bigger."

"How much bigger a story do you want?" asked Paynter, his voice rising an octave. The din of the traffic threatened to drown out their conversation.

Gibson was adamant. "We could wait forever. That's not the point. We cover news as it happens. This is a development, and with all the interest in The Rose, it is a fascinating development. If you decide not to run with this story, then I'm off the team as of this moment."

Jennifer could see Gibson was serious. She studied the faces of her colleagues. She could find little sympathy in their eyes.

Baker took her arm, imploringly. "Jennifer, this may provoke your father's killer, you know. It might flush him out of hiding.

If I were a killer and I read photofits of me were knocking around I'd be beside myself with worry."

"Not if the police are refusing to release them. Not if the story says they are not much like the real man, by the admission of the police themselves," she countered.

"But consider it," said Paynter. Jennifer was surprised at the tone in his voice. He sounded angry. Normally he was so withdrawn. "There might be someone somewhere who recognises something within the photofits."

"That's what I said," explained Jennifer. "But Winters refused to go along with that. He said he had high-ranking backing on this one."

Gibson stood back from the group. "We're off the point. The point is we have a good hard news story and we're not going to use it." He turned to face the men, ignoring Jennifer, speaking as if she wasn't there. He stalked away, hands in his pockets, stepping out with angry strides. The others watched him go.

Davis said: "It's your choice Jennifer. But if you decide to write the story, I have some good background on the photofit system. I'll be waiting back in the office. If Rodgers asks where you are, what shall I say?"

"I'll be back in a minute," Jennifer said miserably.

Davis waved a hand in farewell. "You coming?" he asked Baker and Paynter. Baker shook his head. Paynter grunted, and the two men walked off together.

Jennifer was left staring at Baker. She felt utterly wretched. He touched her hand, squeezed, and self-consciously withdrew his hand when he saw her looking at his fingers. Lately, Baker had a growing tendency to touch her whenever he could. She had been only dimly aware of his slow slide from seeming asexuality to a distinct liking for her. The thought amused her. To fill the silence, she said: "Do you go out with a lot of girls?"

Baker frowned. "What?"

"I'm sorry, that's personal. I just wondered whether you saw much of the opposite sex."

He laughed. "I should be offended. Do you think I'm gay?"

"Far from it. But I have to admit I've sometimes wondered whether you have much time for women."

"For the right woman, plenty," he said, looking into her eyes.

She turned away, trying to see if she could still identify Davis and Paynter in the throng of pedestrians in The Strand. No. Long gone.

Baker spoke quietly. "Gibson is right. It is a good story. But Davis is also right. It's your choice."

Jennifer stared blankly at him. Her mind was racing. What would Alan do? Oh God, what would he do? She focused on the scar on Baker's cheek. "How did you get that scar?" she asked, distractedly. Anything to avoid the pain of indecision.

He frowned, then shook his head, smiling indulgently. "You've asked me that before. And about my broken nose."

"Well, what did you say? I can't remember." She did remember. He had avoided the question. His secrecy had intrigued her, but she had never had another chance to ask him.

"It was all a long time ago. When I was a boy. I prefer not to talk about it."

"Oh. I'm sorry."

"Don't be. Instead, return to the point at issue. Whether you're going to run this story."

Jennifer squeezed her eyes closed, trying to block out the question, wishing the problem would go away. Her mind kept shying away from the decision, refusing to allow her to concentrate.

"What do you think is the role of a journalist?" she asked, suddenly.

He scowled. "Why?"

"It's important."

"A journalist is a crusader. They represent truth, record events, hold aloft the light of knowledge. They arm the public with the facts they need to effectively run their lives. They also piece together puzzles, and –"

"Okay, okay. I get the point. I just wish I could believe you."

"Why can't you?"

"Because that doesn't sound like you at all. You're such a cynic usually. That sounds like so much idealistic hype."

"You're right," said Baker. "I thought it was what you wanted to hear."

Jennifer turned back to face Nelson's Column. A young girl in jeans was trying to climb astride one of the lions at the base of the column. A policeman, hands clasped behind his back, was admonishing her, using his head to gesticulate for her to get off. For a moment, Jennifer watched, in thought. The more she got to know about Baker, the more she saw how much he kept hidden. Was most of what he said a sham? She wondered why she was being so easily diverted from her dilemma.

As if reading her mind, Baker said: "I can only say I think it would help matters if the momentum was kept up. News has a way of making other news. And that sort of cycle may help us to find out who killed your father."

Jennifer winced. Baker had touched the right nerve. She clenched her fists. What about Alan? He'd understand. Would he, though? She was struck by another thought. If the killer managed to remain undetected, she would never really be able to have Alan anyway, because her father's unexorcised ghost would always haunt their relationship. Alan would label himself a failure. He was terrified of that, she knew. Neither of them would ever again know serenity of any kind. That would be enough to finally tear the two of them apart, whatever they tried to do.

She felt tears come to her eyes. She looked at Baker, nodding. "I'll do it," she said. "I'll do it."

"That's my girl," said Baker. "Let's go tell the others. We can still make the next edition."

They began to walk back towards Fleet Street. Baker said: "Sod it. Let's catch a taxi."

He flagged down a cab, and as they settled into the seat, the taxi surging into the stream of traffic, Baker patted Jennifer on the knee. "You're making the right decision," he said. "You'll see."

But Jennifer still felt unsettled and terribly afraid. Apart from anything else, she wasn't sure she liked Baker's increasing protectiveness towards her. Worse, she was far from convinced she was making the right decision. She felt more like she was undertaking a premeditated act of betrayal. She tried to picture Alan's face when he saw the report. She couldn't conjure up the image. Instead, a vision of her father's face swam into focus. The tighter she closed her eyes, the more the face resembled a death mask. She gritted her teeth, and opened her eyes to stare straight ahead, concentrating on the traffic ahead of the taxi.

THIRTY-SIX

"AS OF THIS minute, you are no longer in charge of the case," said Maxwell. His fingers were steepled on the desk, his face empty of expression. "Van Deventer will assume command, you will answer to him. Do I make myself clear?"

Winters could feel his ears and cheeks burning. He dreaded the thought of having to walk back to his office through the Murder room. After this roasting, the whole damn squad room would know about his shame. Pairs of eyes would follow him and he cringed at the vision.

"Yes sir," he muttered.

Maxwell had torn strips off him, bellowing about Winter's "indiscretion." He had raged for half an hour. Did Winters have any conception of what sort of pressure this would place on the police? As if Winters needed to be told. Already calls were jamming the switchboards, and the paper had only been on the streets for an hour. Maxwell told Winters he was foolish to have allowed himself to get involved. How could he have taken a journalist into his confidence, even if she was the victim's daughter? Maxwell posed the theory Jennifer might herself have been the killer. Winters felt helpless. How could he explain he was sleeping with the woman? How could he explain even an ambitious policeman needed a woman in his life, especially one as beautiful and magnetic as Jennifer Chapman? How could he explain he was just as angry as Maxwell, maybe even more so, because to a degree it had been a calculated risk. He had only himself to blame. It was a stupid, potentially dangerous mistake.

When he cooled down, Maxwell clearly regretted his temper.

But then he added the final humiliation. "Until now, Alan, you've had a pretty faultless career. You've always worked with an admirably fierce application to duty. However this mistake is too big to ignore. You're lucky still to be on the case at all. I've had my job cut out keeping you on the force. Don't let me down again."

Maxwell swivelled his chair around to stare out the window of his office. Winters was dismissed. He strode out of Maxwell's office, through the squad room and into his own office at full speed, slamming the door behind him. No one had even looked at him, the men in the squad room studiously keeping their eyes on their work.

He was annoyed to see Van Deventer still in their office, on the telephone. Winters sat down morosely in his chair, staring glumly at the papers on the table in front of him.

"Right Philip. I understand. I'll deal with it. No need to worry," said Van Deventer. He replaced the receiver.

Winters stared at him challengingly.

Van Deventer had finally got his way. He could barely contain his satisfaction.

"So. You made a mistake as I suspected you would. And without any help from me."

"I hope you're happy, Superintendent. It's what you've been aiming at all this time, isn't it?"

"Yes. But I must be frank. I would have preferred different circumstances. I understand your situation. I do. But we still have a job to do. I hope I can count on your support."

Winters turned around, toying with the idea of going out. What purpose would that serve?
He couldn't run away from it. He didn't want to run away. The truth was, he wanted to catch the bastard more than ever. If he could get his hands on The Rose now, he would tear the man's

head off his shoulders. No, he couldn't run away. He had to stay with it. To repair this damage to his career. Before he became a detective "who nearly made it." Before Jennifer was destroyed. Before their relationship was damaged beyond repair.

He looked squarely at Van Deventer. "Yes," he said. "You can count on my support."

Van Deventer nodded. "Good." He returned to his notebook, and Winters was grateful that the Dutchman was not going to make more of it all.

Winters stood up and paced to the window, staring down at the headlights of cars in the street below. It was getting late already. By now, ordinarily, he would be looking forward to going home, to seeing Jennifer. He shook his head. HOW COULD SHE HAVE DONE IT? The thought forced its way out, and the sense of betrayal and disappointment flooded in. He felt on the edge of tears and he blinked fiercely, confused at his reaction. Crying? Why crying? He should go out there and scream at her, tell her to stay away from him forever.

But oh, what if she did? Forever didn't bear thinking about. Yet he had to face it. She had declared her hand. She had used him. All she had wanted was the information, not him. He had fallen so neatly into her trap. Bitch.

He wondered what had gone through her mind as she wrote that story. Had she stopped for a moment to consider what she was doing? Had she thought of the consequences for him? Yes. She would have thought it through carefully. She cared for him, of that he was sure. But right now, she cared about finding The Rose more. She had written the story in spite of the consequences. And now he would be forced to act. He couldn't see her again. Not for a while.

Not until this was all over. Perhaps then he could resume the relationship, and hope against hope that there was still something to salvage. He felt hollow, bruised. He wished he could treat the ache inside him. The last time he had felt this pain and despair was when his parents had ... Winters became aware of Van Deventer calling him. He turned around, blinking back the tears. "What?" he croaked.

Van Deventer had his hand over the mouthpiece of the telephone. Winters had been so engrossed, he had not heard it ring. "It's Jennifer. She wants to talk to you. She knows you're here," said the Dutchman.

Winters' first reaction was to say he didn't want to talk to her. But he knew that wasn't true. He wanted badly to talk to her, even if only to hear her voice for the last time for a while. He took the phone from the Dutchman, barely acknowledging his thanks.

"Yes," he barked.

"Alan? I'm sorry. Please, let me explain, then try to understand," said Jennifer. Her voice was quiet, pleading.

"I cannot understand. Not in a million years." He spoke through clenched teeth, only just able to refrain from shouting because of Van Deventer. If the Dutchman would only go out... Winters stared pointedly at Van Deventer, who refused to take the hint. The Dutchman motioned his hands together. "Talk. Get together," he mimed.

Forget it, thought Winters.

Jennifer said: "Will you give me a chance to explain."

In spite of himself, Winters exploded. "Explain? Explain? Not on your life. What the hell is there to explain? You betrayed me for your own ends. That's all I need to know."

"It's not that simple Alan. I was stupid. I made a mistake. Please don't do this."

"I like that. You've got what you want. You've done what

you had to do. You got your front page story and now I must take the flack and be kind and understanding. Well, you can shove it. I'm bloody lucky still to have my job."

"I didn't think it would be that serious. I thought – "

"Well you obviously didn't think hard enough. Look at what you've done. You betrayed my trust. Relationships are built on trust. I could never put my faith in you again. What kind of relationship have you engineered for us? Did you stop to think of that?"

Winters saw Van Deventer flinch. The Dutchman looked pained that Winters could talk to a woman that way. And sod you too, thought Winters. His hands were shaking. He knew what was coming. And he knew he had to do it. From now their relationship would be half-truths and pain and guilt and everything it had promised lay shattered and OH SHIT why did she do it? Why? WHY?

"Alan, surely this isn't that serious? If I'd thought that this would happen..." Her voice trailed off. Winters heard it breaking, the way it did when she was about to cry. He could see her lips quivering, her eyes tearing. Stop. Don't do this to yourself, he admonished himself. This was pointless.

"Jennifer, this is more serious than you conceived. You didn't even stop to think what you were doing. I trusted you with information I should have kept to myself. I thought if I couldn't trust you enough to tell you we had nothing, so I told you. And what did you do? You went and told the whole bloody world. How can I ever trust you with anything again? Don't you understand?"

"I think you're over-reacting. I think we should meet tonight and discuss this over a glass or three of wine." She was trying to inject a note of playfulness into her voice.

"No," said Winters. He felt cold, numb. A sense of lethargy

filled him. He ignored Van Deventer, who was shaking his head fiercely, a look of anguish on his face.

Winters sighed. "No Jennifer," he went on. "Not tonight. Not ever. Please don't call me again. Goodbye."

The last word was a whisper. He replaced the receiver, wishing this could be different, wishing he had not told her, but what was the point? He was right. In the end it was all about trust. Believing in each other. If he forgot that, then what had he become? What would their relationship become?

Winters looked up at Van Deventer, defiantly.

The Dutchman said nothing. Instead, he stood up, put on his coat, making little clucking sounds as he did so. At the door he turned to Winters. He was wearing an expression that reminded Winters of his own father. The day he had told him he was going to be a policeman, not a publisher. The look was that of a father, hurt by, but still concerned for, his child.

"You're going to have to live with that for a long time," said the Dutchman. "A very long time. Much longer than you think."

Van Deventer walked out of the office, moving into the thick of the men in the squad room, most of whom were now getting ready to go home. At last sight, Winters saw Van Deventer was still shaking his head.

THIRTY-SEVEN

SHEILA CHAPMAN stroked her daughter's hair. Jennifer was only dimly aware of the soothing nature of her mother's work. Even so, her sobs were beginning to subside.

"If only..." she started. "If only I hadn't let them talk me into it. But I was trapped, I had to ..."

"Sshhh," whispered Sheila.

Jennifer could still hear the hurt and pain in Alan's voice. Worse, she could still recall the terrible note of finality in his voice. His words cut through her once more. "Please don't call me again." He had meant it.

She had barely been able to contain her tears while in the office. She fought them back all the way home on the tube, and during the walk from the station to her house had been commending herself on her toughness and self-control. At first she had gone straight to her room, but she didn't want to be alone. She had gone in search of her mother. She found Sheila in her own bedroom, vacuuming the carpet. When Sheila saw her daughter she immediately switched off the cleaner. Then she walked over and took Jennifer in her arms, leading her gently to the bed.

For Jennifer, it was a simple and touching act of concern and love that unleashed her tears. Sobs had been torn from her. Lying in her mother's arms, all she could think of was Alan's voice. The sound of his pain. She wept without restraint while her mother held her head in her lap, running her fingers over her cheeks, wiping away the tears, smoothing her hair, gently soothing her. When Jennifer was in control again Sheila said: "I'll make us some coffee." She stood up and looked down at Jennifer for a long time. Then she had slipped away quietly.

Jennifer could hear the sound of Sheila working in the kitchen below. She could smell her mother's perfume on her pillow, and she remembered how she used to come into this bed as a child, seeking comfort. She was filled with a sense of nostalgia. After a while, Sheila came back into the room, carrying a tray. She pulled up a chair and table and busied herself pouring tea. "I've never washed this pot with soap or dishwashing liquid, you know. I learned somewhere you should never wash a pot. Spoils the tea. All I've ever done is rinse it out."

"Thought we were having coffee?" asked Jennifer.

"I thought some tea would be better."

Sheila handed a cup to Jennifer. It was weak and hot and sweet, and she sipped it with pleasure.

"Has something happened with Alan?" The question was spoken softly.

"Yes. I've done something terrible. I think I've destroyed our relationship forever."

Jennifer described what had happened. Sheila remained silent through the story, nodding occasionally, sipping her tea. This was the mother she remembered from her childhood. Composed, serene and competent.

"The terrible thing is that I knew it would result in something like this. But I couldn't resist."

Sheila put down her cup and came to sit next to Jennifer on the bed. She put her arms around her daughter. "It worries me to see you like this. You seemed so strong until soon after the service for your father. Since then you've been changing. Something has happened."

Jennifer started to speak, but Sheila raised her hand to silence her. "No, wait. I was pleased you found Alan. But I worried you were using him as a crutch. Something else has been happening to you. You've been obsessed with this killer. You can talk of nothing else. That worries me, because I fear you'll do something stupid. You're all I have left now. You are the living part of Hugh. Don't get me wrong. I don't want to hold you down, but I was hoping we could now develop our relationship. I couldn't bear it if anything happened to you. I just don't know what I would do."

Jennifer shook her head. "Nothing will happen to me. I'm not doing anything stupid."

"You already have, I'm afraid. This thing with Alan. It is all part of your fixation. I'm standing on the outside and I can see you changing. It frightens me. I know you must go your own way, and I won't stop you, but you really are all I've got left. Your future is, in a way, my future. I want us to grow close, like a mother and her daughter should be."

Sheila took Jennifer's hand, gently stroking her fingers, examining each one carefully, as if it were something precious and fragile. "You know, we seldom had the chance to talk and discuss problems. You have always been a very, uhm, independent person. But I have something to say now. Something I learned from your father's death."

Jennifer squeezed her mother's hand. She had been about to protest, but she knew what Sheila was trying to say. Theirs was another relationship that had never been fulfilled. Hugh had been her daughter's focus in life. Maybe she even understood all the reasons. In any event, she had never forced her opinions on Jennifer, nor had she ever insisted on giving advice. But she had always been there, in case she was needed.

"Our lives are very short. I was always happy to wait, looking forward to the time your father was retired and we could spend our days together. I had everything planned so neatly. The holidays, the activities. Everything."

Jennifer looked expectantly at her mother. What was she going to say? Sheila looked so composed, and so capable again. To think she had worried that her mother was going to do something stupid with that ancient gun. Time heals wounds. Well, here was the proof. She should take comfort. A few weeks ago she believed Sheila would never stop crying, that she would waste away until she vanished in a pool of tears. She could hardly believe the recovery her mother had made, able so quickly to handle someone else's grief and give comfort and support.

Sheila went on: "I've learned you can spend your life chasing the wrong things. You can spend your life anticipating and never actually living. I regret that today. I wish I had demanded more of your father's time. I can't get it now. And I would do anything – anything – to have him back."

She sipped her tea, looking around the room. "Your father lives on in this room. I can smell him still. I see him in the bed. I've cleared out his clothes, and most of his things, but all the time I wish it was me who was dead and not him. He always seemed so alive, and so vital to everything and everybody. Everyone seemed to need him so much. His work colleagues, his contacts, his friends, even you. I thought it would be unfair to pressure him from my side as well."

Jennifer was watching intently. She looked at the bedside photograph of the three of them, taken one Christmas when Jennifer was still at school.

Sheila saw her looking. "That picture tells a lie," she said. "It shows us together, happy together. But we weren't. We were all separately waiting for something. Now it will never come. What I'm saying is this: Don't waste time waiting. Do things Jennifer."

"What, for instance?"

"Well, if you really do care for this man –"

"Everything that happened today made me think that I do care for him. More than I wanted to, and more than I thought possible."

"Then do whatever you have to do to get him back. Don't let your pride prevent it. Get him back. In the end, all we have is love. Our lives are worth nothing without it."

Sheila stood up and turned to face her daughter, looking down at her on the bed. "I know that now. Don't mistake me. I don't mean I want my life to end, or that I'll take it myself. I'm not that sort of person. But I know my life is much less meaningful without Hugh."

"But what can I do?"

"You'll know what you have to do. Give it time, and you will know what you have to do. I've been thinking about things, and what lies ahead of me. I know what I have to do. The answer comes to you naturally. It is so simple, and so clear cut. Soon, you also will know that you have to do."

"But I don't. I just don't know what to do."

Sheila smiled, then bent to pick up the tray. "Give it a day or two. The answer will come." She left the room, and Jennifer turned to stare at the photograph. She could see no way out of this maze. What could she do to win back Alan? Sheila didn't know him. She didn't know how single-minded he was, or how proud and ambitious he was. She wanted him back, of that she was certain. But what could she do to get him back?

She heard again her mother's voice. " You'll know what to do."

Maybe she was right. Perhaps a little time would be enough.

Then another thought struck her. What had her mother meant when she had said she knew what SHE had to do? She shook her head in frustration.

Nothing made sense at the moment.

Jennifer lay back on the pillow, clutching at the sheet with one hand, smoothing it against her cheek. She remembered that, as a child, waiting for her father to come home, she would often climb into bed with her mother. Lying on her father's side of the bed, holding the sheet to her cheek just as she was now, she would listen for the sound of his car and the clatter of his key turning in the lock. It was the sound that would be enough to release her so that she could sleep.

She tried to imagine the sound of his key in the door. All she heard was the sound of her mother alone in the kitchen below.

She began to cry again.

THIRTY-EIGHT

APRIL 29, 1986 *The dreams stir up a terrible sense of ancient grief. Why?*

Because the man in my dream seems like my father. I still can't see his face. While the rest of him is in perfect focus, his face remains blurred, swimming behind a screen of opaqueness.

Still, the dreams conjure up from my subconcious all the horrors and nightmares of my childhood, the nightgames my father played, and all those times I spent waiting for the nightgames to start.

I see I am changing. I have never experienced emotions quite as fiercely. Elation, depression, follow each other in ever-tightening circles. I look for answers. Why did my parents die? Why has my life been so bleak? Why am I so excited at the thought of killing? Trying to find answers is an exercise in futility. I don't believe there are any.

So, instead, my mind turns to goals. Achieving something while I'm still alive. When I'm doing that, I'm fine. There are other changes...Religion has never interested me. In many ways, it has repulsed me. Yet now I develop a strange fascination. Near our office is St Brides Church, just behind the Reuters Building. It looks like a wedding cake. Sometimes I stop and sit on the benches outside the church. A day or so ago I went inside. It seemed small and dark.

I read somewhere it had been designed by Christopher Wren, who was also the architect of St Paul's Cathedral. I had been to St Paul's once, but never felt the inclination to go back. Suddenly, I felt the need. The next day, after work, I walked up past Ludgate Circus to St Paul's. It is one of the most famous buildings in the world. The cross on top of its great dome stands 330 feet off the ground. The building tends to dominate the City skyline. When I walked into the Cathedral I knew I was looking for something, I'm not sure what.

Answers? The building fascinates me. It is so vast. So many people inside. I stayed for a long time, looking up at the dome. I bought one of the booklets for sale at the counter of one of the stalls at the rear of the building. Those stalls sickened me. It seemed to cheapen the church. I wanted so much for it to be a place of refuge. It wasn't.

I stood in the cathedral, just before official closing time at five, and watched the people. I kept trying to listen in on conversations, to hear if someone was talking about me, "The Rose". I sat down in the pews under the Whispering Gallery and I wondered how it got its name. My booklet says if you stand in the Gallery and face the wall, then whisper, the sound can be heard at the far side of the Gallery, more than 100 feet away. I tried to get up to the Gallery, to look down on all the tourists. It was closed. For some reason, they close it at 3:15pm, along with the Stone Gallery and the Golden Gallery. It looks so high up there, and the people in it always seem so puny.

Standing in the throng of people I was struck by several thoughts: Is there a God? Does he control us? If not, who does? How many people have walked through here? How many lives? How much sadness, how much pain? How many killers? Has anyone ever died in the cathedral?

That was an intriguing thought. But not as intriguing as the thought that someone else might be in control of everything that is happening right now. You see, at times I wonder whether I'm not a pawn in some devilish chess game, part of some carefully planned but incomprehensible strategy worked out by someone much more powerful than me. For instance, why did Jennifer Chapman want to put together a team of journalists to investigate her father's murder? What motivates her to try and do something bound to end in failure? Someone bigger than all of us is forcing her. And that someone has an incredible sense of irony.

Why else would Jennifer ask ME to be on her team?

THIRTY-NINE

"ANY NEWS?" asked Jennifer.

"Nothing," muttered Davis. The others shook their heads. She looked around - these were clearly the last days of her team. The thought struck her like a pail of ice water. She suddenly felt hugely depressed. She wanted to sleep for a week. It had been several days since the front page lead which had so angered Alan. But, as every journalist knew, you were only as good as your current story, and right now the team did not have one. The men before her were growing steadily disheartened. Unless she managed something major soon, they would fall apart. Without Alan, her chances of getting any major news breaks were greatly reduced.

Soon she would have nothing but her own hatred.

Of them all, Baker was the only one in a cheerful mood. Gibson refused to look her in the
eye; Davis was smiling distractedly, Paynter (yet again) was

agitated and restless. This was becoming a grind for all of them, she thought.

Then Baker said: "I know what's happening with The Rose, or, rather, who is behind it all."

It was as if someone had thrown a switch. They all tried to gabble at once.

"Who is it –" started Gibson, unfolding his arms from in front of his chest.

"Have you been holding out on –" tried Davis, scowling heavily.

"Hang on. Hang on," said Baker, holding his hands up in front of him, palms towards the others. "All I have is a theory. But I have a feeling about it. I think, for the first time, we could be on to something ..."

"Well, what is it?" asked Jennifer. She leaned forward, straining to hear Baker's reply, suddenly aware of the noise in Duff's Place. For a quiet little Fleet Street coffee shop, it was as noisy as a nightclub at times, she thought. After all their meetings there, she would have thought each of them ought to be immune to the hubbub.

Baker laughed. "Patience is a virtue. But then, you're all journalists. Patience is the least of your virtues."

"Come on," snapped Gibson, before sipping at his coffee, peering at Baker over the rim of the cup. Gibson was going to be the next to pull out, thought Jennifer. There was something about him now, these past few meetings, an air of hostility and resentment. He sat through the meetings looking bored and disinterested, seldom contributing. Rodgers had not given this his official blessing, insisting they conduct their meetings outside the office. Gibson had not been pleased.

"Okay," said Baker, less enthusiastically, taken aback by the hostility of the reaction.

"Have any of you thought about the possibility of terrorists?"

No-one replied. They seemed to sag back into their seats.

"For Christ's sake, Colin, that's old hat," said Gibson. "We spoke about that at one of our first meetings, and dismissed it, just as the police have done."

"Perhaps we shouldn't have," said Baker, traces of irritation in his voice. He leaned back in his seat, glancing defensively around the table.

A waiter interrupted, leaning between them to wipe the table. "Anything else?" he smiled.

Davis turned on him. "Don't you believe in excusing yourself when you interrupt?" he said. The waiter mumbled an apology. Paynter hastily ordered another round of coffee, as if to cover over the rudeness of his colleague, before lapsing into silence.

The other reporters did not react. They had long ago learned to ignore Davis and his temper, which was showing itself more frequently these days. Jennifer leaned back against the bench in embarrassment, staring at her hands on her lap. God! she thought. Even her hands were looking old today. She heard the others start talking again, arguing about the possibility of a terrorist organisation being behind the murders of Chapman, Ballantine and Whitfield. Baker theorised it was the start of a campaign. Someone soon would claim responsibility.

Davis snorted his disgust. "Terrorists would use bombs, and kill for the publicity. This is not
 a terrorist at work here." There was a note of finality in his voice.

Jennifer watched him for a moment, only half interested. She was grimly aware that Davis was not what he made himself out to be. In the office he projected an air of a serene and capable person. The truth was that he had a temper only barely held in check. She looked at him as he spoke to the others, noticing again the redness of his eyes and that some of his gestures and mannerisms were effeminate in many ways. It was the first time she had seen this side of him – how absorbed in herself she had been since her father's death!

Or perhaps she had always been self-absorbed? Too selfish to worry about other people. People like Alan. She felt her heart thudding in her chest, the way she felt after a hard workout at the dance studio. Was Alan missing her? Did he find himself thinking of her as much as she was of him? These past three evenings she had been visiting her dance studio again, for something to do with herself. Last night she had gone for a glass of wine with her three closest friends, all of whom were delighted to see her back at the studio. Less enthusiastic had been Neville. In her absence he had begun an affair with one of the other dancers. He was embarrassed and could not look her in the eye. No loss, she had thought. Even so, she had not been particularly keen to let him off the hook easily, and had enjoyed his discomfort as he clumsily attempted to explain what had happened.

The arrival of their coffee attracted her attention for a moment. She was in time to see Paynter reluctantly dig deep into his pocket to pay. Baker was derisive. "Couldn't get away with not paying again, heh, Morris?" Paynter ignored him, deliberately counting his change. "I hate a pocket full of coins," he said, by way of an excuse, as he gave the waiter a tip. Jennifer was amused to see him furtively cast a second glance at his change as the waiter slipped the money off his tray into his own pocket.

The conversation continued, dispiritedly, each of them

taking a turn to bomb Baker's idea. Jennifer tried to see some merit in the idea. She searched for angles to pursue, but nothing came. She kept quiet. Instead, she thought about how much she had changed over these past weeks. Usually fun-loving and open, she had become withdrawn and sullen. Without Alan, she felt empty and hopeless.

There had been a common thread running through her relationships with her father and with Alan. In both cases she had wanted them for selfish needs. She had wanted someone to love and be loved by, without the responsibilities and sacrifices inherent in a close relationship.

"Okay, okay," she heard Baker saying. "Bloody hell. It was just an idea. Something we seem to lack these days. Without ideas, we may as well pack our bags and go home." Jennifer heard him but did not realise he was talking directly to her.

"Jennifer? Are you all right?" asked Davis, touching her arm.

"What? Yes. Sorry. Yes, I'm fine."

"I mean, you seem...somewhere else," persisted Davis.

"No. Not at all. I was trying to work out a way of finding some more news, where we can go next for story ideas. I have one idea, but I thought it best to keep under my hat until I have firmed it up a bit." She had no real ideas, but she could think of nothing else to say.

"Well, then tell us what to expect," said Paynter, looking into his black coffee.

"No, I want this to be something solid. I know you will all be pleased if it works out, but don't press me now. Tomorrow, I promise."

She saw Gibson turn away to hide a dark scowl. Davis looked bemused. Sometimes he looked like a lost little boy, thought Jennifer. She expected that from Paynter, with his boyish blonde looks, but Davis was quite a large man. She looked at him afresh. He was also fairly good looking. Had she been blind to that because of Alan? Yes. There was little room for other men in her life with him around.

Baker reacted in the way he always did – an enigmatic smile touched his lips and he looked as if he had some secret knowledge. Paynter looked petulant. "I thought we trusted each other," he said.

Jennifer was abruptly filled with contempt for them all. Not one of them seemed to have the strength Alan possessed. There seemed to be something corrupt in each of them. Perhaps that was true of all journalists? she thought. Perhaps she was like that too. The cynicism finally gets at your soul, rotting you from the inside. She wanted to be alone. She wanted to call Alan. She wanted to be with him, not these men. She stood up, hampered by the table top and the fact she was still hemmed in by Paynter.

"Please excuse me," she said. "I'm not feeling well at all. I must get some fresh air."

"I thought you said you were fine?" said Paynter, concern showing for the first time. He remained sitting, ignoring the fact that he blocked her from leaving.

"May I help?" said Davis. He stood up and held Jennifer by the elbow. She glanced around the table. Baker, Gibson and Paynter remained sitting. Baker was still smiling vacantly, and Gibson was looking at a nearby table.

"No," she said, smiling at Davis. "I just need air. In the meantime, please trust me. Something is coming up. It is worth waiting for."

Under her direct gaze, Paynter wilted. He shuffled out of the booth and stood aside to let her out. She didn't stop to say goodbye.

She slammed open the door, the bell on top of the door jangling a protest, and she heard Gibson's voice: "What's the matter with her?" She thought she heard Baker reply. Probably some platitude, she thought. Baker was always pretending to be so fatherly and know-it-all.

Stop it , she chastised herself. What good is this doing? It's not their fault. It's your own. You should never have told them in the first place, then they would never have talked you into writing the story. The story which had come between her and Alan. Would he talk to her? she wondered.

On impulse, she walked back to her office. The doorman greeted her cheerfully. She rode the lift alone to the editorial department and went to her desk, glad there were only three reporters still in the newsroom. They were each engrossed in typing stories.

She dialled Alan's home number, twisting the cord in her fingers while waiting. He answered on the second ring. "Winters," he said, gruffly.

"Alan, this is Jennifer." She held her breath for a moment.

"I thought I asked you not to call again," he said, finally.

"I know, but you said that when you were still very angry. I hoped you might have cooled down."

"I have cooled down as you put it. The answer is still the same. There is nothing left for us to say Jennifer." His voice was calm, but the words were clipped and cold. He was still livid, she thought. It scared her.

Jennifer felt her nails biting into her palm. "Why won't you at least give me a chance to explain? Let me come and talk to you."

"Because there is nothing you can say that will change what happened. I wish I had never told you. But I did. I can't change it either."

"If we meant anything to each other, anything at all, you'd give me half a chance," she said. "How can you be so damn final."

Silence. She prayed. Just give me a chance. Please.

He sighed. "No. When I think about it, we didn't have much anyway. We didn't really have the chance to build up anything worthwhile."

"Please Alan, don't throw it all away like this. We CAN make it right."

"NO. Don't make a fool of yourself Jennifer, on top of everything else. Just leave well enough alone."

Embarrassment and indignity reddened her face. She curbed an impulse to shout abuse at him. Then the phone clicked in her ear.

"Alan? Alan?"

She put down her own phone, her eyes sweeping the newsroom blankly. Why wouldn't he listen to her? She was going to say she would stop her investigation. She was going to say she had thought about what she wanted more: revenge, or him. For the first time, she knew what she wanted the most. Alan. But now she had no choice. All she had left in the world was revenge.

FORTY

MAY 1, 1986 *I cannot count the number of times I have been back to St Paul's. I wake from my dreams, and the torment of the whispering man, and I feel a compulsion stronger than my resistance. I visit the cathedral in the early morning, and watch the cans and papers being swept up, and all the daily polishing and dusting*

on the ground floor. Electricians, plumbers and painters are busy with unending maintenance work. Services and sessions of public prayer and choir practices go on at all times of the day. Often the sound of choirs fills the cathedral and for a time I lose myself as I listen to voices soaring around the vast spaces of the church, echoing and resonating in perfect harmony.

I drag myself away to go back to work. Back to the team, and Jennifer.

Such disharmony.

Jennifer worries me. She's losing her spark. I can't get her to speak to me. She seems withdrawn, and she's not sharing all she knows with us. Even when Gibson left Jennifer could barely acknowledge he was leaving the team. After the roasting she gave Bergman, I was surprised at how passively she took his resignation. Gibson told us he had had enough of chasing after shadows, of pestering his police contacts for leads they didn't have. He said our meetings were eating into his social life. He said the police were wondering whether he really had come off the crime beat. He recommended we all call it a day. When he left, I could see Jennifer watching him all the way to the door. There was no expression in her eyes, and I wondered what she was thinking. The rest of us tried to console her.

Now, we are only four.

***

May 2. Tonight, the breaks went against me. Walked down Kings Road, to the tube station at Sloane Square. Wanted to get someone on a train. Thought about the number of times I'd been the only one in a carriage. Part of me tried to resist. I wanted to save myself for someone more deserving, someone who would be noticed. But I had no-one in mind.

So I took my revolver and caught the tube, and rode the tube for most of the night, until after midnight. Went around and around and around on the Circle Line. Got off at various stations to wait for the next train. Would stand there, sometimes alone, sometimes with several other people on the platform, looking for the right opportunity. Would feel the rush of air from the tunnel before the train arrived, and my heart would start to race. Perhaps THIS train would have a deserted carriage, bar one person. But the right opportunity never came. Would sit in the train, my hands in my overcoat, the beard itching, sweating, one hand on the revolver, and I would study other passengers. They never knew I had the power to take their lives.

Came close on one occasion. Two people were left on the carriage with me after the South Kensington stop. One was a young man, dressed in denims, carrying a leather hand bag. He looked young and fit. The other was an elderly man, a businessman, it seemed. I would shoot the young man first. Then I would watch the older man as he understood he would be next to die.

But I couldn't do it. Too many risks. Finally, I returned home. In reprisal, the dream lashed my sleep till I had to surrender any thought of rest. Cannot take another night like that.

***

May 3. Something terrifying in the very deepest and darkest part of my soul has been awakened. I can feel it stirring, and stretching, and all I can do is watch, mesmerised, and wait. Every day now it pulls and strains at the bonds that have so far held it in check, but I can feel those chains coming loose at their moorings. For the first time, I begin to understand the dreams that have plagued me over the years, the horrors and terrors that have coloured my sleep.

Whatever this beast is, however unspeakable a demon it might be, I fear it is the source of me. And I fear that the crossbow shot which killed Chapman has unleashed it forever.

FORTY-ONE

FOR JOSEPH Walker, life was a bitch. It wasn't always that way, he thought, as he looked up at what, in his opinion, was the best known landmark in London, possibly the whole of England. St Paul's Cathedral. As usual, he failed to gain any inspiration from the house of God. It was a hard, cold concrete and stone building. Nothing more. It was as cold as this April night, he thought. And this April night was colder than he had known it in years - or perhaps his old bones were just feeling it more? The night was miserable, gloomy, depressing. Now that most of his friends had gone, claimed by age and cold weather and lack of will, there was no-one left with whom he could hold a conversation. People these days avoided talking with strangers, especially those who wore tattered overcoats and ropes for a belt and didn't know when they'd last seen soap and water. Life was sad, sadistic and barren. There was nothing, but nothing, to anticipate. Only things to fear. Staircases, for example. They seemed steeper lately. And yet, he preferred them to escalators. The underground was filled with the damn things. Somehow escalators seemed to scare him more than the awful prospect of a flight of stairs. He felt out of control on an escalator, always about to fall. Yes, they definitely scared him more.

There were so many things that frightened him now. He was even afraid of children. They played horrible jokes on him. Like the two schoolboys on the tube this morning. He had managed to slip on to a train, and had fallen asleep on the seat. He woke up gagging. Something was stuck in his throat. He choked it up to find it was a tiny ball of cigarette paper. Two kids opposite him were giggling uncontrollably. Obviously he had been sleeping with his mouth open and they had thrown the paper ball into his mouth. Little shits.

Walker wondered where his life had gone, how he had come to this. Yes. Life really was a bitch. And he was hungry to boot. What could he do about that? He could stroll down Carter Lane, heading past the pubs and restaurants he knew in the area. There might be something in their rubbish bags he could forage. Maybe the restaurants had done badly tonight? If so, that would mean leftovers for him. The owners didn't believe in letting anything go to waste, and often gave their leftovers to tramps in the area.

Walker hitched his coat, attempting to keep it closed around his chest. He coughed and hawked phlegm on to the pavement. Jesus. It was bright yellow. His sinuses had been streaming all day. Come to think of it, he wasn't feeling that good.

He shuffled towards Carter Lane, grateful as he crossed Ludgate Hill from St Paul's Cathedral that there were no cars about. At this time of night, long after the pubs had shut, traffic was usually pretty thin. In any case, he would not have been able to run. Things took him much longer these days. More years ago than he cared to remember he had been quite an athlete. At school he had been the fastest runner in his class. Now he hobbled across the road, moving away from the giant dome of St Paul's, into the quiet back streets of The City of London.

When he reached Carter Lane, Walker paused. Which way? He decided to wind his way down Carter Street, past the Rising Sun pub, to New Bridge Street, then up to Bride Lane, past St Bride's Church, then along Fleet Street. Bound to find SOME-

THING along the way. If he had no luck he could wend his way down to Cardboard City on the Embankment. He would spend the rest of the night there, out of the wind.

Walker lumbered down the narrow lane, occasionally stopping to inspect a dustbin, or peer down an alleyway. He picked out a Daily Telegraph from a waste bin. The newspaper would come in handy later, when he found somewhere to sleep. Keep him warm. He stuffed it into his coat, spreading it across his chest. For the moment it could act as a wind shield. In another bin he found half a stale sandwich, still wrapped in greaseproof paper, and he munched gingerly on the bread as he plodded into Broadway, passing the Queen's Head pub. He explored the food in his mouth with his tongue. You never knew what people put on their sandwiches, and his old teeth and gums were not up to any surprises. It was too gloomy and misty to see clearly what was on the bread. Looked like some kind of savoury spread. Better than nothing.

As he neared the "Food for Health" restaurant, he realized that a faint mist was swirling around. His footsteps thumped drearily on the road. Abruptly, he paused and stopped chewing. Had he heard something behind him? A cat? No. There were no cats around these parts that he knew of. Probably nothing. He couldn't trust his ears anymore anyway. He had noticed how people always spoke much softer and less clearly nowadays. Needed to enunciate better, the lot of them. Walker trudged steadily, ignoring the pain in his feet and legs. He was used to that. The lights of New Bridge Street beckoned him.

He stopped. What was that? Another sound from up the street. He began shuffling towards the traffic lights in front of him, glancing back over his shoulder. He could see nothing in the gloom. Nothing. When he got to New Bridge Street he hurried over the pedestrian crossing without waiting for the lights to change in his favour, stopping in the centre of the road to allow an empty taxi to pass. Then he shuffled to the far side of the road. He reached the safety of the pavement and looked back, studying the shadows behind him for a minute. There really was nothing there. Anyway, what had he to be scared about?

Walker knew the tides of the streets well. It was about two am, and it would still be a while before people appeared on the streets in any significant numbers again. He continued walking toward Ludgate Circus, passing the marble columns of Fleet House before turning into the narrow Bride Lane. His heart was pounding. He stopped to catch his breath. Even though he had been walking only slightly faster than normal he was wheezing, and he leaned forward, his hands on his knees, trying to control a dizzy spell. In that moment he yearned for his youth, for a chance to try it all again. He wished he had persisted at teacher training college, that he had never met that bitch Edna, that he had never let her have the kid, that he had tried harder to keep a job, and stay off the booze. Oh God, just one more chance.

He heard the sound of someone running. Not the click and pat of leather-soled shoes, but the padding of running shoes. He crept back to the corner, leaned against the wall, sliding his head slowly past the corner, peering warily up and down the street. He could see nothing. The sound of running had stopped. Jesus, this was unnerving him. What was going on?

He pushed away from the wall with both hands, like someone pushing a boat away from its mooring. He turned and pulled his coat closer to him. Somehow he felt even colder all of a sudden, as if there had been a quick drop in temperature. He shook his head, muttering under his breath. Stupid old fool. There was no reason for it to be colder. He followed Bride Lane as it swept sharply right, heading up to Fleet Street. On his left was a 10 foot high wall. He felt closed in a canyon of concrete. He drew closer to the entrance to Bride Court, a shopping thoroughfare, on his right. He paused to catch his breath. He leaned against the wall. The brightly lit Fleet Street was just a short distance away now.

He decided against cutting through the alley that ran parallel to Fleet Street, separating the stone yard of St Bride's Church from the buildings along the high road. One of those buildings was the Old Bell pub. The alley was a narrow passage of hostile shadows he would rather avoid at the moment. There were two lights in the alley that he could see, but in spite of them there was simply too much darkness for his liking. In the mist, each of the lights of the alleyway sported a multi-coloured halo.

Walker was looking down at his shoes, one hand against the wall, the other holding closed his coat. His breathing was easing up a bit. He saw white flashes on the edges his vision. This always happened when he exerted himself. He glanced up towards Fleet Street to see how far he had to go until he was in the brighter light again. Something dark caught his eye and he turned to look into Bride Court.

And choked back a scream. A man was standing at the far end of the thoroughfare, watching him. All Walker could see was a silhouette in front of the streetlight. The figure was standing with legs apart, hands on hips, dressed all in black.

"Jesus," whispered Walker. "Jesus Christ."

He held his hand to his heart and bowed his head, miming a heart attack. He wanted to indicate to the man that he had given him a fright. The figure did not move.

Suddenly Walker felt cold again. And very, very vulnerable. He began trudging towards Fleet Street, muttering curses. He heard the sound of running feet once more. He thought the figure might be darting around to block him off, which meant he would walk straight into the bastard's arms if he continued straight. Walker turned left into the alleyway alongside St Bride's church, heaving himself up the six steps, heading towards the large Reuters Building and another exit there, opposite the Daily Express building. If he was lucky he would get there before the shadowman.

Who was this person? What did he want, anyway? What would anybody want with a tramp? Walker stopped for a moment, reflecting on the questions. Too true. What would he want? He was letting himself get frightened for nothing. But he WAS frightened. His lips were dry, his tongue sticking to the roof of his mouth, strands of spittle like mozzarella gluing his lips together, his heart racing wildly, pushed to its limits by rushing around like this.

He started his lumbering walk again. Only to stop two paces later. The man was in front of him again. This time Walker could see more of him. He was dressed in dark clothes, and he was wearing a balaclava, standing with his arms at his sides, breathing heavily. The holes in the balaclava - for eyes and mouth - were like bottomless pits. Walker had the eerie feeling there was nothing behind them.

He called out: "Good evening!" His voice sounded old and frail, and frightened.

No response.

"Cold out tonight," said Walker, trying hard to sound friendly.

Still no response.

Damn it, thought Walker. Who the hell WAS this maniac?

He turned away, starting to walk back towards Brides Lane. He looked over his shoulder. The man was gone. Thank God for that, thought Walker. That was starting to get most unpleasant. He paused for a moment, leaning against the retaining wall of the church yard, which was above his head. The alley was at most two paces wide, and he felt claustrophobic.

The flashes at the edges of his vision were back. He shook his head, trying to clear the spots. He put his hands on his knees and leaned forward, resisting an impulse to vomit. He would lose the only food he had found that night if he succumbed. A rush of bile burned his throat. He spat onto the ground. Then he looked up.

Into the eyes of the shadowman. The man was standing three paces away. Walker could see his eyes. They were small, glittering reflections of light in the black holes of the balaclava. Walker saw another flash. In the man's right hand, which he held close to his thigh.

A gun. No. Not a gun. More like a cannon.

Walker looked back into the man's eyes. Now there was only an infinite blackness. The hand with the gun rose slowly. The barrel was pointing directly at Walker. Oh Jesus. So this was how it was all going to end!

Walker felt resistance rush out of him, like air hissing from a punctured wheel. His eyes were fixed on the muzzle. As he waited, he felt an ooze of warmth on his leg, running down his inner thigh. In shame he looked down at the ground, his mind numb.

The night exploded. He was whirled around, the buildings spinning, feeling as he had when dumped by a wave in his youth, out of control, being battered from all sides by massive forces, rolling, rolling until the wave had run its course, leaving him disoriented, lying on the wet sand, dazed and shocked. Relieved still to be alive. He heard the echoes of a blast, like a distant peal of thunder, sensing the flash from the muzzle of the gun. He was lying on his back. Flashes like skyrockets were going off in his eyes and he no longer felt cold. He couldn't feel anything.

A numbness spread out from the centre of his chest. He could dimly make out the man, who seemed as if he was standing far away, at the end of a tunnel. Ten or fifteen paces away. Walker was shocked at how far the bullet had propelled him. He tried to stand up, but the muscles in his stomach refused to assist. He rolled on to his side, using his arms to push himself up. He got one knee under himself, a hand against a wall, the other leg into position, then he grabbed at a ledge with both hands, using it to pull himself erect. He stood there, shaking and wavering drunkenly.

Walker turned to look at his assailant again. If he was going to go, let it be with some dignity, some pride. He drew his shoulders back and tried to look into the place where the eyes should have been. The man stepped closer. Everything seemed distorted, like a funfair mirror. Walker leaned back against the wall. His legs would not support him unaided.

He watched impassively as the man stopped in front of him. About two paces away, slightly to Walker's left. The gun came up again, this time pointing at his face.

"Why?" Walker had to know.

But the man was silent, almost as if he was unable to talk, a mute angel of death.

Walker tried to push himself away from the wall. He saw the man flinch. The gun was jerked downwards. Walker realized he was falling forward, then saw another flash from the barrel. His fall was checked as the blast flung him back against the wall, then as he bounced forward again he put out his hands, clutching for support, his fingers closing on the man's pull-over. He slid downward and crashed face first into the hard, unyielding concrete.

Walker could no longer hear or feel anything. Out of the corner of his eye, he saw something flutter to the ground near his face. It looked like a flower, he thought dispassionately. Pieces of teeth filled his mouth. He used his tongue to try to shove out the bits. He wasn't aware of his twitching legs and arms, nor was he aware of the sound of unhurried, fading footsteps. Walker was grateful for the numbness. There was no more cold, no more ache in the legs, no more shafts of pain from his feet. In a way, he felt safe and warm. But I'm not safe. I'm shot.

"Help," he croaked. His voice was a hoarse, futile whisper.

He tried to drag himself towards the Reuters Building. He felt himself inching forward. It's not far, he thought. If he could get to the light, someone would see him, and get some help. If he could just make it to the light...

FORTY-TWO

"IT DOESN'T make any sense at all," said Winters, hunching his shoulders inside his raincoat.

"Oh yes it does. It most certainly does," said Van Deventer. A fine drizzle had matted the balding Dutchman's remaining hair to his scalp, and drops coated his spectacles. In spite of the discomfort, Van Deventer seemed not to notice the miserable weather. "We've got a psychopath on our hands," he continued. "The bastard is a vicious killer, a series murderer. This just confirms my theory."

Van Deventer seemed pleased. He had been the first to moot the idea of a random killer. To his credit, he had been able to resist reminding everyone. But Winters felt badly demoralised.

After his mistake with Jennifer, he had barely been able to come to terms with being removed from command of the case. Now his refusal to accept the idea that they were dealing with a serial killer was going to be another black mark against him. Especially if it turned out the killer WAS a madman.

Winters stared moodily at the Dutchman. The body of Joseph Walker had been discovered at five that morning, by a young woman on her way to begin an early shift in the Reuters building. Luckily the first officers on the scene had held her there for questioning to ensure she would not leak the story to the Press. They had released a brief statement saying simply that the body of a vagrant had been discovered near Fleet Street. The story appeared in the afternoon editions of the papers, buried amid other short stories on inside pages.

Both Winters and Van Deventer had been at the scene soon after the discovery of Walker's body, and had returned together to Scotland Yard after the corpse had been taken away. They had spent the rest of the day huddled in meetings with Maxwell and other senior colleagues, awaiting the results of the forensic investigation, and discussing what they were going to do if it was proved Walker was more blood of The Rose.

Then Patterson had joined them with the bad news. The flower discovered in Bride Lane was a rose; the bullets that killed Walker were fired from the same weapon used in the murder of Whitfield; and fibres found under Walker's fingernails were matched with those found on the industrialist.

Van Deventer had insisted they return to the scene of the killing. "I want to walk around. See if I can pick up anything. Are you coming?" he asked Winters.

Reluctantly, Winters agreed. He had been keeping quiet since Van Deventer had taken over, doing exactly as the Dutchman requested, anxious not to allow him to see just how disturbed he was. Winters had to admit to himself that he was confused. He knew that Van Deventer was aware of his state of mind, and was doing his best to help him through it. Now that the Dutchman had what he wanted, he was beginning to show his softer side, and several times that day had defended Winters to Maxwell.

Even so, Winters felt bewildered and disorientated. Everything was confusing. This case, the evidence, the killings, his feelings about Jennifer, his missing her, his feelings about Van Deventer, everything. He felt like a child again. He wished his father was there. Over the past two nights, he had been alarmed to find himself dreaming about his parents frequently. Worse, he was also dreaming about Jennifer. He could not get her out of his thoughts. He could hear Jennifer breathing in bed next to him, he could sense her presence in his home, every day. Oh HELL, he missed her! Standing with Van Deventer in the rain in Brides Lane, Winters wondered whether things could possibly get worse. What could he do? Events seemed to be completely out of his control. The thought terrified him.

"Each of the killings before Walker showed careful planning and research. What made you think we had a madman on our hands?" he asked. His voice was flat. He kept his hands in his pockets, his collar turned up against the wet, following Van Deventer listlessly as the Dutchman prowled the area.

"He has to make a mistake sometime," said the Dutchman, ignoring the question. "We'll get him."

"How can you be so sure?" said Winters. "So far we have three descriptions of a man seen waiting in Crane Park before the shooting. On this one we have even less."

Winters was referring to the fact that intensive interviews of regular users of the park had so far netted only a hazy description of a man in dark clothes, smoking cigarettes. Again a beard was mentioned. Patterson speculated that the killer might be an actor, someone with access to a wardrobe of costumes and make up. His comment had spurred Van Deventer to order a detective to start checking shops that sold theatrical props. The Dutchman was a new man.

Winters had overheard him talking to his wife on the telephone. He had heard Van Deventer whisper that he now had the chance to put his shame behind him. "Perhaps now I can bury the scandal forever," he had said. Funny how the wheel of fortune spun, thought Winters. A week ago it had been his own star on the rise.

The Dutchman led them to the area where Walker had been shot. Standing over the spot where Walker had died, Van Deventer said: "I can sense his presence all the time. But only his signs, never him." He looked around, stopping as his eyes fell on the entrance to St Bride's Church. "Let's go up there," he said, setting off. Winters followed, still hunched against the rain. He spoke to Van Deventer's back. "The bastard watched Chapman and cold-bloodedly chose his moment. He lured Ballantine with the only bait that COULD have got the lawyer to a car park in the middle of the night. He knew the personal habits of a rich and powerful businessman. Walker is the odd man out. The only one who doesn't fit the pattern. But as for the others, the killer researched them all. How did The Rose know all the most relevant things about the victims? Why did he switch tactics? Why go after an old down-and-out when all your other victims have been rich and influential?"

"If we are dealing with a psychopath, there will never be a motive, except in the twisted mind of the killer. Now we have to change our tactics too."

"What do you mean?" asked Winters, stopping. Van Deventer didn't notice. Winters had to walk rapidly to catch him up. The Dutchman stopped at the open door of the church. He looked up at the four tiers of the steeple. "This was Sir Christopher Wren's work," he said, offhandedly.

"I said, what do you mean?"

Van Deventer ignored the question. "I can feel him strongly here. He's been here, I know it," he said.

Winters shook his head in frustration. He turned and looked out towards Fleet Street, wondering how just a few hours ago a man could have been murdered here without anyone hearing a thing. Now, the street was choked with traffic. People scurried along the pavement, clashing umbrellas as they dodged puddles. Detectives had tried to trace the movements of Joseph Walker, and had reconstructed his last hours until approximately eleven that night. The last time anyone had seen him alive was at a hamburger joint at Ludgate Circus. The shop owner thought he had given Walker an unused bread roll. It was common practice to give the homeless the day's leftovers.

What had happened to him afterwards? Why would anyone want to kill him? For that matter, why would anyone want to kill Whitfield? The businessman had recently announced his intention to resign, and hand over the reins of his multi-national company to a younger man. Detectives were interviewing colleagues, neighbours and friends of the millionaire to try and find some motive. So far, nothing.

Van Deventer turned back to Winters. He had an obsessed gleam in his eye. "At first I was convinced he was an assassin. A professional hitman. I was even more convinced after the death of Ballantine. But then one or two things started coming up that threw me."

"Like what?"

"We learned from Stockton that The Rose got his weapons from him. But Stockton's impression the first time they met was that the man did not know very much about guns. We discovered from the car hire firm that the man used a pseudonym. Harold Hastings. A trifle too flamboyant and mocking for a professional, if you ask me. Then, his victims. We can find no trace, absolutely no trace, of any links between them. Nothing."

"So?"

"So that could mean they are being selected at random. That there ARE no links. And there IS no motive."

"I was so convinced he was a professional. Now, I'm not so sure anymore," admitted Winters.

"Why would a professional hitman warn his victim he was going to kill him? It doesn't make sense," said the Dutchman.

"But if you look at most random killers, their murders are all brutal slayings that involved some form of mutilation. There is a terrible, grotesque pattern of anger in their killings. Chapman, Whitfield, Ballantine, and even Walker, have been taken out cold bloodedly, almost clinically. That doesn't sound to me like a lunatic running amok."

"An assassin knows his weapons."

"That could have been a ploy. What about the second weapon? He specifically asked for a 357 Magnum. THAT sounds like someone who knows what he wants!"

Van Deventer shook his head, shaking loose a spray of drops. "I'm not convinced. But I could do with some coffee. Hot coffee. Let's go back to the office."

He began walking back towards Fleet Street, looking once more down the alley to where the body had been found. "If this is a random killer, then each time he murders someone he will be gaining immense satisfaction about the publicity he is getting. We should try to end that."

Winters kept pace with Van Deventer, who was clearly on

his way back to their car. "What would that gain us?" he asked.

"I don't know. An edge we didn't have. We cut the man off from his supply of information about our investigation. Keep him guessing. Perhaps we can use the papers to throw a scare into him by pretending to know more than we do."

At the mention of newspapers, Winters grimaced. He knew he was not far from Jennifer at the moment. He glanced up the street towards the Courier building.

"Apart from anything else, we'll be doing ourselves a service," continued Van Deventer, oblivious to Winters' anguish. "A great service."

"How?"

"Well, can you imagine how the public will react if we told them about our lunatic theory? They can cope with the thought of terrorists, or a conspiracy. There's a kind of order and logic to that. They feel safer. But a madman has no logic."

Winters nodded, understanding.

Van Deventer smiled grimly. "If they know our man is a madman, each of them feels vulnerable. And who knows, they could be right."

He looked back towards the lane. "We all know now that there will be more murders. Without a doubt. There IS a pattern to these killings. A link, somewhere. No matter how obscure, we have to try and find it. While we are looking, we need to keep every advantage that we have."

"What advantages do we have?"

"Only one," said Van Deventer. "The fact we know he is insane."

"What good will that do us?"

"I don't know. But I suggest we keep it close to our chests. Tell no-one. Keep the bastard complacent. That way, he'll make mistakes. And then we'll get him."

Winters was still not convinced. But he did not argue. Instead, he said: "You may be right. I just hope he makes a mistake BEFORE he finds his next victim."

FORTY-THREE

MAY 5, 1986 *What have I done? What made me do it? The dreams. The clouds, the rain, the man, his voice. They drove me to kill Chapman, and Ballantine, and Whitfield, and Walker. The voice. It was my father. Guiding me. He wanted to make me into a twisted parody of himself. He is the man in my dreams. The man in the chair. God help me.*

He has come to get me.

***

I toyed with the tramp, like a cat does with its prey. Trapped him next to St Bride's Church and he went into a paroxysm of coughing. When he regained control, with spittle still running down his unshaven chin, he looked up at me. Slowly. Into my eyes. In that instant he knew his life was over.

Raised my arm, hoping he would try to run. He just stood there. His gaze did not waver. He didn't even look at the gun. (I would have been compelled to look at the barrel, to watch my death coming.) Instead, he looked down at the ground and I felt anger and loathing. He carried around with him defeat and degradation, like a pall. He carried an awful stench of stale sweat, and cheap booze, and fear. At once I saw a vision of my own father, as he was when he had been at the bottle. Unshaven, pitiful, glassy-eyed, mindless, beaten.

I pulled the trigger. Again. Two bullets in the chest. THROUGH the chest. He's dead, but he haunts me still. It's that face. I cannot blot it out of my mind. That slobbering, unshaven, pathetic, drunken face.

***

Tonight, for the first time, I managed in my storm dream to get closer to the chair, to discover why I could never make out the mystery man's face. It was because he was wearing a misted up plastic bag over his head. I watched as the mist inside the bag slowly cleared. Then I saw living eyes in a dead man's skull.

***

Help me, please...help me escape this vision. It is my father's drunken face underneath the plastic bag, his eyes staring out at me, his tongue hanging out, the bag still, not a sign of breath. His eyes find me, wherever I stand. They follow me around, moving in the sockets of a skull, just the eyes still alive, bloodless flesh flapping from bleached cheekbones, things slimy and green slithering from his mouth, and all the while those eyes fix on me. Now I know the source of my dreams. It is my father. It is because he knows I'm the one who killed him.

***

Been vomiting for the past hour. Nothing more to give the basin. The only way to still myself is to sit and write. As if talking with a friend. Someone who will listen, without passing judgment. All these years... You wipe out a memory. Your mind blots out a horror too awful to contemplate. But only part of your mind has erased that horror. The other part nurtures it, keeps it for moments when your resistance is weak, when you cannot wrestle it back to the grisly dark dungeon of your conscience.

I had put it all behind me. Except in my sleep. Tonight, accompanied by wave upon wave of battering nausea, the reality finally broke free of its chains, forcing me to confront again the events of that terrible, terrible night. The night I murdered my father.

***

He was drunk. Yet again. He beat me so savagely I thought he would kill me. I do not remember him stopping the beating. I think I must have passed out. Then HE passed out, in his favourite chair. I crept out of my room, to find him unconscious in the living room. He was sitting in his chair, his head lolling from side to side. He was moaning. Sometimes I thought I could hear him saying my mother's name. It sounded as if he was calling to her. Calling FOR her.

I knew what I had to do. I went to the kitchen and found a clear plastic bag. In his wardrobe I found several of his ties. I fastened his wrists and ankles to the chair. Then I threw a tie around his neck, followed by the plastic bag. Once I had it in position, I gently pulled the tie over the rim of the plastic bag, then I yanked it tight, sealing the bag. I sat down in front of his chair.

He struggled weakly when his air began to run out. He started to vomit. He tried to free his hands, but he was still in a stupor, and he was like a moth fluttering at a flame. I watched him die. I watched the plastic bag mist up with his breath and I saw his attempts to free himself, and I marvelled at how little effort he put into saving his own life (perhaps he wanted to die?. I sat there until I was sure, until I could see no more movement of the bag, and only then did I get up.

Without looking at his face, I undid the ties and took them back to his bedroom. Then I took the plastic bag to the kitchen sink and washed out his vomit. I turned the bag inside out and dried it, then put it back with all the other bags in the kitchen. Finally I went back to bed, and slept. I remember the smell in that room. It was sickening. Stale sweat and fear and booze and vomit. Only once in the recent past have I come close to that stench again.

It was the smell of the tramp.

FORTY-FOUR

VAN DEVENTER was waiting for Jennifer as she emerged from St James's Park tube station on to Broadway. He was wearing a dark raincoat, and he stood wiping the rain from his spectacles. At first he did not see her. She stood watching him. Behind him was the huge New Scotland Yard building. He had walked but a short way from his office to meet her. She had caught the tube from Blackfriars, and reflected on how much she detested using the underground. She opened her umbrella to protect herself from the soaking drizzle. The movement caught Van Deventer's eye, and he put on his spectacles, smiling as he recognised her.

"You look more like Hugh every time I see you," he said as he took her elbow. "Come on, I'll escort you back to my office."

Jennifer resisted. "No. I don't want to go in there. Not just yet, anyway. I'd rather we found a place to have a cup of coffee."

Van Deventer looked puzzled, then slowly smiled. "I understand," he said. He looked directly across the road, pointing at a sandwich bar. "Let's go in there," he suggested.

Together, they crossed the road, sheltering under her umbrella. A queue had formed at the door, but Van Deventer shouldered his way past the miserable people waiting to get in the shop. "They want takeaways," he explained, as the people uncomplainingly let them past. At the back of the sandwich bar, out of sight of the door, Van Deventer and Jennifer found an empty table and took their seats. The few mirrors on the walls had steamed up and Jennifer could barely make out her own face as she stared into one of them.

Van Deventer ordered the coffee from a disinterested waitress before turning to Jennifer again. He lowered his face to his hands, rubbing his eyes. He seemed to be splashing water on his face. He looked a tired old man. His eyes were sunken, hiding in shadowed sockets. He had not shaved well that morning. His tie was pulled to one side underneath his raincoat. She tried to remember what her father had said about this man. Hugh Chapman had not often talked with his daughter, but when he had she had always been the perfect audience, hanging on his every word. He had spoken of an immense respect for this policeman. She wondered how her father could have maintained a relationship with Van Deventer over the years without regular contact? How could they have been so fond of each other when they had seen so little of each other? She had once asked her father. He had spoken of circumstance, about another time another place, about a mutual respect, about being individually too busy, about little common interest beyond crime. He had even mentioned wasted opportunities, incompatible wives, and sheer laziness. She had not understood. If they had liked each other, felt even a trace of desire to see more of each other, what had kept them apart?

Van Deventer seemed to sense her scrutiny. "Yes, Jennifer, what may I do for you?" It was a muffled query, coming from behind his hands.

"I already told you. On the telephone. I want you to help me with Alan."

Van Deventer placed his hands on the table, slowly, deliberately.

"I want him back. I know you know what happened. I don't know if you understand why. That doesn't matter. I've made a terrible mistake and I want to try and undo it. I need your help."

Van Deventer watched her closely, his eyes slowly softening. "I have to be honest. I'm not sure anything will help you now."

"Why?" Jennifer suppressed a shudder. Van Deventer's words were almost exactly those she had dreaded she would hear.

"Alan was…is…extremely upset. He hasn't said much, but he's not the same person. Not the same person at all. A part of him is ripped away, and I don't know if anything will put it back. What you did ran against everything he believes in. Everything."

"Is he ... I mean, does he ..."

"Talk about you? No. Not much. I tried once, but he cut me dead. The only thing that might help is time. He may get over it. But not at the moment. He's too wound up in this case, too involved with the conflicts it evokes in him. On top of everything else, he is badly demoralised about being removed from command of the investigation. Worse, I'm the one he least wanted to have to answer to. He is too confused at the moment to be rational. He's not the same man at all."

Jennifer was horrified. It did not sound like Alan at all. She tried to judge whether Van Deventer was telling the truth, but he stared back at her evenly and deliberately.

"All I need is the chance to see him again. I know I can

convince him I'm sorry. " Her voice lacked the conviction of her words.

Van Deventer smiled, wistfully. "Will that be good enough? I don't know Jennifer. I would love to help you patch it up. But I honestly can't see it. You betrayed him. If you know this young man at all you'll know that's the one thing he can't forgive."

Jennifer sat motionless. She remembered sitting in her father's study one night, as he chastised her for stealing from her mother's handbag. She had been a seven-year-old child then, but the same feelings of shame were sweeping over her now.

Van Deventer went on: "It would help if you made a gesture. Back off a little, give him room to manoeuvre. Tell him you've given up your hunt for The Rose."

Jennifer considered. Did she want to do that? Could she do that? Even for Alan? Why should she? Why did it all have to be so complicated?

Van Deventer sensed her indecision. "Take it from me Jennifer. I know that as long as you are involved with this investigation the conflict will arise again and again. Even if you get him back, the same thing would happen. And then you will lose him forever."

Jennifer was stung. She was about to rebuke the Dutchman when the waitress arrived with the coffees. She waited, then said: "What makes you think that I'd do the same thing all over again?"

Van Deventer brought out his handkerchief, and removed his spectacles. He rubbed them intently. "The apple never falls far from the tree, Jennifer," he said, peering at her shortsightedly. "Never. You forget I knew your father, and his commitment and stubbornness, and – yes - his ruthlessness. I'm pretty sure you hold dear the same ideals he did, perhaps with even less flexibility."

"What's that supposed to mean?"

Van Deventer considered. He replaced his spectacles. "I never had any children of my own. We couldn't. I have always regretted that. I wanted to be able to teach someone about life. Teach them things I know. Things I've learned. Many of them the hard way. I remember what it was like to be young like you. And I know that you haven't had much time to learn some of the cruel facts about life. One of them is that your ideals have to be compromised sometimes."

"I don't understand."

"You won't. Not for a while."

"I want my father's killer found. How can you call that an 'ideal'?"

"Which do you want more? Alan? Or your father's murderer? You have to decide."

Customers at the surrounding tables were staring curiously at them as their voices grew louder. Jennifer glared at several of them defiantly, then returned her eyes to Van Deventer.

Who did this man think he was? she fumed. No wonder Alan found him so abrasive. He was so damned arrogant. His faint Dutch accent only seemed to accentuate his indelicate approach. She decided to change the subject. "Did you bring the new photofits? On the phone you promised I could see them."

"Jennifer! Stop being so blinkered. Stop before you destroy yourself. Stop while you still have a chance to save your relationship with Alan. Don't mess up a chance like this. Don't."

Jennifer turned away, holding back her rage, and her tears.

Still looking away, she said: "Have you got them?"

The Dutchman refused to answer. She turned back to face him. She said: "The truth is I happen to agree with you. I don't think you can help me with Alan. Even if you could, I don't believe Alan would listen to you. Or me. You were my last desperate chance, but I'm afraid you're right. Nothing can help me. Now I've got nothing more to lose. So I'd rather you helped me with my investigation."

Van Deventer looked appalled. "What?" he said, leaning back from the table.

"You heard me. I said I want you to help me with my investigation."

"Are you mad?" He was shaking his head in disbelief. "I couldn't help you with your investigation, even if I wanted to."

"You have no choice," said Jennifer.

"What?" he spluttered. "What?"

"I said you have no choice. You will help me."

Van Deventer stood up. "I'm leaving Jennifer. Here's some money for the coffee. I don't have to listen to this madness."

Coins clattered on the table as Van Deventer emptied his hip pocket. His mouth was grimly set, and a dark scowl made him look almost comical. He began walking out of the sandwich bar. Jennifer did not look up at him. She took a deep breath, lifting her coffee cup with both hands. As he drew level with her chair, she said, softly: "Remember Ian Campbell?"

The Dutchman stopped. "What?" He bent closer to her. "What did you say?"

"Campbell," said Jennifer. "Drugs. Policemen. Suicide. That Ian Campbell."

The Dutchman said nothing. Jennifer could feel his eyes on her. She could sense his shock without having to look at him. She sipped her coffee. Then she said, coldly: "I know what really happened. I have the evidence. It was in my father's belongings."

Finally, Jennifer looked up at the Dutchman. He was staring at her in horror. She felt empty, cold, without pity. She looked pointedly at Van Deventer's empty chair. "If I have to, I'll use it."

Van Deventer walked slowly back to his chair, sitting down stiffly, still in shock. "What...what sort of evidence?"

"My father taped conversations. He took copious notes about the drugs ring supposedly led by Campbell. Those notes name you as his source. And they would make a wonderful story for my newspaper."

Van Deventer shook his head. He looked stunned. Blood had drained from his face, leaving him looking deathly ill.

"What do you suppose that revelation would do for your career now? There are a lot of your colleagues who would like to get their hands on those notes."

Van Deventer said, dazedly: "Hugh said he had destroyed the notes. I don't understand."

Jennifer's voice was still a flat monotone. She took little pleasure in destroying the Dutchman this way. A part of her tried to resist the force that was driving her. Whatever it was, she found it ugly, frightening, but powerful. She was revolted at herself. But still she could not stop. "All I want is a little help. I want to know what is going on."

"They were all guilty," said Van Deventer, staring at the table, his eyes unseeing. "I saw them. They laughed in my face. They said I would never prove it. The bastards were as guilty as sin."

Jennifer persisted. "Will you help me?"

"It was my word against theirs. Even so, I tried to report them. No-one would believe me. All my senior offices said I should shut up. They were going to cover it up. They said it was for the good of the force. They would act against Campbell in their own way."

Jennifer looked at the Dutchman. His eyes were haunted.

"I told Hugh about it. I couldn't let them get away with it. Then Ian shot himself. And those bastards cleared him posthumously. Not because he was innocent, but because they didn't want mud sticking to the police force. My life has never been the same. Never. I thought I'd managed at least to dull the pain. All the humiliation and hatred. My career in pieces. People were starting to forget. And this case. It was a chance to make amends. To make things better. I hoped it would help me to leave it all behind. Finally. Yet somehow I always knew it would come back one day. I didn't think Hugh would be the source. He always stood by me. Always. But he didn't account for you ..." His voice trailed off.

Jennifer felt nauseous as her revulsion at herself threatened to overwhelm her. She gritted her teeth. She had come so far now..."The photofits. May I see them?"

Still Van Deventer did not hear her.

"Superintendent!" she snapped.

Van Deventer lifted glazed eyes to her. "Why, Jennifer? Why do you do this? You destroyed Alan. Now me. What drives you like this?"

Jennifer started to defend herself, to explain how she couldn't help what she was doing, but clamped her mouth shut.

"Don't you understand?" continued Van Deventer. "There is a growing possibility your father's death may never be solved. Never."

He could see Jennifer's puzzlement and pressed on. "Your father's killer may be a random murderer. He may stop killing suddenly and if he does we'll never find him."

"My father's murder wasn't some random slaying. It was planned. So was Ballantine's murder. And Whitfield's. Three prominent people assassinated. That must be easier to solve than some maniac's murder spree?"

Van Deventer shook his head.

Jennifer pressed on. "Are you saying this is not a

conspiracy? Are you saying that some madman is responsible for this?"

"I don't know," said Van Deventer, realizing his mistake.

"So why do you bring it up?"

"To show you that you may wait forever. And to show you that if the might of Scotland Yard can't catch a multiple murderer, what chance does a group of rookie reporters stand?"

"They're not rookies. They're all experienced journalists, experienced investigators. We stand a good chance."

"No, Jennifer, you don't. You stand a chance of stumbling on something that could endanger your life. Don't you understand? It is just not worth it."

The hardness was back in her eyes, a stubbornness he had seen many times before. In her father's eyes. She would not relent. "You think it is a random man, don't you."

"No. I'm not saying that –"

"You are. You most definitely are. What have you got? Or do I have to write my father's long lost story?"

Van Deventer stared at her, his eyes losing all hope. "No. You don't."

"What then?"

The Dutchman waited a long moment. When he spoke, he could barely contain his loathing for Jennifer. "He's killed again. A vagrant. We think he's a madman. There is no motive. We are treating the case as if he is a psychopath from now on."

"Do you mean the body found at St Bride's?" Jennifer ignored the contempt in his voice.

"Yes."

"What happens next?"

"I don't know."

Van Deventer stared at his coffee, still untouched.

"The photofits. Can I see them now?"

Van Deventer said nothing, shaking his head.

Jennifer started to stand up.

"Wait. Wait, please," said Van Deventer. "I cannot release them. We have three different people in three photofits. Three times as many crank calls and three times as many false leads to follow. In the end, our chances of finding him are divided by three."

"But someone out there might recognise him from these disguises. Someone who knows him well," protested Jennifer.

"I brought only the first photofit with me. You can have that. I cannot let you have the others, though. Not now. No matter what you can do to my life. I didn't bring them."

Jennifer was shaken by his resolve. She was threatening his future, yet he still refused to submit. "You must get them for me, I want to see them," she insisted.

"I can't allow that," said van Deventer.

"You don't understand me yet, do you?" asked Jennifer.

"Only too well. But I'm between a rock and a hard place. Commander Maxwell himself has placed a ban on releasing these. No matter what you threaten, I cannot release them."

"I want them for my own use. I won't publish."

"Is that what you said to Alan?" Van Deventer said, bitterly.

Jennifer ignored him. "You have no choice," she said, softly.

"Jennifer, you would destroy my life, everything I hold dear. But I cannot do what you want. You already know too much."

Jennifer understood the Dutchman was serious. She decided to relent, inwardly relieved that he had the strength to resist her, still disgusted at her own behaviour. "For how long?" she asked.

"Maxwell said another two weeks, at least."

"Two weeks then," she said, putting the original photofit in her pocket.

Abruptly, she stood up. "I'll be in touch," she said.

Jennifer left Van Deventer staring at her empty seat, still shaking his head.

FORTY-FIVE

JENNIFER WAS appalled at her behaviour, and several times the next day had to stop herself phoning the Dutchman to return the photofit and promise to keep his secret, just as her father had done before her. Every time she lifted the phone she hesitated, still undecided about what to do. She felt hugely depressed and lethargic. Her mind kept drifting back to a call she had made to Winters the previous night.

It had taken all her will to pick up the telephone. Her pride resisted, even though her mother implored her not to give him up without a fight. "At least know that you did everything you could. Don't be like me. Don't regret all the things in life you didn't do," Sheila said.

Jennifer could not put thoughts of Alan aside. He was everywhere. In the faces of people walking by, in newspapers, in conversations. She realised, with regret, she had never told him she loved him. Why not? Perhaps he would not have found it so easy to cast her aside if she had?

On the telephone Jennifer had tried every trick she knew, but she could not impress him.

Finally, he had excused himself, saying he had an important meeting to attend at Scotland Yard. He refused to tell her more.

When she asked whether she should call again, he hesitated, then said: "I wish you wouldn't. There's not much left for us to say to each other."

Even now, with Baker, Davis and Paynter, she felt lethargic and disheartened. The team was close to falling apart, she knew. They had grown tired of helping her pursue her obsession. She had traded on their respect for her father, but that respect obviously had limits. She tried to put life into one final thrust. "Has anyone thought that these killings might not connect, because, in fact, there IS no connection?" she ventured.

Paynter stopped drumming his fingers for a moment, then continued at an increased tempo. No-one responded, but Davis reached out and placed a hand on Paynter's forearm. "Please," he said, "give it a break for a few minutes. There's enough noise in here as it is."

The two men stared at each other for a second, then broke off as Jennifer began speaking again.

"What if there IS no connection?" She could hear the listless tone in her voice. To hell with it, she thought.

"How can there be no connection?" asked Davis, his brow furrowed. "Do you mean the killings were carried out by different people?"

Jennifer leaned forward in her seat. "No. I mean that we might all be on the wrong track. We know the same man was involved in all the killings. The police claim to have conclusive proof of that. What I'm saying is: what if there was no reason for those killings? What if these are part of a series of random murders by a psychopath?"

"Don't be ridiculous Jennifer," shot Baker. "You really are grasping at straws now."

"No," she said, slapping her hand on the table. "No, I don't think I am. Think about it. These killings have received massive exposure, and yet nothing is turned up by the police, nothing comes from the public, nothing is dug up by the newspapers. Why?"

She looked at each of them in turn. No-one answered her.

"We could be dealing with a random killer, someone who -"

"You mean a serial killer?" interrupted Paynter, turning from the window to join the discussion. "Like Son of Sam, or the Green River killer?"

"Exactly," she said.

"Come on, Jennifer," said Davis. "You know as well as the rest of us there have been many, many unsolved murders, murders that the police never even got close to unravelling."

"I agree with Frank," said Baker. "The mere fact that the police have not come up with anything concrete doesn't mean we have a random killer on our hands. You have to have more than that?"

Jennifer shook her head. "Why do I have to have more than that? "

"Because that's a whole different ball game," said Baker. "Criminologists are still only just beginning to understand that you have to treat those cases entirely differently to ordinary murder cases. There's a whole different psyche involved. You have to throw all the normal investigatory procedures out the window if you believe you're after a serial killer."

"I know, and that's why the police haven't turned up anything."

Baker interrupted: "Come on Jennifer. Have you got more than that to go on? Have you heard something?"

"No. I don't have anything to go on. But tell me this: what have YOU got to go on? Nothing. So why not try the random man theory? I can tell you one thing. I'm going to try and convince the police they ought to follow that line of thinking.

I doubt Van Deventer would need much pushing in that direction at the moment. Why don't you try it on for size?"

"By doing what?" asked Davis.

"I don't know yet," said Jennifer. "I haven't got that far. I can't seem to get very far at all these days. I'm tired and frustrated."

"So are we all," said Davis. "The problem is we have nothing to go on – this random man theory may do nicely."

"That's not quite true," said Jennifer. "We do have something coming up. Some new photofits. Van Deventer told me of a set of photofits they dragged from another witness. He will give them to me in another nine days. Then we can use them in a story."

Paynter whirled on Jennifer, his face furious. "How long have you known this?"

"A few days. Why?"

"And you tell us nothing about it. Why not?" he persisted.

Jennifer was startled by his ferocity. She felt unnerved and decided to refrain from telling them about the tramp, the new victim of The Rose. She would save it for another meeting if this was how they were going to react.

"Well, I wanted time to study them. I promised Van Deventer I would keep them until –"

"That's not the point," said Davis. "We're supposed to be working as a team."

"I gave my word. Just as I give you my word. I will let you have them in another nine days, when I get them."

"At least tell us something about them," suggested Baker.

"I have only seen one of them. There is something about it which unsettles me, makes me think I have seen this man before. But Van Deventer says that is a common response to photofits. People, if they look hard enough, can read into them what they want. He reminded me that it is a photofit of a man who was obviously wearing a disguise."

"Is that all?" asked Davis.

"For the moment," said Jennifer.

"While we're waiting for the photofits, what do you suggest we do?" asked Baker.

Jennifer looked up at Baker. "I don't know, really," she said. "But for a start, we could try and think about how a random killer selects his victims. Assuming we're dealing with a madman, why would my father, Ballantine, Walk - uh, I mean, Whitfield, become his victims?"

Jennifer looked at each of the three men to see if anyone had spotted her slip. Paynter looked at her curiously, but said nothing. Davis had turned away. Baker was still watching her, intently.

"A good question," he said. "A very good question."

FORTY-SIX

MAY 7, 1986 *How did all this begin? I thought I started it. But no. I'm caught up in a wave of events over which I have no control. Did I initiate this? I don't know. I get so confused. Perhaps it started long before I had any conscious decisions to make, even before I was born? Events took place, seemingly unrelated events, and slowly all our different destinies have swept towards each other.*

Perhaps my father carried genes which now thrive in me, dictating I should find pleasure in what I've been doing? In him, they lay dormant. In me, something mutated them into this.

Or perhaps he DID kill my mother? Why does he haunt my sleep? He's back again. In the storm dream. Only now I can see him. His living eyes in a decaying skull.

I'd do anything to have it all the way it was. No bodies. No crossbow. The dream only, with the man in the chair who I thought I knew. It was all so simple then. How can I hope to control anything on this basis? Today I thought I was going to vomit again, like I did the other night after my dreams It was when Jennifer spoke about the killings being carried out by a serial killer. Fear kicked me in the stomach. My mouth went dry. My hands trembled. I was rigid. For a while, my mind was numb. It took everything to remain outwardly cool.

Secretly, I wanted to plunge a blade into her heart, to silence her before she convinced the others she was right. What gave her the idea? How did she home in on the truth? Female intuition? I sat there, her voice screeching in my brain like nails scraping on a blackboard, as she went straight to the heart of the matter. A Random Man, she said. Think about a random man. Then she made a tiny slip. She mentioned Walker. Damn her to hell. This could be the turning point. I was so careful to select people the police would think had to be killed by a professional. If she convinces the police to adopt this theory it could ruin everything. She could put them on my trail, somehow.

Perhaps I'm worrying about nothing? Perhaps I'm over-reacting? What are the chances the police would give her a sympathetic ear? And even if they did, what are the chances they would act on what she says? I don't know. But events seem to be gathering a kind of uncontrollable momentum. I must settle down. Work this out. Trouble is, I feel so tired. The dreams take it out of me. There must be something I can do. But what? There might be more clues in the other two photofits. And if they are published, someone might recognise me! If they also start snooping into how

I selected my victims, they'll soon tumble to the fact those people featured in the news prior to their deaths, bar Walker.

Add to all that the possibility Jennifer herself might recognise me in these new photofits... everything comes back to Jennifer. She's the key. She forced Van Deventer to promise he would release the photofits. She's come up with the correct theory. She's going to persist until she finds out everything she needs to. And she needs to know so badly. I can see it in her eyes. She will never be at peace as long as her father's death remains a mystery. She doesn't leave it alone for a second. Even when she's quiet and withdrawn, she's going over every detail.

From what I can tell, the other evidence they have can only serve to prove I was the killer if they catch me. It won't actually lead them to my door. But Jennifer will. If she goes on like this, she'll lead them right to me. She'll convince the police to look for me. I can sense it. Only eight days are left before she gets those photofits. I can't go on leaving things to fate. I have to take a hand in all this. But what can I do?

The storm is beginning to rage again. Even while I'm awake. Those twisting, swirling clouds. The wind, the rain, the writhing rosebushes, the skull, the eyes... They stir in me like living creatures, even while I'm awake.

I HAVE TO DO SOMETHING.

But what?

The truth is, I know. I have to kill Jennifer. And the others. It will have to look like an accident, and that I escaped death through great luck. It must seem as if The Rose was after us all. A car accident? A shooting? A bomb? I don't have long. I must think. The answer will come, I know. It always does.

FORTY-SEVEN

THE FACE seemed to leer at her, tauntingly. Jennifer shook her head, closing her eyes tightly, trying to shake the illusion. Her mother was saying something, but she heard only the sound of her voice, not the words. "What was that?"

"I said everything seems worse when you lack direction," Sheila repeated.

"What do you mean?" asked Jennifer, turning over the photofit on the table in front of her. She had been studying the face yet again, trying to pinpoint what it was that so bothered her about it.

"Well, when you have nothing to look forward to, no goals or ambitions, life can be bleak."

Jennifer looked up at her mother. Every day, Sheila managed somehow to look marginally better than the day before. It was a little over a month since her father had been murdered, and already Sheila was looking much like her old self. She was still pale, still had some weight to regain, but she no longer resembled the fragile and lost person she had looked after Chapman's death.

A month! Was that all? It seemed so much longer. It seemed more like a lifetime. Her affair with Winters had been so intense, her emotions so heightened, she felt a lifetime away from her father.

Jennifer had arrived home from the latest meeting of the journalists exhausted and drained, and had gone straight to her room. She had tried telephoning Winters again, at his home, but he wasn't in. She wondered whether it was worth trying to contact him later. Depression had settled on her like a pall. In desperation she had pulled out the photofit and taken it into the sitting room, excusing herself from the supper Sheila had made. Her mother had accepted her mood without trying to force food on her. But now, an hour later, she wanted to talk.

"You've got to have a dream, or else how can you have a dream come true," she said.

Jennifer grimaced. Her mother laughed. For the first time in many days, Jennifer smiled too.

"I know that's a cliché, but like so many of them, it's true," said Sheila.

Jennifer ignored the point. "Do you know that's the first time I've heard you laugh in what seems like years?"

"Is it?"

"Yes. And I can't tell you how much I've missed that sound. At times I wondered whether I would ever hear it again."

"You will. Life goes on."

"Another cliché mother."

"And another truth."

Jennifer stood up from her seat and walked to sit at her mother's feet, resting her elbows on Sheila's knees.

"Do you have any dreams right now?" urged Sheila.

"I don't really have any," said Jennifer, dismally. Then she shook her head. "No. That's not true. I do have one. But it's more like a nightmare. I want to take the gun father left and put a bullet in the man who killed him. If I ever get the chance, I will. So help me, I will."

Jennifer saw the alarm in her mother's eyes. Sheila stared at her, horrified. "I couldn't let you do that," she whispered.

Jennifer stood up suddenly, and began pacing. "I look at that photofit day in, day out, and I can think of nothing but putting a bullet between that man's eyes. He's destroyed all our lives." She picked up the photofit, waving it at her mother, the paper crackling in her hand.

"Don't you feel the same way?"

"Jennifer, please. Sit down. Calm down. You mustn't think that way. If you did something like that you'd destroy your own life. You still have a chance now, don't throw that away."

"People keep saying the same thing to me," said Jennifer. "But I can't see what chances I've got to achieve anything worthwhile. A part of me knows how irrational I have been of late, and I hate myself sometimes. I have violent mood swings. It scares me."

"I understand. But that doesn't mean you should talk about killing anyone. I couldn't let you do something like that. Not ever. I would do anything to stop you, so don't even think on it," said Sheila.

Jennifer stopped pacing, throwing the photofit back on to the coffee table with a look of distaste on her face. "I mean it mother. If I get the chance, I will."

Sheila shook her head, firmly. Her mouth was set. Mother had decided, thought Jennifer. "What about this investigation of yours? Isn't that something to keep you going?" asked Sheila.

"No. Not anymore. It seems so futile at times. I'm just going through the motions, and so are the others. Frank, Colin, Morris. They're bored with it now. I can't say I blame them. In fact, today we decided to stop meeting for a week. They know about the photofits I'm getting from Van Deventer. They couldn't see any point in meeting any more, especially Morris, so we voted to give it a break for a while."

Sheila stood up and took Jennifer's hands. "Are you any closer to finding out anything?"

"I doubt it. At times I fear we'll never know who killed Dad. And I find THAT more frightening than anything else."

"What about your friend? Alan. Have you managed to patch things up?"

"No," said Jennifer. She put her head on her mother's shoulder, enjoying the contact. When she spoke again, her voice was muffled. "I'm frightened I'll never see him again. I can't say why, but I know he was so right for me. I don't have much experience with men, but I know he was the right kind of man for me, and even though our time together was so short, I learned more about love with him than I ever have with anyone else. I can't believe the way I've behaved. I don't understand myself anymore. I've done some terrible things lately."

She looked up at her mother. Sheila smiled, touching a hand to her daughter's cheek.

"Jennifer, sometimes it isn't reaching your goal that's important, so much as having one. So what if you never find out who killed Hugh? At least you have something to keep you going, something to act as a bridge between now and when you understand you need something else. Perhaps you will never straighten things out with Alan. But at least that's a goal, at least it is something to strive for. At least your life will have a purpose."

"What are you saying?"

"I'm saying don't give up," said Sheila, breaking contact to stand off and look into Jennifer's eyes. "Whatever else you do, don't give up. When you do that, you give up on yourself, and then you'll never have anything worthwhile. Keep trying for what you really want. No matter how much people try to resist, eventually you'll get your way. But just don't give up."

Jennifer smiled, wistfully. "I don't know...I just don't know," she said. But her eyes were thoughtful, speculative. An idea was taking shape, and she couldn't helping smiling.

Sheila grinned in response. "That's my girl," she said.

"I may just have a lot to thank you for, mother," said Jennifer, as she walked determinedly from the room.

FORTY-EIGHT

JENNIFER WAS waiting for him at his front door.

On seeing her, he stopped. He was carrying a bag full of groceries. He stared at her, silently.

She gazed back, noticing how tired he appeared. He was dressed casually. He looked slightly disheveled, a touch vulnerable. Somehow, he had never seemed more appealing.

She had dressed carefully, provocatively. She was leaning against the door frame, her hands in the side pockets of her dress. A cardigan was tied around her neck by its sleeves. She watched as he began walking slowly towards her, fumbling in his back pocket for his keys, his eyes never leaving her. At the door he said nothing, looking at her as he inserted a key in the latch. He swung the door open, but didn't move inside. Still he held his bag of groceries. They stood a foot apart. For a long while, they stood gazing at each other. His face was expressionless. She felt nervous, her heart racing.

Then Winters reached up and touched her face, his fingers tracing the line of her jaw.

"I've missed you," said Jennifer, softly.

Winters was looking at her mouth, his fingertips brushing her lips.

"I made a terrible mistake. I made the wrong decision."

His hand slipped to her collarbone, his fingers encircling her neck.

"I know that now. It's you. I want you. Deep down, I've always wanted you. Not my father. Not my father's killer. You."

His thumb glided softly over her skin, and she pressed her cheek into the palm of his hand.

She kissed his hand, then whispered: "I never told you this before. I wondered why. And yet it's so simple. I love you."

He searched her eyes. He wanted to believe her. She could see the last vestiges of doubt in his eyes.

"You'll never find someone else who loves you as much as I do. Please believe me. And forgive me."

Winters pulled her slowly to him, his eyes still on her lips.

"I'm giving up our investigation. As proof."

Their lips were nearing. Jennifer closed her eyes, sighing. They kissed, gently, lingeringly. Jennifer felt tears spring to her eyes. She pulled away from him, withdrawing a folded piece of paper from her pocket. "I'm bringing this back, as more proof."

Winters looked down at the sheet, puzzlement filling his eyes as he recognised the photofit.

Jennifer said: "Don't ask any questions. Not now. This is my way of showing you I'm serious."

He groaned, heaving the bag of groceries on to his hip to relieve his straining bicep. Winters stepped inside his flat, putting the bag down on the hall table. Jennifer followed him in, standing at the door, slipping the photofit back into her pocket. He turned back to her, then reached for the door, pushing it shut. He stepped in front of her, leaning to kiss her, more roughly this time, more longingly. Winters backed Jennifer up against the door, his hands resting on her shoulders, his kiss growing more urgent. She responded with her own sense of urgency. She felt anxious something would interfere, that she was dreaming, that it was not possible he would take her back. Not after everything she had done.

She broke off the kiss, a thought flashing into her mind. Perhaps he didn't know she had the photofit? Perhaps Van Deventer hadn't told him? Perhaps he would throw her out again if she told him how she got them?

She pulled away from him, walking towards his bedroom door. "Alan. I'm sorry for everything I've done. It wasn't me. My father...it was such a shock...I feel so ashamed."

Winters walked to her, taking her hand.

"Do you love me?" she asked, her heart in her mouth.

He looked at her curiously before answering. "Yes," he said. "God help me. But yes. I do."

***

They lay entwined, silently, and Jennifer felt his breathing, deep and regular. He was fast asleep, his face peaceful again. Jennifer stayed with him for more than an hour, unable to stop grinning. Finally she eased herself from his arms and stood up from the bed, looking down at him for several minutes before she started to dress. There would be time enough for talking, she decided. But not for a while. She wanted to avoid that until she felt sure their relationship was on firm ground again. She decided she would call him early the next morning, to arrange a meal with her mother that night. Sheila would enjoy that, she thought.

As she slipped on her cardigan she felt the photofit in her pocket. She smiled and took it out, searching Alan's dresser for a pen. She found one and scrawled a quick note on the back. "I let this man come between us. Never again. I love you, J."

She put the note on the pillow next to him, then let herself out of the flat, humming softly as she walked back to her car.

FORTY-NINE

MAY 12, 1986 *It always helps to know the right people. And I know of a man who once commanded a bomb disposal unit. He's been a source of information to many reporters, particularly in these days of indiscriminate terrorist bombings. He works as a security consultant. Talks freely to the Press to gain exposure for his company. He spent most of his life defusing crude but lethal bombs other people made in their homes.*

Told him I was a reporter on one of the morning newspapers and wanted background information to help me to understand a court case due to begin next week. Told him a man was accused of trying to kill his wife's lover with a bomb made of household chemicals. Was this possible? I asked. If so, how would a person make such a bomb? He said the person probably designed a bomb which contained a large amount of shrapnel. Our conversation went on for some time. Finally, I suggested we get together so he could show me in more detail what he meant.

Last night I visited him in my usual bearded disguise. I could not have done that had the photofits been released. He was pleased to see me. He never once asked me to prove I worked with a newspaper. Some people are like that. They talk to anyone. I got the feeling he missed being part of the action. When I left, I was carrying the one part of a bomb I was not able to buy in a store. A detonator. As I became more interested in what he had to say, he brought out a box of souvenirs to show me. Grenades and detonators and shrapnel. I said I thought I should do a feature on him. He thought that a marvelous idea. Told him I would have to visit him again, and next time I would bring a tape-recorder. He was delighted. He did not notice when I slipped one of his detonators into my pocket. I asked what a bomb disposal expert would have to do to disarm a home-

made device, and he virtually built a bomb for me in order to show me how he would go about dismantling it.

This morning I went to the library for more information. From there I went on a shopping expedition. On the desk in front of me now is a small, but deadly, device. I'm relieved I won't be around when it goes off. It is a lethal mixture of plastic, fertiliser, sugar, nails, tacks and a detonator. All of this is wired to an alarm clock. This is how I will end the threat of Jennifer and her team.

I've made all the arrangements. Including that of throwing off the police again with another threatening note. I posted that last night. Should make them think about the theory of a conspiracy again. At least it will buy me more time.

Tomorrow morning I will put the bomb in my briefcase and take it with me to work. It will be set to go off at 3.15pm. That's the time they close The Whispering Gallery at St Paul's. We'll be standing in the Gallery, waiting. Or at least they will. With the bomb.

Shortly before noon, I'll arrange that Jennifer receives an anonymous message suggesting she and the others should meet the writer at St Paul's. The note will infer the writer has information for her about the murders. If Jennifer decides she does not want to go, I'll disarm the bomb and try to find a different way. Somehow, knowing Jennifer's obsession, I doubt my plan will fail. If the others do not come, well, too bad. They are not as big a threat as Jennifer. Should my bomb fail to go off, no harm will be done. Not one of them will be any the wiser. My briefcase will be safely locked. No-one will think it strange that I bring it. After all, we all have one these days to carry our various notes and information.

When the time comes, I'll stroll to the stairwell and put down my briefcase next to Jennifer. Once I've planted the bomb, I'll wait at the door for two or three minutes, effectively denying the others an exit. Then, I'll walk away to the stairway, to wait for the explosion.

The tacks and nails in the casing should tear them all apart.

My secret will be safe.
It is simply a matter of time...

FIFTY

Winters looked at his watch. It was a simple watch, he reflected. Tasteful. Expensive. His parents had given it to him as a birthday present nearly 15 years ago. He had cared for it, servicing it regularly, and it had never given him any problems.

He switched his gaze to the watch Van Deventer was wearing, shaking his head when he saw the contraption on the Dutchman's wrist. One of those multi-purpose multi-functional electronic wonders that did everything from calculate to defecate, thought Winters.

He had often been tempted to buy himself a new watch, but sentiment had caused him to hang on to this one. It still kept perfect time, he noted, watching the hands edge towards noon. He focussed on the second hand as it swept past the day/date indicator, and his eyes stopped to take in the time of month. May the fourth. He tried to work out how long it had been since Chapman was killed. Was it 42 days? Or 43?

That was something like 1,000 hours. God knew how many of those hours spent investigating the murder. And still no closer to solving it than they were on the night of Chapman's death. An intense sense of frustration hit him, and he clenched his fists, crushing the report in his hands. Shit! How could one man make them all look like a bunch of absolute monkeys?

He looked across at Van Deventer. The Dutchman's dress sense had improved of late, thought Winters. A couple of new suits had crept into his wardrobe. He wondered whether it was his influence. Whatever his new-found taste in clothes, Van Deventer wasn't reflecting this improvement himself lately, Winters thought.

The past few days the Dutchman had been unusually flat, his responses to people dull and mechanical. Initially, Winters had wondered whether Van Deventer was simply beginning to feel the pressure. But now he was sure it was something more than that, something the Dutchman was very reluctant to talk about.

Several times that morning Winters had caught the Dutchman staring vacantly at the office wall. Each time, when Winters tried to attract his attention, Van Deventer had seemed miles away, and had struggled to focus his attention on the question. Even then, his replies were strangely listless.

Something had caused him to lose heart, puzzled Winters. But what could it be? The younger policeman felt as if it was he who was back in charge of the investigation, control somehow having swung back to him without any formal notification.

Good. That suited him just fine, he thought. Still, the Dutchman's attitude was starting to worry him.

Winters had dressed casually in a bright and trendy sports jacket. He had felt elated and positive on waking that morning. He couldn't think how long it had been since he had slept so well. His bright choice of clothing suited his refreshed mood. Only one thing had soured his morning. The strange note from Jennifer, and the mystery of how she had managed to get her hands on the photofit. How? And why return them?

He shook his head. He would sort that out with her later, when they had time together again. Winters was feeling much more positive. His night with Jennifer had restored his shaken confidence. He wanted badly to see her again, but felt unsure about calling her. He decided to leave the initiative to her.

Winters looked across the desk at Van Deventer. The Dutchman was reading through lab report findings at the different murder scenes. Winters had suggested they go through everything again, in the hope yet another reading would throw up something they had missed, some new avenue to pursue. But before long, Winters knew it would be no good. He knew every report by heart, and he found his concentration slipping every time he tried to read. His thoughts kept drifting back to Jennifer.

Would they be able to resolve their differences and stay re-united? He wondered. He had to admit the thought of seeing her again excited him. As much as he tried to put her out of his mind, he kept seeing her face. For some odd reason, he kept remembering the night they visited The Courier offices. Something about that evening plagued him, but he couldn't isolate it, no matter how hard or how often he tried. He also kept thinking about Jennifer's reaction to the photofit when he had shown it to her. He was sure there had been something in her eyes. What DID that mean?

Thinking of the photofit, how had she managed to acquire that first version?

"This is no good," he declared finally, throwing papers onto his desk. "I had hoped I could approach all this from a new angle, but it's like looking at blank pages. My mind simply refuses to take it in again."

"Sorry. What was that?" asked Van Deventer, stretching and easing his back.

"Nothing," Winters said, with irritation. After a moment, he went on: "Have you had any further thoughts regarding your theory our man has a day job?"

"No, not exactly," said Van Deventer. "It was a simple idea. I have not pursued it. All the killings have taken place at night. It would seem to indicate that the killer is tied to a day job. But it could also mean he prefers to work in the dark. Who knows?"

Winters looked at the Dutchman curiously. Van Deventer would usually have responded to any new line of reasoning or questioning with vigour.

"You know," said Winters, choosing to ignore the Dutchman's mood, "no matter how hard we try, we can find nothing to link the victims. I keep thinking to myself what possible way could the killer be linked to each of them, if you get my drift?"

"No," said Van Deventer, dourly. He looked at Winters, who remained silent, frowning. Van Deventer tried to pretend interest. "You're asking what is it that links all the different people involved – the killer, the victims, the gun dealer - and, for that matter, crossbows, international magazines, disguises and roses? Yes?"

"No, I didn't mean that. I mean what sort of person could possibly be linked to all of those different people and objects. But asking that question is as far as I can get. I totter on the edge of something, something I think might be worthwhile, an idea or spark of intuition, but then it fades away and I can't get it back. I get the feeling I'm on the edge of a clue, something that has been staring us in the face, but I can't grasp it. I get so damned frustrated. It has been bothering me for days, ever since you promoted the idea that the killer is a psychopath."

The Dutchman looked at him, still no interest showing on his face.

Winters reached into his jacket pocket, withdrawing the photofit Jennifer had left him. He unfolded it and looked at the face on the sheet. "What links this man with such diverse people? Even if he is your 'random man'?"

He saw Van Deventer studying the back of the sheet, the Dutchman's eyes widening.

"What's the matter?" asked Winters, turning over the photofit and seeing Jennifer's scrawled note.

By way of an answer, Van Deventer asked: "Have you seen Jennifer lately?"

"Yes. Last night. Why?"

"Did she have anything interesting to say?"

"She gave me this. Somehow, she managed to get it from somewhere. Other than that, nothing special."

Van Deventer did not react. Now his face was deadpan. After a moment, he said: "You have settled your differences?"

Winters hesitated. He decided he had nothing to hide. "Yes. In a way."

"In a way? What does that mean?"

"Well, sometimes I wonder if we have any common ground on which we can settle differences. Jennifer is a reporter. I am a police officer. We would be in conflict with each other all the time. Situations like the one that drove a wedge between us would arise time and again. There would be no freedom of discussion about our working lives, for fear the other would use the information the wrong way."

"What if you talked her into giving up journalism?"

"I'm not sure I could. What right do I have to do that, anyway? No, I'm sure she would stay on even if I tried to convince her otherwise."

Winters paused to contemplate Jennifer's comment in the lift on the night they were leaving The Courier. What was it she had said? Something about enjoying the stimulation and the people?

"Well, I've often wondered what she sees in it," said Van Deventer.

Winters muttered his agreement. He returned his gaze to the photofit in front of him, then abruptly jerked upright in his chair, as if he had been delivered an electric shock.

"What?" said Van Deventer, startled.

"That's it. Christ. That could be it. You may have hit the nail on the head," said Winters, excited.

"What do you mean? What are you talking about?"

"Jennifer once TOLD me what she sees in journalism. And that could be our answer."

"Well, what is it man?" said Van Deventer, gathering interest in spite of himself.

"She said: 'You get to meet all sorts as a journalist.' She said…if I can recall her exact words….' Drug addicts, pushers, robbers, businessmen, policemen…' Or something like that," said Winters, excitedly. "Whatever her words, it's the link I've been searching for. I'm sure that's it! A journalist would have access to editors, businessmen, lawyers and vagrants. And access to gun dealers, the latest copies of international editions of magazines…"

Van Deventer looked bemused by the torrent from his younger colleague.

He whispered a curse. Now he knew. This was the thorn pricking at his subconscious, that brief glimmer of recognition in Jennifer's eyes…

"Christ," he said, thinking aloud. "What about that look in her eyes when she saw the photofit? Maybe she knows the person? Maybe the person is a journalist she works with at The Courier!"

Winters jumped up from his seat. "Come on," he said.

"Grab your hat and coat. I've got a hunch. I want to visit the library at The Courier."

Van Deventer did not need a second prompt. As they marched out through the squad room, the Dutchman said: "Even if your hunch falls through, we could look through the newspaper files on the killings. The papers have been full of preposterous theories about the killer. One of those preposterous theories could, in fact, be inspired speculation."

Before they reached the door, Hawkins, pipe in one hand and an envelope in the other, stood up from his desk calling out for Winters. "Inspector! This has just arrived for you."

Winters took the envelope, looking perfunctorily at his name typed neatly on its front. It bore a local stamp. More crank mail, thought Winters, slipping the letter into his pocket.

"We're off to the Courier if anyone wants us," he informed Hawkins. Without waiting for acknowledgement, Winters and Van Deventer walked hurriedly from the squad room.

As they reached Winters's car, the detective felt a knot growing in his stomach. He couldn't explain it, but he could feel the tension mounting an assault on his nerves.

"There could be something in one of those newspaper reports that sparks off a line of thought we haven't considered," repeated Van Deventer, looking for a response.

"You could be right," mused Winters. "When we get to The Courier we'll ask Channing to let us see all his files. We can spend the afternoon there. Anything is better than poring over ours again."

They were in the foyer of The Courier twenty minutes later, waiting for Channing's assistant to fetch them at the security desk on the ground floor. The editor's office was on the second floor and the two men waited patiently, ignoring the stares of newspaper staff as they came and went from the building.

While waiting, Winters rediscovered the letter in his pocket. He tore open the envelope, withdrawing the folded paper inside distractedly. He winced as he read the words pasted on the sheet. It resembled the anonymous notes sent to Chapman, composed from headlines cut from what looked like the same international finance magazine:

THREE MORE. SOON. VERY SOON. SELECTIVELY, NOT AT RANDOM

"Jesus," he said. "What's this? What does this mean? How could anyone know about your random man theory?"

Winters handed the note to Van Deventer. The Dutchman read it quickly, his face growing ashen. Winters shook his head, struck dumb by the letter.

"Is this a joke? Someone's warped sense of humour? Or is it our man? Why address it to me? Doesn't he know you're in charge?"

Van Deventer stood clasping the letter – he looked pale and horrified, and Winters contemplated putting out a hand to steady the Dutchman.

"I ..." Van Deventer started. "I think–"

The editor's assistant arrived before Van Deventer could finish. She flashed a cheery smile. Her gaze lingered on Winters fractionally longer than was polite.

"Inspector, Mr Channing is in an editorial meeting right now. Would you mind waiting for him?"

"Here?" asked Winters, looking around with obvious distaste, still feeling shaken himself by the letter.

"No, upstairs."

"Let's go," said Winters.

When they reached the second floor she led them along a corridor to a group of offices on one side of the building.

As they walked, Winters noted that Van Deventer was still ashen-faced. For some reason, the anonymous note had badly disturbed the Dutchman.

"Is Mr Channing going to be long?"

"Well, he could be. It is an editorial conference, at which they plan tomorrow's paper. There are deadlines to meet, so I'm afraid I can't interrupt."

"We'll wait," said Winters. "But I wonder if you could do me a favour in the meantime? We'd like to be able to look through your files on The Rose murders. Would that be possible for you to arrange, or must I speak to Mr Channing?"

"Those files are all in our library. Normally, only staff members are able to make use of the library. Members of the public have to get special permission to go in there."

"We're not exactly members of the public. We're officers investigating a series of murders."

"Look, hold on a minute and I'll see what I can do."

She walked over to a colleague sitting at a desk near her own, outside what was obviously the largest office. Winters could hear the sound of laughter coming from behind the door. He wondered where Jennifer was in the building. He knew she sat in the newsroom, but he wasn't sure where that was in relation to the editor's offices. He remembered her telling him this section was often referred to as 'Mahogany Row'.

After a minute, the assistant turned from the person she was speaking to. He watched, expressionless, as she approached.

"Mr Winters, I think it will be quite in order if you use our facilities. You can look at whatever you want. I'll just call the chief librarian to tell her that you'll be coming."

"Thank you," said Winters. "You've been a great help."

Winters glanced at his watch. It was now 12:45. He hoped

she would hurry up. He turned to look at Van Deventer. The Dutchman was still clutching the note, and Winters could see from the trembling paper that the older man's hands were shaking quite violently.

FIFTY-ONE

JENNIFER CHAPMAN was standing at her desk peering at a type-written note. Around her stood Baker, Davis and Paynter, all staring at the note equally intently. It had been found on her desk at about 12:30, in a sealed envelope addressed to her and marked urgent. It did not carry a postage stamp.

She had torn it open, read it quickly, then called out to Davis. As Davis read it, she had collected Paynter and Baker. Then she had gone to the front desk to grill the security guard about how the letter had been delivered. After a few minutes, she returned to the three men.

Once again she read the note:

"Meet me in The Whispering Gallery at St Paul's Cathedral at 3pm today. I have information. Come alone. Arrive at 2:45 and wait on the steps in front of the Great West Door while I make sure you have not brought anyone unwanted. If you are not with Baker, Davis and Paynter I will not appear. If you are followed I will not appear. After a few minutes, go into the Cathedral and walk to The South Aisle. When you get to the staircase for the Whispering Gallery, wait for a minute at the door. Again, I'll be watching. Then go up the stairs and wait for me on the Gallery, in full view from below, but near the door to the steps. I will be watching. You

know me, so you will be able to identify me once we are together. Baker will be able to vouch for me. I can blow the lid off your story forever. If you are not prepared to guard my identity with your lives, don't come. Bring all your notes about the case. You'll be interested to find out how much you already have that is valuable."

The journalists stood in puzzled silence.

"How did the note get here?" asked Paynter, finally.

"It was dropped on my desk by one of the internal messengers," answered Jennifer. "They said it had been left at the reception desk downstairs. No-one saw who delivered it."

"Who could it be?" asked Baker. "It says I can vouch for the person. Who the hell could I vouch for in regard to The Rose?"

"That doesn't matter until we're there," said Jennifer, impatiently. "What matters is this could be a breakthrough for us."

"Hold on a minute, Jennifer. I'm not sure I want to go risking my neck on this," said Paynter.

Jennifer whirled on him. "Don't be ridiculous. This guy sounds petrified himself. What do you think? That it's a trap, or something? I doubt it, but I can tell you one thing for sure: there is no way I'm going to pass this up."

"No-one is suggesting we should pass it up," said Davis. "But perhaps we should be more cautious than you're being."

"You really burn me up. For weeks now we've been eating, living and breathing this case. Now that we have this opportunity, perhaps something that will blow it open, you want to plead caution and give up on it."

"I never said I wouldn't go," said Baker, raising his voice. "I'm just as interested as you. But what if it's a hoax, or a crank?" They were beginning to attract attention from the other reporters. Jennifer sat down at her desk.

"Then we've lost nothing but some time," she said, in a whisper.

"Okay, okay," said Paynter. "Keep your hair on. Perhaps you're right. After all, there is safety in numbers. There's four of us and one of him."

"Or her," said Davis, with a wink.

"Or her," said Jennifer, smiling. "Do I take it we're going to go?"

"Count me in," said Baker.

"And me," said Davis.

"How much longer until we're supposed to be there?" asked Paynter.

"In two hours," said Jennifer, looking at her watch.

"What are we going to do until then?" asked Davis.

"How about some lunch at 'Food for Health.' It's halfway to St Paul's. We can go straight from there," said Baker.

"You're on," said Jennifer. "I'm famished. Let's meet at the lift in five minutes."

The reporters returned to their individual desks. Jennifer was assailed with doubts. What would Alan do if he found out? Would she ruin everything again? Should she go to the Gallery? Who was the mystery person?

On impulse she picked up the telephone and dialled Scotland Yard. She would tell Alan what was happening. He would know what to do. It would be another way of showing him she was serious about making things right between them.

She had to wait several minutes to find out that Chief Inspector Winters was out. Relieved, she left a message to say she had called. That would cover her, she thought. "I called to give you the news, but they said you were out. What else could

I do?" she would tell him.

Jennifer was the first one waiting at the lifts. She was joined by Baker.

"The others are on their way. I saw them packing up," he said.

Jennifer kept glancing at her watch, even though there was still plenty of time till they were due at St Paul's. Finally Paynter arrived, followed a minute later by Davis. Jennifer saw Davis and Paynter were both carrying their briefcases. Baker saw her looking at the briefcases, swore, then walked briskly back towards the newsroom.

"Where are you going?" called Davis.

"Wait for me, I won't be long," he called over his shoulder.

Baker was back, carrying his own briefcase, a few seconds later. "Can't go without this," he smiled.

"Why not?" asked Jennifer.

"Because this contains everything we may need for this meeting," said Baker, hefting his briefcase to eye-level and looking pointedly at the cases carried by Paynter and Davis. "And the letter did say we should bring our notes."

The journalists lapsed into silence as the lift arrived. The men stood aside as the doors opened, allowing Jennifer to enter first. The doors closed behind them.

Along the corridor, Van Deventer and Winters emerged from the editor's office.

They walked past the bank of lifts on their way to the newspaper's library.

FIFTY-TWO

WINTERS STRODE into the library at full pace, Van Deventer lagging behind. Barbara Smith, chief librarian, looked up at them over the top of her spectacles.

"Mrs Smith," said Winters, "we're from the police. We want to look at some of your newspaper clippings."

Mrs Smith had been forewarned by Miss Hayes. "Certainly, uh, Mr..?"

"Chief Inspector Winters, and this is Superintendent Van Deventer."

"How do you do? What clippings did you want to see?"

Van Deventer put his elbows on the counter that separated him from the librarian. He was still shaken by the anonymous letter. "We wanted to look at everything you've got on The Rose killings," he said, quietly.

"That's easy, although I must warn you, Inspector Winters, that you've got an enormous amount to go through."

"Why's that?" he asked, turning back to the counter.

He looked around the library, impressed at the vast number of filing cupboards in the room. He hadn't really noticed them the last time he had been in here. Several librarians were busy filing clippings at various cupboards, and several more sat at a bank of desks cutting out articles from newspapers and magazines.

"We get all the newspapers every day, and then we cut them up and we file and cross-file every article. For example, on the Rose story we have several files. We have a heading titled The Rose, which is several folders thick, then we have files on each of his victims. We also have a file on you, Mr Van Deventer."

"Is that so?" said Van Deventer, obviously pleased, in spite of his strange mood.

"Would you like to see all of those files?"

"Yes," replied Van Deventer.

"You'll have to wait a few minutes. This will take me a little while. Then you can take a seat at the reading table over there and examine them at your leisure."

"Thank you, that would be just fine," said Winters, smiling broadly at Mrs Smith. She smiled in return, turned and started issuing instructions to two of her assistants.

Winters turned to face the door, and leaned back on the counter. The reception area was large. In the centre of the floor was a wide table, with several chairs around it. Against the wall furthest from him was the magazine and newspaper rack. The main daily newspapers and weekly magazines were chained to the rack on special metal filing strips. Each publication had holes punched in it to be fitted onto the strips. International Finance Week was one of the publications. He stared at the rack.

"Isn't that the magazine from which our anonymous letter writer cut his headlines?" asked Van Deventer, seeing Winters studying the magazines from afar.

"Yes, it is," answered Winters. He walked to the filing rack and began flipping through the magazines, looking idly at each cover. He went back through nine or ten copies and paused for a moment, turning to gaze at Van Deventer, his brows knitted in concentration. Van Deventer shrugged. He didn't understand what was concerning Winters, who turned back to the rack and began flipping through the magazines at a faster pace.

Van Deventer walked over to stand next to him, and disinterestedly turned the pages of a copy of The Courier on file.

Mrs Smith tried to attract their attention from behind the counter. She was holding a file which bulged with newspaper clippings. "Mr Van Deventer?" she called. She had to repeat herself before the policeman turned to acknowledge her.

"I've got one of the files, the one on The Rose. The others are being worked on by members of my staff, but I've told them to finish what they're doing and bring the files to you as soon as possible."

"Thank you," said Van Deventer, as he walked to the counter. Mrs Smith put the file down and started to leave.

"Uh, Mrs Smith, I wonder if you could help me for a moment?" asked Winters, joining them.

"Certainly. What is it?"

"I see you have Finance Week magazine filed over there. I want to –"

"Oh yes," she broke in, "I have copies on file going back a full year.

"So you keep them all in order?"

"Yes. I add the latest issue to the top of the pile, and take away the bottom issue, every week. Why do you ask?"

Winters shook his head, ignoring the file on the counter, and walked back to the magazines.

He flicked past more issues of Finance Week, returned to the top of the pile, and started again.

Out of curiosity, Van Deventer came to stand next to him again. Winters turned to him:

"Do you remember which issues of the magazine were supposedly used for the anonymous letters sent to Chapman?"

"Yes, there were five different issues, as far as I can remember. I think there were two issues in January, one in December, and two more in February."

"Can you remember any specific dates?"

"No. Well, maybe. I think one was February 12. Another was January 23."

"Look at this," said Winters. "This rack has every copy of this magazine going back a year, in perfect order. However, the file is missing one copy from December, two from January, and two from February. Both the January 23 and February 12 issues are missing."

This time more than shock registered on the Dutchman's face. Now, he looked frightened.

"Don't you see? Every copy identified by our forensic lab boys is missing from this file."

Van Deventer reached into his pocket, withdrawing the anonymous note Winters had handed him. He did not answer his colleague.

Winters seemed not to notice. "Whoever sent those threatening letters must have taken the copies of Finance Week from this rack. The library is only used by members of staff. Outsiders have to get special permission."

Van Deventer silently unfolded the note and stared glazedly at the words glued to the paper.

"Whoever sent those notes probably works on the newspaper," Winters finished. He noticed Van Deventer still staring at the note.

"I was right! The bastard works right here on the newspaper."

Winters paused, puzzlement overtaking him as he thought about the letter held by Van Deventer.

"If that note is genuine," said Winters, "how the hell would the person know about –"

"Because I told her," said Van Deventer, looking up, his eyes filled with guilt.

"Told who? What?"

"She blackmailed me. I had no choice. She got that photofit from me." Van Deventer could not meet Winters's eyes. "I told her about the vagrant. About the random man."

The full extent of Jennifer's duplicity was beginning to dawn on Winters. "Who? Who blackmailed you? Who did you tell?"

"Jennifer. She found her father's papers on the Campbell case. Everything. She was going to write a story naming me as the person responsible for Campbell's death. Me! After all these years. I gave her the photofit to keep her quiet."

Suddenly everything fell into place for Winters. His heart started to race. Van Deventer's strange apathy lately, how Jennifer had come by the photofit, the anonymous note in his pocket...

"Christ," he whispered. "Do you know what you've done?"

"Yes. God help me. I do."

"The killer, or at least an accomplice, works on this newspaper. Now we get a note like this. It means Jennifer must have told someone..."

Van Deventer's face was filled with shame and remorse.

"...And now that person means to kill her."

"What?"

"It says three more. Soon. One of those victims may be Jennifer," said Winters.

Van Deventer nodded. "I know. I've been fearing that since we first got the note."

Mrs Smith and her librarians had stopped work to listen to the exchange. Winters was oblivious of them.

"You old fool. You stupid, bloody old ..."

In exasperation, Winters clenched his fists, glaring at the Dutchman. He shook his head abruptly and turned for the door. He would find Jennifer in the newsroom and warn her. Make sure she was safe. Then they would be able to concentrate on finding out which one of the journalists was behind all this. Only then would he allow himself to concentrate on the Dutchman.

Van Deventer followed him, still clutching the anonymous letter.

Winters raced along the corridor and slammed open the newsroom door in his haste, skidding to a halt just inside the office. Several journalists were startled by the noise. He scanned the faces of the reporters, searching in vain for Jennifer.

A small man with sleeves rolled up, newspaper in one hand and a pencil in the other, confronted him. "This is a newsroom. Not a zoo. What do you want?"

Winters turned on him. "Police! I'm looking for Jennifer Chapman."

"I'm the news editor. My name is Rodgers. Jennifer Chapman is a member of my staff. Why do you want her?"

Winters flashed his badge under Rodgers's nose. "She may be in danger. Where is she? Quickly."

Van Deventer had arrived on the scene. "Where does she sit?" he asked.

"I don't know where she is," admitted Rodgers. "What's this all about, anyway? Why is she in danger?"

"We don't have time for questions," said Winters, growing increasingly frightened for Jennifer, his voice rising. "We have information which suggests she may be in danger. Now answer my question."

Rodgers was finally intimidated. "She's been gone a while. She didn't tell me where she was going."

"Where does she sit?" insisted Van Deventer.

"Over there," said Rodgers. He led the two policemen to a cluster of desks. "This one." He pointed down at a small, grey metal desk, immaculately tidy save a typewriter and a small vase.

Winters stopped, frozen.

In the vase was a rose.

"No!" said Van Deventer.

Winters looked hatefully at the Dutchman.

They both recognised the killing sign of The Rose.

FIFTY-THREE

"HOW MANY members of her team?" said Winters.

"Four, including her," said Rodgers.

"Where are they all?"

"I told you. I don't know."

"They're members of your staff. How can you not know?"

"They must have slipped out. I don't know where they are. I don't even know if they are together."

Winters smacked a fist into his palm. "Shit! I don't believe this."

Finally, Van Deventer spoke. "If the note is from the killer, and he is on Jennifer's team, it could mean he's planning to kill all the other members. The note says three more."

"Thank you Superintendent. I already thought that one out for myself." Winters was acid, unable to curb his antipathy for the Dutchman. He turned back to Rodgers. "How long have they been gone?"

The news editor paused. "About 20 minutes, I suppose."

Van Deventer's face was puce with humiliation and anger. "Don't blame me for this, Alan. Blame your bloody girlfriend. I didn't WANT to give her the information. She damn well threatened me."

"And you so badly wanted to redeem yourself in everyone's eyes that you could only see your own selfish ends. You didn't think of the dangers to her, did you?"

"This is no time for blame. We have to act – and act fast," said the Dutchman. The two men glared at each other for a moment.

Winters turned back to Rodgers. "Have you got their home addresses?" he snapped.

"Yes, but I'm not sure –"

"Don't you understand yet? We believe all of them may be in danger. I'm not asking for those addresses, I'm telling you to get them for me. Now."

"All right, all right," said Rodgers, holding up his palms.

He walked off to retrieve his address book from his desk.

"I'm calling Hawkins and Boyer. Then the three of you can take fast squad cars and visit these homes. Break in if you have to. In the meantime I'll put out an alert. I'll instruct Boyer and Hawkins to call you if they find anything – all information to be routed through you. You can get me here - I'll wait in case they return."

Van Deventer nodded, downcast.

Rodgers returned, handing a slip of paper to Winters. "There. All their addresses."

Winters took the note. "Where can I use a telephone? In private." Rodgers pointed at a meeting room near the entrance.

Winters showed the note to Van Deventer. "You take the top one. I'll get Boyer and Hawkins to visit the other two."

Van Deventer scribbled the address on his note pad.

"What are you waiting for?" asked Winters, agitated.

"You'll have to let me have your car keys," said Van Deventer, meekly. "We came here in your car."

Winters dug into his pocket.

"Here. Just get there. Quickly."

Van Deventer took the keys and turned to leave. He halted, turning back to face Winters.

"Alan," he said. "I'm sorry. I'm truly sorry. I was wrong about you."

"Not now. Go. Hurry," said Winters.

He started for the telephone in the interview room.

FIFTY-FOUR

THE FOUR journalists sat at their usual table in the Food for Health restaurant.

Jennifer suppressed a shudder. At last they were rolling. Something about the note, the tone of the author, compelled her to respond. Please, oh please let it be for real, she thought. After all this time, let this be the piece of the jigsaw that makes sense of the puzzle. What if it is just a hoax? She didn't know how she would react. No, it wouldn't be a hoax. It couldn't be.

All four journalists toyed with the food on their plates, indifferently picking at a vegetable curry.

Jennifer wondered again whether she should slip off and call Winters. She worried that he may not accept her word that she had tried to call him. But of course her earlier message would prove she called. She relaxed imperceptibly.

Eating was impossible with her stomach in the state it was in. She watched the others pushing food around their plates, appreciating they felt the same way. Baker looked the least concerned. He saw her watching him and smiled. Jennifer returned the smile with a brief, nervous grin. She turned to watch Davis. He appeared relaxed, although Jennifer could see he was tense from the way he concentrated on his food. His lips were tightly sealed and his nostrils flared with each inhalation. Paynter appeared the most nervous. He kept starting at every noise, shaking his head in disgust when he identified the source. Jennifer knew Paynter's briefcase was between his legs, where he had set it down carefully when they took their seats. Baker and Davis had left their briefcases in the cloakroom.

Jennifer pushed her plate away, finally giving up on the meal.

Baker said: "I wonder who's waiting for us at The Whispering Gallery?"

Davis shrugged. "I haven't a clue," he said.

"I've been trying to think who it might be, and I can't fit anything together," said Baker. "The note says I'll be able to identify him. That means I've probably spoken to him, maybe even seen him. Yet I can tell nothing from the note."

"Who says it's a he?" asked Paynter. "Does the note say it is a he?"

"No, come to think of it, it doesn't," said Jennifer. "Whoever it is, I hope to God the person has something of value for us. I don't know that I could cope with a false lead."

"Well, we'll soon know," said Davis. "I suggest we eat our lunch, then go early to case the joint, so to speak, before we go in."

"How can you be so cool about it?" asked Jennifer. "We could be at the beginning of the end of all this, and you sit there and say let's eat!"

"We can't do anything about it right now, so let's take it easy and do what we have to do when the time comes," replied Davis.

"I wonder whether we shouldn't tell the police about this?" asked Paynter.

The four journalists looked down at their food.

"When I think about it, I'm not hungry anymore," said Jennifer.

"Just relax Jennifer. We'll soon know," Baker said.

"What about going early?" asked Paynter, picking up his knife and fork, prodding at a yellowed potato.

"I don't know if that's wise," said Baker, watching Jennifer. "The note was explicit. We shouldn't do anything to scare him off. The person may think we're up to something if we don't do exactly as we're told."

"I agree," said Davis. "So let's enjoy a slow lunch and then an easy walk up to the Cathedral. No point in getting indigestion."

"Has anyone told the newsdesk we won't be this afternoon?" asked Jennifer, looking at her watch. "It's already 1:15."

The three men looked at her.

"I didn't think to tell anyone," said Davis.

"Me neither," added Paynter.

Baker shook his head.

"Do you think we should?" asked Davis.

"No," said Baker, abruptly. Then he lowered his voice. "Rodgers will insist on knowing what it's all about, then he'll try to stop us. If this is what we hope it is, we won't have to do any explaining when we get back to the office. Our copy will be all the explanation we need."

"Are you sure?" said Jennifer.

"Positive," said Baker.

FIFTY-FIVE

DETECTIVE SERGEANT Ian Hawkins was struck by the pristine cleanliness of the flat. Everything in place, as if it was a show home. He found it difficult to believe anyone actually lived in it.

The front door had surprised him, he recalled wryly. It was fitted with no less than five different locks. Winters had said it was urgent, that he should do anything to get into the flat, so he had broken in through the fanlight. Ridiculously simple, although it could have been a struggle for the portly Boyer, he supposed. He had smashed the glass, then cleared away the jagged shards before climbing through the window. While squeezing his long legs through the fanlight, Hawkins worried that there was still someone inside the Chelsea flat. He pictured a man with an axe waiting for him. He could imagine the axe plunging on his head as he lowered himself to the floor.

Safely inside, he turned to survey the hall.

Hawkins threw up an arm and recoiled from the figure confronting him in the gloom. It took a second to realise he had been startled by his own reflection. A mirror! Hawkins smiled, feeling foolish. He practised the smile again, aware it did not stop him looking sheepish.

The flat was deathly quiet. He could hear nothing of the rest of the building's sounds, nor could he hear any street noises.

Cautiously, Hawkins looked around the flat, still afraid someone would leap out at him. He searched every room before he relaxed. No-one in sight.

"Look for flowers," Winters had said. "A crossbow, a handgun, copies of Finance Week. Anything suspicious. If you find it, get on the radio immediately. No time for a search warrant, so keep damage to a minimum."

At first glance, the flat was as bare as a stripper's arse, thought Hawkins. Not a sign of a flower. He began looking through cupboards and drawers, rifling through clothing, and peering under furniture, but could find nothing of interest.

Where to look? Well, flowers would be obvious, and there were none, he said to himself. So the next choice was a crossbow. Now where would he hide a crossbow if he lived in a small home like this? It was a bright and pleasant flat, he noted. Austere, but then it was situated in an area of Chelsea which was noted for stately but austere old apartment blocks.

It did not have much of a view, and the occupant was obviously not keen on ornaments, paintings or photographs.

Where would he hide a crossbow? Hawkins had already looked in the cupboards in the bedroom and the kitchen. He searched the living room, only to emerge back into the hall a few minutes later looking even more disgruntled than ever.

"What a bloody shame," he said aloud.

There was nothing here. Better report back to Winters. The Inspector had said to hurry.

One more check in each room, he thought. He passed the mirror again. From where he stood, the mirror reflected a scene from the kitchen. Once again, he smiled at his reflection, pleased that his grin was no longer sheepish. His eye was arrested by a dustbin reflected in the mirror. It was in the kitchen, under a counter. Its lid was slightly ajar. He hadn't noticed that when he had looked in the kitchen. He turned to look at the bin.

Why not? he thought. I've gone snooping through another man's underwear, I may as well look through his rubbish as well. He walked back into the kitchen and saw the lid was being held ajar by what appeared to be stalks.

He lifted the lid.

Inside the bin were several bunches of dead flowers.
If he wasn't mistaken, they were roses.

FIFTY-SIX

BAKER BLEW onto his hands, as if he was cold. A snatch of wind
stirred his hair.

Jennifer looked up at the overcast sky, wondering how long
it had been since she'd seen the sun. It was really quite warm,
in spite of the chilly and grey appearance of the day.

Davis glanced at his watch. "It's two thirty already."

"Well, let's go," said Paynter.

The four journalists were standing outside Food for Health.
It was a brisk ten minute walk to St Paul's from the restaurant.

"We'll be early," said Davis.

"By how much?" asked Jennifer.

"Our man won't be stupid. He'll know we won't time our
arrival to the precise minute," said Davis. He turned to look at
Jennifer. "What do you say?"

"I suppose that's okay. Let's walk slowly, though. When we
get to the entrance we can dawdle before going inside."

"Suits me," said Baker.

They walked in silence. Baker appeared nonchalant, and
Jennifer envied the way he appeared to be able to keep his cool.
She was nervous, and even Davis looked under strain. Paynter
was pale and drawn.

Slowly they drew closer to St Paul's, and Jennifer found the
grandness of the building seeping into her. It was so solid and
reassuring, she thought. Like Alan. His name slipped into her

mind, and she found herself smiling. She wondered what he'd say about the meeting, especially if it proved to be a break in the case.

Her promise to him to give up the investigation knifed through her. He wouldn't approve, she thought, glumly. Had he known about the note, he'd have tried to stop her.

Baker was the first to stop at the base of the stairs leading to the entrance of St Paul's.

Jennifer pulled her jacket tight to her chest. She studied the entrance of the cathedral before she looked around her. She wondered whether their informant was watching them from one of the nearby buildings. She studied the windows of the buildings which faced the street. The three men joined her, all huddling together and looking up at the pillars in front of the church. She wondered whether their informant was happy with what they were doing.

"What's the time?" she asked again.

"It is now 2:40," said Davis. "I suggest we stand here for another minute or so, and then go inside. That should give our friend time to make sure we're not being followed."

"Suits me," said Paynter.

"Let's have another look at that note, Jennifer," said Baker. They all turned in towards the note, gathering in an awkward circle as they read the anonymous letter yet again.

Baker put down his briefcase, while Paynter held his close to his chest. Davis carried his effortlessly.

Baker sniffed. "It sounds so damned mysterious. I'm intrigued as to who this chap is going to be," he said. "Whoever it is, I reckon we've given him or her enough time. Let's go inside."

Jennifer folded the note, put it in her pocket, and grabbed the nearest arm. It belonged to Davis. The journalists turned as one towards the entrance, and Baker led the group to the cathedral steps.

FIFTY-SEVEN

VAN DEVENTER burst into the apartment, followed closely by four uniformed constables. Detective Sergeant Hawkins greeted them in the hall.

"You asked for roses, sir. I found hundreds of them in this chap's dustbin. I've been waiting in the hall for you in case anyone came home. I haven't looked any further."

"Well done, Hawkins. Well done. Find anything else?" asked Van Deventer.

Hawkins looked at the Dutchman strangely. There was a tautness in Van Deventer that Hawkins found unsettling. Usually the Dutchman was relaxed, always in total control. But this afternoon he seemed on edge, on the verge of losing his temper, unpredictable.

"No sir, nothing yet. It is quite simple and neat, not many places to hide bulky weapons without tearing it up. I wasn't sure I should do that."

"You won't mind if these chaps take over, will you? They know what they're about at this kind of thing," said Van Deventer.

Hawkins waved a hand. "Not at all, sir."

He watched as the four uniformed policemen moved into the living room. One of them addressed the others. "Philip, Chris, you take the bedroom. William will handle the kitchen. I'll go through this room."

The men split up and Hawkins moved out into the hall. Suddenly the flat felt tiny.

He watched William as he worked in the kitchen. William started a methodical search of the cupboards and drawers, then began feeling under the shelves, behind the drawers, squaring the room off into segments which he tackled quickly but surely.

He heard Van Deventer talking to someone on the telephone in the lounge. The Dutchman's voice drifted through to him between the sounds of drawers opening and closing in each room of the small apartment.

"Yes, that's right," said Van Deventer. "I want an all points alert put out on him. I don't care. Just hold him for questioning. Yes, there is every likelihood this is our man, or that he has something to do with it all. Tell them to be careful, he could be extremely dangerous."

Silence. Van Deventer continued: "Alan is still with Channing at The Courier. He is interviewing staff there. I know he's worried, because Jennifer Chapman and three of the journalists are missing from the newsroom. No-one knows where they are. The news editor can account for all his staff except for those three. Our man is one of them. They may all be together."

The policeman called Chris came striding from the bedroom. "Where's the Superintendent?" he asked brusquely.

"In the living room," said Hawkins, pointing.

Under his arm, Chris was carrying a large book, covered in imitation leather.

"Superintendent?" he called.

"Over here," said Van Deventer. "What is it?"

"I think you'd better have a look at this," said Chris, walking in to the room, and handing over the book. "I found it in his cupboard, under some tiles on the floor. There's also a crossbow in the same spot."

"Get the crossbow. Be careful not to smudge any prints. Let me see the book," said Van Deventer.

He walked to one of the two couches in the sitting room and began to read. Chris walked back to the bedroom as Hawkins sat down next to Van Deventer and tried to peer at the contents of the book.

The hunt for The Rose appeared to be over, thought Hawkins. He was torn between the desire to see the crossbow and his curiosity about this book.

After reading the first three pages slowly, Van Deventer looked up at Hawkins. There was alarm on his face.

"My God," said Van Deventer. "I was right. We're dealing with an absolute madman, not an assassin. This is his diary. It's quite clear the man is a raving psychopath."

He returned to the diary, then looked up at Hawkins. "Call The Courier. Tell them to intensify their search for him. Tell Winters there is no doubt about his identity."

"Right," said Hawkins, already striding towards the phone.

Van Deventer returned to the diary. "Christ," he whispered.

He shook his head as he read the bold handwriting on the pages of the diary. Then he began to turn the pages at a faster rate. As he got further into the diary, he started skimming over the contents of each page.

FIFTY-EIGHT

JENNIFER LOOKED around the cathedral. She and Paynter were standing underneath the dome, looking up at the Whispering Gallery. They couldn't see anyone up there.

Davis and Baker had moved into the church first, followed by Paynter. Jennifer had waited a moment before entering and found herself taking a deep breath as she stepped through the North-west door. Apart from her father's service, this was the first time she had been in a church for years. She had only visited St Paul's once before. With her father.

In front of her was the High Altar. She looked at the canopy over the altar. She remembered her father calling it "The Great Baldacchino." He had described to her how it was made from English Oak, and pointed out Christ Triumphant standing on top.

Would she be triumphant in a few short minutes?

Her three colleagues were peering around the cathedral, looking down the nave towards the entrance. Nothing out of the ordinary.

"It looks as though our man could have arranged this," said Paynter. "There are just enough people here for him to lose himself among them, but not enough for the place to be over-crowded."

"What are you saying?" asked Jennifer, distractedly. She kept looking around the cathedral, searching for a clue to the identity of the note-writer. Every face she saw looked suspicious. Nothing came to her.

"It's the first time I've ever been in a church and felt scared," said Baker. "I feel almost claustrophobic."

Paynter kept looking up at the Gallery. "I'm not sure I want to go up there," he said.

"Oh come on, are you always so timid?" said Jennifer.

"No. Are you always such a bitch?"

"That's enough!" said Baker. "I know we're all tense, but there is no need to go for each other now. We've come this far, let's see it through."

"You're right," said Davis quickly. "I suggest we all calm down. It can't be long now."

Baker sat down on one of the chairs. Jennifer followed his lead. She chose one of the chairs on the opposite aisle. Paynter and Davis remained standing. Paynter said: "If we're going to go, let's go now. I hate heights."

Without saying a word, Jennifer and Baker stood up. They walked to the door leading to the circular staircase that would take them up to the Gallery. She led the way up the stairs.

Five minutes later they were standing on the Gallery looking down towards the North Transept. Each of them was panting. It had been a steep climb up the narrow staircase. Jennifer had been grateful she had only a light handbag to carry, and had not been burdened with a heavy briefcase like the others carried.

Baker said: "Why does this person want to see us? Come to think of it, how would he know we're all involved?"

"That's a good point," said Davis. "He says you'll be able to identify him. Perhaps you said something to him about our team, in one of your interviews?"

"Could be, although I don't think so," replied Baker. He leaned his elbows on the railing, looking down to the floor below. "Those people look so tiny from up here, don't they? Like miniatures."

They lapsed into silence, broken a minute later by Jennifer. "How much longer?" she asked.

All three men looked at their watches. Davis was the first to reply. "About five minutes."

FIFTY-NINE

EVERY TIME he turned a page, Van Deventer cursed and shook his head. Before long it became a litany of swearing, rising in crescendo as the policeman whipped the pages over one after another. Finally he came to the last entry, paused, cursed again, then turned back a page. He leaned forward and his mouth dropped open. "Oh no," he muttered. "Please God, no."

Hawkins was waiting for Winters to come to the telephone. He could hear the sound of a typewriter clattering away, acting in counterpoint to Van Deventer's mutterings. Hawkins watched the Superintendent from across the room.

The Dutchman's brow furrowed, and he turned back another page. "What the ..." he began.

"What is it?" asked Hawkins, craning to see what had alarmed the Dutchman.

Van Deventer shook his head. "Oh my Christ! He's going to kill them all. Jennifer, the others. He's lured them into a trap."

"Where? When?" asked Hawkins, his voice strident.

The Dutchman looked up. Hawkins could see tears in Van Deventer's eyes.

"He's going to kill them all, because of me," said Van Deventer. "Because of me. I shouldn't have told her."

Hawkins couldn't understand what the Dutchman was trying to say. Why was he to blame?

"When is he going to kill them? How?" said Hawkins.

Van Deventer checked his watch. "Now. No. In fifteen minutes. But where? Where? WHERE?" He turned back another page, using his finger to track the lines, speeding through the paragraphs.

His finger stopped. "Here it is! At St Paul's. We'll never get anyone there in time! "

Hawkins stared in horror. He dimly heard a voice on the telephone saying: "Hello? Hello?".

His attention snapped back to the voice. "Inspector Winters? This is Hawkins. Superintendent Van Deventer needs to talk to you urgently."

The Dutchman took two strides to the telephone, snatching the receiver from Hawkins's hand.

SIXTY

WINTERS CHASED after death itself.

In spite of his fear, he decided on the stairs. The lifts would take too long.

He thudded down the steps, leaping four at a time, praying he wouldn't slip. He cannoned off the walls, using his shoulders and hips to bounce himself upright when he felt his balance going, clinging onto the bannister with one hand as he whipped around the corners, pivoting on the railings themselves. He knew his hips would be a mass of bruises, but he ignored the pain.

He slammed open the door as he burst out of the stairwell into the foyer on the ground floor, skidding to a halt in front of a group of people blocking his way. They stared at him, standing stock still.

"Out of my way," he yelled, shouldering past members of the group. They scattered as he ploughed his way through, shouting their protest. Winters ignored their abuse and ran onto the pavement, into bright, wintry sunlight. He screwed up his eyes against the glare. The sun must have come out while he was indoors. What now?

Stop a car, he thought. He would get a driver to take him to the cathedral.

Winters stepped out onto the street, but a bus was holding up traffic a hundred yards up the road. Nothing else going in the right direction.

He looked around frantically. He was near the corner of Shoe Lane and Fleet Street. He could see the Dome of St Paul's in the distance. Van Deventer had been in a panic. He had barely managed to get the information out to Winters on the telephone.

"St Paul's. The Whispering Gallery. They're all there now. He has a bomb. Set to go off at 3:15. Get there Alan. Now. Don't ask any questions. There's not enough time. Nor is there enough time for the Flying Squad to respond. Get there yourself. For Christ's sake, hurry."

Winters had slammed the telephone down, his face ashen. For a second he was dumbstruck. Jennifer. All of them. Dead. Unless he got there in time. Less than twelve minutes.

As he stood in the street now, Winters found himself looking up at the cathedral, expecting a blinding flash, or a pall of smoke. Was he too late already? Would he see the explosion? Would it kill all of them?

As he stood, his mind racing, a motorcycle messenger pulled up outside the newspaper offices. The rider was clad in black leathers, and a full-face helmet. Winters pulled out his badge, shoving it under the man's visor.

"Police emergency," said Winters. "I'm taking your bike."

Winters dragged the dumbstruck rider free of the motorcycle. He revved the engine, found first gear, and roared away amid smoke and squealing tyres.

Dimly, he heard cars hooting behind him.

He raced towards the box junction at Ludgate Circus, slowing briefly when he saw the lights were against him. No time to stop.

The intersection was busy. He would have to take his chances. He saw a break in the traffic and speared through it, but not in time to avoid being hit a glancing blow on the rear wheel by a car slewing to an emergency halt. He sensed more than heard the thud of metal against metal. The bike spun away from him and he felt himself starting to fall. He shot out a leg to steady himself, feeling his ankle twisting sharply as he made contact with the road, an arrow of pain shooting all the way up his leg to his groin.

But he held the bike upright as it screeched to a stop. Somehow. He was standing, both legs on the ground, twisting the throttle to keep the engine revs up. The driver of the damaged car was getting out. Around them, the traffic was in chaos.

"Sorry. No time to stop," shouted Winters.

He hoped the wheel was not buckled. Too bad if it was. He gunned the motor again as more cars came screeching to a halt.

He could hear the dull thud of metal on metal. Someone had run into the back of a stationary car. More screeching and hooting, from every direction.

Then he was clear of Ludgate Circus, racing at more than 60mph up Ludgate Hill towards the cathedral.

He could feel his tie and jacket streaming in the wind. A screaming, howling noise was emanating from under the seat. He glanced down over his shoulder to see the mudguard rubbing against the tyre, smoke pouring from the wheel in a dense cloud.

Weaving in and out of the traffic, he returned his eyes to the dome. They were in there. Jennifer was in there.

He could see clearly the clock on the front of the cathedral. Less than six minutes.

If they were in the Gallery, he thought, he'd have to run in the door, veer right and try to get to the Gallery stairs under cover of the side walls. He would have to walk, or the sound of someone running might panic the bastard. God knows what he might do if he thought someone was coming to stop him.

Oh Jesus, thought Winters. For the first time, the fear hit him.

The STAIRS. The GALLERY. He was going to have to climb the stairs and walk out onto the Gallery, hundreds of feet high.

He remembered the first time he had been to St Paul's. His girlfriend had wanted him to join her on the Whispering Gallery. He had not revealed his fear of heights, and had started up the stairs before breaking into a cold sweat and finally confessing.

One look from the ground up at the Gallery had almost been more than he could stand. The people he had seen up in the Gallery had looked so small, and so far away.

His stomach turned over. He could feel blood pounding in his ears. Was it his fear of heights? Or his fear for Jennifer?

Please, he thought. Let me be in time. Don't let Jennifer die.

The STAIRS. He was going to have to climb those stairs.

"I couldn't live if Jennifer dies." The thought came to him clearly in his panic.

This was more than a race to save the victims of a killer.

Whatever Jennifer had done, he loved her. He didn't dare

face the thought of having her snatched violently away from him, just as his parents had been ripped from him years before. This was a race to save the life of someone he loved. This time, at least, he had a chance to prevent it happening.

In a way, he thought, this was also a chance to save his own life.

Five minutes. If he was lucky.

The bike was bucking and shaking underneath him, the screeching noise now a banshee wail. Not even his speed could leave behind the awful smell of burning rubber.

Ahead of him he could see buses and tourist coaches parked in front of the cathedral.

Only seconds away now.

He aimed the bike for a slip road, but cursed as he saw it was blocked by a yellow and black striped traffic barrier. Winters slowed the bike to walking pace as he drew up at the barrier. He could duck underneath it while still on the bike. Lying flat on the petrol tank, he accelerated underneath the barricade, feeling the pole gouge into his back, tearing his jacket. He was going to be torn to pieces before this was through.

The Gallery. Those stairs. Dear God, he was going to have to climb those stairs.

He tried not to think about them, feeling his chest bursting with the dread of having to face the height of the Gallery.

He steered the bike straight off the road onto the pavement, jarring his whole body as he mounted the curb, riding it right up to the first flight of steps in front of the cathedral. He braked to a halt level with the statue of Queen Anne, dropping the motorcycle as he leapt clear. The engine stalled as the machine crashed on its side.

Tourists stopped to watch open-mouthed as he ran, favouring his injured leg. In spite of the pain, he was taking the steps two and three at a time. On the level between the flights he looked up at the clock.

Barely four minutes.

He raced up the final steps, pushing aside the astonished tourists in his way.

He ran between the giant columns at the entrance, and then skidded to a halt.

No. Don't run inside the cathedral, he reminded himself. Walk. But walk quickly.

Panting heavily, limping in agony, he passed through the revolving door.

Oh Christ, he was thinking. Help me. Please help me.

With those STAIRS.

SIXTY-ONE

IN THE GALLERY, the four journalists were starting to fidget, restlessly looking around the cathedral, at each other, at the door.

"He's just over 10 minutes late. It doesn't necessarily mean he won't show up," said Baker, still leaning on the railings. He was looking down at the floor below.

Jennifer wasn't sure he was seeing anything. His gaze was in the middle distance. She looked down at the people milling beneath her. It was a long drop.

Jennifer began to pace. "I hope to God he comes," she whispered. She stared at the door, willing it to open. She and Baker were standing to the right of the entrance. Davis and Paynter were a few yards away, on the other side of the doorway.

"Don't worry," said Davis, also pacing, studying his watch.

"I'm sure he'll show." He bent down and put his briefcase between his legs.

Paynter drummed his fingers on his own briefcase; an incessant rhythm that fueled the tension. The blonde reporter looked to be near hysteria, thought Jennifer. Baker seemed to ignore them all, deep in thought.

Davis coughed. "Maybe I should go to the stairs to see if I can see anyone coming," he suggested, making for the door.

Paynter leaped towards him, startling Jennifer. "No. NO," he cried. "Let me do it. I'm going crazy up here anyway."

He stood in front of Davis, blocking the bigger man's path.

"I'll go," Paynter repeated.

The two stood toe-to-toe, eyes locked.

Davis was about to say something when the sound of footsteps on the stairwell caught their attention.

"What now?" asked Baker, standing upright, pushing himself away from the railing. "Is this our man?"

Jennifer grabbed at Paynter's arm, pulling him away from the door. "Don't do anything," she said. "Just wait."

Paynter pulled his arm away roughly, whirling on her, backing away towards Davis. His eyes were wide. He clutched his briefcase to his chest, staring at Jennifer.

She found herself looking into a wild and frightened face.

The footsteps were louder now. Somebody was clamoring up the stairs, drawing closer with every second.

"Who could ...?" began Davis, and he took a hesitant step toward the door.

"Don't move!" hissed Jennifer.

Davis glared at her, and the look on his face stunned her. It was a look of pure hatred.

She took an involuntary step backwards. What had got into these two?

The footsteps drew closer, and suddenly the door burst inwards, smashing back against the Gallery wall. Jennifer saw the face of Winters. He was bent double, heaving for breath. His face was deathly pale.

Her colleagues whirled towards the Gallery's entrance, all three registering shock.

Winters was standing in the doorway, his arms outspread, his hands on the frame.

"DON'T MOVE!" he bellowed.

They stood paralysed, stupified by his sudden appearance.

Jennifer was stunned. What was going on? Everything was happening so fast.

She saw Winters snatch a glance at Baker. For some reason, he shook his head, seeming to dismiss the bearded journalist. Instead, Winters turned to look at Davis and Paynter.

All five remained rooted to where they stood.

"What the hell is going on?" asked Jennifer.

"You've been lured into a trap," said Winters, out of the corner of his mouth, still heaving for breath, but never taking his eyes off Davis and Paynter, "The killer intends destroying you with a bomb".

Jennifer's mind fell into a thousand jagged pieces. A trap? A bomb? Up here? Had the killer left a bomb up here for them?

Where?

She looked around, trying to find a parcel or box, something they hadn't noticed as they walked onto the Gallery.

Still Winters stood in the doorway.

He doesn't want to come out onto the Gallery. Why? Was he scared of the bomb? No, of course not, she thought, suddenly comprehending. His fear of heights. He didn't want to come any closer to the railings, and the plunge to the floor below.

Nearest Winters was Davis, the briefcase still between his legs.

Winters saw the case. "You," he said, pointing at Davis, "don't move."

But at that moment Paynter started to make a dash for the door. Jennifer could see Paynter's eyes. They were filled with terror as he made for the safety of Winters and the doorway. That was when he was sent crashing to the floor, his head connecting with a sickening thud, his case skittering towards the railings.

Davis stood in the middle of the Gallery, his own case now in his hands, looking across at her, his face a mask of concentrated hatred.

Baker grabbed Jennifer and pushed her behind him, backing her away from Davis and their prone colleague, but also away from the safety of their only escape route.

Jennifer let herself be moved. It appeared that Baker was trying to shield her. Her mind was still racing. Bomb? Davis? DAVIS?

Winters stood paralysed in the doorway. He screamed again. "GET AWAY. MOVE FOR CHRIST'S SAKE! THERE'S A BOMB IN HIS BRIEFCASE."

Jennifer, who had slowly been backing away, halted. Baker stumbled on her feet. He whipped a hand to the railings to steady himself, dropping his own case. It clattered on the floor. Her mind was a whirl. None of this made sense. What was Winters saying? That Davis was The Rose? That he had a bomb waiting for them? It couldn't be true. Had Alan made some awful mistake? Or was The Rose someone she had trusted and worked with all along? How could Alan know?

Then Jennifer looked at Davis. The big journalist was

standing rigidly, only his head moving, alternating between the policeman and her, an anguished look on his face.

For a second, their eyes locked. Across the abyss. Even from a distance of thirty yards, Jennifer could see his typically red eyes.

Something unfurled in her belly, hideous and terrifying.

A single word took shape in her thoughts.

EYES.

She turned to look at Baker, still standing in front of her.

He glanced down at her, and she could see his face was a grimace of apprehension.

In his eyes, she could see pure dread.

Jesus, she thought. The eyes. It was all in the eyes.

She looked up again at Baker.

He refused to meet her gaze.

The photofit, she thought. The bloody eyes. No wonder she'd been so transfixed by the photofit.

It was all in the eyes.

IT WAS ALL IN THE EYES.

She felt Baker's hand slap on to her shoulder, his fingers like pincers on her flesh. Dread filled her being.

He pulled her roughly toward him. "Come on. Do as he says," he growled.

Jennifer had no choice. Baker was stronger than her, hauling her, stumbling, further away from Winters.

Davis started to move. He looked at the policeman, his eyes desperate. He shot a glance at Jennifer and Baker, drawing further and further away around the circular Gallery.

Davis hesitated a moment longer.

Then he screamed.

The shattering sound instantly froze Baker and Jennifer.

Unbroken, the scream increased in pitch. It was a sound full of rage and pain. He held the briefcase outstretched with one hand. Taking a pace forward, his scream changed to a frenzied growl. The arm with the briefcase was outstretched behind his back. He took another pace, leaning back with the weight of the briefcase.

Too late, Winters seemed to realise what was happening.

Now Davis's arm came up and over. He used his whole body to pitch the weight in his hand. His fingers released, and Jennifer watched as the case flew across the Gallery towards her.

Everything seemed to be happening in slow motion.

The case flew up and up, and Davis was a big man, a strong man, so she knew the case was going to make it all the way to the wall just feet away from her.

And she also knew that in Davis's briefcase was the bomb. It had been meant for her all along.

She screamed, turning to run, all the time watching the case, anticipating a shattering blast. Behind her, Baker was on her heels.

Out of the corner of her eye, she could see Winters was still rooted in the doorway as the case hit the wall behind Baker, crashed to the floor and bounced against the railings.

The bomb exploded.

Jennifer heard a sharp crack; saw a brilliant flash, felt a whoosh of rushing air. The noise was deafening.

Baker was flung against her, the two of them hurled to the floor. As she went down, Jennifer felt a thousand sharp stings on her hands and legs.

All her wind was driven out as Baker landed heavily on her chest.

Debris and shrapnel rained down on the floor beneath the dome. It sounded like a heavy hailstorm. The whole cathedral was in turmoil.

Screams and shouts and running feet punctuated the eerie silence that followed the blast.

Gasping for breath, Jennifer tried to push Baker off her, but he was an absolute weight. She grabbed the back of his coat. His head lolled on her shoulder. Her hand slipped off his jacket, feeling warm and slick.

She held her hand in front of her face. It was gloved in blood and flesh.

Jennifer was sure Baker was dead, feeling sickened by his deathly embrace.

She screamed, reaching for the railing to drag herself from under Baker.

She could see part of the railing near her feet had collapsed, hanging outward by shreds of metal. Desperate, she looked around for help. Winters was lying near the door, still stunned. Davis was still standing. Blood was running freely from gashes on his face. His eyes were fixed on her. She wondered whether they had ever left her, even through the blast. His obsession seemed inhuman. Terror goaded her into trying again to heave Baker's weight off her.

Baker groaned. And moved. He lifted his head from her shoulder, looking down at her. He opened his mouth to smile pathetically and blood dribbled from his lips. More blood flowed from his nose. His eyes were uncomprehending.

Repulsed, Jennifer tried to push him away again. This time he responded to her urging, and tried to stand. Using the railings, he managed to haul himself to his knees, twisting away from her. Jennifer could see Baker's back was smouldering. He leaned against the shattered railing, inching away from Jennifer, shuffling forward on his knees.

"STOP HIM. STOP HIM, JENNIFER." It was Winters.

Jennifer saw what he feared. Baker was hauling himself towards oblivion.

She tried to sit upright, but her limbs seemed to be moving to someone else's will, trembling and shaking spasmodically.

Somehow, Baker managed to drag himself to his feet. He leaned on the bannister, tottering closer and closer to the damaged portion of the railing. His back was still smoking, a gaping wound festering like an evil witch's brew just above his waist. The rest of his back, his neck and legs were covered in tiny holes which seemed to spread out from the main wound.

Christ, he took the full force of the explosion in his back, she registered. He was the reason she was still alive. She had to help him.

But Jennifer was helpless. Her arms and legs remained numb, twitching involuntarily. She looked dumbly at her forearms, realising she had not escaped all the shrapnel from the bomb.

Baker moved on instinct alone. His knees buckled, and his weight was thrown onto the railings. He was still bleeding heavily from the nose and mouth as he turned to look at Jennifer. His eyes were vacant of expression and his face was calm as the metal gave way and he pitched forward, tumbling head over heels in his plummet to the ground.

The screams of tourists under the dome were like an unholy choir.

Baker's body thudded onto the pews below, sending chairs crashing and sliding over the floor.

Jennifer couldn't look. She rolled onto her side, trying to use her arms to push herself erect. As she struggled she glimpsed Davis turn and start walking slowly towards her. He was coming to finish what he had started.

Her legs were still numb, and she couldn't stand. She turned to search for help. Alan? Alan would help her. She peered at Winters and despaired. He was still at the door, trapped there by his fear, dread contorting his face.

Their eyes met and she mouthed: Please. Help me.

He screwed his eyes closed and shook his head. He kept looking from Davis to the railings to her, unable to move, paralysed by his fear.

Davis was walking slowly, mechanically, never taking his deathly gaze off her.

Jennifer looked down to see Baker lying spread-eagled amid the shattered pews below. One of his legs was sticking out from his body at an impossible angle.

Whimpering in fear, hammering her thighs with a fist, Jennifer gave up her punishing attempts to stand. She looked up to see Davis drawing inexorably closer.

Still Alan was pinned at the doorway by his fear.

After all this, her mind locked in the ice-cold clarity of utter resignation, Alan was going to fail her because of his childhood fear of heights.

Davis was twenty yards from her.

Then Winters screwed his eyes closed and launched himself on to the Gallery in pursuit of Davis, hobbling badly, leaning drunkenly against the wall to keep himself as far as possible from the railing.

Davis seemed unaware that Winters was hobbling behind him, closing the gap slowly. Too slowly? Jennifer could see Winters had hurt his leg. It was hampering him badly. She wondered how Davis could fail to hear the sound of Winters behind him.

In desperation, she grabbed the railings, using them to drag herself erect, forcing every muscle to work. A length of the wooden bannister came away in her hands. She lost her grip and the piece of wood, a yard in length and heavy, clattered to the floor. The delay had cost her another few yards. Davis was only ten yards away now, with Winters ten yards beyond that. Davis's eyes were crazed. His hands were outstretched.

Her legs were shaking too much to hold her upright unassisted. She turned away from Davis, a hand out against the wall, trying to put one foot in front of the other. From somewhere outside came the sound of sirens.

A hand clapped down on her shoulder, fingers piercing into her flesh, and she felt herself whirled around savagely.

 She surprised Davis by not resisting, instead flying at him, sinking her teeth into his shoulder. He screamed with the pain. Winters was nearly on them.

Davis punched Jennifer brutally in the stomach, lifting her feet off the ground with the force of the blow. She fell to her knees again. Stunned and winded, she collapsed forward onto her hands, gagging.

She heard bodies crunch together and a grunt from Davis. She looked up to see him fending off Winters, a cutting backhand catching the policeman under the bridge of his nose, the power of the blow sending Winters staggering into the railings.

Davis spun back to her, glaring down. His lips were curled back from his teeth, his eyes fiercely bloodshot, and rivulets of blood ran down his cheeks to his shirt collar. He presented a hideous vision and Jennifer turned around, still on her hands and knees, attempting to crawl away from this madman, still retching. One vicious hand grabbed her by the hair, and she felt Davis step over her. Then he began to drag her forwards.

Towards the gap in the railings.

She sat back on her haunches, resisting even though the pain from her hair was blinding.

Winters had recovered, and he flew again at Davis. He had

to jump over Jennifer, feet first, his heel aimed at the side of one of the bigger man's knees. The kick brought Davis down, and the three of them became a tangle of arms and legs on the ground.

Davis turned on Winters again, his strength superhuman. He punched the policeman; a short, chopping blow on the forehead. More blows battered Winters. The detective tried instinctively to use his karate training to block and deflect the punches, but his efforts were ineffectual. Davis was a wild man. The blows kept getting through, and Winters looked desperate.

The sirens outside the cathedral were closer now, still more approaching. But help was a long way off.

Winters flung himself at Davis, trying to smother the punches with his body, screaming at Jennifer to run, to get away, struggling to hold the maniac in front of him.

For a moment, Jennifer nearly froze as she dragged herself away from the struggling men. She closed her eyes and kept pushing with her feet, attempting yet again to stand. She hauled herself to her feet. In the distance, she could hear footsteps clattering on the ground floor. Several men were running towards the stairway to the Gallery. Even more sirens had drawn up outside the cathedral.

Davis shoved Winters against the wall, grabbing the policeman's hair in one hand to batter his head on the concrete. Dazed, Winters relinquished his grip on Davis. The journalist pushed him violently backwards. Free of his pursuer, Davis turned on Jennifer again. He was as fast as a cobra, diving at her from his kneeling position, flinging out an arm, and Jennifer screamed as his hand closed on one of her ankles. He pulled her savagely to the floor. Jennifer smacked her chin on debris, and lay limply for a second. Davis dragged her back towards the gap in the railings and the deathly drop.

She clung to the bars of the railing in terror, but Davis was too strong. Fingernails broke as her grip was shaken loose. She was over the abyss, with nothing to stop her fall. Davis was grunting like an animal. On his knees, he pushed against her back and legs, propelling her prone body towards the edge. She watched the brink approach in mind-numbing terror, twisting to try and clutch at Davis's clothing.

But it was hopeless. She tottered on the verge of the Gallery, a scream choked in her throat, unable to breathe.

She heard a dull thud, and Davis's grip slackened slightly. The shoving halted. She swivelled to stare into the face of Davis.

His eyes still burned with the manic flames of obsession, but now they were glazed. Blood was pouring onto his forehead from the top of his skull. What had happened?

She broke the stare and looked up at Winters. The policeman stood over Davis, his arms raised above his head. In his hands was the length of wood Jennifer had broken off the bannister. As she watched, Winters swung the club again.

Another thud and Davis's head jolted forwards, blood spraying on her neck and shoulders. His grip on her leg and dress fell free, but still he tried to look at her, tried one last feeble push.

Winters clubbed him again, and this time Davis collapsed face forward as Jennifer grabbed for the railings, using them to haul herself to safety.

"Stop it Alan!" she cried, as Winters crashed another blow onto Davis's back. The footsteps were on the Gallery now. People were shouting, whistles blowing, but no words were discernible amid the tumult.

More damaged railing tore itself free and crashed to the floor as Winters pounded Davis again, all the while sobbing and swearing "you bastard, you bastard" over and over. Davis must be dead, she thought.

Smoke was still hanging in the air, debris lying everywhere.

Winters collapsed to his knees, lifting the wooden club wearily, holding it weakly above his head, aiming it yet again at the back of Davis's bloodied head. But now uniformed policemen were on him, restraining him as he struggled to deliver one more blow.

Hands helped drag Jennifer away from the edge...

EPILOGUE

Her fingers closed around the butt of the pistol in her bag. As usual, it felt as if she had been born with the weapon in her hand. She was familiar with every line, every working part, every bullet in its magazine.

On each bullet, using the point of a nail file, she had scratched the same name.

"All rise."

The judge entered amidst a clatter of chairs and a hum of anticipation.

The people in the public Gallery had been standing in queues since before dawn to secure their seats. For most of them, this was their first sighting of the man they knew only as The Rose. No matter how cold it had been, no matter how much their legs and feet ached, it had been worth it. Now they were going to be part of the drama that was a murder trial.

The judge was well aware of the atmosphere. It had been the same every day since the trial had started. He nodded grimly and sat down heavily.

As she seated herself, she released her grip on the gun, and withdrew her hand from her bag. She looked around again.

Additional police had been brought in to ensure orderly conduct, both in and outside the court. They kept a watchful eye on everyone. Security had been exceptionally tight.

Her timing would have to be just right.

The press Gallery was jammed. Outside the court, at the entrance, several television crews were busy filming the arrival of everybody who drew up in front of the building. Television reporters sought interviews with anyone standing in the street. People watching at home were given a brief summary of the previous day's proceedings. They were also shown film of the locations at which the bodies of Chapman, Ballantine, Walker and Whitfield had been found. Interior shots of St Paul's Cathedral after the blast, and the scene of devastation in the Whispering Gallery were screened again and again. The commentator repeatedly said he found it difficult to believe only one person had died in the explosion.

They showed photographs of the victims, as well as photographs of members of their families.

So often lately, she felt repulsed by the insatiable appetite of the public for all the bizarre and macabre details of the murders. The irony did not escape her. Until now, her livelihood had depended on that appetite.

In court, she cringed every time she heard someone whisper and point at the table which held the evidence. On the table were a crossbow and several bolts, a revolver, various wigs and false beards, three pairs of spectacles, three envelopes, and a large, leather-bound book.

She knew the contents of those envelopes intimately.

In the solemn and dustily dignified voice of the law, the prosecuting barrister started the day's evidence at precisely the point he had ended on the previous afternoon.

She shook her head, deeply wearied by the proceedings. In the end, it was all going to come to nothing. All of this was a pointless farce. She would exact her own revenge.

The words came back to her. "I WANT TO TAKE THE GUN FATHER LEFT AND PUT A BULLET IN THE MAN WHO KILLED HIM. IF EVER I GET THE CHANCE, I WILL. SO HELP ME, I WILL."

The words had kept her awake at night. Now, soon, the nightmare would be over.

Her hair clung to her forehead, limp and unbrushed. She clutched at her bag as a child would a security blanket.

For three days she had sat in the same seat in the public Gallery, always there before everyone else, always the last to leave. She was a solitary figure, discouraging any advances from the people who happened to sit next to her. Sometimes it was merely the intensity of her interest in the trial that sent people away; other times it was the hostility in her eyes.

During the trial her eyes never left the man in the dock. He looked gaunt; hollow-cheeked and skeletal, his eyes sunken. Some newspaper reports had said it was a miracle he was still alive.

In spite of being on show for the fourth day now, the man flirted with a faint smile throughout each day.

She sat in a seat directly in front of him, a seat she acquired before the doors to the courtroom were opened in the morning. Every day she followed the same routine. A slender, darkly blonde man, always well-dressed, would meet her at the entrance to The Old Bailey, then escort her to the security desk at the main door. He would take out a wallet and show the security guards a badge, then he would take the woman by an elbow - in spite of the fact it was he who walked with a limp - and lead her to her seat. Then he would leave, usually to join the elderly policeman with the Dutch accent, who also attended the trial daily.

The court had already heard how both these men had been commended for "excellent police work, above and beyond the call of duty."

Each day the public Gallery was crammed; each day hundreds of hopefuls would go home determined to try again the next day for a seat. Every morning the newspaper headlines would blare out sensational details of the trial. Sales were up. The reporters were in their element.

The previous day, the prosecutor had started to read from the leather-bound book submitted as evidence in the trial. As he turned the pages, his voice droning out the words in a flat, emotionless monotone, the man in the dock had begun to fidget. He became more interested in the people in the courtroom. They, in turn, were enthralled by the revelations, fascinated that they were able to see the man who had penned these words of madness and death.

It was as if a direct line of communication opened up between them all.

The prisoner's eyes scoured the public Gallery, constantly roaming from face to face. Occasionally he would lock eyes with one of the onlookers, and he would stare until the person was forced to look away. He would turn to the members of the jury, and his eyes would challenge them. From the smirk on his face it was clear he was unafraid; some even said it looked as if he was enjoying the proceedings. But he never did turn to look at her.

When the prosecutor began to describe the defendant's plan to lure his colleagues to the Whispering Gallery to await death by bomb blast, those who happened to be watching the woman saw her teeth clench, her eyes narrow, and her hands tighten into fists. But no-one noticed how her hand would slip into her bag at odd intervals, stay there for a while, then come out again empty.

She did this whenever the judge left the bench, and everyone in the courtroom, including the prisoner, had to stand up.

At the end of the fourth day, when the judge had once more adjourned the trial till the next morning, the woman stood up, her hand in her bag, and she watched the accused with an abnormal intensity, almost as if it wasn't him she was seeing. Then, as the rest of the spectators in the Gallery turned to walk out of the court, she removed her hand and sat down in her seat. Beads of perspiration dotted her brow and upper lip.

The blonde policeman with the limp found her there twenty minutes after everyone had left the room. He escorted her from the courtroom, out of one of the side exits, away from the crowds thronging the entrance.

There a taxi was waiting for her, as it had been every day. The blonde man held the door open for her as she got in, they exchanged glancing kisses, he closed the door and the driver pulled away without taking directions. He knew the address. Kensington.

She did not wave goodbye, nor did she see him standing on the pavement, his head shaking sadly.

Making sure she was sitting directly behind the driver, she reached into the handbag and withdrew a World War Two automatic pistol. A 9mm Luger. For a long moment she studied it, turning it over in her hands. There was an air of familiarity in the way she handled the weapon. She slid it back into her bag.

One more night of fear, she thought, then it would all be over.

The taxi driver slowed as he turned into Old Bailey, creeping past the crowd which overflowed in front of the court into the street.

The woman snapped her bag shut as she watched the TV crews, the photographers and all the hangers on jostling each other on the pavement.

Her lips curled in a grimace of distaste, and she shook her head. Vultures, she thought. Then the taxi was past and gathering speed.

She leaned back in the seat; could not resist letting her hand caress the butt of the gun in her handbag. Within minutes, she would be home. She would discuss the day's events with her daughter. Then, together, they would await the arrival of Alan Winters.

The woman smiled. Jennifer and Alan looked happy together, in spite of all the pain.

Tonight would be her last night with them, she knew.

Again, the woman smiled. But this time, it was a tight smile, an acknowledgement to herself that her rehearsals were over.

They had gone perfectly.

Tomorrow, she would be back...

THE END

Kevin Murray began his writing career 40 years ago, working on The Star, Johannesburg's biggest daily newspaper. He soon became Chief Crime Reporter in what was considered to be the crime capital of the world. He once achieved a record of more than 30 consecutive days of front page crime stories, including an aircraft hijacking, several murders, numerous armed robberies and even drug-related gang wars. Since then, his successful career has spanned magazine publishing, public relations and strategic communications. Being a storyteller is his craft. He has written two bestselling business books on leadership and has a cupboard full of ideas for the next novel.